The York King:

Volume Two of the House of York Trilogy

THE York KING

VOLUME TWO OF THE HOUSE OF YORK TRILOGY

AMY LICENCE

LUME BOOKS

LUME BOOKS

Published in 2022 by Lume Books

ISBN 978-1-83901-290-7

Typeset using Atomik ePublisher from Easypress Technologies

www.lumebooks.co.uk

For Rufus and Robin

My crown I am, but still my griefs are mine. You may my glories and my state depose but not my griefs: still am I king of those.

Richard II

Table of Contents

Foreword

By 1464, England had been ruled for three years by Edward IV, the first king of the Yorkist dynasty. The eldest son of the Duke of York, Edward, had grown to manhood while his father fought to assert his rights and steer the country through dangerous periods of instability, occasioned by the madness of the old Lancastrian king, Henry VI.

After the murder of the Duke of York and his second son Edmund, at Wakefield in 1460, Edward avenged their deaths with the help of his cousin, Richard, Earl of Warwick. Together, they defeated the Lancastrian army at Towton, the bloodiest battle ever fought on English soil, and placed Edward upon the throne. His mother, Cecily, sisters and brothers, George and Richard, came to Westminster, receiving new titles. The French queen, Margaret of Anjou and her son, the Prince of Wales, fled into exile, while the old king, Henry, went into hiding.

Young, unmarried and athletic, the new king quickly attracted a reputation for womanising, accompanied by his new friend, Henry Beaufort, Duke of Somerset, a former Lancastrian leader. Their close friendship breached the divide between the two sides and helped restore peace at court. But when Beaufort absconded from the king's company, lured back to his former allegiances, it became clear that the old divisions had never really gone away. And there were always those, even closer to home, who were willing to exploit them.

ONE

Night Visitors, January 1464

Something had broken the night. A new sound spread through the white softness of the forest, where snow had been falling since dusk, covering the path to the village. Here, the shadows were green, softened by the clouds that hid the stars; the tall standing trees had a martial air, as if awaiting the fated command, their branches a tangle of black hair. In a hollow, sat the grey stain of a hare against the snow, ears flat against its head, bulbous eye turned to the moon. It paused, bunched itself up on long legs, listened.

A sound was coming. A sound that had muscle, and reach. It pulsed into the tiny hearts of birds huddled overhead, breast to breast, as they shrank back into their nests. It stayed the talon of the owl, head swivelling like a globe, tearing flesh from bone. It reverberated among the leaves. Men were coming.

They rode as if the wood was theirs. As if a thousand years ago, seeds had split from buds and fallen into cracks in the soil, rooted and grown, purely for them. As if rain had massed in the heavens and wept down to quench the earth, for their convenience alone. As

1

if generations of animals had mated, struggled to find food, or been slaughtered purely for the pleasure of being dressed with saffron or cinnamon and served at their table. And somehow, on some level, the woods knew to expect them. And the trees trembled in expectation.

They came at a gallop, five young men, strong, broad and colourful, wrapped thickly in furs. The ground thundered at their approach; the trunks of age-old trees quaked. They were absolute, defiant: the cold was nothing to men who could wield a sword and command any household fire to burn in their name. They had youth and speed on their side, the security of a warm bed and a meal barely a mile off; not even the glint of the moon on death's scythe could daunt them, as it slipped between the trees. The heavens seemed to close in at their approach, as the sound became almost deafening.

Their leader turned and briefly looked back. They were travelling too fast for him to call to the others, but there was no need. With the rush of a storm, the rush of life, like heralds of the present moment, they sped through the clearing, hooves pounding up the snow in a cloud. The place was theirs. But already they were disappearing from sight, present for a moment alone, then vanishing through the trees. Silence descended again. The shadows folded in. As they receded, the wood closed upon itself, like so much viscous greenness, only momentarily torn.

Ahead lay the manor house with its long hall and chimneys flooding smoke out into the sky. Through the darkness, spots of gleaming light held promise, like treasure bound in red stone, hidden in a fold of countryside. Here there was a change in the road, where the thinning of the trees began, and the marks of civilisation grew prominent. The white spaces seemed to stretch for longer as they passed fields and a little stream; an upright on the horizon might have been a church steeple. Their horses' hooves clattered over a stone bridge that spanned still black water.

2

A pair of strong iron gates were already standing open at their approach, although they had not been expected, and the house was half abed. They entered without surprise, or alarm, almost too easily. The horses clattered into an outer courtyard, so quiet that the sound must have woken all those inside. Before the main entrance, they dismounted, slipping to the stones, perhaps a little loose with wine, their voices touched with laughter. They walked as if they knew their way, as if these stones underfoot, these worn steps, were their old friends and the night and the snow were mere inconveniences. Hands opened doors, ushering them inside. Unseen figures hurried to light tapers and poke the cinders in the hearth back to life. Sleepy-eyed servants saw to their needs.

Like a formation of birds, the men followed their leader. Before the door, he paused and cast his eyes around the place, taking in the yard and stables, the house and road behind them. As ever, his hazel eyes were adept at seeking the shadows, the places of weakness and the distant line of the horizon, whether still, or swarming with the movement of men. Finally, satisfied, his gaze flickered up to the stars, where pinpricks of brightness were visible between the clouds. The sky hung heavy and dark overhead, full of menace, threatening to bring danger close. With a movement of his hand, he gestured for the door and the gates to be locked behind him.

'The king! The king!'

Edward, England's fourth king of that name, strode into the great hall, stuffy with heat from the fire and the breath of sleepers. The hearth's embers glowed with faint red heat and the signs of feasting were still visible in the half-empty plates and pitchers. The rushes strewn underfoot were trodden flat.

He cast off his hat and unwound his cloak, eyes scouring the corners of the room. For Edward, the eldest son of the Duke of York; Edward, the child born in Rouen, with the blood of Lancaster and York in his veins; Edward, who had grown to be a man against the backdrop of bloodshed and chaos; Edward, who knew the sting of irreplaceable loss, had learned to be wary of friend and foe, to proudly wear the glittering crown he had won and to seek his enemies behind their smiles. He had learned that life was short, and harsh, and no titles or wealth could shield a man from the assassin's blade. And though he went from place to place, anticipating that each night might be his last, he projected an ease and confidence that drew men and women to him.

In his twenty-second year, Edward's face had taken on a broader but leaner cast, the plump lines of childhood giving way to the strong cheekbones of his father, the determined chin and straight nose. Those who recalled York could see the differences between father and son, but also the similarities. Those who knew him well said there was something more of his mother about the eyes. He had the stamp of Cecily Neville's beauty, coupled with a sense of knowing, perhaps, that had developed in recent years, wise beyond his years, with a note of melancholy amid the warmth. And there was an animation about his face that could hold listeners, sometimes for hours, especially when it was coupled with the gentleness of his touch. He was taller than the others and wore his height well. His sense of command was effortless, as natural to him as breathing. He stopped, waited.

'Where is Norfolk?'

On another occasion his voice would have been warm. It resounded with centuries of royal blood, but on this January night it had a ring of cold command. When he received no reply, he spoke the words a second time, up to the rafters.

'Where is the Duke of Norfolk?'

Figures hurried through the partition at the end, four or five of them, dropping to their knees. They came a little hesitantly, wreathed in confusion, uncertain of the occasion but overriding their fears in the knowledge that they were being compelled.

Edward strode forward to stand before them. One, in the centre, he recognised as the newly ennobled Duke of Norfolk, John de Mowbray, whose dark head was bowed low upon his chest.

'Rise,' the king commanded. The action revealed the duke's youth; he was barely eighteen or nineteen, flanked by women, whose cloaks were hurriedly thrown around their bed garments. The sight of them, startled from sleep, mute and scared, softened Edward's face.

'My good lord, my ladies. You must forgive us this rude intrusion. Is the house at peace?'

'As peaceful as I have ever known it,' the duke stammered, looking about to the ladies for confirmation, then to the men in the background, the stewards and ushers, who nodded in earnest.

'Send men to check the outhouses and ensure all the gates are locked. We rode in with too much ease.'

Norfolk gave the instruction. 'Is there cause for concern, my lord?'

Edward nodded sternly. 'You have been celebrating?'

Norfolk's baby face blushed a deep red. 'Forgive me, my lord, we are in no fit state to receive you.'

'Celebrating?'

'Our new year festivities ran over their allotted day.'

'You have no guests in the house?'

'None other than those you see before you.' He turned to indicate the hall.

Edward observed the women again.

'Believe me, I would not have disturbed your peace for anything less. We were travelling in the area today when reports reached us

5

that Lancastrian rebels and traitors had been sighted, raising men with the intent of laying an ambush on the road ahead. It was sworn that they rode this way.'

Norfolk's eyes widened as he rapidly computed whether this information implied an accusation. 'It was sworn? By whom?'

Edward thought of the friar on the roadside, standing in his brown robes, tonsure to the heavens, begging to be heard and mumbling some incoherent tale about traitors. 'That doesn't matter.'

'No, we have kept a quiet household today. This afternoon we rode to the church, but we were back long before dusk; we saw nothing unusual on the road and heard no reports. Is there' – he paused – 'is there anyone particular whom you seek?'

Edward's brow furrowed. 'As ever, we seek the traitor Henry Plantagenet, formerly called King, who plots from afar to usurp our throne with the help of his French-born whore. But these reports did not concern him, not directly. You have heard no news of Henry Beaufort, Duke of Somerset in these parts?'

Norfolk's face betrayed his surprise. 'Beaufort? I thought he was in the north?'

Even the name of Somerset was difficult for the king to speak, so deep the wound ran. The son of the man the old Duke of York had killed at St Albans, young Beaufort had swiftly replaced him in the confidence of the French queen, Margaret of Anjou. Yet, in the wake of Yorkist success at Towton, the young man had begged for his pardon, arrived at court, and charmed the king. Edward had trusted his Lancastrian cousin, received him into his private household, ridden beside him in the hunt and, eventually, restored him to his lands and titles. Together they had ridden on progress to Coventry, like brothers, side by side, only for the young duke to abscond again. With his current whereabouts unknown, Edward feared the worst.

'We all thought he was,' confirmed the king, 'but he has played us false and returned to his former loyalties.'

'Like the slippery Lancastrian serpent that he is!' added a lean figure at Edward's side.

The king's brother, George, Duke of Clarence, now fourteen, was a pent-up well of fire and passion as his dark glowing eyes revealed even in the gloom of the hall.

'So there have been no sightings of Beaufort in the area?' continued the king. 'He has not made contact with you in any way, not by letter, messenger or any other means?'

Norfolk put his hand upon his heart. 'My lord, I am prepared to swear an oath that he has not, not by word, deed or any means. Should he attempt to make a connection with me or my men, we should detain him if possible and send immediate word to your Grace.'

Edward clapped him on the shoulder. 'Spoken like a true and honest subject. Together we can expel the Lancastrians and restore peace once more to the realm. After all, are we not cousins, Norfolk, my mother and your grandmother being of the same blood?' He turned to address the women. 'Ladies, please forgive our intrusion into your peaceful night's sleep. It was only our concern for your safety that occasioned it.'

Norfolk indicated the old lady at his side. 'Indeed, here is your great-aunt Katherine, who is my guest this season. Come forward, Grandmother.'

Edward bowed his head in homage to his mother's elder sister, who stepped out of the shadows as bidden. In her familiar face, lined by cares, he saw the echo of Cecily's features, the fair hair common to the family, streaked more with white at Katherine's temples than her sister's, the pale blue eyes and elegant, aristocratic shape of the chin and mouth. He took her frail hand, all skin and bones, between his fingers and pressed it to his lips, but theirs had been a complicated relationship.

'Aunt, I hope I find you in good health?'

The pale eyes looked back at him sourly. 'Your father cost me a husband at Northampton.' She delivered this with typical Neville directness. 'I trust you intend to find me another, now that you are king.'

He did not mind the tone of slight mockery from the old woman, keeping the wry smile from spreading across his lips.

'I will try my best to please you in all things, Aunt.'

She snorted. 'It seems my sister has been more fortunate in her family than I, but time will tell, time will tell.'

Edward shot a glance at Norfolk, whose face betrayed no emotion in response to his grandmother's slight. 'In which case, I shall do my best to swiftly endow you with a husband suitable to your particular needs. Your fourth, I believe? And who else have we here?'

Before the dowager could respond, he turned to the woman at her side, a small, demure looking figure, with wide, generous features. The torchlight flickered over her papery skin and Edward judged her age to be well advanced.

'May I present the Countess of Shrewsbury,' obliged Norfolk, 'mother of that Viscount Lisle who fought so bravely at Castillon, and her daughters, Lady Eleanor Butler and Lady Elizabeth Talbot.'

Under the shadow of the hoods pulled over their undressed hair, Edward glimpsed two fresh faces: one still rounded and plump with youth, the other refined into something of rare beauty, wide-eyed, with full lips.

'We are negotiating a marriage,' chimed in Katherine Neville, proprietorially, 'between my grandson and the Lady Elizabeth.'

The younger girl flushed.

'Lady Elizabeth,' said Edward, grandly, 'the pleasure is all mine. A very fitting match, I am sure.'

His eyes flicked away to the second sister. She seemed older, wiser, and yet more fragile. Her gaze was low, her cheeks pale.

'And this must be the Lady Eleanor?'

Edward waited for her mother to reply but, to his surprise, the girl lifted her head and spoke to him directly, her beautiful face defiant.

'Lady Eleanor Butler, elder daughter of the Earl of Shrewsbury, widow of Sir Thomas Butler, son of Lord Shrewsbury.'

'Eleanor!' hissed her mother.

Edward laughed and held up his hand to stay the old woman's interruption.

'Lady Eleanor Butler, it is a pleasure to make your acquaintance.' And taking the woman's hand, he pressed it to his lips.

Her eyes met his for a second, briefly uncertain. They were of an unusual blue, steely and grey, with flashes of chestnut around the iris. A mixture of emotions chased through them, appealing and contradictory. Then he saw her regain her composure.

'You recall my husband, Sir Thomas Butler?'

Edward struggled to bring a face to mind. She did not wait.

'He died of a wasting sickness before you became king. I have been a widow these past four years.'

'Eleanor!'

The king raised his hand. Taking a step closer, he looked deep into those complex eyes. 'Then it is high time you remarried.'

He was turning away when she spoke again. 'Thank you, my lord. I have no desire to remarry. I wish for the return of my husband's manors. They were taken from me.'

Edward turned back slowly. 'By whom were they taken?'

'By my father-in-law.'

Edward inclined his head. 'Then he should return them.'

'Thank you, my lord. Might I ask again, to be sure? Your advice would be that, if someone took them from me unlawfully, that person should be obliged to return them?'

Edward inclined his head to concur, but sensed a trap.

A taut smile touched her lips briefly.

'But he cannot return them, my lord.'

He waited.

'He cannot, my lord, can he?'

'And why is that?'

'Because you took them from him.'

Norfolk coughed awkwardly as if he could stifle Eleanor's voice, but Edward had heard her. She lifted her chin defiantly and met his gaze.

'Forgive her, my good lord,' urged the countess, trembling from fear and cold. 'She knows not what she says.'

Edward did not take his eyes from the young woman's face. She was older than him, perhaps twenty-five, or more, but her conviction was almost unnerving. He could not help but admire her bravery in speaking to him in such a way. 'Oh, I think she knows exactly what she says. If your manors were taken, Widow Butler, then I am certain they were taken for a reason.'

Her eyes flickered. He had unknowingly stumbled upon something.

'But, my lord…'

'I will look into it. I give you my word.'

She dropped her head, and despite the hang of her hood, he was surprised to see how her cheeks flushed scarlet. It made him wonder which emotion had caused it and how much her outburst had cost her.

Edward turned back to his host. 'And now, as I am satisfied with matters here, I do not intend to keep you from your sleep any longer. It is late. Might there be a place we can lay our heads for the night? We will be gone at dawn.'

Norfolk's sigh of relief was almost audible. 'Of course, my lord, please follow me.'

The house had seen grander days, echoing with the ghosts of old feasts, as Norfolk penetrated its cloistered darkness. Its walls needed a fresh coat of paint and the cobwebs begged to be brushed away. The chamber he opened contained three beds, an empty table and a cold hearth, being hurriedly kindled into life by busy hands. It looked as if it had formerly been used by household officials, but at least it was a roof over their heads against the cold winter's night, and welcome after the long, frozen ride.

'Please forgive our humble accommodation,' Norfolk said uneasily, conscious of the chamber's faults. 'I am in the process of visiting all my father's estates. Some refreshment will be sent up to you as soon as possible, my lords. And truckle beds, if you require them.'

Edward turned from his examination of the room and smiled. 'Peace be with you, Norfolk, all is well. This will be adequate for our needs. You recall your fellow Knights of the Bath? My brother George, John Stafford and William Stanley, and of course, Lord Hastings. You are among friends.'

A servant handed round a tray of wine and spices; another bore a salver of dried fruit and comfits.

'Please,' urged the king, 'will you drink with us before returning to your bed?'

The nervous duke acquiesced and accepted the glass. As the men shed their boots and cloaks, flames gradually kindled in the hearth, bringing a warmth and welcome to the chamber.

'So, you are to be married?' asked Edward, sinking into a chair.

Norfolk nodded shyly.

'Soon, I hope?'

'The date has not been set but, yes, within a twelvemonth.'

'And the girl is to your taste?'

'She is a simple girl, good and obedient.'

'Then she is perfection,' pronounced Hastings, crinkling his good-natured eyes about the corner. Edward's old companion was now in his mid-thirties, his neatly trimmed golden beard flecked with grey. 'You must marry her at once and have a large family. Trust me, the obedient ones are hard to come by.'

'Don't listen to Hastings,' urged Edward. 'He speaks of women like horses because he has difficulty in taming them.'

The men laughed aloud. Hastings began to hold up his hands in protest but gave up.

Edward turned again to Norfolk. 'Is your grandmother in favour of the match?'

'She drives a hard bargain, but I believe she wishes to see it accomplished as soon as she can. She has been unwell these past months. One of the things she can offer the countess, is support in her feud against the Berkeleys, and there is no objection to the lady, none whatsoever, no precontracts, no existing affinities.'

'How could there be? Then you have my blessing.'

'All men of position should marry as soon as they can,' spoke William Stanley, pointedly, an austere, monkish-looking man whose premature hair loss made him look older than his twenty-eight years. 'It is their duty.'

'Indeed so,' echoed Hastings, with particular emphasis. 'All young men should marry.'

'And we have it again!' Edward smiled, half amused, half exasperated. 'Another assault upon the king's freedom! You all know that, as we speak, the Earl of Warwick negotiates for me a bride from France, with none less than Bona of Savoy, but a future queen of England cannot be so quickly chosen. She is a trout that must be caught with tickling.'

'But at this rate, she will never be chosen at all!'

'But why this indecent haste?' asked the king. 'You will recall, dear Hastings, the storm that was unleashed upon this country by the former king's marriage? Now that did England no good turn.'

'I do, indeed!' Hastings stopped before the fire. 'Margaret of Anjou. I was just a lad that season when she crossed the Channel. It was the year forty-five, I believe. A fearsome warrior queen who made men tremble, even those who sought her particular favours. And her so small a thing, skinny and slight like an overgrown child. You would get no sons with the like of her! She is fierce enough to drive away any man's powers.'

Edward ignored his crudeness. 'She was a queen whose advice brought this country to its knees. Who ruled her husband as if she were the man, and he the maid, who listened to the lascivious tongues of evil councillors bent on the destruction of good men. You see why I will not take a queen in any degree of haste?'

Stanley was shaking his head. 'There surely can be no others who can be the like of Margaret?'

'None, no, I will not have her like. Not even her equal. I will have her better. I must take a queen with a spirit to match hers and a head full of good sense and loyalty. And if she is beautiful, then I would be trebly blessed.'

'Know you of such a woman?'

Edward smiled. 'Will the day come when you take your own advice, Lord Stanley, as I believe you have yet to secure yourself a wife?'

Stanley held up his hands at the recurrence of the old argument and retreated towards the fireplace where Stafford and Clarence were warming their cold limbs.

'You see, Sir John,' continued the king, turning to Norfolk, 'save for Hastings and Stafford, we are bachelors all. You will beat me to the altar, while I wisely refuse to be hurried.'

13

'It will be a rare woman who can catch this king,' Hastings added, and his indulgent smile spoke of evenings spent in drink and dancing, of bare feet on the king's staircase at night and crumpled bed sheets in the morning. Lovers, even whores, were one thing. A wife, and a queen, were an entirely different matter.

Edward did not reply. He had few secrets from Hastings, his closest friend.

Norfolk put down his glass. 'I will bid you good night, my lord, if I may. Do not hesitate to ask for anything you need. I will leave two of my best men posted in the corridor outside your door.'

'God bless you, Norfolk, and please extend our grateful thanks to the ladies of the house for their gentle tolerance.'

Norfolk bowed, and the men watched his retreat. The chamber door clicked shut and his footsteps echoed down the corridor.

As soon as silence fell, Edward's countenance changed. The king became serious. Appearances and merrymaking fell aside like a mask after a disguising.

'Stafford, check the room, all wooden panels, all ways in and out; Stanley, the bedding and underneath each frame; Clarence, chests and closet. Feel each surface with the tips of your fingers, consider that blades and needles might be found there. Seek cracks and holes through which we might be viewed or overheard.'

They sprang to action at his words.

Edward motioned Hastings towards the alcove of the window. Now his joking friend's eyes had taken on a focused cast. The pair stood half concealed in the heavy curtain that had been pulled across the glass, outside which the night was still swirling with snow. Accustomed to the task, Hastings swept the alcove behind them with his eyes.

'It seems we are safe to talk here.'

14

'I believe so.'

'You are convinced by Norfolk? You think he had no knowledge of Beaufort being in the area?'

Edward pursed his lips. 'On balance, I think he knows nothing. The man was so riddled with fears that he would have given himself away, had there been anything to hide.'

'Then what led our source to implicate the house? You did not tell him all.'

'No, I thought it best to keep the rest to ourselves. The monk seemed certain that it was someone under this roof who paid him to carry the letter to Beaufort. He was old and far from home; there is always the chance that he was mistaken, but he gave a very particular description of the place, the road and even the approach to it.'

'Could the monk have had another motive?'

Edward frowned. 'It's possible. We might have been deliberately misled, but he would be taking a risk. And why?'

'The monk might have been innocent, but deliberately sent by another?'

Edward nodded. 'On the morrow I will write to his community at Coventry, to see if he has returned there, also to the Abbot of St Albans, where he professed he was headed. We should have him watched.'

'You suspect him of being a Lancastrian agent?'

'No, I think his heart was sound, but that he may have been used to set us on a false trail. What was the last we heard of Beaufort?'

'That he was headed north, to join the queen in Scotland.'

'Exactly. Why would he turnabout and head south again? Especially if he knows we are close behind him.'

'Yes. It does seem strange.'

Hastings parted the curtains between two fingers and looked out upon a slither of night.

Edward watched him, knowing his friend too well. 'You think I have been too generous, don't you? Speak it.'

'You are always too generous, almost to a fault. It will be your undoing.'

'I have no intention of being undone.'

'But remember, Beaufort is not the friend you believed him to be. You must let those illusions go. He has played you false and, whatever he once was, he is now intent upon your destruction. While the Lancastrian Prince is still just a boy, they are heralding the duke as the saviour of their cause, and his arrogance is such that he seeks to lead them.'

It was more Edward's pride that was wounded. There had been a joyous Christmas spent at Westminster, laughing and making merry; the long rides in pursuit of the hart, Beaufort's horse slightly ahead of his own, urging him onwards; the confidences and plans they had shared; Beaufort's colours in the list as he lowered his visor; the ease with which they had spoken of the future. For a while, the two heirs had stood side by side: York and Lancaster, and the court had rung with laughter.

'You think his friendship was ever genuine?'

Hastings shrugged. The memories returned to him, too. 'It seemed so to me, even against my judgement. I did believe it.'

'It seemed so to me at the time, too. His heart did not feel false. To think now that I trusted him so far as to let him share my chamber, when he only intended to gain favour for his younger brothers, or to learn my secrets.'

'No, No, I think he was true then. I give you my word. I think he was once your true friend, or tried to be. But the Lancastrians got to him after you had parted, and they turned his head with their promises.'

'It was because I sent him away. It is my fault.'

'No, no.'

'I should have kept him close.'

'No, you had no way of knowing what choices he would make.'

'But I did. I knew it was a risky move at the time, but I thought I had no choice other than to send him away when we were together at Coventry. He was unpopular there. You should have heard the crowd baying against him and threats were made against his life. I thought he would be safe at Holt Castle; it was not meant to be a punishment, although I fear he took it as such. I should have sent him south.'

'It was isolation at Holt that did it. The Lancastrians are strong in North Wales and he had time to brood, a sitting target for any conspirators. If we could only get our hands on the old king,' Hastings said with exasperation. 'They could do nothing but surrender once he is in our custody, nothing. Then surely Beaufort would come into line.'

Edward sighed. 'Perhaps. But I do not think Norfolk is implicated. You remember how his father fought at Towton?'

'I do indeed, God rest his soul, but do not allow yourself to dismiss the dangers here. We still have reports of rebels in the area, which have not satisfactorily been answered.'

'Perhaps,' Edward pondered, running his hand through his hair, 'perhaps if we could meet again, come face to face in the same room, and I could speak with him, I am sure I could convince him to return.'

'And you would be able to trust him again?'

The king was silent.

'Would you have him share your chamber again? Would you trust him with the lives of your sisters, your mother?'

'No, I would not.'

'You are too trusting, Edward, you have always been, of those you love, in spite of all your caution.'

Edward nodded, shamed by the truth. 'It is not a virtue in a king.'

17

'Nonsense. It is the highest virtue. Mercy, forgiveness and charity. And then, when your enemies have proven themselves beyond doubt, you deliver absolute ruthlessness.'

'Absolute ruthlessness,' Edward echoed, catching the eye of his brother, who signalled that their search of the room was complete. 'See, Clarence confirms it is safe. Now, let's drink and retire. All is safe. We have ridden many miles today. We may trespass on the duke's hospitality for a few days more in order to uncover the truth.'

From the outside, from the quivering greenness of the forest trees, a dark window on the manor's second floor slowly kindled into light. Birds huddling together on solid branches saw a faint glow appear as if it was the blush of dawn, blinking in order to be certain that the moon and stars were still spread overhead. At the edge of the road, the hare paused, sniffing the air, scenting the trail which the men had left, of sweat and velvet, metal and horsehair. The dints of their hooves were still just visible on the road, although they would soon be covered by the lightly falling snow. The owl did not notice, slowly dissecting its delayed meal. Nor did the stoat, sticking its head up above the parapet now that the men had gone.

She lit a candle from the embers and carried it across the room to her side of the bed. The light danced and flickered up the walls of the chamber that the sisters shared, a modest room, improved by the tapestry hung in advance of their visit, and the presence of two finely carved chairs that had come from some baronial hall in the north. In her long shift, with a shawl thrown about her shoulders and fair hair spilling down her back, she set the candle in the well of a little writing desk and drew out paper. Her bedfellow, Elizabeth, rolled on to her back.

'What are you doing, Eleanor?'

'Go back to sleep. It's nothing.'

'You're not going to do anything to get us into trouble? If you jeopardise my marriage…'

'Don't be ridiculous. Go back to sleep.'

She waited, watching until Elizabeth had rolled back onto her side, too tired to sustain protest. Then, taking the pen, Eleanor scratched out a few hurried words, fast and furious across the page, with the conviction of the devoted. From the little finger of her left hand, she pulled off a thin silver ring, a simple band set with a small dark block, like a man's signet. Pressing it first to her lips, she placed it in the middle of the letter, where it imprinted the entwined initials H and S. Then she folded and double folded the paper to contain it, waited for the red wax to run soft and dropped it to form a seal.

The owl in the old yew outside saw the moment when her breath snuffed out the light. The manor house stood in darkness, the letter hidden under the pillow where Eleanor Butler lay awake.

TWO

Guests Bearing Gifts

Morning arrived late, hidden in a rush of black storm clouds from the west. Edward stood in the main doorway, rain spattering the flagstones and the tiles at his feet, as he squinted out towards the horizon. A little way behind him, Norfolk was reluctant to leave the shelter offered by the hallway. When he spoke, his voice was thin with uncertainty.

'The conditions are perilous, my lord. My men tell me there are trees down across the road.'

Still Edward stared ahead, his eyes searching the dark places of the woods.

'And you would be soaked through before you reached the end of the drive. It would be madness to attempt a journey today.'

'Madness?' Since the days of the unstable Henry VI, it was a loaded word. It sent Norfolk into a bluster.

'Forgive me, my lord, of course not. I don't mean that, I mean… I only mean, it would be exposing your person to avoidable dangers.'

The candle brackets flickered in the wind. Norfolk wrung his hands and looked back to where Hastings and Clarence stood at the foot of the staircase, half-heartedly carrying their saddles.

'My lord?'

Edward held up an arm to stay his host's voice. He took a step further out, across the hearth, so that the wind caught his cloak and buffeted his sturdy back. Rain darkly stained his shoulders as he turned from left to right, shielding his eyes, looking along the road and up to the heavens.

He stepped back under the porch. 'There will be no travelling today. We will avail ourselves of your kind hospitality once again and use this as a day of rest. By God's grace the storm will have calmed by the morrow.'

'Very good, my lord,' Norfolk replied, bowing his head. Then, turning with a sharper gesture to figures waiting in the shadows, he added his orders. 'John, build up the fire. Simon, instruct the kitchens. Inform the women.'

The sound of feet and industry echoed along the corridors, up the stairs, right to the rafters, as the house seemed to marshal itself in response to the challenge.

'My lord,' Norfolk gestured, 'the parlour is at your disposal, and all the hospitality my poor estate has to offer. Will you please come this way?'

Edward strode after him as the servants pulled the heavy door closed and shot the bolts.

It was a smaller room off the great hall, something like an old solar, and easier and quicker to warm. Even the fire roaring in the grate could not drown out the howl of the wind. The old stone walls were thick, having withstood centuries of weather, but the storm seemed to bring them to life, teasing out the smell of the plaster and paintwork, giving a chalky undertone to the smoke. A chair carved with vine leaves was hurriedly placed for him at the hearth, set with a velvet cushion. A flagon of wine, plates of fresh bread, pies and cheeses sat on the cupboard before the array of silver, and little dishes of spices and comfits waited on a red cloth.

'My betrothed sent those for you,' Norfolk added, his tone still nervous like the previous night.

'Then please do convey my gratitude to her. I trust we shall see the ladies again today?'

The young duke nodded. 'Of course, my lord, once they have completed their devotions. Is there anything else you require?'

'Nothing. I bid you good morning.'

Norfolk, upon being dismissed from his own parlour, gave a prompt bow and scuttled away under the archways towards the kitchens.

Edward sat by the fire and closed his eyes. He breathed in the scents of lavender, damp wood, bitter smoke, chalk, and the lingering tones of roasted meat from last night's supper. And then there was something else, more of a feminine smell amid them all too, perhaps a tincture of roses, or another flower resonant of the summer. The trace of women. The voices of his men reached him as they sat before the flames, finding a still point amid the house's activity. Perhaps, between these walls, in the company of Norfolk and these women, he might let his guard down and breathe easy, even forget the world for a while. If only he might permit himself.

Yet there was always something in Edward's mind, something unsettled, a strain of unease like a dust mote in his eye. Towton had been won and Mortimer's Cross too. Three whole years had passed since then. And yet the tortured path to victory and the many losses still hung heavy upon him at times, in the shadow-side of the day, or when he woke at night after the fire had burned low. Sometimes it felt like every day was a battle to be won. There were enemies at every table, not bearing swords and poll axes, but putting on their diplomatic smiles, bowing and scraping, while their minds ran on evil. Edward looked up at his men, at Hastings, Stanley, Stafford and young George. They were ready to serve him, poised to obey every command, willing to be led into battle, even into death for his cause. They venerated him as their king. Good, honest men, all of them, ready to give their all to keep a son of York on the throne.

So why did he sometimes feel torn? He was still young: his birthday would fall soon after Easter, bringing the end of his twenty-second year; he was strong, powerful, and he held the throne. But still, like one of the hounds, he always slept with one ear open, even when he slept the most deeply, and while his body rested, his mind raced. He was Edward the king, always doing, active, riding, hunting, ruling, fulfilling his duty, always in motion, and yet he was also Edward the man, caught in the demands of the flesh, hungry, sensual, with a perpetual restlessness, a sense of need he could not sate.

'Edward?'

He seemed to hear his father's voice, cutting through the room.

'Edward!'

It was his brother, George. He was tall at fourteen, precocious, expectant. For a second, his way of ducking his head to look round reminded Edward of Edmund, the brother they'd lost on the battlefield, but Edmund's gesture had been out of shyness and introspection, while George's was affectation.

'Edward? Will you break your fast with us?'

'No. Go ahead, eat.'

The boy did not need to be told twice.

'You are musing.' Hastings pulled up a chair beside Edward. 'I know that look. What are you thinking?'

Edward sighed. 'It's frustrating, being stuck here. I'd hoped to press on to Gloucester.'

'We will lose a day at most. Why the hurry?'

But Edward could not find the words to explain why perpetual hurry was necessary, why it kept his vices at a distance and how idleness could play on his mind. Instead, he found respite in duty.

'The assize courts have commenced. The abbot expects us.'

'The abbot can wait. And so can the game in his forests. Come, Edward, let us use the time wisely and turn our minds to the defeat of the traitor.'

'Little can be achieved while we are stuck here.'

'Perhaps this weather will provide a useful pause for reflection. We can gather the accounts of Beaufort's whereabouts, list those among his allies who are likely to shelter him, plan our course. Come, we will turn this moment to our advantage.'

Edward nodded, grateful for Hastings' practicality. 'But where might he be? The monk was certain that Beaufort had contacts in this household.'

'He may have been certain, but his information may not have been correct. To my eye, Norfolk looks like a sound man.'

'And to mine.'

'Then submit to this moment. We can draw up plans for the next meeting of the council and contact all our allies.'

'Very well, so be it. Have them bring us paper and ink.'

The hour was slipping towards noon when Norfolk knocked upon the door.

'My lord, forgive this intrusion.'

Edward looked up from the maps spread across the table before him.

'What is it, Norfolk, any news?'

The duke bowed low and Edward noticed how his eyes scanned the papers on the table. 'Word has spread about your arrival. Your horses were observed on the road last night and when I sent out the servants for more supplies, questions were asked about your presence. My men lacked the wit to explain the quantities I had ordered. Now our neighbours are at the door. They bring gifts and would like to wish you well.'

'Your neighbours?' interrupted Stanley, always cautious. 'You trust them?'

'Of course. Lord Dalton from Cheneywood, Sir Walter Brookes and Sir Reginald Wise, all good men and true Yorkists. Dalton was my own godfather. I would otherwise not admit them.'

Stanley turned to Edward. 'My lord, consider the risk. In such a remote location as this, with men unknown to you personally, we could not provide you with adequate protection.'

Edward looked at Norfolk. 'You have known these men long?'

'All my life, my lord. I am happy to send them away if you are unavailable.'

'They travelled out through this storm?'

'Six miles, the furthest one of them, through the rain.'

The king met Stanley's eye, then turned to Hastings. The messages he read there seemed to conflict.

'I am the sort of king,' he began, 'who does not want to be hidden away from his people.'

'And what if one of those people carries a bodkin?' Stanley frowned.

'The duke has given his personal assurance,' said Edward, gently. 'I am certain he does not wish to be accountable for the death of his king.'

Norfolk dropped to one knee. 'Of course not, my lord, I shall send them away.'

'No, do not do that. Let them warm themselves and take refreshment. I will give them an audience in your hall.'

'This is folly!' burst out Stanley, as Norfolk hurried away.

'Then it is a king's folly,' Edward replied, reaching for his cloak, 'which it is your duty to indulge.'

As Edward walked the short distance down the corridor to the hall, he sensed the presence of many people. The air smelt and sounded of them, of their hopes and fears, their excitement, their humanity. More tapers had been lit, burning brightly along the corridor and flanking the walls. Men in Norfolk's livery, bearing swords, met him at the threshold and accompanied him inside.

In the short time since the guests' arrival, Norfolk had been busy. A wide aisle had been created down the centre of the hall, with a strip of patterned carpet borrowed from some other location in the house, leading to a chair at the far end. It was the best chair on the estate, carved in dark wood with heraldic devices and curious creatures, set with cushions of gold. Swathes of red cloth had been draped above it, hoisted to a beam in semblance of a canopy, destined for the king. To the right, Norfolk waited at the head of his family and household while the new arrivals formed a line on the left, before the hearth, their faces turned towards him, bright in expectation. Edward sensed no immediate danger; the visitors had an air of admiration, of appreciation and gratitude. There were perhaps two dozen in total: three sturdy lords in velvet and furs, a number of ladies of all ages, a few youths, children and a handful of liveried servants, who dropped to their knees in turn as Edward processed past them. Alongside his host, he recognised the bent heads of the two old women and the two young ones he had met the previous night, especially the sisters. Elizabeth, with her hair pulled back under a fashionable headdress and Eleanor, her fair curls dressed more simply, her demeanour pretending disinterest. Edward looked away as he reached her, fixing his eyes on the chair ahead.

Before he sat, he turned to face them, touched by their numbers.

'My loyal subjects. You have ventured out of your homes amid this tempest to honour your king. I thank you for it. I thank you, with sincerity and gratitude, for the loyalty and good service you do to the house of York. I bid you welcome, and invite you, in turn, to be received.'

They came forward, one by one, or in small groups: men with pledges of loyalty and haunches of meat, women carrying pots of preserves, cheeses, plums and spices, children with bread and cakes.

Edward smiled and pressed the hand of an old woman as weathered as the storm. She looked back at him with watery eyes.

'I knew your father, my lord, when he was a boy, many years ago. He was a good lad, kind to me, I've never forgot.'

'Thank you.' Edward bent to kiss the top of her white head. 'That is the most priceless gift of all.'

'Kindness is never forgotten, my lord.'

He watched her as she returned to her family, a small group who had travelled from the next estate. She moved slowly. Her back and knees evidently pained her.

'Bring wine,' he spoke softly to a servant at his side, 'and see the old lady is given alms.'

He called upon the next in line, a woman and boy who had brought a rabbit caught in a snare. The king looked down at the still creature, the flank of brown fur and silent limbs held in the childish fingers. The boy wriggled under the king's gaze.

'And what is your name?'

He was perhaps five or six.

'Peterkin…'

His mother nudged his elbow. 'My lord, say my lord.'

'My lord Peterkin, my lord.'

Edward smiled. 'You must stay and dine with us, Peterkin, and take your share in this bounty.'

The boy held up the rabbit's face, the soft, stubby nose and brown eyes, the ears lying back from the head like silk. 'Shall we eat him?'

'Maybe! Did you catch him yourself?'

'I set a trap,' said the boy in a rush. 'And baited it with scraps so it came sniffing round. I had to wait ever so long, and not move a hair, and hardly breathe, before I could pull the string.'

Edward laughed and ruffled the boy's dark fringe. 'A born hunter. And do you look after your mother?'

'Very well indeed, my lord!'

The king fished into his coat and pressed a silver coin into the woman's hand.

'Oh, but I can't, my lord, thank you.'

'It's for the boy. A fine son to be proud of.'

'Thank you.' She dropped low before him, accepting the coin.

'Stay and eat with us. You are welcome.'

There were more supplicants offering gifts and best wishes. One by one, the king gave them his blessing with gentle words and the touch of his hand. It had always been his talent, this special sensitivity and ability to read others, to draw them close, to make them feel welcome. It was one of the reasons why Beaufort's betrayal had hit him so hard. It cut to the very heart of his warm generosity.

As Edward was turning away, his eyes came to rest on the Talbot sisters. They stood side by side across the hall, one dressed in blue and the other in green, observing the procession of guests. The younger, doe-eyed and soft, still a child at the side of her fiancé, Norfolk; the other, watching the king with a sharply focused gaze and a mouth that spoke of both passion and cruelty. She met his eye almost imperceptibly, turning away before he had been able to hold her gaze, keeping her face tilted away from him, in a pretence of being occupied with the room. But he had seen it. That look had contained both admiration and warning.

Norfolk called for minstrels. They had arrived with Lords Dalton and Brooks, bringing their lutes, pipes and viols wrapped up in sacking against the worst of the weather. Edward watched them set up with a slightly unsettled air. He could not fully enter the moment, fully immerse himself in that time and that place, as a sensation of otherness kept him hovering on the edge. No doubt it was occasioned by the uncertainty over Somerset. The others did not seem to feel it though. Hastings was content by the fire. Stanley and Stafford drank with Sir Reginald Wise, with George eagerly smiling at Wise's daughter, a tall young woman with dark eyes, perhaps five or ten years his elder, who merely gazed away above his head.

As the players struck their chord, Edward rose to his feet. He strode boldly down the hall, with all eyes upon him, to the place where his aunt sat, who was dressed in a red velvet gown.

'My lady?'

She could not prevent the little smile from leaping into the corner of her mouth. His mother was the same. Rising slowly to her full height, the old duchess accepted his hand with all her Neville dignity and followed him to the centre of the hall, where they began to dance.

She moved slowly at first. He could feel the frailty in her body, the fragile bones, the limbs stiff with age despite the pride coursing through her. His mother refused to dance now, which had once been such a great pleasure to her, citing her age, her widow's vow. With the passing of each year, he had tried to entice her, in the festive season and again when the heady flush of spring rushed in to mark her birthday, but she merely folded one hand over another and said her

29

dancing days were over. And he had not pushed her. Perhaps the day would come again, or perhaps not. She had not danced since they lost York, as if she had done it solely for the pleasure of her husband, or for the pleasure of dancing with him.

'You have brought me out here for a reason,' spoke Katherine Neville, after a while.

'I…'

'Don't talk. You invited me to dance in order to win me over. I know your intentions. They are too transparent, young man.'

'My intentions?'

'You hope to win me over so that I will back you against the Lancastrians when the time comes.'

'Would you not back me anyway,' he said, frowning, 'as your king and your nephew?'

She smiled, turned away in step with the music, then drew back closer towards him.

'You know it is so much more complicated than that.'

He took her hand as the dance required, moving in a stately line forward then back. But his brow furrowed a little.

'Is it, indeed? Even now, my lady? Even when I am your anointed king?'

She smiled and completed her circuit, coming full-circle to stop before him. 'You will not entrap me in a net of treasonous words.'

'Nor was that my intention. I already know how devoted you are to your family.'

They passed each other and returned, closer, and then he was obliged to take her in his arms.

She averted her face, her expression composed. 'Are you any closer to catching Beaufort?'

Edward hesitated. 'I will catch him.'

'He is young and headstrong. Might you be disposed to mercy?'

'Mercy?' He felt the anger rise in him. 'You should not seek to lecture me, madam.'

'Why?' she whispered. 'What would you do?'

She moved around to his side in time with the steps.

'I am sure you would not cut me down if I defend him?'

Edward forced a smile but his chest was tight. He knew she was thinking of her husband, who had been killed by a Yorkist army, in his defence of the Lancastrian king.

'I would cut down any traitor.'

'You should mind your tongue, Nephew. You speak against God's will and his punishment will be more fearful than that of any mortal man, even one who wears a crown.'

The dance was not yet complete but Edward broke off the steps and took the old woman firmly by the hand. She was a little startled, dragging one foot slightly, as he led her promptly back to her place. Bowing his head with exaggerated courtesy, he lifted his eyes to meet those of Eleanor Butler standing just a little way before him. No doubt he was flushed with annoyance and his eyes blazed in indignation.

'My lady?' He held out his hand and Eleanor dared not refuse.

Leading her out into the hall, he closed his fingers over her slim ones, and felt the sinuous, graceful way she followed his lead. She danced well, with a mixture of feeling and restraint. At first they did not speak and he indicated the minstrels to keep playing, once that dance had ended its cycle.

'You would keep me longer, my lord?'

'I would not deprive you of the pleasure of the dance.'

'You assume that I take pleasure in it?'

She turned around, extended her reach, and then returned to him.

'You take no pleasure in dancing with your king?'

Her eyes lowered, perhaps reading something of his mood. 'The pleasure of a loyal subject, of course.'

Other pairs were joining the dance, complicating the space. Edward moved and Eleanor followed closely, like his shadow, her steps patterning his. At least in terms of the music, they were in sympathy. He snatched glances at her as they passed and re-passed, taking in the set of her mouth, her neck and shoulder, the sweep of her headdress. On one occasion she turned, as if she had felt his eyes, and met them with her bright ones. And in that moment, amid the mix of emotions, he decided he wanted her.

'You are angry with me,' he said more softly, as the dance brought them close together again. Briefly they were man and woman, not king and subject. 'The question of your lands will be dealt with.'

She made no reply.

'I said, the question of your lands will be dealt with.'

'I thank you.'

She turned around to face him, as the other couples processed between them. For a moment their eyes met and he read in them the glimmer of a chance. Then she offered him her hand, as the dance demanded, in order to follow their lead.

'Perhaps you might even look upon me as a friend.'

She turned her head away. He circled around her but she avoided his gaze.

He tried again. 'Would that be such a bad thing? An impossibility?'

They moved past each other, shoulder to shoulder, but she kept her head turned away.

'Life cannot be easy for you,' he offered.

She turned and accepted his hands again.

'A young, beautiful widow.'

Did he see her purse her lips, almost imperceptibly?

'You need a protector.'

But she would not respond.

The dance came to an end. She bent her knee before him, bowed her head as etiquette demanded and hurried away.

The trestles were being cleared in advance of the food arriving. Servants set out the best plates and bowls the family could muster, with spoons, knives, glasses and clean white linen. A separate table was being set for Edward at the top, but he waved the men away, insisted that he would dine among his friends.

'So far, so good.' Hastings appeared at his side.

'You've heard nothing?'

'Not quite.' Hastings drew him to one side. 'There's a stable lad, come over with his master from Cheneywood, half a mile away, says a woman here paid him to carry a message, a seven night ago.'

'Go on.'

'He was to meet a man on the Gloucester road who was to ride north with it. There's more. You should speak with him.'

'Good work. Where is he?'

'Standing by the door, but do not draw attention. The woman he speaks of may be close.'

Edward felt a thrill of excitement and anger. 'Wait a little, then bring him to meet me by the great door.'

The entrance passage was empty, lit by flickering tapers. Edward dismissed the guards that stood either side of the door and listened to the howl of the wind outside. After a moment, footsteps behind him told of Hastings' arrival. The youth at his side was barely out of childhood, his chin hazy with the first growth of beard.

'This is Roger, son of the Smith.'

The boy bowed, clearly overawed.

'Be at ease, Roger,' insisted Edward, laying a hand on his shoulder. 'I believe you can be of service to your king.'

'Anything I can do, my lord. It would be such an honour.'

'Lord Hastings tells me you carried a letter from this place.'

'Yes, it was just after the feast of Twelfth Night. My master bid me bring over a horse from Cheneywood, which he had promised to the Duke of Norfolk. As I was leaving, a woman met me in the yard and asked me to bear a message.'

'A woman from this household?'

'I believe so, my lord. A well-dressed woman, a lady.'

'And do you see her in the hall this day?'

'I cannot be sure. She wore a hood pulled well down over her face.'

'Was she young, old?' interrupted Hastings.

'She did not move like an old woman. Her movements were easy. And her voice suggested youth.'

The king nodded. 'And the message?'

'I was to carry it to the Gloucester road, as soon as possible, where a man was waiting to carry it north. This I did.'

'What manner of man was he?'

'A soldier perhaps, but one of the meaner sort. Grey-haired, tall, well-armed but lean as if he was hungry. He asked no questions other than whether I had been seen or followed, and he gave me a shilling for my pains.'

'What did the message say? To whom was it addressed?'

'It was sealed, stamped with the device of a swan. But I do not know to whom it was addressed.'

'You cannot remember?'

'I cannot read, my lord.'

Edward stood, lost in thought.

'You have done well,' added Hastings, offering the boy another coin. 'Your information has been helpful.'

'I wonder,' mused Edward, 'if this woman will approach you again, attempt to give you another message.'

The boy shrugged. 'She might, I suppose.'

'The storm is severe. You will undoubtedly sleep here in the hall tonight. Be on your guard but find opportunities to stand alone. Check on the horses in the stable. Step into the courtyard for the cold air. Put yourself in her way and report back to me.'

'I will, my lord. I will do all I can to assist you.'

'It shall not be forgotten. Now return to your place before you are missed.'

They watched him go.

'Only one of four women to choose from,' pronounced Hastings.

'And that is three too many,' retorted the king. 'Come, the feast begins.'

THREE

Night of the Storm

Night had fallen across the estate. Encircled by the woods, the house wreathed itself in the smoke of many hearths, where kitchens were boiling and baking, fire roared up the great chimney and the bedrooms were kindled into life. The moon and stars were hidden overhead; thick clouds chased behind the trees. Gates rattled on their hinges, shutters protested against leaden panes, buffeted by the wind. Horses in the stables trampled their straw, emitting snorts to register their unease, but the stable boy slept on.

On the Gloucester road outside, a lone rider had braved the storm. Conditions had worsened during the afternoon and although the driving rain had finally ceased, it lay heavy on the earth, turning hollows into ponds and ditches into streams. The road was swamp-like, treacherous. And yet, he had bound himself tightly in cloak and hood, saddled his mount, and was driving the beast hard against the wind. He had a mission, something worth risking everything for. And that was loyalty, to his master, his house, his cause. The road was long and lonely, flanked on each side by shadows, and once or twice he looked back over his shoulder in fear, but he rode as if escaping the devils of judgement day. He only pulled up the reins when the lights of the hall came into view. The lights, too many lights, blazing out in defiance of the night. This was not the quiet, sleepy house he had expected to find. The gates were barred but the bright fires and sounds spilled out at every opportunity and he sensed the presence of activity and many people. He paused, peered through the darkness which offered no answers.

He urged the horse to walk slowly forward. There was a low point in the wall, at the agreed meeting place, where the ground was high outside and crumbled stone allowed him to see over the top. This was where the lad met him last time and handed over the letter, but now there were men in the courtyard. Some attending to the horses, others fetching wood and barrels, a few merely standing under the arch, catching a breath of air, two even quarrelling almost so close he could reach through and touch them. Then the kitchen door flew open, and the cook bustled outside to empty a bucket down the drain. Amid the brightness inside, there was a crowd of bodies, all hurrying about the business of hospitality. The door swung shut again but the sight had caught him off guard. He pulled the reins, drawing the horse away. It was too dangerous. There was no chance of getting any message tonight without arousing suspicion. Nor could he see anyone waiting at the wall; perhaps the lad who brought the message last time had decided not to come, or was occupied. He was supposed to wait, as long as necessary, but the night was too foul and he would catch his death to linger under these clouds. With a blunt curse, he picked his way back to the road and galloped away.

Roger, son of the Smith, stood uneasily in the doorway. It led into a service passage used for carrying barrels, wood and plates of food, so it was quiet and cold, lit only by a single torch. Now that the feast was over, it was secret enough. But this spot, half on the threshold of the passage and half visible from the hall, meant that anyone who wanted him could find him easily. They were dancing again now, with the king observing from his chair of state. The minstrels were in mid-flow, with their jaunty, rhythmic notes. The red brick walls around him flickered with reflected firelight. He had made his departure obvious, standing apart from the tables and benches, the dancers, his lord's party, lingering in plain sight. If she wanted to find him again, he could scarcely have made it easier.

Then the song ended. There was some breaking apart, laughter and raised voices. A new chord was struck. Roger shivered and rubbed his arms. The temperature was dropping, away from all those active bodies.

'A good even to you.'

She was there again, the woman in the hood. She walked past him, a little shorter than himself, well-formed but slight. This time, the cloak she had thrown about her shoulders displayed the fine clothes below, the embroidered skirt, the flash of colour at the hem, the lace cuff. She continued a little way down the passage, looked around, and turned back to face him. Her features were partly hidden, but he could make out the fresh, young complexion, the lively mouth and intelligent eyes.

'You are not cold out here?' Her voice was soft.

'No, my lady.'

'You wish to earn a shilling?'

He did not reply. Wisely, he waited.

She held out a piece of folded paper, sealed with red wax.

'Give this to the man who comes to the estate walls tonight, on the eastern side, by the kitchen yard.'

'Yes, my lady.'

She held out a coin.

'And tell no one.'

He blushed. 'Who is he?'

'That is not your business!'

'Forgive me. I mean, how will I know him?'

'There will be no other waiting in this storm. Do not fail me.'

'No, my lady.'

She swept past him, past the hall, and into the darkness at the end. The passageway fell silent again. Roger, son of the Smith, turned over the paper in his fingertips. The seal showed the print of two letters, H and S, the tendrils of the latter stretching back to entwine with the first.

Hastings stepped out from the shadows, peering up and down. He plucked the note from Roger's trembling fingers.

'You recognised her?' he asked the lad.

'Aye, my lord.'

'As did I.'

'It was the same woman as before?'

'Without doubt, my lord.'

With one deft crack he broke the seal and read the contents. Then, silently, he handed over payment and waved the youth away.

Stanley was standing waiting at the side when Hastings returned to the hall. 'Anything?'

Hastings nodded. 'Most edifying. Where is the king?'

Stanley nodded over to where Edward stood by the fire. He had left the dance but was smiling with the figures moving lithely before him, one hand clasping his goblet of wine.

'Tell him nothing yet,' urged Hastings. 'I am going out to watch the road; there should be a messenger waiting tonight.'

'From Beaufort?'

Hastings held up the letter's seal, with its distinctive H and S, twined together.

Stanley examined it in the gloom. Then his eyes widened as he recognised the imprint in the wax. 'Henry, Duke of Somerset.'

'The very same.'

'So the monk was right; Beaufort has an ally within this house?'

'A woman within this house. And we both know whom. Keep your counsel for the moment. We shall see what the night brings.'

Stanley's austere brows knit closer. 'Should we not tell the king?'

'I think not yet. Not until we are sure. From the way they danced earlier, I believe he is already under her spell and will not believe us until we have further proof of the exchange.'

'Is this letter not proof enough?'

'She has not signed it, and her head was covered with a hood. If she denies it, it is our word against hers. No, I will take some men and intercept the messenger on the road, bring him here and force it out of him.'

'Well, I am for telling him as soon as possible.'

Hastings shook his golden head. 'Allow me to know my friend. When he is caught in the thrall of an attraction, he can hear nothing against the woman. We are safe here tonight. Let me uncover the proof.'

Stanley shrugged. 'On your head be it.'

But Hastings held up a warning hand. 'See how she returns.'

They watched together as, at the far end of the hall, the Lady Eleanor appeared from a gap between the tapestries, from some hidden passage used by the servants. She had shed her hooded gown and her bright hair shone in the candlelight. Her cheeks were flushed.

'I am off to watch the road,' said Hastings, making his move. 'You might do worse than to set an eye on young George tonight. He seems to be setting his mind towards mischief with that squire's daughter.'

'That pup!' replied Stanley in disdain. 'I would rather be stood outside with you in the rain.'

'Then come along, my man, and make good your words.'

As the musicians struck up their next tune, Edward saw her rise and step away from the others. The Lady Eleanor leaned across to where her sister sat, spoke to her softly and leaned down to kiss her cheek. Then, after offering the same courtesy to her mother, she slipped through the hall towards the staircase. He could not ignore the sinuous way she moved, the grace with which she carried herself, the firmness in her expression and her tread. Swilling down the remainder of his wine, he passed behind the trestle and followed her outside.

At first, he kept his distance, watching her dim form ahead in the flickering light as she made for the main staircase. He followed as she slowly climbed, keeping his eyes on her as she reached the landing, ducking into the shadows as she turned, as she reached the first floor. She made her way along the landing, past the chamber doors, to the very last one, its door set back in an alcove. Edward paused as she took out a key and turned it in the lock. The door had scarcely closed before he reached it, and knocked softly upon the wood. His heart pounded as he waited for her response.

The door opened at once. She looked out into the corridor with distrustful eyes. He saw, with gratification, the moment she realised that her king stood there, and the resulting change in her demeanour. At once she dropped an awkward curtsey but kept her eyes low, so he could not read her emotions.

'Please, none of that.'

She paused, uncertain of his intentions.

'Might I come in?'

There was a moment of hesitation, but she stood aside and let him enter the room. It was small and dark. A large bed stood against the

41

far wall. There were chests, books, clothes draped over a chair that stood close to the hearth. A small fire grumbled amid the tinder.

'You share this chamber with your sister?'

'Yes, my lord.'

'She will be dancing still for hours.'

He closed the door behind him and strode into the space. Heavy curtains hung across the window, matching those that were looped down on one side of the bed. She had not yet had time even to remove her headdress.

'You were retiring for the night?'

'Yes, my lord, I was not in the mood for dancing.'

'And why is that? Do you dislike dancing or are you unwell?'

'Neither, my lord. I merely wished for the quiet of my chamber.'

'And now you have it.'

'My chamber, but I am not quiet.'

'You are not?'

'No, I am quite disquieted.'

She was clever, cleverer than him. He hovered, suddenly uncertain, full of desire for her but unsure how to broach the gap between them, in spite of all his experience.

'How may I help you, my lord?'

Her voice had the same hostile note as when she had questioned him about her lands.

He took a step closer, hoping that his presence, his gaze, would speak silently for him, but she kept her chin raised, proud and unyielding. It only made him want her more.

'Do you like me being here?'

'Any way that I might serve, my lord.'

He tried to catch her eye but she kept her gaze averted. He had the sense of the awkward dance between them continuing.

42

'Why have you not remarried, Eleanor? May I ask?'

Her expression changed slightly. She turned her head away, just a little, but he had caught it.

'There is someone? Your heart is committed?'

'I am unsure who would have me.'

'A woman like you? I don't believe it.'

'I'm looking to make the best match I can.'

'And what would you like? An earl, a duke? A king?'

Her cheeks flushed. She swallowed. He moved closer, taking over her space, but she did not submit, only stood her ground.

'A woman in my position must make the right choice.'

'Do you not miss having a husband?'

He thought a brief smile touched her lips.

'I am concerned only to do my duty, my lord.'

'Your duty?' He traced a line on her shoulder.

Her muscles stiffened. 'Yes, my lord, my duty'

'But what about your pleasure?'

He was so close to her now that he might have kissed her. He was aware of the contours of her body, her shoulder closest to him, the length of neck, the curve of her breast.

He spoke softly, huskily. 'Take off your headdress.'

'My lord, I…'

He lifted clumsy fingers, attempted to unpin the hennin from her hair, but only succeeded in making a tangle. She was forced to intervene and complete the job, revealing the long fair locks tied back.

'Loosen your hair.'

She did as she was bid, keeping her eyes on the floor, while her fingers teased out the hair and pulled it forward across her shoulder. Only then did she meet his eyes, briefly, but he saw anger there.

'Are you satisfied, my lord?'

Her expression forced him to step back.

'Satisfied, no? Not at all. I fear you do not like me.'

She looked away.

'Which is a shame. I followed you up here because I admire you. I thought I saw a similar regard within you, perhaps not one you cared to admit, even to yourself.'

She looked away.

'I was mistaken.' He continued. 'You see me as the enemy of your friends, the thief of your lands.'

Now she met his challenge, eyes ablaze. 'Yes, I will not deny it. My family has fought against yours. For decades we served the Lancastrian king, the one you keep a prisoner in filth in the Tower. There are good men whom you have persecuted, killed, all for the sake of your own glory.'

From her lips, somehow, the words did not wound him. He found himself suddenly tolerant, indulgent.

'You are aware that you speak treasonously? Men have died traitors' deaths for less.'

'So be it,' she retorted. 'You have already taken everything from me.'

'Then I restore it. I restore your estates and give you a new husband.'

Her lips moved in confusion. 'Restore my estates?'

'I will instruct my secretary as soon as I return to Westminster.'

'You will forget.'

'I give you my word.'

He waited for her to address his second offer but she remained quiet. As he watched her face, thoughtful, intelligent in its beauty, a rush of desire swept through him, and he knew he must have her at any price.

'You may not like me as a king. But how do you like me as a man?'

Her lips quivered, parted: finally, he had disarmed her.

'As a man?'

'As that which I am, that which I was before I wore any crown? That which I am without my cloak?'

He pulled off his coat and threw it on the floor at her feet. The gesture impressed her. Her brief smile was involuntary, sincere. She could not keep her eyes from appraising him and he followed her gaze as it travelled across him.

'You're just a man,' she replied softly. 'Like any other.'

'Like any other?'

She paused. Her voice was barely a whisper. 'No.'

He touched her cheek lightly with his fingertips, stroked down to the corner of her mouth, ran his thumb across her lips. 'Let's overlook everything else, estates, names, allegiances, just for tonight.'

Her breath was warm on his face as he moved in to kiss her. The dizziness of surrender was almost upon him, but at the last moment, she turned her mouth away and stepped backwards. He stumbled into her space, caught off balance.

'So you would make a whore of me?' she cried. 'Is that your plan? To humiliate me? With one hand you wish to restore what I am owed but on the other you will take away my good name? How can I marry after that, after it is known? It would kill my mother. I will not!'

He tried to touch her again, to soothe her, but she batted his hand away. Even that contact made his senses swim with desire.

'Eleanor. It would be no dishonour to you. I would not allow it. No one else need know; I would reward you and your mother. Your sister too.'

'No, you cannot buy me. You must go!'

'I mean you no dishonour. Quite the opposite. I would seek to honour your person in every way.' His hands reached for her again but she stepped back towards the cold grate.

They stared at each other through the gloom.

'You think that because you are king, you can have anything you want.'

'It is your widowhood that makes me bold. I would not presume to speak so if you were still a maid.'

'No, it is your boldness that makes you bold!'

'I am your king!'

'No, as you told me just now, in this moment you are just a man, like any other.'

He pursed his lips in vexation.

'And I have watched you since your arrival. Your intense arrogance! King or no king, you treat the world and everything in it the same way. You are the kind of man who takes any woman they want, then casts them aside. I have heard of your reputation.'

'And you dare speak to me like this? You, who have known me for mere hours. When I am your king!'

She stood silently, head almost bowed, but he sensed it was not in submission.

'I serve another master.'

He assumed she meant God.

'You will give yourself to no man but your husband?'

Again, she made no sound. He saw her eyes fall upon a small desk where there was writing paper and ink.

'You will not answer your king?'

'What answer would my king have?'

His temper rose at her game. 'That which I might command, should I choose.'

'And take what is not willingly given?'

'Madam, you accuse me of arrogance, yet you forget that I am your king. Your life, and your lands, are in my gift. In return, I accuse you, as my subject, of ingratitude and insolence.'

46

She opened her mouth as if to interrupt but he continued.

'I will take my leave of you, madam, in quite the different spirit to that in which I came. In spite of your harsh words, I will invite Norfolk and your sister to Westminster to receive my blessing. Should you still wish to regain your lands, and you can keep a civil tongue in your head, you may consider accompanying them. Good night.'

He reached the door, hand outstretched to turn the handle.

'Wait.'

He heard the new note of submission in her voice.

With a swift, graceful move, she knelt on the floorboards before him and bowed her head. Her fair curls tumbled forward. 'Please, forgive me, I went too far.'

Edward waited, caught in the moment as the mood turned.

'You are my king. I should never have spoken those words; they came from my fear. My life is in your hands and you must treat me as I deserve.'

He did not raise her at once but left her upon her knees. In the stillness he could hear her breathing, heavy and uncertain as she awaited her fate. She knew he desired her. He had made that plain. And he believed that, underneath her defensive front, on a personal level, she desired him too.

Slowly, she lifted her head.

And the dilemma came upon him again. The tug between man and king. He could claim her now if he wanted, and he did want her. He had never hesitated with a woman before, always pursued them with the conviction of a huntsman who had marked his quarry.

Then her eyes met his. The blend of submission and uncertainty sent a wave of desire through him. He could easily have pulled her up to him and pressed his lips down upon hers. And yet something, some instinct he could not decipher, held him back.

She sensed he was not yet won over. Without waiting for his permission, she rose to her feet and edged backwards towards the bed. He followed her with eager eyes, wondering at her intention. She walked with languor, with an understated deliberation, making him transfixed by her movement. And then she lay back upon the bed, her arms flung open, and she fixed her eyes upon him. It was such a look that left him in no doubt. A look of desire and permission. He stepped forward, involuntarily.

She kept her eyes on him as he came closer.

'My king.'

She was stretched out before him like a sacrifice, ready to be claimed. Her lips parted in anticipation, her body keening towards him. It was too swift a surrender, too easy, but he was too hungry, too much made of flesh and blood to resist her.

'I would be more,' he whispered.

His doubts were submerged by the waves of passion she promised, and he dropped down upon the bed, covering her body with his, making a seal over her mouth with his. And the rest of the world receded.

Her body rose up to meet his, melting into him, so close that a breath could not have passed between them.

'But what?' she gasped, between his kisses. 'If I give myself to you, what then?'

Edward's lips were upon her throat, tracing the line of her warmth.

She tried to pull away a little, but he held her closer.

'I would only...' she gasped, as his mouth rose up to silence hers. 'Only give myself... to my husband.'

At that moment, he would have said anything to possess her. 'Then I will be your husband.'

'You, you?'

His hands fumbled with the material of her skirts, reaching the warmth of her thighs. 'I will be your husband tonight,' he murmured against her mouth, 'and do a husband's part.'

'And after?'

'And every night after,' he promised, overcome with the desire to claim her.

She squirmed her hips away from him. 'Do you mean that? You would make me your queen?'

'My queen in my bed.'

'Then promise me.'

Her hand stole down his thighs, finding the place where he strained to be free, hard and ready. Gently she released his yard from its confines, held it in her warm hand.

'Promise me. Promise me. Then you can have me.'

He yearned towards her, anticipating the sweet sensation of entry. 'I promise.'

'Say it, say it all. You promise to make me your wife.'

'Yes, yes, my wife, I promise. God, Eleanor, I'd promise the world.'

And she moved closer, guided him down towards her, and closed her mouth over his.

Stanley was waiting at the back door when Hastings arrived. He unwrapped his cloak, still cold from the night outside. The clatter of pans and the sluicing of water reached them from the kitchen nearby.

'Did you see anyone upon the path or in the grounds?'

Hastings looked quickly up and down the passage. 'Not a single fellow.'

'Nor I to the east.'

'I wonder if perhaps the woman was mistaken, or the messenger

49

failed to brave the storm. I think it best we counsel the king to move on in the morning and reach the safety of Gloucester.'

Hastings nodded. 'If the storm has died, we will leave at first light. Come, let's return.'

The hall was still alive with drinkers and dancers, who showed no signs of fatigue. They found George, seated alone at the bottom of the staircase, befuddled by wine.

Stanley clapped him on the shoulder. 'Is the king within?'

'Within whom?' belched George, crudely, 'because he has all the luck with women while I have none.'

The men exchanged glances.

'You don't know? He tarries late with the widow Butler. The lovely Eleanor. Who wouldn't?'

Hastings' face dropped. 'With the widow, Butler?'

'In her chamber.'

'In her chamber, all this while?'

'I believe so.'

Hastings nodded. 'Of course. Her part tonight was already performed.'

Stanley's eyes widened in realisation. 'You think the king is in danger?'

'If he is alone with her in an unguarded moment. Who knows what she might do, for the sake of Somerset?'

In one impulse, they hurried towards the winding stairs, but the approach of feet from the floor above stilled them at once.

'Wait!' Hastings put his finger to his lips, urging Stanley back against the wall. Both men's hands went to their swords. The footsteps came closer as they judged the approach of a heavy-set man from the floor above. A pair of leather boots came down the steps, followed by the dark form of a man.

'Fellows! Why do you seek the shadows?' Edward strode up to them with a swagger in his step.

Hastings and Stanley exchanged glances. The latter spoke first.

'My lord, we did not know it was you.'

'Well, it is I. Who else might it be?'

'And all is well?' Hastings enquired.

'All is more than well. And so to bed.'

He walked past them and into the hall, calling for wine.

Hastings went to follow him, but Stanley laid a cautious arm upon his shoulder. 'Should we speak to him of this?'

'What do you counsel?'

'We leave in the morning. We put miles between him and the woman, but we have her watched. We do not yet have the proof we need, and now it is worse.'

'And they will come to court, as arranged?'

'And we will have the chance to observe her then.'

'But perhaps we should seek to replace him, with another, more beautiful, more willing, so that he forgets her the sooner.'

With a nod of agreement, they followed their king.

FOUR

The King's Business, March 1464

The Earl of Warwick strode up and down the council chamber, both fists balled into his hips. The room was vaulted, with paned gothic windows, and the spring sunlight streamed in from outside. It left tones of green and mauve, yellow and pink upon the paved floor.

Seated at the high table, in blue velvet, Edward addressed the assembled men. The chamber was filled with lords and bishops, the clerks at the side and the supplicants who had gathered in the entrance by the carved doors.

'As there is no objection, I declare that grant is approved and passed. Let it be recorded that a grant of 500 marks has been made to the king's sister, Anne, Duchess of Exeter, upon her separation from the Lancastrian traitor, her husband, Henry Holland, the former Duke of Exeter, who has been attainted for treason, for the sustenance of herself, her daughter, and her wards, from the issue of the king's lordships of the places beforementioned.'

At the wooden desk, a young man in black diligently scribbled down the details. The point of his quill scratched across the paper, up and down, leaving a spidery black trail. Edward paused a moment to look round at the assembled faces. There were friends here: Hastings, William Stanley and his brother Thomas, Baron Stanley, Stafford and others whom he knew he could trust, like Montagu and Worcester. But Warwick was still striding, unsettled since his arrival, with his black curls streaked with grey and his brows knit. He would not rest until he had expressed what was on his mind.

'What business is next?' the king asked.

'My lord,' spoke out a second clerk, in a grey coat. 'A petition from your erstwhile physician, William Hattechief, that he may be permitted to claim the revenue from three acres of sheep fenced into an enclosure on the common land at Brunton in Warwickshire. It is disputed by the farmer, a Giles Morton, who claims he owns the land but not the sheep.'

Warwick stopped pacing. 'For the love of God! When will we be done with these trifles! There is serious business to discuss.'

Edward ignored him. 'If Morton owns the sheep and Hattechief owns the land which feeds the sheep, it is right and fitting that the profits be split equally between the two. Let that be set down and let Hattechief be content with it. And now…' The king rose to his feet. 'I defer the hearing of petitions until the afternoon. Leave us.'

Both clerks rose, bowed to the king, and hurried from the chamber. The doors at the back were opened and those gathered streamed out. Then they closed fast upon the court's inner circle: Warwick and Hastings, the Stanleys and Stafford, Montagu and Worcester.

'At last!' Warwick took his seat at the table to Edward's left. The last three years had effected little change in his person: he was still the weathered, grim-faced man he had been since youth, and just as determined.

'You are impatient, Richard. You forget that these questions are a matter of life and death to my subjects.'

'You will no longer have any subjects if Somerset is allowed to continue raising support in the north. He will wipe your rule clean away.'

'Have a little more faith. Have you forgotten Northampton, Mortimer's Cross, Towton?'

And the memory of that last, terrible encounter washed over them: the sleet driving in their faces on the incline of farmland outside a Yorkshire village; how the river ran with blood, and the lanes for miles were piled high with the dead.

'And the old Duke of Norfolk, and your brother Fauconberg, whom we have lost since, God rest their souls,' added the king.

Warwick drew back his shoulders and lifted his chin as if to speak.

But Edward was used to his headstrong interventions and lifted his hand to still the earl. 'So let us speak of Somerset.'

'Yes, because Somerset must be taken seriously, for all the victories of Towton. He is headstrong and lacking in wisdom, but he has allies. He will not lack for men to support his cause.'

'I know full the danger Somerset poses, and the flaws of his character. You will recall he was an intimate of mine for a twelvemonth, and my guest at court.'

'And a vainer, more arrogant coxcomb never walked these halls!'

'Hastings,' asked Edward gently, turning to address his friend, 'what news of the Duke of Somerset?'

Hastings exchanged a glance with William Stanley and then rose to his feet. The room fell to a silent attention.

'Our agents in the north inform us that there have been sightings of the duke at Newcastle, and close to the Scottish border. He has Henry Percy with him, and Lords Hungerford and Roos. It is believed that he is attempting to make an alliance with the young king of Scots, and with Kennedy, the regent, who has taken over governance since the death of Marie of Guelders.'

'The Lancastrian queen found a welcome there, did she not?' asked Warwick, reminding the king of Margaret of Anjou's sojourn at the Scottish court, and the troops Marie had offered her cause, just a year or two before. 'I believe she was welcomed like a sister.'

'At first,' Edward recalled, 'but that friendship quickly turned sour. It seems we need to pay a visit to the Scots and remind them just who their allies are. I shall prepare to depart as soon as possible.'

'My lord,' spoke Hastings, rising to his feet with concern in his voice. 'I would not recommend that you go in person, not at this time.' He continued in haste as he saw Edward begin to react. 'No wait, my lord, please listen to my reasons. I understand that it is always your desire to go in person, but I must counsel caution. This is exactly what Somerset intends. He plans to draw you away from the capital, away from your support and isolate you in the north where he has raised his army, and' – he looked tentatively at the king – 'it is the same strategy he used with your father. He would lure you out for talks, make you believe yourself secure and then ambush you. Send another in your place.'

'He speaks wisely,' added Warwick. 'You should not meet him in his stronghold.'

'Then what sort of king am I,' replied Edward, seething with the reality of their remarks, 'that I sit in Westminster while my friends fight my battles for me. His stronghold lies within my kingdom! Would you make me the coward king, like the Lancastrian, Henry?'

'No,' said Warwick, approaching him and laying a placatory hand on his shoulder. 'No one would ever accuse you of that. You have proven your skill and bravery a thousandfold. But this is wisdom; it is caution, and best for the commonweal. If, by some twist of fate you were to fail in the north, Somerset would claim the throne at once, by right of conquest. Sit tight in London and, however many victories he wins, you retain the throne. Make him come to you.'

Edward turned his back to them and looked out through the paned glass into the walled garden. The season was on the turn. Spring sunshine had already brought some of the shrubs into bud and the trees bore white blossom, hanging down above the paths. He let the words of his friends sink in.

'Then who? Who do we propose to go?'

'It falls to me, my lord.' Warwick's brother, John, Marquis of Montagu, veteran of Towton, clambered to his feet. Taller than his brother, and leaner, but with a body dense with power, he had led the forces into Scotland at the start of Edward's reign, lifting the siege of Carlisle and claiming many border fortresses.

Edward turned to face him.

'I, also, have been gathering intelligence,' Montagu continued, 'from my spies on the border. The Lancastrians are massing in the East March, with the intention of taking Newcastle and disrupting the negotiations for peace between our nation and the Scots. I will go and rout them out.'

'We are in your debt, Montagu,' Edward replied, humbly. 'The peace process must be concluded as swiftly as possible. The Scots' king's uncle, Duke Philip of Burgundy, wishes for an alliance with us, against the French, and Beaufort cannot be allowed to jeopardise this.'

'He must not be allowed to influence the king of Scots,' Montagu added.

'How old is he now, young James? Ten, eleven?'

'He is twelve, at the least,' offered Hastings, 'old enough to speak his mind but under the sway of the Kennedy family.'

Edward thought fast. 'Let us bring the negotiations away from Beaufort. Montagu, your task will be to intercept the Scots party and conduct them safely to York, where the peace can be concluded. The Lancastrians will not dare to show their faces there, not in the city whose name I bear.'

'And if I meet the duke on the road?' asked Montagu, squaring his shoulders.

'If you meet him on the road?' the king echoed, 'then you will dispatch him to meet his maker.'

'Oh?'

Edward nodded. 'That may be God, or myself, depending on his actions.'

Edward stepped outside into the spring air. The walled garden was a haven for his family, a place of sanity amid the business of the palace. Over the last three years, he had come to admire its gentle serenity and its regular surrender to the seasons. It caught the sun's rays like bees in a honey pot, yet the wind never seemed to blow too harshly here, especially in the corners where seats had been placed among the flowers, screened by green arbours. It was to the far corner, past the stone sundial, where Edward went now. At the chamber window behind him, where the councillors were dispersing, Warwick stood in the stone frame, watching as the king walked away.

Cecily Neville, dowager Duchess of York, was sitting in a spot of sunshine. Bright light bathed her pale face and papery skin, but lit her eyes a brilliant blue. She had aged since Edward came to the throne; the lines about her eyes and mouth were still deeply etched but a serenity had set into the lines of her noble mouth and her chin still spoke of nobility. Wrapped in black furs, her frail form was settled upon the edge of the bench, surrounded with greenery and flowering shrubs, bright and fair, as if it was painted in one of the palace manuscripts.

At Cecily's side, sat the eleven-year-old Richard, leaning slightly into the curve of her body. His dark eyes were closed, concealing their sensitive expression, but the frailty in his bird-like features seemed to grow more marked as the years passed. He made such a contrast with their middle brother, the robust George, who was in the orchard beyond, practising his swordsmanship. Edward smiled to see him waving the heavy sword about and testing his balance.

'Mother, enjoying the sunshine?'

Cecily smiled gently. He noticed that her right hand rested against Richard's back.

'Your business is conducted?'

'Done for now but just beginning,' he replied cryptically. 'Montagu is to go north to conclude the Scots peace.'

'And the traitor?'

She always spoke of Somerset in this way, since his betrayal of Edward's friendship. He knew that since the deaths of his father and brother at Wakefield, she took any traitorous activity personally.

'Montagu will meet him in the north. He will not be allowed to get close to London.'

She idly picked at a herb growing in the raised bed beside her. 'Montagu is to go?'

He could have predicted her response. He knew her that well.

'He is the best man for the job, Mother.'

She raised her eyebrows, almost imperceptibly, but he had seen it.

'I would go if I could, but as my council were swift to explain, I am not expendable. I would be walking into a trap of Beaufort's making.'

She squinted into the sun. 'But you are the better man for the job, regardless.'

'Montagu is Warwick's brother. I am confident in his loyalty and abilities.'

'Of course. And Warwick himself?'

'What of him?'

His mother kept her lips closed, but Edward was well aware of her dislike of Warwick's influence.

'I will not accompany Montagu, but I will follow him. No, I will stay in the Midlands, in safety, while he brings the Scots party south. I will go with a small company and travel swiftly, so that I am in the vicinity if I am needed. We cannot let Beaufort slip through our fingers again.'

'But is this not against Warwick's advice?'

'I will make it known that I am going on a hunting trip.'

'A hunting trip?'

'Indeed. No one will doubt it. Warwick will not know otherwise.'

Young Richard opened his eyes. The gaze he sent up to his brother was one of mixed emotions, pride and pain, innocence and knowledge. 'The earl says he will teach me to joust and to use a sword like George. I need to begin my training as a knight. I am in my twelfth year, the same age as when George started, and I don't want to be left behind. Please grant me your permission to begin, Edward, please. If Warwick is to stay here, he might commence his teaching of me.'

Edward's eyes met that of his mother. They both feared that the pain the boy experienced in his back might bar him from field activities. Handling a sword may even prove beyond him, if the worst of the physicians' predictions came true. It was only in the last twelvemonth that he had started to complain of the pain and begun to lean to the side as he walked. It was ever so slight so that most others did not notice it, but his mother's eye missed nothing.

Edward saw that his mother was about to begin her careful explanation so he spoke quickly. The boy's pride was at stake and Edward remembered what it was to be on the verge of youth, with the fire stirring in his veins, waiting for life and manhood to begin.

'I will speak with Warwick, put together something suitable.'

'Will you, really?' His note of hope was almost pitiful.

'Of course, there will be plenty for you to do.'

'And soon?'

'Soon enough.'

'And you promise, I can ride and joust, like the others?'

'Well, perhaps not jousting,' Cecily interjected.

The boy reacted with control and reserve. George would have spat out his words at once and rejected such caution, but George did not have such racking pains down his spine.

'I will speak with the physician again, ask him to make up more ointment,' the duchess continued.

'And I with Warwick. No doubt we can find suitable activities for you.'

Richard hung his head. 'I know I may never draw a bow, but I should like to be able to handle a sword. For Father's sake.'

'And there is no reason not to try,' replied Edward. 'I give you my word.'

A breeze stirred the branches above them.

Cecily looked up at her eldest son. 'Is Warwick still pursuing your marriage in France?'

Edward nodded. He half looked back at the council chamber window. 'It had escaped my mind. He wishes to speak with me on the matter. Yes, negotiations continue. She is the sister of the queen of France, a native of Savoy. It would be a good match, a useful alliance, with Margaret of Anjou and her son still in exile out there.'

'Yet the idea does not seem to please you?'

As usual, she had seen through him. 'Is there pleasure to be taken in such a marriage? I think pleasure must lie elsewhere.'

'You are a king now, Edward, you cannot expect to please yourself in all things. It is a good match for England.'

'Indeed it is, Mother, and for that reason, I will pursue i .

'I am glad to hear it. Tell me, has my sister arrived at court yet.

Edward recalled the promise he had extracted from Norfolk and the Lady Katherine to attend him at Westminster. 'I expect them any day.'

Cecily stared into the play of light upon the path. 'You think she will come?'

'Why would she not come?'

'My sister has always been firmly of her own mind. She will only do what she has convinced herself she wishes to. Stubborn as a mule, like all of us.'

'But why would she not come if I have invited her?'

'She is one of those who burns with indignity. Did you not see it when you met at Norfolk's?'

'I did, but she was careful to remain within the bounds of civility, if only just.'

'You had her captive there…'

'No, not at all…'

'I mean, by surprise. She had her choice taken away with your unexpected arrival. She will not have liked that. I doubt she will come.'

Edward thought for a moment. He did not know his great-aunt Katherine well, but she was, after all, his mother's sister. 'She strikes me as one who loves being flattered and served. Would she so easily throw over a chance to visit court?'

Cecily laughed. 'Ah! You may have her there. Her vanity might prevail if she has jewels enough to carry it off. So, are they wed yet, young Norfolk and his wife?'

'I believe it happened last month. I have promised them a nuptial feast upon their arrival.'

'And to win the son over, as you did his father?'

uccessor. I think he is already won over.'

le may not always be as they seem.'

darkened. 'I know that, Mother, I know. Even the

nd might prove to be a viper in the nest.'

ot reply, but her fingers twined themselves among

Ric. curls.

From behind them in the garden, a man cleared his throat. The king turned to see Warwick standing awkwardly upon the path.

'Not that man again,' muttered Cecily, barely audibly under her breath.

'My lord, might I approach?'

Edward beckoned him closer, surprised at his strictly observed etiquette, but his mother rose to her feet.

'Richard, walk me inside. It is time for prayer. We will leave you two to discuss your schemes.'

Edward stood aside and Warwick bowed low as she swept past them in a rustle of velvet skirts.

'My lady duchess, my lord of Gloucester, God speed you.'

When they were almost out of sight, Warwick spoke up. 'I fear I may have displeased your mother in some way. If so, it was not my intention.'

'Not at all. She is devout. It is likely that she seeks the seclusion of the cloister after the glare of the sun.'

'Yes, it is bright today.' The earl shielded his eyes. 'Shall we walk through into the orchard?'

'If you wish.'

'After you, my lord.'

Edward headed along the path where herbs were springing into life on each side. At the end, the gate to the orchard was guarded by two yeomen in livery, bearing the king's device of the sun in splendour. At his approach, they drew the heavy bolt, stepping out into the green space beyond to ensure it was safe for Edward to follow. He had learned hard lessons about safety and security and they sat upon his heart with a heavy reminiscence. But the orchard on that spring day was full of air and light, of fresh breezes and blossom, with the tall grass growing up around the gnarled apple trunks.

'Time marches on,' pronounced Warwick, suddenly poetical amid the flowers.

But Edward knew him better than to trust his flights of words. The earl was always focused, conscious, driven. This was only the prelude.

'Does it not, my lord?'

'Indeed it does, Cousin, but you did not bring me out here to speak of nature, did you?'

Warwick laughed. 'In a sense, I suppose I did.'

'Ah. The marriage talk again.'

'Yes, that, you can't run from it forever. The French are keen to sign a contract of betrothal. I have gone almost as far as I can with the negotiations and now they begin to ask questions. They doubt your enthusiasm for the match, and question whether I have your ear.'

Edward sighed. 'I suppose it must be so.'

'What would you rather? A princess from the Netherlands or from Italy? The Spanish infanta is still too young.'

But Edward could not quite articulate his lack of passion for Warwick's plans. The thought of a princess, far away in a foreign land, was not without romance, but the reality of it, of her arrival as his bride, was quite another matter. Perhaps the example of the Lancastrian Henry and his French match lingered in his mind. The dark almond eyes of Margaret of Anjou appeared in his memory again. Then he thought of Eleanor, laid out before him on the night of the storm, of her soft kisses upon his face and the contours of her body beneath him. The words he had spoken; the promises he had made her that night…

'You are certain there are no objections to the lady?'

'To Bona of Savoy? None whatsoever. She is a paragon of virtue and noble blood.'

'And her appearance?'

'I am assured that it is all it should be.'

Edward nodded. Off to the left, the Thames rolled on, with the unfurled sails of barges passing behind the trees.

Warwick frowned. 'What is it?'

'I suppose it feels strange,' Edward attempted to explain, 'to wed a wife I have never seen.'

'Especially to one who is accustomed to women?'

'Don't do that. Am I not a man, like any other?'

Warwick was wise enough not to reply. He waited for Edward to gather his thoughts.

'My mother speaks in favour of the marriage. She reminds me of my duty as a king, and that marriage is a necessary step, rather than a pleasure.'

Again, Warwick stood in silence.

'Louis of France is pressing for the match?'

'He is, my lord. He believes it will be wondrously advantageous for the friendship of England and France.'

'But the last match between England and France did not go so well, did it?'

Warwick frowned. 'I believe that was due to the character of the lady. Bona of Savoy is sweet-natured, docile, but strong. Louis of France assures me so.'

'Well, he would do that, wouldn't he? He'd hardly make confession of her faults.'

'Is that your best argument against the match?'

Edward sighed at the inevitability of it all. Warwick was rolling this match towards him like an unstoppable force.

'Then so be it. Bring the documents and I will sign. A betrothal only at first, until the terms are agreed. Do you understand? It must not be binding. It must allow us to set our own conditions. Louis must make concessions; he must promise he will work against Margaret on our behalf.'

'It is understood.'

'Come, then let us return to the chamber. There is the business of Montagu's expedition north to be arranged. And I plan to go hunting in the Midlands.'

'Hunting, at such a time?'

'Yes, Warwick, hunting. I prefer to keep myself occupied. Speak with the French, then give me your report. But what does this man want?'

A servant was hovering in the doorway. Edward beckoned him forward.

'What is it?'

'Please, my lord, the Duke of Norfolk has arrived.'

The king spun round to Warwick. 'You hear that? Norfolk is here. Let's go and greet him. The dinner hour must be approaching.'

The hall was set up for the approaching meal. Servants were laying white linen and placing plates, spoons and glasses along the trestle tables; up in the gallery, the minstrels were tuning their instruments with a sort of gleeful cacophony.

The Stanley brothers and Hastings were waiting at the door.

'Ah, my lords, you are joining us to dine today? The Duke of Norfolk and his new wife are to be our guests. A chance to thank them for their hospitality in January.'

The lords exchanged glances and began to follow their king as he strode down the length of the hall towards the dais at the far end.

'Norfolk, and his wife and sister?' asked William Stanley.

'Indeed, they were all invited.'

'Anyone else?'

'Who would you like, Stanley? Do you have your eye on some pretty squire's daughter?'

Cecily, Richard and George appeared from the side door to take their places at the top table as the trumpets announced the hour.

'And here they are!' exclaimed Edward, as the Duke of Norfolk and Elizabeth were led in by a steward. 'My lord, my lady, you are most welcome.'

The duke and duchess bowed low. Marriage seemed to suit them. Norfolk looked happier, fuller in the face and less nervous. His bride of a month smiled coyly at the king.

'You are both looking so well. It is a pleasure to see. But you are alone? No mother and no sister?'

'Pray accept our apologies,' offered Elizabeth, no longer shy about speaking up. 'My mother is infirm with her old complaint and my sister has had to travel north to see about her estates.'

Edward hid his disappointment under a royal smile. 'I wish your mother the best of health and your sister a speedy resolution. And tell Eleanor…' He paused. 'Tell Eleanor that I expect her to honour me with a visit before long.'

'We will,' said Norfolk, as the steward showed them to their seats.

'Did I hear right?' mused Hastings, as the king turned back towards the table. 'Lady Eleanor Butler has ventured north?'

'To attend her estates, according to her sister.'

'Which estates are these? I was not aware she had any in that region.'

Edward was quiet for a moment.

'And look who it is,' burst out Baron Stanley. 'None other than Anthony Woodville, the son of Lord Rivers. Have you come to joust with us, sir?'

Edward turned to see the tall, young man approach, dressed in russet velvet. The Woodville family had professed their loyalty after fighting on the losing side at Towton and had been pardoned. They had been an occasional presence at court since. Usually the brother, father and mother, although Edward was aware that there were sisters, vaguely recalling elegant, blonde beauties who had visited court in the wake of his succession.

Anthony bent low. 'My lord.'

'You are welcome,' said Edward, with a friendly air but a degree of reservation. Nor had he forgotten how the Woodvilles had once been his captives in Calais.

'So,' urged Hastings. 'Now he is here, we must arrange a joust.'

'There will be little time,' said the king, 'as I am about to depart on a hunting trip.'

'Have you decided your route yet?' asked Stanley.

'I expect to pass through the Midlands.'

'Well then,' Hastings laughed, 'you must be sure to call at Grafton, home of the Woodvilles, south of Northampton. There is excellent hunting to be had in Whittlewood forest. Anthony will happily show you all the best places, won't you, Anthony?'

'Well, yes, of course, we would be honoured,' spoke Woodville.

Edward replied with a nod. 'I will see if we have space in our itinerary.'

'And will your sisters be there?' asked Hastings. 'I have heard their beauty praised far and wide.'

'I expect they will,' laughed Anthony. 'And will be most happy to welcome their king.'

'Well, then it is settled, Edward, is it not?'

But the king only smiled.

William Stanley intervened. He was more sober than his flamboyant brother. 'For shame, Hastings, let them go. You keep a man from his dinner.'

And as Edward walked away with Anthony following, and the servants began to bring in the first plates of steaming food, Stanley turned back to berate his friend.

'You are far too obvious. He has to think the idea was his.'

'Well, I bet you a brace of pheasants that he will have one of the Woodville sisters in his arms, and Eleanor Butler will be forgotten.'

Stanley smiled wryly. 'I will not make that bet, William, because we are on the same side, and you know how fond I am of pheasant!'

'About as fond as the king is of women!'

'Then let us pray it comes to pass and his heart is occupied until Warwick brings about this French match.'

A steaming dish of rabbits cooked in pastry was carried past them.

'But for now,' added Stanley, with a nod to his brother, 'to dine.'

FIVE

Two Women, April 1464

The hills rolled up towards the horizon in a mist of purple heather. Eleanor pulled the wandering edges of her cloak together and cast an anxious look up at the sky. Dark clouds were rolling in from the west and there were still hours to go before they reached Newcastle. They'd been travelling for three days, and their guide, a man they'd hired at Leicester, kept reassuring them that he would deliver them safely to the Lancastrian stronghold. Eleanor watched his sturdy back and leather jerkin as he rode ahead, unable to shake the fear that here, out in this vast wilderness, he could just as easily kill them both rather than fulfil his promise and await his fee.

She had hurried north as soon as the storm had passed, leaving behind her mother and sister with the Duke of Norfolk. Guilt lay heavily upon her chest, guilt for allowing herself to be swept away in the caresses of a king, guilt for betraying her love. But the person and the promises of a king had proved seductive. She had paused only to collect Luce, her maid, and a few dresses and precious items to sell on the road. Her drop-pearl brooch and the little silver ring given to her by her aunt had paid for their food and lodgings. Once she was with Somerset, all would be well, but she should have gone sooner. She should have been stronger, held fast to the promises she had made him last summer, sped to him as soon as he fled Holt. He had urged her then, if she ever found herself in difficulties, to come to him.

They had met at the Warwickshire home of her aunt, her namesake, Eleanor, who was also his mother. Cousins, and yet they had barely seen each other, growing up in different parts of the countryside. She'd been aware of a tall, dark-haired boy, a sulky child who'd not wanted to join in their games, at the few family weddings, at the Lancastrian queen's coronation and, while he'd kept his distance, there had been an aura of mystery about him, an edge of something dangerous. His dark, flashing eyes had fascinated her, promising unchartered depths. But more than the attraction, she'd wanted to know him because they were the same age, born just weeks apart, and there was a sort of connection in that. She'd surprised him once, in a tent set up for jousters, painted over with roses and hung with red tissue, where he'd been standing, staring out at the combat, with such a look of intensity upon his face. She'd sidled up like a cat, a girl of ten or twelve, and stood beside him. But he'd frowned and marched out, as if her presence had stripped the joy out of things.

And then she'd seen his face among the guests at her wedding. He'd come with his parents, expected to do his duty, on the day she had married Thomas Butler. He'd been one of the crowd in the church as her father had given her away, and then he was seated somewhere in the hall at the feast. She'd not given him much thought then, but as the years unfolded, and she'd sat childless, alone, neglected, watching the seasons pass, she'd heard news of him from her mother. And his name began to matter to her: Henry, Henry Beaufort, Duke of Somerset, son of the murdered duke. It seemed a romantic exciting life from a distance, especially such a lonely distance as hers, and touched by a tragedy with which she could sympathise. He'd been travelling with the French queen, advising her, fighting battles, cut down and hovering on the brink of death after St Albans. They'd heard terrible stories of him being dragged from the battlefield on a stretcher, through streets running with blood, where the alleyways to the cathedral were blocked with bodies. It had troubled her dreams for such a long time, still did, on occasion. At first, the family had thought him lost, killed at his father's side, fighting against the Duke of York, but his wounds had slowly healed. Letters from her aunt had brought updates, and parcels of herbs, folded between linen, from her garden. The cuts to his arm, shoulder and face, his dear face, had closed over, and he had grown stronger, and finally been able to walk again.

And then, last spring, while her sister was a guest of Norfolk and his family, she had gone to stay at the country home of her aunt, thinking to pass a season in quiet widow's contemplation, in walking and spinning, and picking the fruits of the field for the still room. But he had appeared, riding into the courtyard with a kingly air and she had been quite unprepared for the feelings that had arisen in her. And in the walled garden, tucked away among the roses, he had kissed her for the first time. It had been such a long time since she had felt the touch of a man. Thomas had been a good husband, diligent and devout. She had never wanted for anything, save a little passion. No one could accuse him of having been a passionate man, except perhaps in his pursuit of his faith. He had thrown himself wholeheartedly into that, leaving her wishing he shared her bed with as much fire. But Henry was something different. When the house was dark and the fires smouldering, he had visited her chamber and made her understand exactly where her husband had been lacking. And by the summer, when he had ridden to join the king, she had already given him her heart, and made such promises that she never knew she had in her. And the ring. She looked down at her hands, clasping the reins, the ring with his initials. Such promises.

Promises she had broken.

Eleanor returned to the road ahead, winding away into the hills. Perhaps it was best not to mention Edward after all, to pretend that night in the storm had not happened, that she had not allowed him in. She had been lonely, aching for her love, and she'd allowed herself to weaken, weaken for an hour or so, in order to feel alive again. Would it help if she made her confession to Beaufort? If she gave him cause to reject her? There was no child; she was certain of that, so he need never know. Edward was not likely to tell him now, now that their friendship was over and their old enmity had returned. Just so long as she could get to him, everything would be alright. She beckoned Luce closer, a docile, plump young woman, who rode on a mule beside her. Luce pulled on the reins and closed the space between them.

'Do you trust this guide?'

'I believe so, mistress. He has not yet played us false.'

'He has time still though, does he not?'

A man named Stevens, dressed in wool and leather, a former soldier in service to the Lancastrian queen, or so he had told them.

'I do believe him, mistress. If he had wanted to do us harm, I think he would have done so by now instead of waiting three days. He has had plenty of opportunities to do so. And in Leicester, he showed me his old livery badge with its red rose.'

'Really, you have seen it?'

'Yes, there is no doubt he was in the queen's employ.'

'Thank you, Luce, you have set my mind at rest. That is a wondrous comfort. When we reach Newcastle, I shall see that Beaufort gives you ample reward.'

'It will not be long now, mistress, perhaps even before sunset.'

'Pray God it will.'

'And also that the rain holds off.'

They looked over to the west where the clouds were still massing, dark and heavy, with a bright edge where the sun protested behind them.

'Pray God it does, as there is little shelter out here on the road before we reach the city.'

Elizabeth stood at the window, watching the clouds chase across the sky. The house at Grafton was shielded from the road by a bank of trees, but above them the darkness was gathering. She was a slender form, arms folded, her chin upturned.

'That storm is coming,' she said softly, her mind wandering through the sky. Happier times, sunnier days came back to her, when her boys were small, running across the garden on sturdy legs.

Behind her, at the table, her mother Jacquetta looked up from where she was cutting the spring rhubarb.

'What was that?'

'The storm. Father might get caught in it.'

Jacquetta put down her knife and walked over to stand beside her daughter. At almost fifty, the lines of beauty were still evident in her face, in her high brows and the gentle curve of her cheek which was still soft. In her youth, she had come close to becoming queen, married to the brother of the king, but her fortunes had changed when she fell in love with Richard Woodville and married him in secret, against the ruling of parliament. In time, they had been forgiven and the marriage had been happy, but she had lived out the years quietly in the country, raising her children.

She directed her eyes to the horizon. 'I would say an hour before it hits, if we are lucky. Your father might make it home in time. If he hurries.'

But Elizabeth did not seem to hear her. She was lost in the storm, her pale eyes clouded over.

'You're still worrying about the boys' inheritance?'

Elizabeth nodded, squeezing her eyes tightly shut.

'Please don't. All we can do is wait now. Your petition will be read. I will write to Hastings myself and urge him to help.'

'Those lands should be theirs by right, from their father, from his father. It is the way these things have always been.'

'John promised you them, didn't he? Long before his death?'

They hadn't been married for long, just eight years, but it had been a happy time. They'd been young, in love, and so excited about becoming man and wife. It was still hard to believe that he was gone.

'Of course. And although we did not speak of it often, it was always understood that they would pass to the boys, even by his mother.'

'But now her new husband wants them for himself. Just like a man.'

'I don't understand her, not at all. I thought she cared for me, for her grandsons, her own flesh and blood. What would John say? What would he say if he was here?'

'I know. I know.' Jacquetta took her daughter in her arms. 'Where are the boys?'

'Anthony is practising archery with them in the field.'

Elizabeth allowed herself to relax into her mother's arms. She had been with her at Grafton since John was killed in battle, almost three years before. Although Elizabeth had left off her full mourning, her simple grey kirtle and dark skirts showed her widowed status. Her fair hair was pulled back at the nape of her neck, tied in a large knot. When there were no visitors expected on the estate, the women dressed simply. There were velvets and silks in the chest upstairs folded with lavender, and jewelled necklaces locked in the cabinet, but it had been a long time since they had been to court, or even any other occasion that demanded such finery.

'Oh look!' Jacquetta pointed to the distant gates. 'He has made it back in time.'

Elizabeth followed her gaze. Entering the estate, her father rode tall on his horse, still strong and active in spite of his years. He came at a pace, slowing down as he reached the house. The women walked through to the entrance in anticipation of his arrival.

Richard Woodville was a handsome man but his features were of the small, mild kind. His face bore a permanent expression of patience, married with experience, after years of service to the king. He strode into the hall, casting off his fur-lined cloak.

'We were wondering if you would make it back before the storm.' Jacquetta greeted him, gliding past her daughter to kiss him on the cheek.

'It's a way off still, but it's coming fast. Better make sure everything is under cover. No washing out today?'

'Not today.'

The women followed him into the hall where he sat down before the fire and pulled off his boots.

A servant brought wine and Richard took a glass and drank.

Elizabeth was impatient. 'Any news from Northampton?'

Her father put down his wine. 'Nothing concerning your sons, I am afraid, but the news is far better. It may bring good fortune and favour our way.'

'Oh?' Jacquetta took the chair beside him.

'I heard this from Farrer, the owner of the Lamb at Stony Stratford. The king is headed this way, has already left London, and will arrive tomorrow. He stays in Stratford, they know not where, but probably for a few days while he hunts. There is every chance that he will visit us when he does.'

'Visit, here? It must mean we are forgiven.'

'I believe so, and if not, we have another opportunity to demonstrate our loyalty.'

Only four years had passed since Richard, Jacquetta and their son, Anthony, were taken from their beds at Sandwich and carried across the Channel by the Earl of Warwick and Edward, then Earl of March. The insults and disrespect heaped upon them by the Yorkists still privately rankled with the couple although they were too wise to show it, and there was little choice but to submit now that March was king.

'What are the chances that he will come here?' asked Jacquetta, thinking of all the preparations she must begin.

'I left word at the inn and will post a messenger on the road to intercept him and offer our hospitality. If he comes this way, we shall do our best to host him.'

'The king, here!' breathed Jacquetta. 'I will go and tell Anthony!'

But as she stood up, they heard the first rain spatter on the window-pane and the room darkened.

'Ah, here we are,' observed Richard. 'It has caught up with me faster than I thought.'

'Oh, the boys are outside!'

But even as Elizabeth hurried towards the front door to seek them in the field, they raced across the threshold: two boys of nine and six in brown jerkins, with rosy cheeks and dirty knees, their bows strung over their shoulders. Behind them, their uncle, a tall, dark-haired man who had inherited his mother's features, carried a bundle of arrows. Anthony Woodville was younger than his sister by almost two years, but life had taken him further out into the world, into the world of letters and the jousting lists. He walked with the graceful ease of a man confident in himself.

'We just made it back in time.' He smiled. 'Saw the clouds coming from across the field.'

Jacquetta was unable to contain herself. 'But what do you think is going to happen? Your father brought news. Tell him, Richard.'

Woodville looked round at his son. 'Well, we don't know for certain, but we hope…'

'Oh, Richard! Go on!'

'Very well!' He laughed. 'Prepare yourself, Anthony, because the king is coming!'

'Is he indeed?' asked the younger Woodville. 'Well, who would have guessed!'

'This is the place, my lady.'

Eleanor looked through the dark stone gateway to the tall house beyond the courtyard. Rain threw down heavy stinging drops on the flagstones around them, battering her head and shoulders, her back and legs, and the poor horse beneath her.

'You are absolutely sure? The Duke of Somerset is lodging here?'

Their guide nodded. 'I am certain. I had word at the market cross. I had thought he might be at the Lodge, but the suppliers confirmed it.'

And suddenly, when she was this close, when his touch was a certainty, Eleanor felt unsure. Fear gripped her stomach and she could not move forward.

'Mistress?' It was Luce at her side, urging her mule under the arch.

Eleanor recalled herself and reached into her skirts to pull out her purse. 'I will be sure to pass to the duke just how kind you have been to his kinswoman.' She pressed three pieces of gold into his hand. It was more generous than the situation needed as she saw reflected in his eyes, but she had no more need of money now. Henry would take care of her.

'Thank you, my lady, thank you for your generosity. I will be at the Huntsman overnight if you find that you should need me further.'

'You have been most kind.'

The courtyard was small and dark, overshadowed by the grey slate of the towering house. A drain into which the roof gutters flowed was spilling over with water, making the cobbles slippery. Few of the windows were lit and any smoke escaping from the chimneys was dispersed at once. It looked like a cold, unwelcoming place. Eleanor could hardly believe it contained her lover.

'Right,' she said to Luce, 'this is it!'

An ostler ran out to lead away their mounts and point them towards the black wooden door, which stood firm against the rain. And it struck Eleanor that the last few months had been nothing but rain, rain and clouds, and that spring was long overdue.

Luce's knock revealed a peephole at head height, which was slid back cautiously by an unseen hand.

'The Lady Eleanor Talbot, kinswoman of the Duke of Somerset, is here to see him. Please would you…'

The door swung open at once. Eleanor was relieved to see a servant dressed in the white and blue Beaufort livery stand aside to allow them to enter. The corridor was lit by a single torch and they blinked as they were shown into an anteroom with wooden panelling and a cold hearth. The Beaufort arms, with its lions and fleur-de-lys, was carved in stone above the mantlepiece.

'Please, be seated, and I will inform the duke.'

It felt as though they were kept waiting a long time. Presently, another servant brought spiced wine and cakes, and Eleanor had almost drained her cup by the time they heard footsteps along the corridor. Low voices conferred outside the door, too low for the words to be heard inside the room. Then the handle was turned cautiously and a figure stepped inside the room's shadow.

Henry had not changed significantly since Eleanor had seen him last. He was tall, majestic, with broad shoulders, regal in bearing, with his descent from John of Gaunt, a potential king. He was darkly handsome with a melancholy cast to his brows. The scars on his face from St Albans, nine years earlier, had become barely visible. His face now registered surprise, almost disbelief.

Eleanor rose at once, ready to throw herself at him. 'Henry! It is so good to see you safe and well.'

'But you, here? I don't understand.'

'I had to come. I had to see you. I wanted to share your exile.'

He did not come forward to greet her, nor kiss her, nor take her in his arms. Instead, he looked troubled.

'Henry?'

'It was not safe for you to come here. You know my situation. You have placed yourself in grave danger. The day will come soon when I must meet the king and I cannot guarantee the outcome.'

'But you said…'

'I did not mean for you to put yourself in danger.'

'I will take my chance. Did you not get my letters?'

'I did.'

Still he did not embrace her, and the coldness of his welcome sat like a stone in Eleanor's chest. But she did not wish to speak up before Luce, so she lifted her chin in pride.

'It has been many months since we saw each other at your mother's house, but I trust that as your kinswoman and friend, I am welcome. My maid and I have made an extraordinary journey, and many sacrifices to be here.'

'Of course. We must get you settled. Come with me.'

She followed him in relief, back down the dark passage to a hall, where some of the faces in the fire glow seemed familiar, and then up a narrow flight of stairs. Henry showed them into a small solar, with a carved fireplace and paned window overlooking the street. A bed stood on the far wall and two chairs had been placed either side of the hearth.

'You will be comfortable here. I will send up wine and a man to light the fire. We dine at five in the main hall we passed through.'

Luce carried their single bag to the bed and began to unpack.

As he was turning to go, Eleanor caught his arm and spoke in a whisper. 'Is that all? Is that all you would say to me? Have you not forgotten what we were to each other last summer? The promises we made?'

He was stilled by her words but they did not soften him. He kept his eyes low and would not look at her face.

'You should have sent word about your intention. I would have told you it was too dangerous.'

'Are you not pleased to see me?'

'You cannot stay.'

Her composure broke at this. 'Why not? Where else should I go? All this time I have waited to be with you, wanted to be with you, and after I come all this way, you greet me so coldly?'

'As I said, you should not have come.'

'And this is all the welcome, all the thanks I am to expect?'

He sighed. 'I am sorry. I am occupied and the moment is approaching when I must make my move. I cannot think of love or any such things at the present time, until my future is settled.'

'I only wish to be with you, to be of comfort and support.'

He nodded briefly, almost brutally. 'I must see about your fire. We will speak again.'

* * *

When they were warmed, with their tired limbs having taken ease before a newly-kindled flame, Eleanor and Luce drank wine and prayed together. In the silence, the sounds of the building around them pressed in, and of the street outside. Voices, horse hooves, carts. Once a bird flew past their window with a shriek. There must be many men there, Eleanor realised, waiting patiently, in the hall and adjoining buildings, friends of the Lancastrian cause, while Beaufort planned his next move. When the feet started to stir in the corridor outside, they decided that the dinner hour had come.

The hall was filling up. She hadn't really taken it in before, amid the disappointment of their arrival. Rich tapestries hung on the walls depicting hunting scenes, and two long trestles had been set up, parallel to each other, down the centre with benches on either side. A main table, draped in linen like that used by a king or queen, was placed apart, close to the fire, and Eleanor gravitated towards it as befitted her rank. The benches started to fill with men in livery and supporters, one or two of whom Eleanor thought she recognised as members of the Beaufort family. Then, Lords Roos and Hungerford appeared, took their seats at the top of the nearest trestle and nodded to her in surprised greeting. Music began to play in the gallery above and she waited, but Beaufort still did not come.

Three tall young men approached the table, pausing in hesitation to see her there. After a moment, she recognised them as her cousins, Henry's younger brothers, Edmund, John and Thomas, who were grown into young men since their last meeting.

'My lords, I am your cousin, Eleanor Butler, daughter of the Earl of Talbot. I came to support your cause.'

'Eleanor, you are most welcome,' spoke the eldest, Edmund, in a long drawl. 'You arrived today?'

'Yes, with my maid, Luce, but I had hoped to see Henry. Will he be dining with us?'

The young men exchanged glances. 'You will see him presently.'

They took their seats, and Eleanor did too, feeling out of place, with all the men's eyes upon her. One glance around the hall showed that she and Luce were the only women present amid the sea of faces. The dishes came swiftly, and were not too warm; broths and spiced caudels, pies and puddings. Basic fare for working men, without ornament, without expense, but they fell upon it with gratitude. Eleanor ate lightly, selectively, then rose and left with Luce following. In the corridor outside, a pair of liverymen were lighting more torches as the day began to fade outside.

'Where is the duke's room?' Eleanor asked of one, a lean man with close-set eyes, who twitched nervously in response.

'It's alright. I am his cousin, Lady Eleanor Butler, daughter of Talbot, the late Earl of Shrewsbury.'

'Up the stairs and at the far end of the corridor.'

She left Luce in their shared room and, with a deep breath, proceeded along in the shadows. The torch lighters had not yet moved upstairs and the only light came from a small row of lattice panels set high up to the ceiling.

It was an unprepossessing door, wooden, unvarnished and unpainted. The surround was not even carved and the panelling on either side was plain. Was this a place worthy of a duke? Eleanor supposed that Henry must adapt to whatever circumstances dictated; she raised her knuckles and rapped sharply.

'Come in!'

It was a well-furnished room. Comfortable drapes and carpets had been brought there, and a big, soft bed was hung with green velvet. A table was draped with a carpet, set with plates of food and a flagon of wine. Before the fire, a man, woman and child were sitting eating, in comfortable intimacy. Beaufort, with his shirt loose and throat bare, rose at once when he saw her. The woman, a dark-haired delicate figure, continued to eat, passing morsels to the little boy on her knee.

'You should be dining in the hall!' He steered her out of the room into the corridor. 'Who sent you here?'

'I asked where I might find you. I thought I would see you at dinner. Who is that woman?'

'She is family. This cannot do, Eleanor. You really cannot stay.'

'Then she is my family too. May I meet her?'

'No.' He closed the door.

'No, why not?'

'Let me walk you back to the hall.'

'I have eaten already. I was heading to my chamber. Henry, be honest with me, who is that woman and the child?'

He paused and sighed in the gloom. 'Very well. That child is my son, Charles.'

'Your son?'

'My natural son. And the woman is his mother.'

The words hit her like stones. All the waiting, the sacrifices, the long journey, only to discover this. She thought again of Edward's arms and the warmth of his words as he entreated her to be his that night, and every night after.

'Do not cause trouble about it, Eleanor. It's not your concern.'

With a deliberate gesture, she removed the small signet ring she wore upon her left hand and held it out to him. Pain made her cold and focused.

'You have misunderstood me. I wish to return this ring you gave me last year, and to inform you that I release you from our understanding.'

'You do?' He took the ring with some uncertainty.

'I find myself obliged to confess a great secret which you must not share, but it is important that you know, for yourself.'

She paused for effect, seeing that she had his interest.

'I am promised to another man. I am to be married. It has been very recent.'

'Then I wish you well, Cousin.'

His words stung but she pressed on. 'You do not wish to know whose wife I intend to become? Who has promised to be my husband as he shared my bed? It is King Edward. I shared his bed and I will be his wife and queen.'

'Will you, indeed?' His dark eyebrows raised in disdain and surprise. 'Then I am surprised to see you so far from his side. I expect you will wish to return to him as soon as possible now that you have delivered your news.'

He did not believe her. She felt it keenly.

'I will depart in the morning. I shall be obliged to communicate with my husband concerning your whereabouts.'

'He knows where I am. We shall soon meet in battle and then we will see whether or not you have tied your fortunes to the winning side. I bid you goodnight. I do not expect to see you again, Cousin.'

He closed the door sharply and left her alone in the corridor. She had gone too far. It was over.

SIX

In Whittlewood Forest

These paths were familiar to Elizabeth. Their twists and turns as they swept around tree trunks, the smooth texture underfoot of grass and moss, and crumbly summertime earth. She had always loved this forest, tracing its contours since childhood. All its moods were known to her, in the gentle spring and burnished autumn, vibrant high summer and the iced-over winters. She had seen all the seasons pass in turn, the freezing of puddles and the basking of birds, wing-stretched in the heat.

She hummed softly as she walked between them, tracing her finger-tips over the heads of grasses, the new growth on shrubs. The dark spaces held no fear for her and the secret places where flowers and herbs grew welcomed her, their scents making the air heady. Here, the long branches had borne her up, up among their leaves, finding seats among their crooks and curves, high above the ground. In the old oak, she had waited, suppressing her laughter, as her brothers and sisters raced about below. In the clearing, she had gathered mush-rooms, and set free the shrews and rabbits lured into the boys' traps.

But now the forest took on a different aspect. She stood at the crossroads, where the way to Stony Stratford met that coming from Northampton, where, although it was usually quiet, riders and carts sometimes thundered through, startling the birds and sending up clouds of dust. In the past, she had awaited her father here, when he was due back from court, and once or twice, Thomas Grey had ridden over, in their early courtship. She had waited in this green open space to greet him privately before they headed back to Grafton. Now, on this spring morning, the soft sun had already given way to hail, forcing them to shelter. The dry, rutted road was briefly drenched, and the tiny white balls gathered in the indentations made by horses' hooves. But even as the shower passed, the sky started to brighten and hope returned.

Elizabeth leaned against the trunk of the great oak. The bark was bumpy and gnarled through her kirtle and even through the shawl she'd knitted last winter. Thomas and Richard were grubbing about in the young grass with the toes of their shoes, looking for new shoots and insects. The road had been quiet. But it was the only way he would come if he did come hunting, if he did visit Grafton. She kept staring at the distant place where the trees closed in and the road disappeared from sight: a bluish spot of promise. When would the king come? She had met him only once before at court, early in his reign, but she had no doubt that she would recognise him. The king must come this way, he must. And then she could plead for the future of her boys. She had told her mother they were out for a ramble, both today and the day before, and Jacquetta had not asked any questions. But if he did not come today, could she stretch the truth for one more morning? Surely, he must come soon.

When the sun was high overhead, Elizabeth unwrapped her bundle of bread, cheese and nuts and called her boys over. They sat together on a fallen log, the branch of a tree that had been growing for a hundred years, brought down by the winter storms. And they ate, in a moment of absolute stillness, in the greenness of the forest. It was quiet enough to hear the flight of a bird overhead, and the fall of nuts where a squirrel had awakened and was foraging. And then, then, as she held her hand up to still her sons, she was certain she heard the distant vibration of horses' hooves.

She stood. Shielded her eyes.

'Thomas, Richard, do you hear that?'

They rose too, following her example and her gaze, as far as the distance would allow. And they saw it at the same time as their mother; the space where the trees merged became full of life and colour, of horses and men moving at speed, heading their way.

'What is it?' asked Richard, cowering behind his brother.

'No, do not fear. Stand up and be ready to welcome them. I believe it is the king.'

'The king?'

She hurriedly brushed down her skirts, smoothed her hair, which she had deliberately worn loose, and pulled it forward over her shoulders. The riders were coming closer, perhaps half a dozen of them.

'Come on, here, stand with me, one on each side. Remember your manners.'

And they stood, like a pageant of patience and virtue, as the riders approached.

The lead horseman pulled in his reins and called a halt. He had the sun behind him, weak though it was, but his broad shoulders and ease in the saddle were unmistakeable. Edward had aged a little since their last meeting, but it was only the process of a youth becoming a man: stronger, fuller and wiser. She caught the glimpse of gold jewellery and cloth of silver beneath his cloak. His face was broad but in proportion, features and jaw strong, eyes hazel and alert, and they focused upon her intently as he drew his horse alongside. For a moment she blushed and cast her eyes down before she recalled her purpose and bowed low.

'Who have we here? Rise up, show yourselves.'

His voice was strong but gentle.

Elizabeth stood and lifted her chin. 'Please, my lord, I am the daughter of Richard Woodville of Grafton, and these are my sons.'

'The daughter of Richard Woodville? From Grafton?' He looked at her with interest. 'I believe we may be heading that way later. You may expect us.'

She was almost overwhelmed by this stroke of fortune. 'You do us a great honour, my lord.'

'Have I seen you before? I am sure I would not have forgotten your face.'

He studied her intently, forcing her to blush under his scrutiny.

'I was at court once with my parents when you were first king.'

'And they are keeping well? Your parents?'

'I thank you, my lord, they are well.'

'Ah, and you are the sister of Anthony Woodville? Tell me, does he still joust? I have heard he fancies himself our greatest jouster.'

Elizabeth flushed. 'I would not know, my lord.'

Edward picked up his reins again. 'We shall see. I am headed to Stratford tonight but I will be hunting tomorrow with five or six men, and we will call upon you for dinner.'

'Thank you, my lord, I shall make sure my mother is prepared. But, forgive me…'

'What is it? Is there sickness in the house?'

'Oh no, nothing like that; all is well.'

'Then what?'

'Might I present my sons by Sir Thomas Grey, Thomas and Richard. I wished to speak with you about their inheritance. I am in despair as their grandmother, Baroness Ferrers, has remarried and refuses to grant them the lands promised them by their father.'

Edward nodded. 'I know the case to which you refer. I believe the baroness has married my Bourchier cousin, John.'

Elizabeth was crushed by the knowledge; she should have anticipated this.

'But that does not mean I am unsympathetic. The boys must be provided for as their father wished.'

'Oh, thank you, my lord.'

'I will look into it. We will speak more tomorrow. Until then.'

He gave her a last look before gathering up his reins and galloping away. Within moments, the forest was quiet again and the group of three were standing alone in the long grass.

Looking down from the roof of Grafton Manor, it seemed as if the sleepy place had been brought to life. Birds had gathered here for centuries, feet clawing at the tiles, watching the chimneys and the sun rise and set. They sat in a line, ten or twelve black rooks, like sentinels over the garden. Far below, the old stones were visible, hundreds of years in place; the paths where the monks had once walked, the space into which their chants had risen and disappeared up to heaven. Here was the enclosed garden with its herbs and fruit, the fields of wild flowers, the drying space for linen, the barns and outhouses and stables, chickens and pigs grubbing in the mud, the little chapel, all laid out in the sunshine like features on a map. Beyond stretched the road, the village, the church, the forest and the rolling hills up to the skies. The birds saw the carts rumble in and out, the men unloading supplies, the women beating the carpets and rugs in the air. Servants were sweeping paths, trimming the shrubs, gathering herbs. Leaves and branches from the recent storm were being dragged away, fuelling a bonfire at the back which trailed smoke into the sky. And a woman came walking: a woman in a green dress with long fair hair, her arms full of flowers, down the path and into the house.

Elizabeth set down the blooms on the table. 'I went to the far meadows; these were the best I could find, for the season.'

Jacquetta inspected them, splaying out the stems with her fingers.

'Marigold, and anemones, oh, and narcissus. Where did you find these?'

'On the walk past the hermitage, in the lea of the path that runs by the wood.'

'They are perfect.' And the task began of stripping, cutting and preparing the flowers, their orange and yellow heads clustered together like sunshine brought indoors.

In its corners and crevices, hallways and corridors, the house was being transformed. Tiled floors were washed down, old rushes swept out and new herbs sprinkled. Dusters and feathers ran over every shelf, every mantle; fireplaces were cleaned and the winter cobwebs were brushed away. Tables and benches were scrubbed clean, sheets and pillows bleached white and rinsed with lavender, the feather beds aired and the pointy quills picked out by small fingers.

'Be diligent, children,' Jacquetta insisted, as she inspected the room where her daughters, Anne, Martha and Margaret, had been set to work. 'And don't be silly with the feathers. Gather them in a pile. We can use them again.'

The kitchens thronged with activity. Fires burned bright with the roar and crackle of hot coals and meat turning on spits above them. Stove tops were set with pans, boiling and bubbling; ovens baked;

meat was brought in from the larders; sauces were stirred, and wines were summoned from the cellars.

'Mistress, might I have the spice key?'

'Again, cook?' asked Jacquetta, but she was already reaching for her belt where the keys hung.

'More ginger is needed for the puddings, and saffron for the custards.'

'So be it. Be generous but also sparing, if that is possible.'

'Yes, my lady, I will try.'

'We do not know if the king will come back this way again, so we had better hold some reserves until the order from London arrives.'

'Yes, my lady.'

Jacquetta turned to her daughter, whose bright hooded eyes shone in the shadows. 'And you. Get yourself upstairs, out of that old dress, into the new blue dress with the long laces. Go, and hurry. The king will be with us soon.'

She was perfection. He had never seen such a face, so captivating, such a mask of control and yet suggestive of reserves of passion beneath. The eyes, so clear and wide, with such innocence, but when she cast a look to the side, their blueness darkened; their promise was clear. The exact same shade as her dress, that summer cornflower blue, both cold and warm. He had glimpsed those eyes in the forest and they had stayed with him, returning to him as he hunted through the day so that he had longed to see them again. And now, seated at her father's table, watching her in profile, outlined by the fire, he saw how she kept them cast down, only venturing up with little darting looks. Was it modesty? The deference of a subject? Or a woman's subtle wiles, to draw his interest?

'More wine, my lord?'

'Please.' He held up his goblet and the servant filled it to the top. Then he watched as she did the same and raised it up to her lips.

They had placed her at a distance to him. Was it deliberate policy? He could not tell. It meant he was unable to speak to her directly, but he was best placed to enjoy her beauty to best advantage. Instead, he was flanked by Woodville and his wife, both conscious of the great honour he was doing them, and obsequious in their praise and service. It was a charming house too, a little small, but the location was pleasant and well positioned. It would be a place in which he might while away the hours happily, riding, hunting, with such hospitality and company.

He reached for one of the roasted birds, dressed in herb sauce.

'Is the food to your liking, my lord?'

'It is indeed, my lady. You have been most generous. Your supplies here are excellent.'

'We produce most of it on the estate but send to London for our spices and wines. It makes a difference to plain dishes, I find.'

'You are wise to do so. I consider myself as being very well fed today.'

'Thank you, my lord.'

'And how has your hunting trip passed?' asked Woodville, on the other side. 'Have you met with much success? The woods are full of deer between here and Northampton.'

'And very beautiful,' added the king, but his eyes were on Elizabeth.

Jacquetta followed his gaze. 'Yes, we are very fortunate here. Our grounds are beautiful at this time of year. You see the arrangements of flowers on the windowsill and in the alcove, there?'

The king dutifully looked.

'All picked by my daughter, Elizabeth, this morning, all from our estate. There is a bed of narcissus by the hermitage.'

'There is a hermitage on the estate?'

'Part of the abbey of St James, and a dovecote, but the hermit has long since flown. Perhaps Elizabeth might show it to you if there is time before your departure.'

She had heard her mother's suggestion, he was sure of it, but she would not meet his eyes and he sensed she was waiting to hear his response. Casually, he reached for some more bread.

'If there is time.'

She was waiting for him in the doorway, no doubt at her mother's command. Her blue dress hung in graceful folds from a waist still slender in spite of her two sons. He couldn't tell from her demeanour whether or not she was pleased to be accompanying him.

'Lady Elizabeth?'

She dropped a curtsey. 'My lord.'

'So, you have been ordered by your mother to show me the hermitage?'

'It is my pleasure to do so, my lord,' she replied, but it sounded like a convention.

'Please, lead the way.'

They headed out of the entrance hall, through the door and down the path. At the end of the garden, it divided and ran away in two directions; Elizabeth chose the left hand one, which ran alongside a stone wall, and the king followed. On the other side, he was aware of the tops of trees weighted down with white blossom.

'You have an orchard here?'

'Yes, my lord, an ancient orchard, planted by the monks. But the apples are a little bitter.'

'Quite suitable for monks,' he nodded wryly. 'They couldn't be allowed to enjoy them too much.'

'My mother adds honey, or elderflower, or blackberries, so we do well with them.'

'Your mother often works in the kitchen?'

'Sometimes. We like to make puddings and jams. And jellies. She makes a wonderful jelly, oh, but not today. There was not enough time, I am afraid.'

'I will just have to return on my way home so that I can taste one of your mother's jellies.'

Elizabeth blushed. 'It is this way.'

The path sloped away through a coppice where the trees met overhead and the long grass was sprinkled with the faces of small white flowers. It was idyllic but he could not keep his eyes off her. The movement of her graceful neck; the sweep up from her neck to her ear drew him and stirred his passion. She was just as beautiful as he had suspected when he saw her in the forest, perhaps more.

'So you are living with your parents and your sons?'

'Yes, my lord. I passed my childhood here. I returned when I was widowed.'

'When was that?'

'Three years ago at St Albans.'

Edward tried to recall it, following her over a wooden bridge that broached the stream. He had been in the West Country at the time, while Warwick had led the Hertfordshire campaign. 'He fought for the Lancastrian king, I believe.'

She hesitated at first, concentrating as if she was watching her footing. 'He did.'

'Men fought bravely on both sides.'

She was grateful for his magnanimity. 'Thank you, my lord.'

They broke out of the trees to the edge of a meadow of wild grasses and flowers. The roof of the hermitage was visible beyond a down curve in the land, lit by the spring sunshine.

'It is not far now,' she replied, turning, and very briefly, smiling.

'That is the first time I have seen your smile.'

She bowed her head again and almost put a little urgency into her step.

'Don't hide it. You have a beautiful smile.'

'This way,' she replied, forging ahead.

The tiny building sat snug in a fold of land, as compact and satisfying as a beehive.

Elizabeth turned the key in the lock and pushed open the wooden door. The stone interior smelt cool and musty as their eyes adjusted to the gloom. Then he saw the altar, the decorated walls and tiled floor. Although it was an old building, recent work had been undertaken on it and the flowers and candles showed the place was still cared for.

'Your family use this place often?'

'We do. A monk comes to us from the abbey three times a week, but we like the stillness and peace here so we come more often. Mother and I come a lot.'

'And bring flowers.'

'Yes, more flowers.'

She was framed by the paned window, which filtered the incoming light about her head.

'And why have you not remarried, may I ask?'

The space about them was very still. He felt her discomfiture.

'I, I don't... I am raising my sons.'

'You cannot do that and have a husband at the same time?'

She turned her face away.

'I am sorry to have made you uncomfortable.'

Elizabeth made no reply. He looked around at the place again, barely enough to contain a congregation of a dozen before the small altar with its brass cross and candlesticks. The simplicity of it struck him, plain and honest in its solemnity, the perfect foil for her fragile beauty. With the light making her hair shine and her large, hooded eyes, she was possibly the most beautiful woman he had ever seen.

95

'Elizabeth?'

'We should be getting back soon. You will need to ride back to Stratford.'

'Elizabeth?'

She had reached the doorway but stood still at the sound of his voice.

'Might I visit you again? Without company?'

Outside, the wind blew through a line of willows as if the air had sighed.

Eventually, she replied. 'The king can command my presence whenever he wishes.'

'That is not what I meant. I would no more command your presence than command the wind to blow. But I wish to see you again, if you will let me.'

She would not meet his eyes. 'To what purpose, my lord?'

'Because I would like to know you better, and because you are the most beautiful woman I have ever seen.'

She turned away, stared out of the door. 'But where would that lead? I have my reputation to consider, and that of my boys.'

If the recent memory of another similar conversation, and another golden-haired beauty flickered in his mind, he pushed it aside as meaningless.

'I will restore your boys' inheritance and give them much more besides, so their futures are secure. With my protection, you will never need to fear.' He moved closer behind her, close enough to lay a hand upon her shoulder. 'It would give me the greatest pleasure to be your protector.'

She turned abruptly, shook off his touch. 'My protector? And what would I be? Your whore?'

'There's none would dare use that word to you.'

'Behind my back, then. And what if I wished to remarry? Who would have me then, the king's cast off? And what of God? I would be sinning in his eyes and that is something I can never accept. You dare to proposition me here, in this holy place? Have you no respect? You may be the King of England, but there is always a higher master to be served.'

And she hurried out of the door and back across the meadow, leaving him reeling.

She was there among the household lined up along the path to bid the king goodbye. Of course she was. Her mother would have allowed for nothing less. Edward saw her blue dress fluttering as he bid goodbye to her brother, Anthony, and the younger children. Woodville and Jacquetta bowed low before him but he took their hands and gratefully raised them, with fresh eyes about their future friendship. He had expected her to be blushing, bashful, even repentant, but Elizabeth was cool and calm, her eyes like ice, her lips firmly shut. And although he had barely known her for more than a few hours, never spoken words of love to her, or kissed her even, a conviction rose in his chest that she was the one, the only woman who could be his equal. The sudden realisation unnerved him, but he looked into her mask-like face with a mixture of authority and tenderness. What did she want? What price would she demand before he could claim her as his? At that moment he would have laid his crown at her feet.

'I am passing back along this road in two days' time. I wish to call here again and hope that you will consent to have dinner with me, in no way that might give God offence. Until then, I bid you and your family good health, good day.'

At the edge of the estate, where the track met the road, Hastings was waiting. Edward reined in his horse.

'Any news?'

'I have ridden today to Northampton and Towcester and enquired in all the villages between. There have been no sightings of Somerset but an old woman received notice from a tenant of hers who has vacated her farm to ride north to join him.'

'How long ago?'

'Just two days. He is a John Vintner, an unremarkable man, but his father served the old duke, so he is acting on that allegiance. Somerset is summoning his men for the fight.'

'Where did she think this Vintner was headed?'

'He told her only that he was to overnight at Leicester and Nottingham, then would join with allies at Leeds.'

'And where is Montagu right now?'

'We received word today that he is on the road to Newcastle. It is also reported that Sir Humphrey Neville and Sir Henry Bellingham, Lancastrians you generously pardoned after Towton have gone to join him, and the towns of Norham, Langley, Hexham, Bywell and Prudhoe have been taken.'

Edward frowned. 'Let us away to Stratford for the night and wait to see what news the morning brings.'

'But, my lord, there is more.'

'More?'

Hastings bent in close. 'Rumours have reached us that the French queen has landed in Scotland.'

'Margaret? Is she really back?'

'To join with Beaufort. It was to be expected. We knew she would not remain indefinitely in France.'

'And where is their king? Where is Henry?'

'Being sheltered by friends in the north. The threat is serious, I am afraid, my lord. It would not be wise for you to travel any further at the moment, but remain here, within striking distance of London, well out of their reach. Montagu will deal with Beaufort.'

'It rankles me. It goes against everything I feel, to sit here, playing at hunting, while others act the part of men, of soldiers. Especially under such a threat.'

'I understand. But you must show caution. The time may come for you to lead an army north, but until then, wait for news.'

'I feel that time has come. Caution be damned. Send to Warwick in London and have him raise an army. I cannot be a bystander in this, just as I was not at Mortimer's Cross or Towton. Dispatch a man at once!'

'My lord…'

'At once!'

Edward shot a look back at the manor house, where lights were shining out of the windows. 'Now come, let us away from here.'

SEVEN

The Promise

Margaret of Anjou stared critically at the Beaufort arms carved above the fireplace. She wore a heavy cloak with a fur hood and had become leaner during her exile so that her cheeks were quite gaunt and the lines of her neck more pronounced. Her famous almond eyes, still beautiful, held something of the privation she had suffered in the last few years. It was a long time since her noble head had borne the crown. The hall was empty and the table behind them spread with maps and letters.

'You are quite certain that the house is safe?'

Somerset, tall and lean in his habitual black, made a gesture as if to humble himself before her.

'My family's connection to the place is not widely known, and then it was only a junior branch; my men are all through the town and posted on the road for ten mile out.'

'And yet your cousin was able to find us.'

Henry frowned at the mention of Eleanor. 'She is family. She has always known about this property. But she left a seven night back; she has no idea you are here.'

'And yet, she specifically knew to find you here. My son is asleep upstairs so how can I be certain?'

'I assure you, all is safe here. Edward remains in the south and we have thousands of loyal men gathering. Soon we will defeat him and you will be restored to the throne.'

She sighed and turned a withering look upon him, every inch still the queen. 'Unless you decide to become his friend again.'

'Do not berate me with that…'

'I beg your pardon?'

'Forgive me, my lady, my words were too harsh. I made the best of the situation that I could, as I feared for my brothers.'

'But you two were like brothers, you and Edward, or so I hear. And why, why, Henry, did you give him Bamburgh? Just signed it over to our enemies. That's one thing I am struggling to understand.'

Beaufort stroked his chin. For a moment he thought of the hunt, chasing through the forest at Windsor with Edward in close pursuit. 'We have all done things to ensure our survival that we might not otherwise have done. I can assure you I am fully committed to the Lancastrian cause, and I am your true and loyal knight.'

'Then you will have nothing to fear. I am putting my life in your hands by trusting you in this way. So come, tell me. What are your plans?'

'Edward has sent Lord Montagu to bring the Scots party to York. I will intercept him when he reaches the city and ensure he never crosses the border.'

'Montagu? Why has he sent Montagu and not Warwick, or gone himself?'

'He is not a fool. He anticipates that I will be attacking and he does not wish to leave London open for you.'

'No,' the ex-queen mused. 'He is young, inexperienced, even

headstrong, but one thing he is not is a fool. He has the advantage over his father there. He is not married yet?'

'I believe Warwick is finalising the arrangements.'

'Is it the Bona of Savoy match?'

'I believe so.'

'I cannot stay in France if Edward allies with Louis, not even to go to my family at Angers. He will make it a condition of the match that Louis opposes me. And if he concludes peace with Scotland, there is only the Netherlands left, and Philip the Good is no friend to my cause.'

'Ireland?'

'A savage backwater.'

'Then we must ensure we succeed.'

'Do you have news of my husband, the king?'

'I believe he is in a strong house outside Bamburgh. It is better if he remains there until we have secured a victory. We cannot run the risk of himself, you and I all being taken in one go. The more we are spread about, the better.'

Margaret nodded at this wisdom. 'And is he, is he… well?'

Beaufort paused in understanding of the full scale of her question. 'His health is sound; his constitution is strong. He has given no indication that he would not be fit to resume rule.'

'God be praised. So now we cannot fail. We simply cannot fail.'

He saw the rising emotion in her, playing about the corners of her mouth, and he touched her hand gently in a gesture that spoke of a former intimacy.

'God will answer your prayers. Have faith in him, and in me.'

The almond eyes welled briefly with tears but the former queen made a mighty effort to control them, fighting them down, ashamed at the sign of weakness. 'If it had not been for your letters, I would have considered you lost to us.'

'Not lost, never lost. Your ever-loyal knight and champion.'

'Then we will prevail. When I am queen again, you will be rewarded handsomely.'

Beaufort indicated two carved chairs at the table. 'Will you sit, my lady?'

'I am inclined to stand. I'm so very cold. I can't seem to get warm.'

'Oh, let me call for a servant to make up the fire.'

'No, I will be well. I thank you.'

'Some wine then?'

'Some wine.' She nodded.

He beckoned to a servant in the anteroom and wine was immediately procured and drunk.

'Have you had any word at all, concerning the king's health?'

'I confess I have not. It concerns you?'

'His physician only writes that he is in good body and good spirits. He says nothing of his mind.'

'Is that a good thing? Or a deliberate omission?'

'I cannot tell. But we must prepare for the worst so we are not caught out. If he is, if he proves to be…'

'Unwell?'

'Unwell, yes. Then we might need to consider a Protectorate again while my son is still young. Of course, that would be your role.'

Beaufort stared into the flames.

'Did you not wish for the role yourself?'

'I did, once. The first time, I tried to persuade the council to appoint me, but I have learned they have no love for a French woman, even if she is their queen. They will never accept me, but you are a different matter.'

'They were fools. No doubt it was the Yorkists among them, encouraged by York.'

103

'Perhaps. But you would be willing to act as protector? Until he is ready to rule?'

'I gained some knowledge of kingship while I was with Edward. I know what I am capable of. We must not be complacent though. We must prepare for every outcome. You understand? If something were to happen to the king, God preserve him.'

And she knew at once. She understood completely that he referred to Henry's death, that his sentiments were both treasonous and sensible. And she knew what he was suggesting, what he had hinted at once before, that if she found herself a widow, then as the Lancastrian heir, he was the best man to become her next husband. The thought was terrifying and thrilling. She turned away.

'We will consider these things in their correct season.'

'Of course.'

A servant appeared in the doorway. 'Please, my lord?'

'What is it? I gave instruction that we were not to be disturbed.'

'Your brothers thought you would wish to know at once; forgive me, my lord.'

Somerset strode over to take the note from the man's fingers. He read it swiftly and then more slowly.

'It seems that Montagu has been sighted, five miles to the south of the city. We must mobilise at once.'

'This is it?'

'I must leave you for now. You will be safe here. I will send word.'

She seized his hand. 'God be with you.'

He pressed her knuckles to his lips. 'And you. Always.'

Her fingers lingered against his face, enjoying the touch that they had been denied for so long.

'Are we alone here?' she whispered.

'I can give orders that we will not be disturbed.'

His cheek was close to hers, with the frisson of skin almost touching. He could feel her breath upon his face.

'Yes,' she urged, softly, into his mouth, 'yes Henry, yes. Do it.'

The room had been hung with white and silver tissue, and the flames of torches flickered their warming light up the walls. A table was set before the fire, draped with Bruges linen and topped with silver plates. Treasures, no doubt, that had been saved from Jacquetta's former life.

Elizabeth stood there alone. She had dressed carefully in a plain white kirtle, sewed by the nearby monks. She kept her face immobile and her fair hair hung loose, almost to her waist. She had argued with her mother about it, right up to the last minute when the king was announced; Jacquetta insisted that she brushed out her best feature in a fan across her shoulders, while Elizabeth had begged to tie it up under a hennin headdress, austere and grave as a widow should be.

When he was shown up to the room, Edward could sense her reluctance and the influence of her mother's hand. A large bed was conspicuous in the corner behind her, hung with velvet, but she kept her back to it as if she could pretend it was not there, or there by chance, and deny its implications. Servants were clearing away the plates and the remnants of the meal they had just eaten.

'Do not deny him,' Jacquetta had urged as she pinched her daughter's cheeks and rubbed her with scent. 'He is the king. Think of what he can give you, give us. Everything. If he has a taste for you, why not let him reward you for it? Marriages are arranged on that basis. Think of the boys' future.'

'I think of nothing but the boys' future. That is why I waited for him in the forest in the first place; I had no idea it would go this way. If I had, I would have stayed at home.'

'Now that is foolish talk. God has laid an opportunity at your feet. Do not be so selfish as to spurn it.'

Elizabeth set her lips tight, not relishing the fine tightrope she would have to walk.

'And smile, do not grimace at him like that. Give him your best smile. Are you laced tight enough? Let me look at you.'

Elizabeth turned to let herself be examined.

'Come now,' Jacquetta chided, pulling strands of her daughter's golden locks forward across her shoulders. 'He is handsome enough, isn't he? And a king? What more do you want?'

'Honour, respectability, perhaps.'

'Those things will not put food on the table. Let him give you that security. You have never shown yourself averse to marrying again.'

'Marrying again? That is not his intention. He would share my bed and leave me to deal with the consequences.'

'Well.' Jacquetta tucked a flower behind Elizabeth's ear. 'Then it is up to you to play the hand you have been dealt. Proceed with caution and discretion. There are worse things than being a king's mistress.'

'Not in the eyes of God.'

'Yes, plenty in the eyes of God. Where did you get this prudery from? Not from your mother, certainly. Now go, I hear the horses in the yard. Go, and smile.'

Elizabeth went and stood by the fire, as if its warmth and strength could offer some kind of protection. With slow fingers, she removed the flower from behind her ear and pulled off its petals, one by one.

'You were very quiet during our dinner,' Edward observed, offering her a glass of wine.

Elizabeth waved the drink away. 'I'm sorry, my lord.'

'Do not apologise. I want to know why, not to chastise you for it.'

She did not answer. He took a step closer to her.

'You are unwilling to be here? With me?'

'It's not that, no.'

'Then what? Your family approve of my visit, so what concerns you?'

'I do not understand why I am here. I am no one, you are the king.'

'For tonight, I am just a man.'

Elizabeth smiled wryly. 'You can never be just a man.'

'But what if I was? What if I was another man, a local landowner, a knight standing here, professing his admiration. Can you imagine?'

'Then I would ask him the same question that I now ask of you: what is your intention? I am a widow with two sons and I must look to their future and to my good name.'

'But could you like him, as a man, this unkingly king who stands before you?'

'Not if he did not take my concerns seriously.'

'I can take care of your sons, and you, and your family. I can ensure your protection and bestow upon you lands and estates so you will be comfortable.'

'But what is your price? What would you demand in return?'

'A gentle and fair bargain, not a demand. The pleasure of your company.'

'And the sharing of my bed.'

He looked at her levelly. 'Yes. You are a widow, not a virgin. You understand the ways of men. I will not keep that from you. Yes, I desire you, greatly.'

At that, he took a step forward as if to kiss her but she held up a hand to keep him at bay.

Her mother was right. He was handsome. Far more than John had been, or any man she had ever seen. The broad face and strong cheekbones, the wide powerful mouth and sharp hazel eyes that had both authority and a suggestion of sensitivity. She could not imagine what it would be like to be loved by such a man, to be the object of his affections, to feel the warmth of his kisses. In fact, kisses seemed to be such a distant memory.

'What are you thinking?'

And for a moment, a glimmer of hope rose in her, that there might be a way to make this work, somehow, to surrender herself and keep her good name.

But then he tried again, taking her by the shoulders and leaning in towards her face, his eyes blurred by passion.

'No, wait! Nothing is decided.'

'Just a kiss. I need you, Elizabeth. I want you so much. What do you mean that nothing is decided?'

'I don't know. I can't just give myself to you.'

'Why not?'

For a moment they stared into each other's eyes, his hazel ones meeting her ice-blue resolve. She saw that he was a king, senses swimming in desire, used to getting what he wanted; he saw that she was vulnerable, afraid.

'If I could, I would make you all the promises and reassurances your heart desires. I could love you, Elizabeth, never tire of you for your entire lifetime. I could pledge my heart to you. No other woman I have ever seen comes close.'

'But you cannot. You cannot make those promises. You are not free to do so.'

'The Earl of Warwick is, at this very moment, negotiating my marriage with the sister of the Queen of Spain. But nothing is final. The vows have not been exchanged. I am still a free man.'

'But for how long?'

'That depends upon you.'

She frowned. The fire spat a little and she drew back. 'But how? How can it possibly depend upon me? You are the king.'

'I am a king willing to be ruled by you.'

She shook her head, turned away. 'You say that now.'

'I do, and I always will.'

'But how, how can that be?'

'Do you trust me?'

'I barely know you.'

He looked at her downcast mouth, the lustrous eyes. 'I will prove myself to you if you will let me. By God, I will. What if I made those promises to you, if I pledged myself to you, as your husband, and you as my wife?'

'But you cannot.'

'I am the king. I can do as I please! I defy anyone to stop me. Would you then consent?'

Elizabeth was stunned, unable to believe in his sudden enthusiasm. 'But you scarcely know me, and you must take a queen.'

'I must. And I choose you. What do you say?'

She blushed in confusion. 'I do not know, my lord. I do not know how to answer you. What would your council say?

'I must have you, Elizabeth. There is no other woman I desire, or who I can imagine at my side.'

'This is too much, too soon.'

'Be my wife. You can think about it afterwards. Do you not want me, as a man, as a king? Can you honestly tell me you do not? If you say you cannot love me, if you find me unappealing, then I will leave you in peace.'

And the future turned about at that moment: his future, her future, that of her children, and that of England.

Edward knew he had made a promise of such immensity, of such scope, that it seemed to dwarf them in the room like the clouds of a coming storm. And he knew it was born out of a physical passion, which might easily be sated, but that was not all. It was only the beginning. There was something in her, in her quiet demeanour, her promise of strength, her elegance, that made her more than his match, something almost queenly in her bearing. He could not imagine tiring of the gentle way she looked aside when she was thinking, of her cautious wisdom and her commitment to her ideals. And he was tired of other women, tired of the chase. He longed for the solace of the same woman, to know her mind, her desires, and to share himself with her. The French match was noble, virtuous, beneficial, but it did not feed his hungry soul. For so long he had been restless, seeking the quiet shade of peace. Elizabeth Woodville was a risk. He knew a marriage to her would not be without opposition, but he had overcome worse obstacles. In the very fibres of his being, he knew she was the one to offer him that connection.

'Elizabeth, will you be my wife?'

And the moment surged up inside her. The widow of a Lancastrian knight, uncertain, friendless, and clinging to the charity of her family, the thin security of her religion. What if this were real; what if he really was offering her a crown? What if she might walk down that path, at Westminster, dressed in gold and jewels, feasting in the hall, waited upon by servants, while her sons received the best of everything. What if she could wake in some gold-tissue bed in the heart of the palace, forever protected, forever secure, with a devoted husband at her side and her family taken care of? And this land she loved, of green valleys and hills, of rolling fields, streams and wide skies, of flowering meadows, to which he had brought peace, what if she were to be its queen?

'Yes, I will.'

'Wait, you will?'

'Yes, I accept.'

And he swept her up in his arms and pressed his lips down upon hers.

'Let me go and speak with your mother and in a few days I will return. But kiss me again, kiss me!'

EIGHT

May Day

Montagu shaded his eyes and peered at the horizon. A few hundred yards ahead, in the middle of the moorland, the land began to rise up, sloping away until it reached a plateau. It fell, purple and green, in peaceful folds and slopes, cut by a stream or a cushion of orange moss. And there, low against the grey clouds, he saw that the scout was right. Men: spread out in a ripple of dark movement, flanking the horizon. Among them, somewhere, were the Duke of Somerset and the Lancastrian deserters, buoyed by their recent small victories, making their last prayers. So, this was it. This scrubby sweep of ground, springy with heather and broken by stones, would soon run with blood.

The earl turned to his captain. 'Yes, I see them. Get the men in formation.'

'Right away, my lord.'

Montagu looked up and down the road. He had passed through the village of Glanton that morning and had hoped to cover the ten miles north to Wooler before his army rested, but Wooler lay beyond the ridge, and beyond Wooler, the Scottish border, where the peace delegation waited. Beaufort's men were positioned to block the way entirely. There was nothing for it but to stand and fight. Montagu had evaded them once already, just outside Newcastle, where a man had battled through the rain, bringing word that Beaufort was setting an ambush in the woods ahead. He'd had fewer supporters then, less than a hundred men at arms and a troop of archers, but by avoiding the trap along another road, and reaching the city, he'd recruited more men and swelled his numbers. And judging by what he could see on the horizon, the earl could see that he now outnumbered the Lancastrian force.

The men were dividing into three parts: one on either side, in the flanks that would close in like a pincer movement; in the centre, with its archers, its first fighters; and behind it, the vanguard, waiting in the rear to make the final, deadly attack. Montagu had consulted with his brother, Warwick, both of them veterans of the field, who understood mobilisation and strategy, pouring over maps and plans of former successful campaigns. He remembered the advice of his father, the old Earl of Salisbury, who had died with York at Sandal Castle, to look the enemy in the eye and keep marching forward.

'The archers are in position, my lord. This way.'

Montagu followed his captain to the head of the force. On that spring day, there was something deeply moving about the long lines of men, hundreds upon hundreds, ranged under the heavens, awaiting their fates. A number of silver crosses had been raised in the camp and prayers had already been said.

His horse was brought, with its light armour and red trappings, and he climbed into the saddle to better survey the terrain. Then, with a swift, sharp move, he pulled the beast round to face the front line of archers.

113

'Men, good men and true, who serve the king's cause. Your loyalty will never be forgotten. Today we face a threat to that honoured, God-given dynasty whom it has been my privilege to serve. On the far hill, the traitor Beaufort would prevent our mission of peace and seek to usurp good King Edward IV, in whose name you are assembled here today. I call upon you, with the grace of God, to give your all in the service of your king, and God be with you!'

A resounding cheer went up from the ranks.

Slowly, with the heaviness of inevitability, Montagu rode to the sidelines, gave the signal and watched as the first row of archers loosed their bows. At the same time, movement in the enemy lines showed that they had mirrored this move. The earl watched as the tiny specks rose through the sky, slowed, peaked and began the downturn. It was clear that the enemy's aim had fallen short, but the swish and thud of arrows falling in the wasteland soon reached him. The captain signalled and the second wave flew up into the air, and then a third.

'I believe we are too far apart,' the captain called over. 'Should I call off the attack?'

'No,' replied Montagu, with certainty. 'Let them expend all their arrows before we advance.'

'Very well, my lord.'

And the arrows continued to fly and fall on the moorland, until there eventually set in a silence.

'Now we move forward!' cried Montagu, his horse turned to face the enemy. 'Now we advance. Onwards, men, onwards, for God, King Edward and England!'

The ground was lumpy and uneven but Montagu pushed ahead determinedly. He picked his way carefully between the arrow shafts scattered across the ground, surprised at just how close they had come before falling short. At the centre of the front line, he never ceased to be moved by this moment, this united ripple of men moving towards their destiny, no matter what. Every battle he had fought, and there had been many, were occasions when he felt the hand of God. And now, in this remote, beautiful spot, death and rebirth would come again, just as surely as the blood would pool at his feet. Out there, on the moving horizon, Beaufort and his traitors waited: Roos and Hungerford, men with whom he had feasted at court, and the Percy brothers, whose feud with his family still raged unchecked.

The enemy were on the move, but not in the way he expected. Senses sharpening, Montagu scrutinised the left flank of his opponents. At first, he couldn't make sense of their formation, odd and straggling as it was, and he couldn't believe what he was seeing, scarcely daring to hope. But then, he saw that he was right. One entire section of the Lancastrian army was crumbling, already, before blows had been exchanged.

'They've lost their nerve!' Montagu shouted to his men, pointing to the opposite lines. 'They've lost their nerve and they're retreating. We have them! Spread the word, men, spread the word!'

He brandished his sword in the air. 'Come men, the day is ours!'

It was dawn. The sun was only just rising over the meadow at Grafton on May Day. Faces of flowers were opening to the sky, pink, white and yellow, still tinged with dew. Tall grasses stood still against the sky which was pale and colourless with a promise of blueness.

Two women emerged from the back door of the manor. Wrapped about in shawls, with their long flapping skirts about their ankles, they hurried arm in arm through the cobbled kitchen yard. Letting themselves out through the gate, they took the path that ran away from the house, along the side of the orchard wall. Behind them, the manor was silent with not even the servants awake. The whole valley slept; the creatures in the woods slept, and the village beyond the estate slept. With a look back to check they were not being followed, they broke away and crossed the meadows. An older woman and a younger one, both with long fair hair tied back and the similar features of a cool, dignified beauty.

The priest was waiting at the door of the chapel. He was old, discreet, knowledgeable in the ways of the world. Their greetings were swift and formal before the elder woman produced a key and the solid door was unlocked, letting the morning inside the holy space. Inside, it was cool and dark, with the scent of a summer day and ancient stones, and the lingering sweetness of incense. The altar was dressed with a gold cloth, silver candlesticks and a plain silver cross. Before these, the three visitors bowed their heads in silent prayer.

As Jacquetta and Elizabeth stood waiting, two horsemen came riding up, thundering through the meadow with solid hooves. In the stillness, they seemed to contain all life, bringing newness with them, as if the moment had returned, somehow, in that space soon after dawn, to an innocence before time. They were dressed simply, in the dark coats of huntsmen, to avoid detection, and their determined air showed their eagerness, their focus upon this secret task. For Edward, descending his horse in one leap, would not be deterred from his purpose by anything. Not all the persuasion Hastings could muster, not his warnings of Warwick's anger, and the disgrace with France, nor the rashness of such a lifelong commitment could change the king's mind. His entreaties had fallen upon deaf ears. Hastings recognised that look that had come into Edward's eyes when he spoke of the lady; it was a kind of obsession, a rapture of desire he had seen

116

before, but none so strong as this. And better this than the dalliance with the treasonous Butler woman. Edward still did not know of her guilt, and it was better that way, now that his affection was drawn elsewhere. The Woodville woman wasn't ideal and surely the secret nature of the union meant that it could be undone later by the clever words of priests, if necessary.

As they tethered their horses to a tree, Hastings put a hand on the king's arm. 'There is still time to change your mind. You can bed this woman without marriage, easily, and there are many others. This is your kingdom, and you may be too hasty.'

'I have no wish to change my mind.'

'You need an equal as your queen.'

Immediately he saw where he had made his mistake.

'I have found her,' Edward smiled. 'You just wait until you see her. Come on.'

Knowing he was defeated, Hastings followed the king through the open chapel door into the darkness. When his eyes adjusted, the circular space inside showed him an older woman, whom he recognised as a duchess, a priest in plain robes, and a woman with golden hair, radiant in beauty and dignity, whose eyes he saw at once had the power to bewitch and transfix a man so that he could quite lose his senses completely.

Connoisseur of beauty as he was, she brought him to his knees, literally, before her. 'Duchess, my Lady Elizabeth, Father.'

'This is my friend, Lord Hastings, a witness to our ceremony. Come, Hastings, rise; don't seek the dust on the floor.'

Edward went to Elizabeth, who had cast off her gown to reveal a plain white dress and loosened her hair which now lay around her in a golden mantle.

'My bride.'

She demurred, shyly. 'I wasn't sure you would come.'

'Nothing would have kept me away. Good morning, my lady duchess, you will be amply rewarded for your kindness. Your father?'

Elizabeth shook her head. 'We thought it best to wait and break the news after.'

'As you wish. Now come, priest, speak the words, make us man and wife.'

The fire in the kitchen hearth was blazing as the cook rolled out the dough for that day's bread. A boy sat beside it, kindling the flames with small pieces of wood so they licked the bottom of the great pot in which water was coming to the boil. The maid swept the floor while another brought a bowl of almonds from the larder, ready to be ground into powder in the stone mortice. When the back door opened unexpectedly, the busy workers stopped and bowed in surprise. Their mistress ushered the king in through the back door and through the kitchens. With surprised glances, they saw him lead the lady Elizabeth by the hand, between the oven and table, and up the back stairs, before Jacquetta appeared and urged them to resume their duties.

The chamber had been made ready with garlands of fresh flowers and tapestry hangings. It was the same room where they had dined before but, on this occasion, the table was set aside and the bed hung with new yellow drapes and downy pillows. At the doorway, Jacquetta kissed her daughter and whispered in her ear before the door was closed upon them and the footsteps faded away. Elizabeth turned the key in the lock.

Edward observed her from across the room. 'So, here we are, my wife and queen.'

'Here we are, my lord.'

'You are more beautiful today than any other woman I have ever seen.'

His words were flattering, but she wanted more.

'It was an official ceremony, with priest, and witnesses, and vows.'

'Of course, my love.'

'So I am really your wife?'

He moved closer to her, took her face in his hands. 'You are my wife and queen.'

'But how will this work? It cannot be a marriage like the one I knew before.'

'I will send for you to come to Westminster in good time. We will live there together and raise our children.'

'And my boys?'

'Of course. They will come too and be raised at court. They will have every advantage of having the king as their stepfather.'

'And how will I be received? By your family, your council?'

He kissed the tip of her nose. 'Leave that to me to manage. You need not fear their reactions as they must be ruled by their king. Anyway, how could anyone fail to love you?'

She appeared unconvinced.

'Anyone who dares disrespect my queen will be swiftly dealt with, be sure. And in the meantime, there are your clothes and jewels to be arranged. Whatever you like: cloth of gold and silver tissue, the best ermine, damask silks, the finest stockings. Anything you desire, necklaces, headdresses, rings. Hastings will see to it.'

'Cloth of silver tissue?'

'Whatever your heart desires. Whatever my wife wants.'

He bent to kiss her lips, but she only allowed him brief contact with them.

'And then you will send for us? My parents and my brothers and sisters too?'

'Of course, my love, you have my word. Now do not resist me any more.'

She permitted him a longer, deeper kiss.

'And I am truly your queen? I am Queen of England?'

And she thought of the rolling green hills outside, the sweep of fields sown with seed, the paths of the forest and the rivers, the cluttered chimneys of towns and the rising spires of churches. All this was hers? Queen of all she surveyed.

His mouth fell hot and hungry upon her neck. 'Not until we consummate the match. Once we've lain together, it cannot be undone.'

She reached her arms up around his neck and drew him back down to her.

'Then love me; enjoy my body; claim me as yours.'

Needing no further encouragement, his arms encircled her until they were lost in a long, deep embrace.

From the top window, Cecily could see out across the fields and down into the valley. Around Fotheringhay Castle, the greenness of late spring was budding into life. With the paths bursting with growth and the trees full again, summer would soon be upon them. A sweetness blew up the rise and in through the open window of her chamber. She felt it upon her skin, but it did not count as being cold. It was the rush of new life and, despite every setback she had encountered, Cecily, Duchess of York, always sought the arrival of new life, new opportunities, new faces.

Behind her, at the table, Richard sat leaning over his books. The tutor had just left them after a morning of Latin and the boy was tired. He grew tired very easily she had noticed, in comparison with her other sons. Edward hadn't been much of a diligent student, and nor had George, but there was a quickness about their wits that allowed them to race through their lessons before heading out to ride, or hunt, or roam outdoors. It had been her beloved Edmund who had loved his books. That boy had been such a blessing. The thought of him always caught her by surprise. Over three years since she had seen his sweet face, and yet she could not stop seeking him in every crowd, hoping beyond hope that there had been a mistake.

'Can I go now?'

But the boy seated at the table had dark, curling hair, almost black. His face was pinched and slight, his arms thin. She knew he wanted to go down to the kennels and play with his dogs. The fresh air would do him good, in time.

'In a moment. I am just waiting for Doctor Strawfoot to have a quick look at you.'

'Another doctor?'

'It won't take long. I want his opinion as it may differ from those we heard in London. Please try to sit up straight.'

He made a small effort but she could see it was difficult.

'Why has this happened to me?'

She put her hand on his shoulder. The frail bones were raised on this side, but not in the usual way of young men practising throwing and combat. It had only been last autumn, soon after his eleventh birthday, that he began to complain of pains in his back. When the doctor had asked him to remove his shirt, even his mother could see the uneven development, one shoulder slightly off-kilter, as if he walked with a permanent strain inside. It was not visible under his clothes, but the doctors could not decide.

'I can't say, Richard. All I can tell you is that everything is God's will, and that if he has granted you this pain, it is a means to a greater glory.'

'But what if I do not want this glory, whatever it may be?'

'We cannot choose the paths God has selected for us. It is only ours to know we are part of his plan.'

'But what can this plan be? How can it help God to make me feel pain? And why me?'

'Everyone feels pain sometimes.' She spoke softly. 'A life without pain contains no trial, no difficulty. Otherwise, it would be too easy to enter the kingdom of heaven.'

He made no reply to this, but she sensed he was mutinous.

'How would you like to go and stay for a while with your sister Elizabeth? A little break in Suffolk might do you some good?'

'She doesn't want me. She's busy with her brats.'

Since her marriage to John de la Pole, Cecily's daughter had borne two children, John, who was two, and the new baby, Geoffrey.

'Richard! What a thing to say. Of course she would want you; she has ample care for the children.'

At that moment, the servant knocked and showed in Doctor Strawfoot, a local practitioner in black robes with a white collar. His long beard was still partly red but streaked with white.

'Ah, Doctor.' She greeted him smoothly. 'We are most grateful to you for responding to our summons. You have ridden from Oundle?'

'That is correct, madam. It is my speciality to look at the bones and the influence of the humours upon their correct growth, so I was most interested to hear of the young master's case.'

'Richard, stand up.'

He obeyed his mother slowly but she sensed it was only due to the presence of a stranger. Since the pain started, he had become so much more wilful, but she could not blame him for it.

She often feared for her two younger sons, growing up without a father. They had Edward, the king, but a brother was no substitute for the lack of York. And although she loathed him personally, she admitted that the Earl of Warwick had taken George under his wing for which she was grateful. Instead of accompanying them to Fotheringhay, he had remained in London, at the earl's house of L'Erber.

'How old is the lad?'

Richard answered him directly before his mother had a chance to speak. 'I am eleven. Twelve in October.'

'Very good. Please remove your shirt.'

He pulled it up reluctantly, exposing his thin, bird-like chest, the delicate ribs and curved shoulder. Cecily hurried to secure the window lest he should feel the cold.

The doctor gazed coolly, his eyes detached and inscrutable. Then he lifted his hands.

'May I?'

Richard nodded.

Slowly, Strawfoot moved his fingertips over the surface of the boy's back and shoulders, working into the muscles, feeling the shape of the bones. Once or twice he nodded to himself, as if what he felt confirmed his suspicions.

'I have seen a case like this before,' he stated.

Some presentiment made her send her son away. 'You may go, Richard, go to your dogs.'

Grabbing his shirt, the boy hurried from the room.

'If it's bad,' she explained, 'I don't want him to know just yet, not until he needs to. I want him to be a child a little longer. Is it bad?'

The doctor spread his hands in uncertainty. 'It is too early to say. My investigation confirms there is a slight deformity in the bones as part of this condition that often begins at this age. There is no apparent cause.'

'It is not fatal?'

'I don't think so. Uncomfortable, certainly; painful, possibly, but unlikely to prove fatal. The one case I saw before was in a young woman whose spine grew curved in the shape of an 's' but she was able to continue her life, even bear children, without too much difficulty.'

Cecily winced. 'Did it affect her movements?'

He hesitated. 'A little. But every case is different. The boy may not be that bad. He may walk straight and true. He might ride a horse, even swim in rivers, but not where there is a current.'

'What can I do?'

'I have brought ointments and will leave you the recipe so you might continue to make up your own batches. Balms, clysters, ointments with honey and herbs, whatever may soothe the pain.'

'Thank you.'

'And he must be allowed to rest, frequently, even when he does not wish to do so.'

She nodded. 'He will not be happy about that.'

'I understand. You might wish to employ another nurse, or given his age, a man to help manage him.'

Cecily understood him at once. Of course, the doctor knew about her husband's death, but she rankled at the suggestion that she could not raise her son alone. Or perhaps it disturbed her because of the truth in it.

'I will consider it, thank you. If that is all, please take some refreshment in the hall before you leave.'

'I am happy to call again while you are at Fotheringhay. Just send me word.'

'Thank you.'

'Or if you need anything for yourself.'

For a moment, she looked at him as a man. He must be around her own age, not quite fifty, and distinguished in his appearance. It was three years since she had felt a man's arms around her and, for a moment, she longed for that happy intimacy again. But the moment passed. There was no man who could ever match Richard.

'I thank you, Doctor. And good day.'

NINE

On Hexham Field

Sister Agatha pushed open the door to the garden and led Eleanor outside. The contrast between the cool, dark cloister and the bright sunshine made her blink for a moment, blindingly following the nun in her brown habit. It was a quiet walled garden, with fruit trees against one wall, and the central part divided into four by gravel paths. A mixture of medicinal herbs and flowers grew in each part and around the sides, and a handful of nuns were engaged in tasks like weeding, pruning and watering. By her white veil, Eleanor recognised that one of them was a novice, as she hoped to become.

'This is our sisters' favourite place for work, or quiet contemplation,' explained Agatha, stopping in the centre, where a plinth held a sundial.

'It's lovely,' Eleanor admitted.

'We're well irrigated, being so close to the river. A channel runs behind that far wall so we always have a water supply for the laundry, kitchens and washrooms.'

Agatha drew her over to a bench on the further side, where two nuns were dead-heading the roses. The scent enveloped the two women as they sat down.

The nun turned to Eleanor with a serious expression. 'How long have you been considering entering a religious community?'

'It seems like the best place for me, as a widow, to live quietly and dedicate myself to God.'

'You are still young, though. What are you? Twenty-five, twenty-six?'

'Twenty-eight.'

'Young enough to marry again and bear children. You have no desire to do so?'

Eleanor gave her answer without hesitation. 'I am weary of the world and the promises of men. The way they use us for their whims. I wish for something higher in my life, something bigger, to transcend these mortal struggles, the petty fighting and losses. I long to dedicate myself to God.'

'You sound wounded. There is a man who has hurt you?'

Eleanor tried to suppress the face of Somerset, which arose in her mind.

'Not exactly. I've lived in the world. It's a fickle place, a place of gamesmanship. I want a simpler, honest life.'

'What you suggest is a huge commitment, and one that must not be undertaken lightly. It is like a marriage to God, which lasts the duration of your life.'

'I understand.'

'And our community here at Whitefriars is a silent one. We spend much of our time without speaking, in line with the teachings of St Albert. Our days are passed in prayer and work; you might be gardening, sewing linen or making bread. Can you manage that?'

'I have never been much of a chatterbox, Sister.'

Agatha nodded. 'I get the sense of that. It can be a hard life, too.

You see us now in spring, in a time of abundance and warmth, but the winter months can be cruel.'

'The winter months are always cruel,' Eleanor echoed, 'but I should not mind, if I were spending them in the service of God.'

'There is time for recreation too, a little. And your family? What do they think of this?'

'My mother is ancient, my sister newly-wed. I have no one else.'

'And you are happy to stay in Norwich? Do you have any connections to the city?'

'None other than my confessor's recommendation for this community. I am happy to be here.'

'And you are aware of our special devotion to Our Lady, the Virgin?'

'It pleases me greatly to hear of it.'

Agatha stood up and Eleanor got to her feet in response. 'Very well. I am satisfied with your answers and am willing to admit you to our community, subject to the usual promises and rules. Do you wish to join us today or do you have any final business to conduct?'

'There is nothing. I would like to join as soon as I may.'

'Then come, let us find a novice's habit that will fit and begin the process.'

'Thank you, Sister.'

As they passed between the roses, where Eleanor caught the scent of the river, she lifted her hand to the back of her head and touched the long golden locks that hung there for the final time. And the knowledge of men's fingers, twisted among her locks, suddenly belonged in the past.

The sun had barely climbed its way into the sky. It hung low and white-gold, threatened by a bank of clouds to the east. All across the valley, life was waking on that May morning. Leaves unfurled;

freshly lain logs kindled; animals yawned and stretched. On the ridge overlooking the river and meadow, Montagu sat as still as a falcon, keening down upon his prey. He had been there since before first light, when the world was still silvered, when the dew was being laid.

It was a while now since he had first spotted the encampment ahead, nestled into low ground by the river. A handful of tents had been hastily erected on a plain; the twists of small fires rose to the sky and the ground heaved with the movement of men. He'd known at once, with a spreading satisfaction, of eyes in the darkness, of claws and talons straining towards soft, unsuspecting creatures. He'd seen the first men rise, their little lights, their movements, almost fancying the strains of their conversation and whinnies of the horses might be reaching him. The surroundings served him well: the slope of the land, the road, the path of the river all served to conceal Montagu and the Yorkist troops, lying just beyond the trees.

The footfall behind him drew his attention. It was George Neville, his younger brother, seeking him out.

'Here you are. The men are awake, asking questions.'

Montagu nodded. 'I have answers now. You see the flag above the tents?'

George shaded his eyes and followed his brother's gaze. Hanging limply in the still air, he could make out the distinctive white and blue border of the Beaufort flag, enclosing its fleur-de-lys and rampant lions.

George let out a sharp laugh. 'Really? You have found Somerset?'

'Sleeping like a baby, and just as aware. Ready for our firearms.'

'Then, by the grace of God, we have him!'

Montagu nodded. 'The Scots party will be safe in Newcastle. We will send word to Edward to meet them there, but now we must mobilise the men. We will proceed as swiftly as we can along the riverbank and dispatch this menace.'

'And he's sitting there, like a duck preening its feathers, completely unaware of the danger. What a novice! You'd think after the beating he took at Hedgley Moor that he'd be wiser. Where are his scouts?'

'I have seen no one and I've been keeping watch for hours. Not a soul.'

'Then he cannot think us near.'

'No, I suspect he believes us to be back in Newcastle still, or further north, towards the Scots. He is in for a rude awakening this morning.'

'Let us dispatch him to the hell he deserves with his traitor father and all his Lancastrian friends.'

Silently, they crept back along the shadow of the ridge, where the depths of stillness could not begin to imagine the coming storm.

At the edge of the fire, the boy squatted back on his ankles. He was eight or nine, with a shock of dark hair and eyes intent upon the flames. There was something fascinating about the crackle and hiss of fire, the glow and fall of ash, turning from bright orange to black to grey. With the end of his stick, he poked the log that had been smouldering all night and watched it shatter into dust.

The men might be stirring, stretching, eating, ready for the day ahead, but his job was merely to tend the fire. Soon one of them might bring him some bread, or pottage, if he was right, and Somerset had roused the cooks. There would be prayers and mustering of the men, discussion of plans, while he fed the logs into the flames. Perhaps he'd be sent off to the village for supplies, where his family lived, just beyond the ridge. And he might linger there a bit, eating whatever he could get his hands on and taking the lazy path back by the river. He'd been scaring away the crows in the field yesterday when the army passed through. He'd followed them down the road, drawn by their numbers, and offered to do service where he could in exchange

130

for his keep. So last night, instead of sharing the stuffy bed with his brothers under the eaves, he'd lain down on straw in a tent and eaten baked meats with the soldiers. There was a battle coming; he knew it. He'd heard them talking about it, but these men had weathered storms before, told tales of their adventures and victories. And it wasn't the day for a battle; it wasn't the day to die, with this beautiful blue sky stretched overhead and the absolute stillness hanging over the river. Maybe some of the stable boys would swim in the river if he dared them.

He poked the flames again.

'Hey, you, go fetch more wood. You want that fire to die out?'

It was an old soldier. One of the northern lords.

The boy scrambled to his feet. 'Yes, my lord, right away.'

Somerset delved into the plate without looking at it. A table had been set up inside his tent with one good carved chair, which he occupied for himself, and trestles, where Lords Roos, Percy and Hungerford had been waiting for him to begin the meal. It was good, hot fare: sliced meats, bread and pottage, brought out of the kitchen tents by men with red faces, who'd been labouring over ovens since dawn.

'I suggest,' began Somerset between mouthfuls, 'that we let the men rest a day, until we have it confirmed that the Scots have arrived in Newcastle.'

'You intend to attack the Scots?' asked Percy, with some incredulity in his voice. 'Was this part of the plan?'

Somerset shook him off. 'Plans can change. The Nevilles will not expect us to double back. We have given the appearance of heading south. If the Scots number among our casualties, it would be the result of their attempt to negotiate with the Yorkist traitors. We cannot be held responsible. Think of the message it would send to Edward.'

'But would it not be better to try and keep a peace between them? For future harmony?'

'Since they have ousted Queen Margaret and turned to our enemies, I do not see that it is possible, and it would prevent them allying with the French, who should be with us.'

He called for sauce. The men around the table exchanged glances.

'But are we strong enough yet to take on another realm? Should we not wait until the throne is secure and see how the land lies?'

Somerset dipped his bread. 'God's blood, Roos, are you the royal advisor now?'

'Where shall we meet the Nevilles?' asked Percy, rapidly moving the subject on.

'I plan to dig in on a plain south of Newcastle and draw them in from the north. I know just the place where the land will be to our advantage. They cannot have raised many men; the north is my stronghold and all the good men have already come over to my cause.'

'And then?'

'King Henry is waiting in safety on the north bank. Once we have our victory, we shall collect him and march upon London.'

'And Edward?'

'Will go the way of all traitors. Henry and Margaret will be crowned again in Westminster and processed through the streets, and I shall be close behind as their chief advisor.'

'And the dynasty shall be restored!' cried Hungerford, with enthusiasm.

Somerset raised his tankard. 'Amen! Let's drink to that!'

Through the lea of the ridge, they came swiftly, quietly, as ghosts in the sunshine. The river birds, startled by the vibrations in the earth, rose up on frantic wings and vanished into the sky. Along the track that hugged the bank, the long line of men kept on coming.

Occasionally, the sun glinted on a helmet or the hilt of a sword, but the clouds moving overhead gave them a kind of cover by blotting out the light again.

Every nerve straining, Montagu paused to watch them pass. He could see his brother at the head of the train, leading the men forward, and the snake of soldiers following, four deep, their feet tramping in unison, like a pulse along the earth. More men had joined them along the route and others had heard of their cause and pledged to march with them back in Newcastle. These were men who revolted under the Beaufort influence, or backed the Nevilles in their feud against the Percies, or had long Yorkist allegiances, or didn't want to return to the chaos of the old king's madness. They had come to him by word of mouth, by the rumours in taverns and on the highways, making their promise, airing their grievances. Some in helmets with arms from past conflicts, some in livery, some in farm clothes and leather jerkins, carrying pitchforks and scythes. He couldn't see the end of them yet, but perhaps they numbered three thousand, perhaps more. And they were keen, and they were angry on this May morning, and hungry for the chance to restore peace in the north. All the prayers and stirring words he had given them fuelled their steps so that it seemed that fortune, the lie of the land, and even God himself, might be on their side today.

Ahead, George Neville had halted. Montagu saw him raise his hand and, as the message filtered back through the men, they also came to a pause, looking to him for confirmation. He sped up the line to where his brother stood.

'Much further and they will see us. We are so close now, we can smell their fires.'

'And there is no chance they suspect us?'

'I think not. They are spread over a place called Linnel's Bridge, by the spot known as Devil's Water. I know it well. We are in a blind spot for them but we will have to cross the river now, as quickly as possible, and group in the meadow.'

'And once we move, they will see us?'

'Indeed. But they will have, maybe, a quarter hour's warning, no more. It is scarcely enough time to don armour, let alone get into formation. They will be in chaos.'

'And we will charge them at once.'

George turned. 'Wait! Someone comes!'

Through the bracken ahead, a form came bumbling, seeking wood on the ground. From his slow, erratic movements, it was clear that he was unaware of their presence. But it was only a matter of seconds.

Montagu hurried forward, sword drawn.

His movement brought the boy up short, for it was only a boy, on the verge of youth, dressed in a battered jerkin. His arms had been full of wood but upon sighting the army ahead, he dropped them on the floor. Montagu seized hold of him before he could turn and run.

'Do not fear. No harm will come to you if you do not resist.'

He could feel the child shaking in his grip.

'Who…who…?'

'Never mind who we are. Have you come from the village?'

'I came from the camp.'

'The Lancastrian camp!'

'But wait!' The boy shook violently. 'I live in the village. I only joined them yesterday to help keep their fires going.'

'You have a mother in the village?'

He nodded his head, hard.

'Then I would prefer to send you back to her alive rather than dead.' Montagu reached into the leather purse that hung at his waist and pulled out a coin. 'Take this; tell no one and go home at once. Stay indoors until nightfall. Do you understand?'

The round head nodded again. He tried to pull back towards the camp.

'Not that way! Go back around the meadow and rejoin the road. You see all these men? Thousands of them. You think that not a single one of them could find you if I set them looking, if you betrayed me?'

'No, my lord, I won't!'

'Then go! And do not let me see you again.'

The boy scampered past him, not needing further encouragement. Soon he was out of sight.

Montagu looked at his brother. 'We must strike now; we're too close not to. The boy may be missed.'

George nodded. 'I'll hurry the men to the bridge. Once we break out of these trees, we must advance with all possible speed and muster in the meadow beyond.'

Montagu peered ahead. He could see the edge of the space, a wide, goodly space filled with early summer flowers, and the distance beyond, which led to the Lancastrian camp. The tops of tents were visible, closer, with the blue and white flag and the thin lines of smoke rising to the sky.

'God speed, Brother. I will meet you in the field.'

'And God be with you; by his will, today is ours for the taking.'

Somerset reached for the quill.

'And ink? We have ink? I must write to the queen and inform her of our location.'

A pot was brought and placed on the table before him, as he sat shielded in the corner of the tent. He teased out the sharp point of the feather between finger and thumb and dipped it once, swiftly, into the dark liquid. The cream-coloured page sat waiting before him.

Somerset paused for a moment, a young, dark-haired man whose face still wore the scars of battle. In his long limbs, so easily arranged across the carved chair and writing table, rested the hopes of the Lancastrian dynasty, of lines of kings heading back into the past, of whispered moments in the corridors of power, of struggles on the battlefield and foreign marriage alliances. Across the country, hidden away in rooms on their estates, or praying in the coolness of churches, hundreds of men and women hoped for his success, his face at Westminster, supporting the king, or even ruling as his protector. The fate of ancient bloodlines and the vengeance of untimely deaths was held in his dark eyes.

'Roos? You wish to send your greetings to the queen? Roos?'

But Lord Roos did not come.

Suddenly, the tent opening was pulled aside. A young soldier stood there, visibly trembling.

'My lord, my lord! The Yorkists are crossing the bridge!'

'What? You must be mistaken.'

'No mistake, my lord. There are hundreds of them, maybe more.'

Somerset dropped the quill and got to his feet. 'How can they be here so soon? I thought they were just south of Newcastle.'

'They are here! Here, now! Come and look!'

The duke followed the soldier out into the brightness of daylight. It only took seconds for his fears to be realised. Beyond the camp, in the meadow, he could see the mass of men moving, arranging themselves quickly into three parts, ready for battle.

A cold panic seized him.

'God in heaven, they have us by surprise. Where were our scouts? Roos! Percy! Hungerford! Rouse the men. We must adopt our formation and go to meet them. God damn them.'

Racing back to the tent, he gathered up his sword and called to his servant.

'Quick, prepare me! There is no time to be lost.'

Percy came blundering in. 'God's blood, is it true?'

'True enough, you can see them in the field.'

The older man's face struggled with uncertainty. 'But what shall we do? We are not ready to meet them.'

'What can we do? We have the location; we have the numbers; we have right on our side. Bury your fears and wear your bravery for the men to see.'

Hungerford appeared in the doorway of the tent. 'My lord, they have loosed the first round of arrows, which are falling on our supply carts.'

'It must be Montagu. Where is Roos? Is he mustering his men?'

'I saw him head that way, my lord.'

'God in heaven and all the saints!' Somerset shook off the servant's hands which had been lacing up his armour. 'To the field! We must stand against them or else they will overrun the camp! God bless you, men. God bless you today.'

The sheet of creamy paper, left untouched upon the table, fluttered to the ground as he hurried outside.

'And again!'

Montagu gave the signal to the archers, who loosened the last round of arrows.

He shielded his eyes against the sun to watch them climb against the sky. One, two, three, then suddenly two dozen or more, like a sinister flock of birds. They hung there for a moment as their upward momentum slowed, before turning and beginning to plummet downwards, down, down, down, towards the distant carts and scurrying men, who tried to flee as the sound closed in upon them. They landed heavy upon the earth, thudding down with force, finding their mark.

With a terrifying savagery, their metal points embedded in earth, in wood, in flesh.

From his position in the meadow, he and George could see as the tiny figures fell, one after another, as the arrows struck home. Once or twice, the terrible cries of the dying reached them, and the babel of panic.

'They're trying to mobilise,' George indicated, as one group broke off to the right, carrying a Beaufort flag amongst them.

'They're heading for the shrub land adjoining the meadow. Look, that's Roos leading them.'

As they watched, the group of men moved in a scattered mess, circling and circling back upon themselves, unsure of where to go, who to follow.

'They're in disarray,' said Montagu, his confidence rising. 'We have them now, we have them. This is the point we charge.'

'Agreed! As we arranged, right through the centre of their camp.'

'Take prisoner whatever Lancastrians surrender.'

George raised his considerable eyebrows. 'You are in a mood to be merciful, Brother?'

Montagu laughed. 'I am in the mood to make a public spectacle of traitors.'

'And look, look, Roos's men are already starting to retreat.'

It was true. Taken by surprise. Unshriven, unfed and unprepared, the Lancastrian knights were not prepared to yield up their souls so easily.

Montagu lifted his sword, rose up to his maximum height. His voice carried along the ranks. 'For God, York and England, men. This is it! Our enemy is in disarray. The day is ours if we fight hard and fast! We must move now. Onwards, men, onwards!'

And with the roar of their voices ringing about the leader, the Yorkist army trampled through the bright field.

* * *

Amid the flowers, Somerset stood firm to see the Yorkists advance. Sword in hand, face towards the enemy, his veins pumped with the coming encounter. Hungerford was mobilising to his left, and beside him, Percy was mustering all the decades-long enmity his clan felt against the Nevilles opposite. Somewhere behind them, along the riverbank, Montagu sensed chaos among Roos' men, for there was too much noise, too much movement and no advance. But it was too late now, far too late. There was nothing he could do to call them back, organise or inspire them, so it must be. This strange place, where the riverbank flowed into the meadow, and the rise gave way to trees, and the trees flowed upwards to purple hills: this land of mystery and wonder, this land of promise, God-given and beautiful, would become the place of resolution.

Time seemed to pass slowly as they advanced. He could make out Montagu, and a few others, advancing at the head of a line, and the faces of the men coming closer. The determination in their eyes, the lines of their faces, the glint of light upon their weapons. Here, the ground was already studded with arrows and the bodies of men who had fallen. Already, blood was seeping into the grass, pooling in the earth. He felt his own lips muttering, and the words of a prayer reached him, although they seemed strangely distanced from him, as if they came down to him from above. And there were only minutes now, minutes before the clash of steel on steel, the endless physical combat, the pain. He held his ground as they came closer, trapped between the arrow shafts and the camp. Let them brace themselves for the broken sticks in the ground and the groaning bodies. Let them tire themselves over the terrain. Let them bring the fight, as the aggressors, the traitors, attacking the forces of the rightful king. Let them explain their actions afterwards at Westminster, when the Lancastrian army call them to account.

'My lord! Look!'

He didn't know who had called him, but he turned, briefly. Torn between the advancing men and this new alarm, he saw the flank behind him beginning to crumble. His men were leeching away from the line, fading back towards the camp.

'Stand your ground!' he shouted, his voice so loud that it seemed to burst out of him. 'Stay and fight like men!'

There was nothing beyond the camp but the river. They would be drawn to the banks, trapped by the water, unable to escape.

'Stay!' he shouted, in a last desperate effort, then turned to face the enemy as a huge Yorkist, with drawn blade, bore down on him.

Somerset raised his sword and the man broke upon it like a storm. Despite his experience, the weight of the attack drove him backwards, almost down upon the earth. He regained his footing and pushed back. Their blades clashed a second time with a force that sent vibrations through his entire body, into his bones. He was aware of his men falling on both sides, of the superior numbers on the Yorkist side.

And then he heard Montagu, working his way across the terrain, dispatching men with ease.

'Beaufort! Give up your arms. The day is ours! Give up your arms!'

But he lifted his sword again and prepared to repel him.

The incense formed a cloud about her. With her eyes closed, lost in the darkness, it crept deep inside her head, inside her mind. It was strong, heady. A mixture of spices grown in the priory garden, and something else, something special, that took her beyond those stone walls, that still haven amid the chaos. Although her knees were sore and her clasped hands ached, she chased away physical discomfort and tried to open herself to the Lord.

'Enter me, O Holy Spirit. Fill me, cleanse me and fit me to do thy work.'

A door banged at the far end of the nave. Footsteps were approaching. Urgent, rapid steps, not the slow stately procession expected of the nuns. Eleanor refused to turn. All earthly distractions must be cast out. There was only to be the spiritual plane now. She was turning her back on the life of the flesh, of concerns and fears, and questions about the world. Her novitiate demanded the complete sacrifice of herself to God.

'Sister Eleanor, Sister Eleanor!'

She turned, frowning. 'I am at prayer!'

One of the girls from the kitchen was holding out a letter. 'I was giving out alms at the gate and a man asked me to give you this.'

'What man?'

'In livery, blue and white. I did not recognise him.'

'You should not accept letters from men, or at least take them to the prioress.'

The hand hovered between them. 'Should I do that now? Should I take it to the Sister?'

Eleanor regarded the letter with the edge of its red seal just visible. Blue and white must mean the Beaufort livery. Perhaps it was not too late.

'No, you're here now. Hand it to me; tell no one.'

Eleanor hurried into the chantry chapel at the side, dedicated to Our Lady. The carved screens gave her a little privacy and the burning candles afforded light. The seal broke with one snap and the unfolding pages revealed just a few short lines, written in haste. She digested them, and then read them again at length.

'My Lady,

I have fled the battlefield where the Yorkists were victorious. My brother, Henry, was taken, with many others, and I believe him to have been beheaded. We will flee into France. God be with you, Edmund Beaufort.'

Eleanor folded the pages again, closed her eyes, and returned to prayer.

TEN

The Secret Wife

She imagined it was just like carrying an armful of the sky. The blue cornflowers, the delicate mauve of the iris and the creamy coloured stocks, all bunched together in the crook of her arm, frothy and soft. She could bury her face in their scent and breathe their essence in, the sweetness of the summer meadows around Grafton. The scent of home.

Jacquetta was waiting in the open doorway of the chapel. Her brows wore the cast of impatience.

'I have been searching for you. Look, another letter.'

Elizabeth's heart surged. It was days since she had heard from Edward. His last letter had informed her that he was heading to York to sign a peace with the Scots and that Somerset had been sighted south of Newcastle. Not a day had gone past when she did not think of him: when she first woke in the morning, while she walked in the forest, even as she scrubbed out the linen. And it made her smile, a Queen of England, washing out the sweat and stains from her family's clothing in river water. And it made her wonder, as the cycle of Grafton seasons continued, and her boys still needed to be fed, whether it hadn't all been some glorious waking dream after all.

But here was Mother, holding out a letter, addressed in a hand she had come to recognise.

Jacquetta held out her arms for the flowers. 'Come, come, give me those. Open it! See if he invites you to court.'

Elizabeth took the letter and broke the seal. The few lines appeared to have been written in a hurry. She read them quickly, then handed the paper over to her mother. Jacquetta scanned them in seconds, eager for news.

'But this is wonderful. The threat of Somerset is gone and, after Edward has been to York, he will come to Grafton again.'

She looked into her daughter's blank expression. 'But this is good, is it not?'

Elizabeth nodded. 'Yes, and no. He says nothing about taking me to court.'

'Well, I am sure he will do that once he is here. He has many things on his mind at the moment. Let's take the flowers inside.'

Elizabeth followed her mother into the cool of the chapel and watched as she arranged the blooms in two vases on the altar.

'And now Somerset is dead and that danger has gone, he can spend his time with you. I am sure he is already making plans to bring you to court, and he wishes to discuss them with you in person.'

Elizabeth picked at a cornflower. 'I hope so. Do you think we should tell Father yet?'

'Not yet. I need to find the right time.'

'You think he will be angry?'

'Only angry that he was not told. After that, he will be delighted that his daughter is Queen of England.'

'Queen of England.' She let the blue petals fall upon the stone floor. 'It still doesn't seem real.'

'It won't yet. Nothing has really changed for you. Wait until you've been to court as Edward's wife.'

'You think they will accept me? Edward's family?'

Jacquetta smiled. 'You mean his mother?'

'You know her?'

'In the past, when I was at court, yes. I saw her often, but I did not know her well.'

'What is she like?'

'They call her a proud woman, but then we are all proud women who want the best for our children. I have heard women called much worse when their enemies wished to slur their name. But it has happened now. You are married; I was a witness to that. Cecily must accept it, whether she likes it or not.'

'I hope she will grow to like me.'

Jacquetta stroked her daughter's long, loose hair. 'If she does not like you, it will be nothing to do with you, but everything of her own making.'

'These carts are too laden up. Look at their height. They might easily topple over, coming round a corner. Take these chests off and load them on one of the empty ones.'

Cecily gestured to the servants who had climbed up to secure the carts, ready for her departure to Westminster. Four had already been piled high with chests and furniture, cupboards and plate, her best jewels and furs, and then with everything Richard needed. His books, his clothes, bows and arrows, and everything for his favourite dogs. The boy did not like to be parted from them for long.

'Come down, come down,' she urged, as the men swarmed over

145

the carts, throwing ropes and untying knots. 'See, the final cart has not been used yet. Balance out the load more.'

Edward had written in earnest from York, summoning them to London. There was to be a parliament sitting nearby, maybe Westminster, maybe Reading, and festivities to celebrate the Scots peace and the victory over the Lancastrians. It was imperative that Edward be seen to be a king, ruling, making judgements, applying his seal. The empty corridors of Westminster, left to Warwick all these weeks, needed to feel his presence.

It was not all that Edward had written. Cecily shared his private frustrations that the victory at Hexham had fallen to the Nevilles. Yet she was also thankful, as she had offered up her prayers that morning, that her son had been spared that danger. She knew too well that even the wisest and best of soldiers might sometimes find the day turn against them.

Richard appeared behind her, coming out of the main entrance into the courtyard. His dark hair was dishevelled and his jerkin unbuttoned.

'Have you exercised your dogs?' she asked, pretending not to notice his appearance. 'You know we will be leaving soon.'

'Yes,' he replied slowly, but his eyes went to the distant hills.

She knew the boy would have preferred to stay at Fotheringhay, even if he was being prodded and poked by doctors. He was always far happier in the countryside, away from the crowds that put him on edge, roaming free among the fields with his horses and dogs. He was the complete opposite of her other son, George, who relished the intrigue of the court. Yet there was no escaping his fate now: Richard was the brother of a king and almost twelve years old. He could not hide behind childish things for much longer.

'We will be at Westminster a while,' she said, 'and then we'll go out to Greenwich.'

She watched him cross to the kennels. His back was behind this,

146

the strange new pain and spasms he felt, which were more than just spurts of growth.

'That's it. That's much better,' she encouraged the men who were now lifting the trunks onto the last cart. 'Make sure they are securely tied. The king does not wish to lose any of his possessions along the way.'

As she turned back to the house, a movement at the gate caught her eye. A young woman stood there, wrapped in a shawl, staring into the courtyard. Her features seemed familiar, perhaps a villager bringing produce to sell.

'Reid,' Cecily called to her estate manager. 'Go and see what the girl wants. It's too late to buy any supplies now. We'll be gone within the hour.'

She headed back to the house, slowly, but paused at the step, to watch the final preparations.

There was something about the way Reid hurried back that gave her pause.

'Please, my lady, she will only speak to you.'

'Only to me? And what might be such an important matter that she cannot speak it to you?'

'Those were her words. Pert little thing, giving herself airs.'

Cecily looked over to her in her drab brown dress and homespun shawl. 'Goodness knows what these girls get into their heads.'

'Shall I bring her in to speak with you, or send her away?'

'No, I don't want her in the house. I'll walk over. It's no trouble. Keep an eye on the carts for me.'

The girl seemed taken aback as Cecily slowly crossed the yard, even though it was what she had requested.

She dropped a sort of awkward curtsey as the stately lady approached.

'Who are you, young lady, to summon me, the king's mother, on my own grounds?'

147

Her pretty face flushed. Yes, Cecily definitely recognised the girl's eyes and little pink mouth.

'My name is Mary Denny, my lady.'

'Do I know you, Mary? You are from the village? What is it? You can see we are packing up to leave.'

'Is Edward here?'

A prickle of annoyance ran through her. 'Do you refer to King Edward?'

'Yes, my lady, sorry, my lady, is the king here?'

'Why should the king be here when he has an entire kingdom to defend? Hurry up, girl, deliver your message.'

Mary was looking past her into the courtyard. 'Are you going to him? Might I confide something in you?'

Cecily turned back towards the house. 'Don't test my patience, girl.'

'Please, my lady, you may know me, I have been to the house before. I brought geese to sell and once I came to a dance. Your son invited me.'

'Is that so? Why tell me this?'

It was then that the girl reached behind her and pulled a small child out from behind the wall. 'Please, my lady, this is my daughter, Grace. She is four years old.'

Cecily looked at the child standing there demurely with large, dark eyes and fair curls. And suddenly, something inside her knew.

'And you are here to tell me this is Edward's child?'

Mary gaped. 'Yes, my lady! Yes, she is Edward's child, your grand-child, born in the spring, nine months after I came dancing here. She is just past her fourth birthday now.'

Cecily looked down at the woman's dirty hands and hardened her heart. 'This could be anyone's child. You're simply begging.'

'No, my lady. I want her father to know.'

'I don't have any money to give you. I will send my almoner out with some kitchen scraps but, otherwise, I do not want to see you again.'

'But, my lady.'

Cecily was already walking away.

'I will not give up,' Mary called after her. 'I will go to London if I must. This is the king's daughter.'

The stately figure paused, turned. She stalked back towards the frightened-looking girl.

'My eldest son, the king, is about to be married to the sister of the Queen of France. Nothing and no one must stop that from taking place. It is essential for the security and future of England. If you make any attempt to interfere, it would be an act of treason. Do you understand?'

The girl's lip trembled.

'I will send out a man shortly with money for the child. Take it and leave us in peace.'

Mary put her hand protectively on the girl's head.

'I only want her to know her father. So she might make a good marriage.'

'Take my advice. Take the money, pass yourself off as a widow and remarry. I don't want to see your face again.'

But once she reached the safety of the hall, out of sight, Cecily clenched her fists and squeezed her eyes tight shut. Damn it, damn Edward for this foolishness, bringing shame here, to her doorstep. She could only pray that the distance to London, and Mary's poverty, would keep the girl in the countryside. In mere weeks the French marriage would be concluded. That alliance would prevent Margaret of Anjou from flying back there when all this was done. And there would be heirs, legitimate grandsons,

149

with the royal blood of two houses in their veins. It must be done. And done soon.

Dusk was falling. It settled across Grafton with the soft, grey light of early summer and the fresh, clean feel of bright stars, distant overhead. Through the holloways and into the fields it pooled its darkness, bringing the rabbits from their burrows. Sleepy-eyed birds watched from their perches high above.

At the open window, Elizabeth sensed the change in the air. The scent of the meadows outside reached her, as well as the sweetness from the bowl of stocks upon the sill. Behind her in the room, her younger sisters were preparing for bed, combing out their hair, finding stockings, unlacing kirtles. It was too late for Edward to arrive now, surely, so she would sleep in here with them tonight.

'Anne! Martha!' called their mother from the doorway. 'Leave your squabbling. Stop that noise.'

Elizabeth half turned. The girls' conversation hadn't penetrated her seclusion, for all its shrill protests and rivalry. Anne was holding a pair of kirtle ties and Martha was attempting to take them from her.

'But they're mine, Mother,' Anne protested. 'I had them first, last summer, they've always been mine.'

'No, you've grown!' Martha cried, trying to reach for them. 'You always grow out of things and then they get passed on to me. I never get new things of my own, but at least I can have them when you've grown out of them.'

'I have not grown!'

'You have so. You know it. You're almost as tall as a man!'

'Mother, Mother! Martha said I was almost as tall as a man. I'm not, am I? I'm not!'

Martha tried to swipe them from her sister but Anne was too swift.

'And you don't grow out of kirtle ties, anyway. They always stay the same length.'

Elizabeth raised a gentle hand. 'Martha, you may use my plaited ones with the blue ribbon, if you would like them.'

Martha's face lit up.

'They're in my chest, in the green room. Under the shifts. Go and find them.'

Martha bounded off but Anne looked aggrieved.

'By rights those should be mine. I'm next in line. We should pass things down.'

'Anne, you have your ties. Be a good girl, and when I am able, I will give you all the kirtle ties and laces and girdles you could wish for.'

'When will that be?'

Elizabeth smiled. 'Sooner than you may think, so into bed.'

At the door, Jacquetta met her eyes. The knowing look which passed between them was not lost on Anne.

'You never tell me anything. There's something going on but I never get told because I'm young. It's horrible being young.'

'Never you mind about the business of your elders, young Miss,' smiled Jacquetta, coming into the room. 'You will find out in good time and be happier for it; you have my word. Now, the pair of you, into bed.'

Martha sneaked past and slid into the middle of the big bed.

'And now she's got the best spot!' cried Anne. 'Move over, move over!'

'Hush now. You have both forgotten to say your prayers, so out and on your knees, girls, to thank our Father for his goodness.'

It was in that stillness, that moment of intense quiet, as the two golden heads were bowed in prayer, that they heard the horse's hooves on the drive outside. A single rider, thundering through the night and reigning to a halt. Then came a hammering on the door.

Elizabeth looked at once to her mother. 'It can't be?'

'Hurry, girl,' Jacquetta urged her, 'go and find out.'

Barefoot, Elizabeth hurried from the room and down the staircase. The great hall was still being cleared by servants as she raced through to the house entrance where her father stood, his face all confusion. And there, upon the threshold, in his black doublet and hose, stood the king.

Her heart leapt at the unexpected sight of him. So familiar, and yet still so new. Her husband. Quite forgetting her secret and her father's presence, Elizabeth flew into his arms. His lips reached down to hers, firm, reassuring, much longed for during his absence. Warm arms enfolded her. When she drew back, finally, she examined his beloved face: the hazel eyes, the long straight line of his nose and the soft, sensual mouth. He was not changed. Whatever he may have seen these past weeks, he was still her Edward.

Behind them, Jacquetta, who had followed her daughter, lay a restraining hand upon her husband's arm.

'But what is this? Someone please explain,' asked Richard Woodville in bewilderment.

'All is well, Father,' Elizabeth began, unable to conceal her smile.

But it was Edward, still holding her against his chest, who spoke.

'Woodville, I owe you an apology. I have not been honest with you. Ever since the first day I saw your daughter, I was captivated by her beauty and could think of nothing other than my desire to make her my wife.'

'Your wife? Your wife? But you are a king. Marriage would make her your queen. But how could that be?' He looked to Jacquetta. 'Our Elizabeth, Queen of England?'

'It is true,' his wife replied. 'I must also ask your forgiveness, Richard, for they took me into their confidence. It has already come to pass. Not two weeks since, they were married here at Grafton, early in the morning.'

His grey eyes looked uncomprehendingly from one to another. 'Here? At Grafton? But where was I?'

'Asleep in bed; pray forgive me, husband. I acted for the best, until it was certain.'

'I was in bed? In bed, while my daughter became queen? Is this truly so?'

Elizabeth nodded. 'It needed to be swiftly done, Father.'

'Swift indeed. So swift I think the swallows themselves could not catch it.' He turned to Edward. 'Is this legitimate? Does the council accept it?'

'Your good lady speaks the truth,' Edward acknowledged, 'and my council will accept whichever wife I choose. I am to break the news to them when I reach London.'

'I am astounded,' stammered Woodville, 'to find myself surprised with a king as a son-in-law!'

'But Edward is tired,' Elizabeth urged. 'Let him come inside and take some rest and refreshment. Have you ridden long today?'

'I have ridden three days from York.'

'Come inside, come inside,' urged Jacquetta. 'Bring food and wine; there will be a time for questions later.'

Edward hesitated out of courtesy. 'Only if my father-in-law wishes it.'

'If it were any other man, I would be furious. But come, yes, come,' laughed Woodville, tickled by the upturn in his fortunes. 'And I shall drink to you and call you my son! Bring up the best from the kitchens, only the best, for the King and Queen of England.'

ELEVEN

Queen of England, September 1464

Standing just inside in the archway, Hastings could see the spot where Edward was pacing. Back and forth, moving in and out of sight, through the dark shadows into the light. It was clear there was something heavy on his mind.

It was almost a half hour when Hastings had passed this spot, where the cloisters met the passageway, on his way to the assembly in the chapter house. Yet still the king paced, still he deliberated. Autumn sunshine filtered down from the row of windows above, warming the old stones around them. The names of past builders, and patrons and saints graced the walls, while painted faces and creatures adorned the bosses on the ceiling with their bulbous cheeks and grotesque smiles. Around the corner, the assembled lords waited, having travelled far and wide to attend the new parliament. They had been summoned to Reading Abbey to discuss a serious matter and now they sat in silence.

William Stanley appeared, looking up and down the passage before he spotted Hastings. 'Is the king here?'

Hastings nodded down the corridor. Edward passed and re-passed the space again.

'Still here.'

'What the devil is he playing at? They're getting restless.'

'My guess is that he's come to the moment when he can't put it off any longer.'

'You think? The secret marriage to Woodville's daughter?'

'It must be. Warwick's brought the French contract today to ask him to sign. But he can't. He's going to have to confess.'

'Why has he waited so long?'

Hastings shrugged. 'Hoping that Warwick would put a foot wrong and the match would fall through. But the man's like a relentless tide. When he wants something, he never lets up.'

'Edward knows that. It's what helped put him on the throne.'

'Oh, not that old nonsense again. Edward took the throne by his own right, by parliament breaching their promise to his father, by his own military ability. Warwick should stop spreading this old story as if he's some sort of divine agent. The man's arrogance knows no bounds.'

'Hush, he comes!'

Down the passageway, Warwick stepped out of the crowded chapter house and glanced over at them with a dark look of irritation.

'Where is the king?'

'Preparing himself,' replied Hastings, non-committal.

'Preparing himself for what? The meeting is losing its patience.'

'Or is it you losing your patience, my lord? Surely the king cannot be hurried?'

'The king's presence is required for governance to take place. Otherwise, it cannot.' He glimpsed a view of Edward as he passed beyond the archway. 'Ah, there he is at last.'

Neither Hastings nor Stanley, standing either side of the passage, appeared keen to step aside and let the earl pass.

'Will you make way, gentlemen?'

'For the king?' answered Stanley, wryly. 'Of course, and only for the king.'

Warwick's face soured. 'Will you not make way?'

'Does the king command it? Did you hear him, William?'

Hastings smiled. 'I did not hear the king. The king did not ask us to make way.'

'God's blood, you mock me, two idle knights, you presume to mock me.'

'Idle knights?' asked Hastings. 'Hardly idle, I believe. We have the king's ear, Warwick, you would do well to think on that.'

Warwick's hand went to his sword. 'Would you make me draw?'

'Only your breath, Earl, only your breath.'

And with one movement, Hastings and Stanley parted and left the archway exposed. At a distance, Edward turned and saw Warwick approach.

'Your friends have grown impertinent, Edward. I was close to teaching that Hastings a lesson.'

Edward breathed in deeply and looked levelly at the earl. Warwick sensed something heavy on his mind.

'What is it? What is the delay? They are still awaiting you in the chapter house.'

And the moment had arrived, as all moments eventually do, and Edward knew there could be no more procrastination, no more excuses, no more chances. Diplomacy and friendship had stayed his hand for weeks, while the tail end of the French negotiations twisted and turned like a caged beast. There was no other choice now but to stand his ground and defend his marriage.

'Warwick, I owe you a debt of thanks, and my apology.'

'Well, come on then, before they start to leave.'

'No, it's not that. You have been a diligent servant to your king in your negotiations with France. You have sought me out a bride worthy of my status and to the glory of England, and...'

'And the apology?'

'I am torn, Warwick. I was not raised to be king, as you know.'

'But you are king.'

'Yes. I am king now. But I was not raised with the intention of rule. I am torn, as a king, and as a man.'

Warwick threw up his hands impatiently. 'What does that mean?'

'I am still a man, with a man's frailties and weaknesses. I had hoped to marry the French princess. I give you my word that I entered into negotiations sincerely, in good faith, in appreciation for your efforts. But Warwick,' he added, seeing the suspicion growing over the earl's face, 'this was always your project. You came to want this match more than I.'

'I wanted it for you, for England.'

'And you were a good and true subject to do so. But I cannot marry her. All negotiations must cease.'

'Cease! Cease! I have the very final documents here in the hall for you to sign. What is the meaning of this?'

'I am married already.'

The stone passageway became very still, very silent.

Edward waited through the painful moments. Eventually, the earl spoke a single word.

'What?'

'I have made promises before a priest and witnesses to a woman I love. I have lived as her husband, shared her bed, and I cannot put her aside. She is worth it, Warwick, she is worth it all. I never dreamed I might feel this way. She is wonderful.'

Warwick's dark features struggled with this realisation.

'And she is wise, and patient, and intelligent, and fertile. She has already borne two sons. And she will bear more.'

Warwick drew himself up to his full height, stinging with the irreparable wound to his pride. 'And was this all a jest at my expense? Were the two buffoons in the doorway laughing at poor Warwick, duped by the king for so long, sent away on a fool's errand? Why have you used me so badly, sir, when I have only sought to be your servant?'

'No, no, of course, it was no jest. I had every intention of going ahead with the marriage, every intention until I met Elizabeth.'

'Elizabeth? Who is the woman?'

'The eldest daughter of Jacquetta Woodville, once Duchess of Bedford.'

'Who disgraced herself by marrying her former husband's squire?'

'The Rivers' family come from a long distinguished line. Her mother gives her royal blood.'

'And a widow? You have married an English widow? The daughter of a squire?'

Edward stood tall. 'Yes, I have. She is my wife and my queen. I will announce the event to parliament and bring her to court. There will be a coronation.'

'Dear God, are you insane?'

'No. We have had one insane king; you should mind your words.'

'But you were promised on a wave of lust. It may not be legal. There will be a way out of this.'

'You are not listening to me. I do not want to find a way out. Elizabeth is my wife.'

'And I am your fool! How could you humiliate me in this way?'

158

'It was never my intention. The French marriage was a valid option until recently.'

'When were you married? When abouts?'

'It does not matter.'

'Weeks ago? Months? You might have told me before now, and I could have drawn back. But you waited until now, when the paper was waiting for your signature. Damn it, Edward, you have made a fool out of me before the entire court. But worse, worse than that, I have lost your confidence.'

'Not at all. It was a secret match. No one else knew. I needed time to ensure it was the right decision.'

'But you have already married her!'

'I have. It is done. You must accept it now.'

'I can scarcely follow my thoughts on this. I wish to retire from court, to my estate.'

'No, you are staying here. I am in need of your advice. You are still my most trusted cousin. This will be resolved. The council must accept it and, once the sons arrive, and the succession is secure, this will be forgotten.'

'It will not,' said Warwick bitterly.

'Now come, we will enter the hall and I will make the news known.'

'You would put me through such a public shaming?'

'No, we will stand shoulder to shoulder to break this news.'

'I like it not, my lord. I like it not.'

'You will be recompensed for your loyalty, Warwick. I will make certain of it.'

The chapter house fell to a stony silence. Edward's hazel eyes scanned the place for allies: young George, almost fifteen, sat at the front; then there was Montagu, fresh from his victories in the north; Worcester and young Norfolk to the right; Hastings, the Stanley brothers and Stafford exchanging secret glances towards the back; John Rotherham, Bishop of London fronting a bank of stunned-looking bishops; and Earl Rivers, with his eldest sons Anthony and John.

It was Thomas Bourchier, Archbishop of Canterbury, who rose to his feet, puffing and panting with infirmity and doubt.

'My lord, I speak for the assembly. Please help us understand how this came about while we understood you were to be married elsewhere. Are we to understand that this marriage was conducted legally? Vows were spoken before a priest and witnesses?'

'Indeed,' replied Edward. 'My wife's own mother, and my comrade William Hastings were present as witnesses and a priest was brought from a local community.'

'But why was this conducted in secret when the match with France was being negotiated? It seems to me,' he urged, looking around for support, 'that perhaps this was a young man's peccadillo, a folly of the moment. Is it to be honoured? Is it legitimate, or desirable?'

Earl Rivers was already on his feet. 'My daughter's marriage was legitimate. Her king chose her to be his wife, and your lawful queen.'

'No one doubts the virtues and charms of your daughter, Rivers,' Bourchier returned, 'only her qualities as a potential queen, and her right to the title. Let alone England's need. Edward should marry for political advantage, nothing less. How can this be anything other than an opportunity lost and a slight to France, from which we will not recover.'

Several of the bishops murmured their agreement.

'You speak, Archbishop,' interrupted Hastings, 'as if the king might still seek to wed, as if he did not already have a wife. No matter how you may dislike it, a legitimate marriage has taken place and must be honoured. It is done.'

'My lords,' Edward addressed them, seeing the mixture of reactions across the chamber. 'I have been lawfully married to Lady Elizabeth Grey, formerly Woodville, and she is on her way to be presented here, at court. I suggest you make peace with your consciences, set your doubts aside and prepare yourselves to welcome your queen. Those of you who demonstrate your loyalty will not be overlooked.'

Yet at his side, he sensed the controlled anger of Warwick, stifling under restraint, and seated before him, young George, still and scowling, his brows knit.

'And Warwick?' pressed Bourchier. 'What of all the earl's negotiations?'

The earl paused.

Edward turned to him to see which way he would leap.

'My lords,' Warwick said firmly, 'I am content to serve my king as he wishes.'

It was a small, fragile victory. The lords muttered amongst themselves but had no choice but to be content.

'In that case, my lord,' concluded Bourchier, 'we shall extend our welcome to your chosen queen.'

As they filed out into the cloister, Edward called to his brother. The boy paused but refused to turn, kept his face away.

'George!'

Eventually, he stopped and sullenly turned. His dark eyes, so resistant and hostile gave Edward a sudden yearning for the open, responsive face of their lost brother, Edmund.

The thought gave him a moment's pause.

'Well?' asked George. 'What is it?'

'I see you do not like this marriage?'

The youth chewed his lip.

161

'But it is my will. When you meet my wife, you will understand. I hope you will love her well, as your sister.'

'Is it now the right of kings to choose their commoner wives? Who should I marry, the scullery maid?'

'Mind your tongue. You sound as if you have been conversing with Warwick.'

George glared back. 'I know how long and how hard the earl fought for this marriage.'

'And he will be rewarded for it, but remember, Brother, that I am your king, not him.'

'He has been kind to me.'

'And I have not, giving you the Duchy of Clarence, bringing you to court, promoting your interests?'

'But those are my birthright.'

'May I remind you that you're only able to enjoy your birthright because I risked my neck in battle.'

George sulked deeply. Then he reached into his armoury for whatever weapon he could find there. 'And what will Mother say? No doubt she has already heard?'

The thought took unpleasant hold of Edward. Cecily was here, at Reading, in rooms set aside for her. She did not yet know, so far as he was aware, and he had deliberately been leaving that unpleasant task until last. He must speed to her, make his explanation and apologies, before the news was broken by another.

'I will go to her now. This marriage is a good thing, George. I have a wife whom I love and who loves me, whose loyalty will never be called into doubt; a woman of kindness and intelligence, who will guide me through these years, and give me heirs. I am full of joy to call her my wife. I hope one day you will rejoice for me. But now, I must speed to our mother.'

* * *

Cecily stood before the fire, facing the flames. Edward stared at the lacing up her back and the coils of fair hair, streaked with white, that were balled upon each side of her head, under the silver hennin headdress.

'Who told you?'

Her voice was high with emotion. 'Not you. That's all that matters. Not you.'

'I'm sorry. I was coming to speak with you now about it. I should have told you sooner.'

'Months sooner. Or better still, before, so that I might have had a chance to prevent it. But that is why you didn't, isn't it?'

'I would not have had anyone prevent it for the world. She is wonderful, Mother. You will see that when you meet her. And she is completely loyal; there will never be any doubt, no plots, no secret alliances, no French influence.'

'Was she not formerly a Lancastrian?'

'She was married to a Lancastrian knight. Now she is married to me.'

'And her family? Must I suffer the humiliation of being asked to bow to Jacquetta Woodville?'

'Of course not. But I hope you will bow to my queen.'

'And your father? What would he say to you about this? Can you imagine his disappointment?'

'I hope he would be proud of me as his son and as England's king. Please, Mother, turn so I may speak with you.'

It was a while before Cecily replied. The fire crackled long and loud between them.

When she finally turned around to face him, he could read that there was no softness in her face, no understanding, no motherly warmth.

'You have committed an act of extreme folly and misjudgement.

163

Unforgiveable for a king. Your father would have been horrified. Did we raise you for this? Did we struggle through all the years of hardship, the fight to have our rights acknowledged for this shameful act of folly and sacrifice? You have always been headstrong, Edward, but this is a terrible betrayal of all we have worked for. Leave me now. I cannot bear to look upon you. I am departing at once for Greenwich.'

'But Mother…'

'Leave me. I said, leave me!'

For a moment, he thought she was about to strike him. She was usually a mixture of ice-cold pride and boiling passion, which together kept her emotions in check, but today he could see she was struggling to contain the extremes of both.

'I am truly sorry you feel this way, Mother.'

'Leave me be, for the love of God! Think of your father, and my dear son Edmund.'

That final sting was the worst. Cecily knew how to wound, and Edward was wounded.

'I will leave you, madam. Go to Greenwich. Enjoy the hospitality of my royal palace but do not speak to me of Edmund, whose counsel and love I have missed with every passing year.'

She turned a little, perhaps making a gesture to speak again, but he did not wait to hear her words.

The great hall at Reading was full. Men and women stood pressed shoulder to shoulder, dressed in their finest clothes, the softest fabrics and brightest colours they could afford, and decked with jewels. Dukes, earls, barons, knights and their womenfolk, bishops and archbishops, deacons and archdeacons, scribes, clerks, visitors, relatives, supplicants. Jacquetta and her daughters found their way to the front, where the lights blazed brightest, in their full gowns with long sleeves, in blue

164

and red, with the gauzy veils of their hennins hanging about their shoulders like wisps of air.

Around them were the lords in their doublets and hose, eyes flashing in expectation and greeting as they spied friends and enemies across the hall. Under the watch of the guards, of the carved statues and the musicians above, the crowd moved, breathed, whispered, as one enormous creature, waiting and watching. The empty chairs on the dais were the still point about which they turned. And the talk was of nothing but Elizabeth.

Earl Rivers leant in to speak in his wife's ear. 'They say the Duchess Cecily has refused to attend court. She has gone instead to Greenwich.'

'Let her stay away,' replied Jacquetta, smoothing the back of Martha's gown. 'All eyes should be upon Elizabeth. Let Cecily stew. Her absence serves us well.'

'Mother,' asked Martha, turning, 'when are they coming?'

'Soon, my love, soon.'

'It's all about making a grand entrance,' added Rivers. 'Let the men wait for their queen.'

'But might the women, at least, sit down?'

'Hush now.' Jacquetta turned her round by the shoulders. 'Think of all the opportunities this gives people to see you at your best.'

'I see Anne is already attracting admirers,' Rivers added, nodding over to where their second eldest daughter stood poised, chin raised, cool eyes straight ahead, as two young lords attempted to impress her with talk.

'She is of an age to be wed; no doubt she will be next and this marriage brings her opportunities she can never have imagined. It does so for all our girls.'

Rivers nodded. 'It was a strange, secret match, but I can forgive all that for the advantages it showers upon us.'

Jacquetta looked round again to the door at the back of the hall, beginning to feel the heat of the bodies. 'Heavens, where are they?'

'Shall I go and see what is keeping them?'

'No, wait, look. Here comes Warwick.'

The crowd parted at the sound of his approach, revealing the tiled stone floor. The earl strode swiftly down the aisle, his face set like thunder.

'Here's trouble,' whispered Rivers. 'He won't forgive us for this. Not ever. He's too proud.'

Taking his place at the front, Warwick fixed his eyes above the pair of thrones and refused to look at them, or at anyone. Even George, Duke of Clarence, with his dark shock of hair and his mocking eyes, waiting to make a jibe about his brother's secret wife, could not draw him.

As the doors opened, Elizabeth could see the throng of bodies inside and drew in her breath.

At her side, Edward squeezed her hand. 'They are here to see you. All of them your subjects. Show them they owe you their allegiance.'

Elizabeth lifted her chin, wondering if he could feel her fingers trembling.

Her ladies had gone to great lengths to ensure that she felt every inch the queen that morning. Her dress of gold silk, overlaid with silver tissue, was embroidered with pearls and gold thread, silk ties and fringed laces. She'd stood patiently while they tied and preened her, wondering if this was something she would ever get used to. And the fingers in hair, untangling and braiding, pinning up the strands, setting them with pearls before her headdress was put in place. Arranging and rearranging the folds of her veil, with its embroidered sunbursts in gold. And upon her finger, the gold band of marriage finally in place for all to see. Now she understood the way knights donned their armour, piece by piece, amid great ceremony. It was an important ritual. A shield against the outside world, against the coming storm. These gold threads, pearls and cloth were her armour.

Inside the hall, trumpets sounded out an impatient peal.

'Ready?' Edward asked.

'No,' she replied. 'Honestly, I am not. But I will go regardless and no one will know.'

And yet, this was the day she had been imagining for the past four months, hidden away in the meadow at Grafton. She had pictured this moment: the faces, the voices. But now it had come, it seemed unreal. She almost wished she could hold it at bay a little longer, enjoy the idea of it, but the other half of her was already walking down the hallway with the people parted on either side, staring at their new queen.

Following Edward's lead, she began the journey through the crowds. It was hot in the hall. The air hung heavy with bodies and breath. It was the vaulted ceiling above that offered relief. Space, air and light. At first she could see no one, not one single face came into focus. Then, halfway down, she glimpsed her mother's hennin, tall and bright above the gathering, with a pair of gauzy double folds, almost like the wings of angels they carve in churches.

Ahead on the dais sat two gold thrones, side by side, decked with gold cushions. Behind, hung the cloth of estate, embroidered with Edward's arms, and above it, the canopy with its gold fringe, extending over the place where they would sit.

At Edward's gesture, she paused, breathed, and turned to face the hall.

Dozens upon dozens of faces stared back at her. Upturned, with their wide eyes, questioning mouths and hands clapping. Some welcoming, some she knew struggled to conceal their enmity, some old friends and others who could become future enemies, which she could not read. A strange new land to be explored and conquered. To the right, Warwick's head was bowed, in pretence of doing her honour, but George's eyes were fixed upon her in curiosity.

'Lords and Ladies,' boomed Edward in his authoritative tones, 'I give you England's new queen, Elizabeth.'

She stood and absorbed the cheers and applause. The trumpets above were almost deafening. The heads bowed; the hands clapped. They were obliged to, she understood that much, but she also knew how little she understood. Sifting between the genuine friends and those whose smiles were for show would take many months, perhaps years.

They had agreed in advance that she need not speak on this occasion. It was not necessary for her to reply, or to address the crowds. It was partly her inexperience, partly their potential hostility that had led Edward to warn her to keep a dignified silence, but now she stood before the court, she saw that he had been right. Silence and dignity were masks, regal masks, making her present but distanced, human but iconic. How easy it would be, once she began to speak, to say a wrong word. Not that she was unintelligent, but because there were so many seasoned politicians, so many here with the viper's tongue in their mouths and the devil in their hearts, just waiting for her to trip and blunder. How easy it would be for her voice to break, to quaver with nerves, to come out weak and reedy, and give them cause for laughter. How easy it would be for this fragile moment to fracture, to set her off on the wrong path with these unknown faces. The time would come for speech, face to face, but at that moment, she understood that nothing was more powerful than the gold and jewels she wore, her own beauty, and the hand of the king in hers.

Edward squeezed her hand. 'You feel that? Queen Elizabeth?'

And their eyes, and their applause, no matter how insincere, seemed to swell her, to infuse her with status, to embed her as their queen. Here, upon this September day, on this platform, Elizabeth felt the exhilarating rush of power. And she stood tall, held in their gaze, with her king at her side. And truly, truly, she did feel like a queen.

Gently, Edward drew her back, led her by the hand to the two gold thrones. In unison, they were seated, man and wife together, king and queen for all the world to see. And every detail, every gesture and moment seemed bright and significant to her, etched in her memory. This strange mixture, this bubbling excitement in her belly, this blend of joy and danger, so strong and yet precarious up on the dais, looking over the heads of friends and foe alike, this was unexpected, but real queenship, thrown about her shoulders like a mantle.

Later, as the musicians played, the people approached in ones and twos, sometimes in small groups. They knelt, offered their blessings and their loyalties while she tried to process their faces and read the truth behind their words.

Jacquetta indicated Elizabeth's sons to kneel before her.

'No, Mother, no.' She smiled, drawing Thomas and Richard up to her. They had been given special clothing for the occasion, royal blue and silver with gold ties, their hair, faces and hands scrubbed in rose water. They looked more like young gentlemen than she had ever seen.

Giving them a brief hug, one on each side, she was aware of faces in the crowd being turned to her. No doubt there was some protocol about who was allowed to mount the dais. Her eye caught Edward's.

'It's alright.' He smiled. 'They're your blood.'

Elizabeth kissed each on their downy cheek, still soft and curved with childhood. 'Now, run along with Grandmother. Take your places for the feast. I will see you later.'

Warwick was waiting behind them, with sour face. His bow was shallow, with little pretence at respect.

'Two fine sons,' he acknowledged.

'Indeed,' replied Edward, reaching across and taking his wife's hand again, 'and soon we will have sons of our own.'

'I wish you joy of them,' the earl replied, but there was an edge to his tone.

'Thank you, my lord.' Elizabeth spoke directly. 'I hope you will be their friend and help guide them as they grow.'

He looked up at her in surprise, trying to detect any element of sarcasm but finding none. Instead, he inclined his head and shuffled off into the crowd.

Edward tried to conceal his smile and leaned in towards her. 'That was well done.'

The trumpets announced the imminent arrival of the feast and servants ushered people towards the trestle tables that had been set up in a horseshoe formation around the sides of the room. The central stretch, dressed in cloth of gold, had been made ready for Edward and Elizabeth. Rising, the king led his wife down the three steps from the dais to take their places. As soon as they were seated and their goblets filled with wine, Edward gave the signal for the court to take their places and the food to be brought up from the kitchens.

Watching her family being served the spiced and rich dishes, Elizabeth could not help but smile. Richard and Thomas, placed between her parents, could not conceal their enjoyment at the range of dishes, helping themselves to portions of each until Jacquetta intervened to counsel caution.

'I cannot believe it,' she whispered to Edward at her side.

His face split with a smile. 'It is all real, and all yours. Wait until your coronation; then it will feel even more like truth.'

'My coronation?'

'Of course. A queen must have a coronation.'

'At Westminster?'

'Yes, at Westminster. You will be my anointed queen. Let Warwick grumble, but it will be so.'

And there, with the heat rising from the golden plates, Elizabeth could see the future for the first time. A future with herself as queen at Edward's side.

Candles flickered in the gloom under the high vaulted ceiling. The Virgin's shrine, deep in the crypt, was spread over with gold, silver and precious gems. As she lifted her head, Elizabeth saw the light catch them in red, green and blue flashes. Canterbury was a favourite with Edward, who liked to visit the tombs of the martyr, St Thomas, and the Black Prince, and the shrines lining the cathedral. One either side, the carved stone capitals featured mythical beasts, and the walls were painted with scenes from heaven and hell. Kneeling on a prayer cushion before the shrine, Elizabeth felt suddenly dizzy. The heady scent of incense overcame her and she felt that nausea arising in her that confirmed she was expecting a child.

Ten months had passed since her presentation at Reading. Since the crowds applauding and smiling, as she walked between them and stood on the dais. The time had passed quickly, with the council meeting, ceremonies, festivities, Christmas and spring, travelling between Westminster, Eltham and Windsor. She had been busy with arranging her new rooms, seeing to her boys' schooling, planning colour schemes for the gardens and choosing furs, velvet and silks, whatever the merchants laid out for her. And the people loved her. Wherever they went, they flocked to bring her little gifts of apples or rosewater, fresh fish and herbs, newly killed game and lamb, even a pot of green ginger. And each morning she'd woken in her canopied bed after strange dreams of battle and struggle, to find that this was indeed real.

'You are my queen,' Edward would whisper. 'Now you just have to believe it.'

Sometimes, as they danced by torchlight or lay on cushions as they were rowed down the Thames, she would turn to him and say that it all felt like a dream.

'For me too,' he replied. 'I never imagined this!'

And they would laugh over cards, or dice, or wine, surprised again at their good fortune, and she would lace her fingers between his and lead him to bed.

She had not forgotten Cecily, who had departed that autumn for Fotheringhay, nor George, who sulked around the place with Warwick, who was schooling him in the arts of war, but their anger felt distant, contained, outside the little bubble of her life with Edward.

'Forget them,' laughed her mother. 'They are your subjects now and you have Edward's love. Nothing can touch you now. Enjoy it.'

Edward was an attentive husband and she'd been waiting for the child to come month after month, as her flowers arrived regularly with the moon. Jacquetta had gathered herbs and flowers, ground up tisanes and applied clysters to her womb. And finally, on the day when she had been crowned in Westminster, Elizabeth suspected that she might have conceived. Now, as the height of midsummer approached, she was certain that she carried England's heir.

Bourchier led them outside through the side door that took them through the passageways and blinking into the mint yard.

'The archbishop's palace has been made ready to welcome you. Please, if you will come this way.'

Chickens scuttled out of the way as they passed through the archway. The scents of mint and fresh grass hung in the air, and she had the strange out-of-self feeling that this was a perfect moment, a moment she would remember later, forever. If ever things changed, if she were somehow to lose it all, at least she would have had this moment.

'My lord! King Edward!'

The voice came from behind them, insistent, excited. A servant in the murrey and blue of Yorkist livery was hurrying across the grass.

Edward waited for him to approach. He was panting, his freckled face red.

'They've caught him,' the man puffed out. 'The Lancastrian king.'

'What? They've captured Henry?'

'Yes! Yes! He was taken by Sir John Tempest in a house in Lancaster. He fled to the woods but Tempest followed. He is on his way to the Tower, right now.'

'He is well? He is unhurt?'

'I believe so.'

'Ride to London. Await them at the Tower and ensure that he is treated according to his station.'

'I will, my lord.'

'Go, go now. Do not wait. We will follow.'

As the man darted away, Edward turned to his wife. 'This is it. We have the Lancastrian king in custody. We are finally safe.'

Elizabeth put one hand on her belly. 'And our son can inherit peaceably.'

'Our son? You are sure?'

She nodded, smiled, consumed by her news.

'Yes, Edward, I have suspected for a few weeks now.'

He took her face in his hands. 'But this is wonderful. The old king is taken and a new one is to arrive. God truly blessed me when he gave me such a wife as you, Elizabeth.'

And he bent and kissed her lips, long and deep, in the shadow of the ancient tower.

TWELVE

Entertaining the Burgundians, June 1467

A light breeze rippled the line of coloured flags. Across the field, the horses and jousters were gathering around the great pavilion, waiting patiently as they were strapped into armour and festooned with ribbons. On the site of Smith's field, where slaughter and bloodshed were so familiar, the bare earth had been sanded and prepared for a special event. The royal carpenters had been at work for weeks, constructing wooden galleries along both sides, after which the painters had gone to work with gold leaf, red, green and white shades, and the wardrobe department had been summoned to supply hangings, curtains and cushions. Now it seemed that half the riches of Westminster Palace had been brought out to adorn the lists.

Mounting the wooden steps to the gallery, Elizabeth breathed in the sweet summer air. It was almost midsummer, the height of the season, her favourite time of year. But there was another more acrid smell which hung between the lists and the royal tent, where Edward was still drinking wine with the ambassadors, above the woodsmoke and the hot food. She recognised it as the tang of horses, of the sweat of their hot, sleek bodies and their anticipation of the event. For they knew from all the activity, all the bustle of men. The animals understood. It took her back ten years, in the blink of an eye, back to the courtyard at Groby Hall, back to her first husband, John, leading out the hunt. And such a time had passed since then, that she could scarcely catch her breath. She had still been a girl then, even though she was already a mother, living in the quiet countryside, loyal to her king. Loyal to her queen. And yet now, here she was, sitting in that queen's place, displacing her. How quickly things could change, and how dramatically. And now she was pregnant again, just a month away from her confinement.

Jacquetta appeared in the gallery followed by a nurse holding Princess Elizabeth.

'So pensive?' The older woman observed.

The queen smiled. 'It's nothing. I was just thinking about the child.'

'Plenty to think about with this one, who has been eating all the tarts!'

But the little princess beamed and knew no shame.

Elizabeth took her place in the royal box which had been hung with green silk adorned with white roses and padded with cushions. It had been carefully placed, to measurements drawn up by the surveyors, pacing the ground with their chalks. From that position, she could survey the entire field. It placed her high above the field of conflict, affording views over the lists, and beyond. In the distance, she could see the common Londoners, excluded from the enclosure, climbing up into the trees in order to get a glimpse of the competitors. Past those trees, the jumbled roofs of dwellings pressed up as close as they dared, and the spires of churches climbed high.

The small of her back ached. Carefully, Elizabeth rearranged her blue skirts and stretched out her arms to the nurse who stood behind her. In the woman's arms, the plump little princess gaped out at the field.

'Here, let me take her.'

Her daughter was over a year now. She had arrived the previous spring, a sevennight after Candlemas, while the snow lay over Westminster.

'Look. Can you see the horses?'

Little Elizabeth proved she could follow her mother's gaze and mouth the word.

'Horse! Horsie!'

'Lovely horses, look at their trappings, Elizabeth, all gold and blue and white. Which one do you like best?'

'All!'

'Do you see that red and white one? That's your Uncle Anthony's horse. We must cheer very loudly for him and wave our kerchiefs when he rides.'

Elizabeth held up her white handkerchief between plump hands. Her fair curls blew a little in the breeze, covering her face. Her mother carefully tucked them behind her ear.

'And they will be riding for us, wanting to win our favour, wanting to win for us! You see Uncle Anthony?'

But the large bay horse, trapped in red and white, hung with silver bells, was being led away, out of sight. Anthony Woodville, who had been instrumental in arranging the event, needed to adjust his horse's reins.

'Just you watch, Elizabeth, he'll turn in a minute, and wave to us.'

Two pairs of blue eyes were fixed upon the distant figure, willing it to be so, but Anthony did not turn. They saw a man in Burgundian dress appear and speak to him, gesticulating with his hands. After that, they saw the distant figure of Edward approach them, tall and resplendent in white and gold, to inspect the horses.

'There, you see, Uncle Anthony is far too important to see us all the way over here. It takes a lot of work to run a tournament like this.'

With a rustling of fabric, Elizabeth's sister, Anne, appeared through the curtain behind them. A year younger than the queen, she had the same long fair hair and blue-green eyes, although her face was more childish. 'Here you are. Drinks are being served in the tent. Are you joining us?'

'I needed to sit down. I'm tired.'

'Here, let me take her.' Jacquetta sat down beside her daughter and took her grandchild into her arms.

'Now, little princess, sit with your grandmama and cheer for the horses with her.'

Anne looked around. 'Where is Edward? I thought he might be here with you.'

'Sitting with the women.' Elizabeth smiled and nodded across the field.

Anne and Jacquetta followed her gaze although the mother's eyes were not what they once had been.

The younger girl shrugged. 'Has he decided to take part, after all?'

Edward had been adamant that he would not be a competitor ever since the idea of the even had been conceived, the year before, when the marriage between his sister and the Duke of Burgundy had been proposed.

'No, he says this is Anthony's affair. He likes the symmetry of the names, I think. Anthony, Lord Scales, against Antonie, Bastard of Burgundy.'

'Unlike him to place names above action,' said Jacquetta, archly. 'I felt certain he would be first on the field, breaking all the lances. Perhaps he is growing up.'

Elizabeth smiled. 'Edward's day has already come, but he does not dare risk his person until our son is born.'

'And then he will go throwing himself under horses to his heart's content, I suppose?'

Anne sat down beside her sister. 'I had hoped to talk to him about my marriage. It's only two months off, nearly two months. William is getting impatient that the arrangements have still to be finalised.'

'Don't worry,' reassured the queen, patting the girl's knee. 'I will speak with him later. You will have all you desire. And your William too.'

Anne had joined her sister's household last year, and a swift romance had developed between herself and the young Bourchier boy, a cousin of the archbishop, with the blood of Plantagenet kings in his veins.

'Tell him to be patient. All will be well. I promise.'

Jacquetta looked out across the field. On the far side, another range of wooden boxes had been constructed for the lords and ladies of the court, who were filing in to take their places.

'I see Duchess Cecily would prefer to sit among the people, rather than with her queen?'

Elizabeth followed her eyes. Under a special green canopy, Cecily had already taken her seat, with Richard beside her. They could see his dark hair and the particular way he held himself, leaning slightly to the right, although he had grown considerably taller that year, almost as tall as his mother as he approached the age of fifteen.

Beside them, sat her daughter, Anne, almost the same age as the queen and divorced from her Lancastrian husband, Henry Holland. On the other, Cecily's younger daughter, Elizabeth, now the mother to three small boys alongside her husband, John de la Pole. The convenient distance between them, across the lists, was such that neither side needed to feign a greeting.

Elizabeth looked away. It was to be expected. Although the duchess would be polite and even show due deference to the queen when she could not avoid her, their relationship was still formal and never warm. Cecily spent as much time as she could in her country properties and retreated to Greenwich when her affairs required her to be in London. The few times they had come together, it was as if Cecily brought a chill into the room. Elizabeth had hoped the older woman would soften once she bore her grandchildren but, in recent months, she had come to realise she would never be fully accepted by her, even though Edward told her himself that Cecily no longer ruled him. He was king, and his mother had no choice but to accept it.

'But where is Princess Margaret?' Elizabeth asked, remembering Edward's other sister. 'Surely Margaret will sit with us, as the whole point of these jousts is to arrange her marriage?'

'She is in the dining tent,' Jacquetta confirmed. 'Edward has a place planned for her at his side. She will be sitting here with us.'

'Quite correct,' nodded the queen. 'It is her day, today. It is not right that her mother hide her away. And the ambassadors are to sit with us?'

'Of course. They are in the tent too, drinking Edward's spiced wine.'

'No doubt it will ensure they enjoy the day and sleep well tonight. Edward's spiced wine is notorious for that.'

Jacquetta glanced at her daughter, trying to read the tone of her response. There had been rumours at court that the king enjoyed the favours of other women, but Elizabeth had never spoken of it, and her position as queen felt unassailable.

The curtain behind them parted again to allow the royal party's entrance to the platform. While they had been talking, Edward had traversed the field and now led his sister by the hand, followed by the Burgundian ambassadors, Oliver de la Marche and Louis de

Gruthuyse, and their party, then Archbishop Thomas Bourchier, Warwick, Hastings, Baron Thomas and William Stanley, George, Duke of Clarence and other members of the court.

Princess Margaret, slender in her dark green gown with white sleeves, was just twenty-one, and her dark eyes and raven hair recalled the colouring of her father, the Duke of York. She was a good girl, a quiet girl who knew her duty, but not as forthcoming with Elizabeth as the queen would have liked. She had always attributed this to Cecily's influence.

The party bowed to the seated queen. Elizabeth inclined her head in response.

Edward handed Margaret to her place with grace and formality, and invited the ambassadors to be seated. William Stanley placed himself beyond them, on the edge of the group, deep in conversation with Bourchier, Baron Thomas to the other side, as if they had some purpose with him. George, at seventeen, and even taller now than the king, sidled round to sit on the step before them, which was spread with a Turkish carpet.

'I hope you have a good view of the arena,' Edward addressed the ambassadors. 'Call for more cushions or wine whenever you wish.'

'Our view is well,' replied the lead ambassador, the cultured De la Marche, with his distinctive accent and dress. 'A most happy view of our two champions and the friendship of our countries.'

'What happens,' whispered George, too loudly, 'when one defeats the other in combat? Will England and Burgundy then declare themselves to be enemies?'

Edward turned, frowning, having caught the words. 'Surely, Brother, you are old enough now to understand the rules of chivalry? Whatever battles are fought in the lists only serve to secure friendships. I know you have been taught this by your excellent tutor, the Earl of Warwick.'

George blushed at his question being addressed so directly and his theory so deftly dismantled. 'But my lord of Warwick is not here to take the credit for he is sailing to France as we speak, is he not, Brother?'

Warwick's absence was a sore point that Edward had not wished to air. Virulently against the Burgundian alliance, the earl had taken himself to negotiate with King Louis, amid rumours that he was attempting to block Margaret's marriage in favour of a French one.

Even more controversial was the absence of Warwick's brothers, Montagu, the victor of Hexham, and John Neville. Just two years before, Neville had been richly rewarded with the Archbishopric of York and the Chancellorship, but his refusal to support Edward's friendship with Burgundy had forced the king to strip him of the Great Seal. The court was still smarting with gossip and the king hoped that the tournament would provide a useful distraction.

'But Lord Stanley has seen me in combat,' added George, 'so he can speak for me.'

All heads turned towards William Stanley, who found his conversation with Bourchier interrupted, and himself being addressed by one of the foreign party.

'Indeed, yes,' Stanley replied, quickly picking up the thread. 'The Duke of Clarence has proved a most deft and skilled pupil. He has an excellent understanding of the field.'

'Might we be so lucky as to witness this prowess during the tournament?' asked the ambassador, with a wave of his gloved hand.

'Oh, but that would not be correct,' Jacquetta spoke up, 'as the king himself does not compete.'

George shot her an angry look. 'But Lord Scales competes. I see the king is not averse to his household competing.'

Seeing a conflict brewing, Edward swiftly deflected his brother. 'There may be an opportunity tomorrow if the time allows it. But, my lords, tell us of Duke Philip and his passion for the joust. We have heard him named as the champion of Europe in his youth.'

Knowing that flattery was the most powerful diplomatic tool, Edward allowed himself to breathe while the Burgundians regaled the gallery with tales of their duke's prowess and skill.

A charger trapped in silver drew to a halt before the royal gallery. The knight, Richard Woodville, dressed in red and white, lifted his visor and saluted the king.

'Earl Rivers!' Edward pronounced. 'Are you ready to begin?'

'Almost, my lord. Your guests have been admiring the lists? They are over one hundred and twenty feet long from end to end.'

'And how will you begin today?'

'Both champions have submitted to being questioned and searched to the satisfaction of the company. Both have promised to abide by the rules. Today they will commence with armed combat on horseback, if your grace will be so good as to open the lists.'

'Very well.' Edward rose to his feet. The jewels on his collar blinked in the light.

The trumpets blasted out a chorus. A peal of notes in sharp rapport, rising up the scale.

Around him, the crowds fell silent and the grooms turned to watch.

'To the glory of God and the perpetual friendship of our two nations, England and Burgundy, the challengers have been tested and prepared, and are judged ready for combat. I declare this tournament ready to commence. May Godspeed all those involved.'

A ripple of applause ran along both galleries, back and forth like an echo.

Rivers spurred his horse and, turning, galloped back towards the pavilion where his son waited, alongside the wide Burgundian. Antonie, the illegitimate son of Duke Philip, was built solidly, with a reputation for skill and speed. Together, the pair rode out, circling the edge of the field in its entirety before they came to a halt before the gallery.

Again, Edward rose, and gave them his blessing, before they separated to different sides of the lists.

Elizabeth turned away from the lists towards her mother and daughter. The little princess was laughing and dancing on Jacquetta's lap, twisting her curls about her fingers. She watched for the horses to approach and pretended to shiver as they thundered past. Elizabeth had seen so many jousts that her attention easily wandered away from the lists to the people in the gallery: her mother watching Anthony fight, Edward exchanging glances with Hastings, the Stanleys conversing with Archbishop Bourchier, although she could not make out their words above the chatter of the ambassadors.

The men on horseback thundered down towards each other. The steel of their swords clashed once, with force, and then they broke apart again.

William Stanley had broken loose and was squeezing between the chairs and the curtain, making his way towards Edward.

'I'm having trouble keeping Bourchier at bay. He's asking questions about Montagu, insists on talking to you.'

'I will not speak with him now, not while the ambassadors are here.'

'I've explained that, but he is most insistent.'

Edward glanced down the line to where the archbishop sat, disgruntled, staring back at the king.

'Either he holds his peace or I will insist he returns to Lambeth Palace. Tell him that. Surely you and your brother can contain him?'

'Yes, my lord.'

At that point, a crash on the field and a roar from the crowd roused the attention of the platform. Bourchier and Montagu were forgotten as all eyes turned to the two men locked in combat. Lord Scales and the Bastard were sword to sword, pushing against each other with a ferocity that belied the diplomatic friendship, so that one of them must soon yield.

'By God!' muttered Edward. 'Draw back man, draw back.'

But neither man moved, each unprepared to relinquish their reputation to the other and yield.

Elizabeth put her hand on her husband's arm. 'They go too far. Someone will get hurt.'

'The Burgundian's horse is wounded,' added George, seeing the animal list and stagger.

Elizabeth turned to her mother. 'Give the child to her nurse, please. Take her away.'

The little princess was removed into the back tent as the creature bowed to its knees.

Edward rose. His right hand raised in an agreed signal. 'End this! End this now. The tournament is over for today.'

At once, the royal guards hurried onto the field. The two knights were led away and the galleries erupted into sound.

'What is the matter with Anthony?' the king muttered to Elizabeth. 'Is he trying to cause a diplomatic incident?'

'I don't know,' she replied, bewildered, looking back across the field. A single sword lay deserted on the ground.

The hall was spread out with tables decked in fine linen and silver plate. The Mercer's hall was built of fine timbers, high to the rafters, and the walls were adorned with the plate and armour gifts of wealthy patrons. Thick tapestries hung between them, depicting the mythical scenes of Diana at the hunt, and fresh midsummer boughs, gathered from outside the city walls, topped the doors, windows and mantles.

Edward sat between Elizabeth and Margaret at the top table, with De la Marche, ambassador Gruthuyse and their gentlemen, under the gold canopy of royalty. The arms of York had been embroidered on shimmering tissue that flowed down the wall behind them. In the light of the torches, the gold threads woven in made sudden bright spots. To their right, Earl Rivers, Jacquetta and their daughters had a table of their own, with Hastings and Anthony placed to the end in order to converse with more of the Burgundian party, who made a noisy group around the next trestle. On the other side of the hall, Duchess Cecily and her children mirrored them, joined by George and, in the absence of the Duke of Warwick, his countess and her two youthful daughters. Further down the hall, the court spread out among their guests, drinking and making merry, although the talk was equally warm when it came to the events of the tournament.

In the central space, lit by three perfumed braziers, a strange group of figures danced, in costumes designed to look Turkish, adorned in silver jewellery, bulbous hats and trailing hoods.

Edward watched them lazily as they contorted their limbs, twisting and jerking awkwardly to the music.

After one particularly awkward dumbshow of a battle, where the dancers mimed out the rise and fall of swords, leaving some writhing on the floor in pretended agony, Edward leaned in to Elizabeth.

'I could almost imagine,' he whispered, 'that this new dance is some device of Warwick's designed to give offence to our guests.'

The queen smiled. 'It's certainly not in the English style, nor in the Burgundian either.'

'Perhaps it's some French barbarism inspired by Louis, given that Warwick loves him so much.'

Elizabeth looked across the hall. The countess sat eating demurely, barely raising her eyes to the extraordinary show, but her two daughters, who must have been approaching womanhood, sat fixated upon the dancers.

'Good of him to allow his family to attend while he is absent,' she observed with sarcasm.

'Oh no, they are here because I summoned them as my guests, so he knows he cannot misbehave in France.'

'How clever of you. They are your hostages.'

'I prefer guests.'

'And how old are those girls now?'

'The elder one, Isabel, is almost sixteen, the other still a child.'

Elizabeth nodded, watching them from afar. Their manner suggested this was their first time at court, their clothes a little out of style but richly made, with the intention of impressing. They had not yet learned the skill of concealing their emotions and every small reaction was written large on their features.

'The elder one is quite a beauty. Shall I have them as ladies in my household?'

The king smiled. 'Would you like that? Can you squeeze any more in, with all your sisters and cousins? I never knew I was marrying half of England.'

'Nonsense, yes you did. They are my own private army, my city of ladies, but I can squeeze two more in. I would like to see them grow and flourish.'

'Then so be it. You shall have them if their mother allows.'

'She would not prevent them from taking up such a good opportunity. I will help arrange their marriages.'

'Oh,' Edward laughed, 'I think their father would have something to say about that.'

'If he ever comes back from France.'

'True. He may decide he likes it better than England and stay.'

They were laughing together, caught up in their own little world when the trumpets sounded the end of the dance and the arrival of the next course.

Two of the ambassadors, dressed in special red gowns, approached the front table carrying a tray between them. Princess Margaret, her cheeks bright with excitement, rose to see them draw near and clapped her hands in delight as the secret was revealed. A huge marchpane, gilded with silver and surrounded by fruits, had been fashioned into the shape of an angel. In its outstretched hands nestled a large diamond.

'A gift,' explained De la Marche, 'from the Duke Philip and his son Charles, to honour the Lady Margaret.'

The tray was set down upon the table, where the golden figure shimmered and the cut planes of the diamond refracted the light.

'That is a generous and delightful gift,' replied Edward, 'and does your masters much honour.'

'There will be plenty more gifts and much more bounty when your sister crosses the sea to become Charles' wife.'

'A jewel for our jewel,' the king replied deftly, and called for more wine.

It was then that the door at the far end burst open and two messengers appeared. At once Edward sensed serious news, for them to interrupt the feast in that way. The pair parted, one heading for Edward, the other for the Burgundian party.

Elizabeth waited patiently as the servant whispered into her husband's ear. She saw his face pale and change while De la Marche appeared to droop and sink back down into his seat.

Slowly, Edward rose. The hall fell silent in expectation.

'My lords, ladies, guests, bishops and members of the guild. We have just received terrible news from Burgundy. Duke Philip has died. Long live Duke Charles. We will conclude this feast and return to

188

our lodgings. Prayers for his soul will be said in Westminster Abbey. We will meet again under happier circumstances. Godspeed you all.'

And while the hall arose in lament and surprise, Edward turned to his wife and sister, offered a hand to each, and led them out through the back door.

'But will I still be wed, Brother?' Margaret asked anxiously once they were out of hearing.

'Undoubtedly,' confirmed Edward, 'and you will no longer have to wait to become a duchess. We will sign the paperwork at once.'

THIRTEEN

Brothers and Sisters, June 1468

The bright summer's day wrapped itself about the Tower. Rising above the Thames, it was the strongest, broadest and oldest of the king's castles, ringed by grey stone walls. Piled one upon each other, cliff-like, those stones had already stood for centuries, casting their long shadow across London. They saw the casual play of sunlight upon its barred windows, the flight of crows through its air, and the spectre of death watching from its corners.

Inside those walls, it was always night-time. A night-time of fears and doubts, of footsteps approaching and receding, of fuddled dawns and desperate midnights. Along a maze of corridors, the stones ran away like a warren. Door followed after locked door. No light penetrated the tiny, damp cell at the far end, but a single candle made the bare walls flicker as if they trembled at witnessing the unfolding scene.

The prisoner, on his knees and in chains, cringed in anticipation of another blow. He was past the flush of youth, but not old enough for wisdom.

The Earl of Oxford stepped forward again, his face set with a determination sprung from the gravest of purposes.

'Where did these rumours begin? Who told you to spread such treason?'

The prisoner tried to draw breath, spluttered, and tried again. 'No one,' he replied, his mouth already clotted with blood. 'No one, my lord.'

'I don't believe you. Did someone pay you?'

The man looked up. He wore the simple jerkin and braes in which he'd been arrested the day before, but now they were marked with dirt and sweat, blood and urine. His unremarkable face was now distinguished by a black eye and a cut lip.

'By our Lord, no, please no!'

'You're lying. He must have paid you well.'

'No, I beg you, no!'

Oxford lifted his cudgel, a brutal-looking stick set with nails, and tested the weight of it between his hands.

Behind him, Norfolk held up a restraining hand. In the last four years, the young duke's face had taken on a broader, fleshier cast. Experience had hardened his eyes.

The pair of them were accustomed to this pattern, alternately harsh and kind, fooling the prisoner that one of them could be trusted, then coming down upon them hard.

'Your name is Thomas Woodman? You are a baker residing in Cheapside?'

'I am, my lord.'

'And you supply pastries to the court?'

'I do, and I have never had any complaints. I have done so diligently. The queen is fond of…'

'But yet, on the second of this month, you were in the Angel tavern on Eastcheap saying that Princess Margaret was a whore who had born a bastard child.'

'No! Never!'

'And was Princess Margaret fond of your… what, your custard tarts?'

'The princess is a worthy lady.'

'She is indeed a worthy lady,' Norfolk agreed. 'Quite undeserving of your slander. Why did you say it? Who paid you?'

'No one!'

Norfolk and Oxford exchanged glances, shaking their heads in exaggerated disapproval. 'Yet you were overheard, Thomas. Your voice almost reached the rafters and there were many to hear you. I daresay that your slanders were spread outside in the street.'

'I was drunk! I might have said anything. I don't believe it!'

'Is it common for you to commit treason when you're drunk?'

'No! No! I am a loyal subject!'

'And yet we have reports, depositions of witnesses who overheard your words. Is there another Thomas Woodman in Cheapside? We've had enough of your insolence now.'

Norfolk gave Oxford the nod and the earl stepped forward again.

'How well would your bakery prosper if I were to strike off your right hand?'

The prisoner began to quake in his chains. 'Oh, no, no, please, I beg you!'

'Then tell us who paid you to spread these rumours.'

'I cannot remember!'

Oxford reached around to the wall and lifted down a great cleaver. 'Oh, I think you do.'

'I didn't see his face. He was just a plain man. I didn't know his name.'

'But he paid you? How much?'

Woodman's body broke. He slumped under the admission. 'A shilling.'

'Tell us who he was.'

Oxford lifted the cleaver.

'He was just a servant. I saw his livery badge but he tried to conceal it under his cloak.'

'Now we're getting somewhere,' said the duke.

'Tell us, what was the badge? Was it the Earl of Warwick?'

Woodman shook his head.

'Come now, you are almost there. Tell us whose livery badge he wore.'

'I dare not.'

Oxford made as if to swing. 'Then prepare to lose your livelihood.'

'No!' Woodman screamed. 'It was the royal colours. The house of York!'

The cleaver struck home.

All along the route to St Paul's Cathedral, people waited to see her pass. The city spread out on either side of the road, a jumble of roofs and spires, with chimneys pouring out smoke and bell towers pealing out their rhythm. On the ground, the people were herded close to the house fronts, in the dark spaces overhung by jutting storeys above, while others leaned out of windows above, hoping to see the princess pass. Some shielded their eyes from the sun, which slanted low and long down through the street. It wasn't the king or queen, but Margaret had lived much of her life in comparative quiet, and curiosity to see this Yorkist princess had drawn people out of their homes.

Wearing a long blue robe edged with silver and a diadem of jewels, Margaret sat high on her horse. She was a confident rider as all the York siblings were; her father had first put her in a saddle in the orchard at Fotheringhay when she was barely three. The animal moved steadily beneath her and she sat firm in the best Spanish leather seat with silver bells hanging from the trappings, but the nerves were rooted deep in her stomach. Looking down, she saw her knuckles whitening where they clasped the reins. Ahead, the royal guard marched in formation, clearing their passage through the crowded streets. The people came to life as she drew close; they waved and cheered, threw flowers and shook coloured banners out of their windows. It was good to see that the dynasty was still popular. The danger did not come from the people, today. No, it was closer to home.

Behind the guards but ahead of the princess rode the Earl of Warwick in velvet and furs, with a heavy gold chain hung across his shoulders. She narrowed her eyes at his broad back, trusting in his ability, but doubting his person. He had been set against her marriage from the start and had done little to hide his dislike. She knew he had spoken against it in the council chamber on more than one occasion, although Edward had paid him little heed. His affiliation with France was as well known as his loathing of Burgundy. She had heard it whispered in certain corners that he would do anything to prevent her marrying Charles, and he was certainly a ruthless man. But now the contracts were signed; the ink was dry; the Pope had issued his dispensation, and her chests were packed. She was leaving. She was actually leaving, and soon she would embark upon a ship at Margate, for a bridegroom she had never seen. The waves would carry her to his arms. There was nothing Warwick could do now, nothing he dared do, surely? Her dark eyes bored into his back as if they could pierce him.

Keep your enemies close, Edward had told her. She had gone to him in a rage, cheeks burning in fury when she found out that Warwick was to accompany her on this journey. But Edward had understood her passion, even shared it. He had placed a kiss upon her forehead and told her to tolerate Warwick one last time. The appointment was Edward's plan to guarantee the earl's loyalty, to make him feel important, involved, trusted and, therefore, less likely to rebel. He was better there with them in plain sight, than plotting in corners or licking his wounds. Besides, no one of any importance had been foolhardy enough to back him, not outside of France. So, Edward told her, this was the safest, best option for them all: now it was done, let Warwick demonstrate his loyalty. But Margaret had never liked the earl and resented him even that chance. At least there was Hastings riding behind her, the loyal Hastings with his laughing eyes. She would miss those merry eyes.

Their first stop was St Paul's Cathedral, which was spread in a great cross along the ridge of the city. The road sloped upwards to meet it and, just as they began the climb, the sun disappeared behind the clouds. Somewhere behind her, carried in a litter, Cecily would be looking at the clouds. Margaret was sure of it. She would be scanning the skies with her pale eyes and muttering something about omens. And there was her sister, Elizabeth, Duchess of Suffolk, then a mother of four sons, riding beside Cecily, and her husband, the duke, with the Stanleys, Stafford, Essex, Bourchier, Mountjoy, Arundel and other council members. She lost count.

The cathedral stretched above them, its spire rising to a point, and the cross at the top, dark against the clouds. Surely Mother would be comforted to see it. They passed through the gate into the churchyard, with its trees and preaching place at the cross, where the prelates in their red, purple and white robes were lined up to welcome them, with crosses, censors and relics, and hands clasped in prayer and welcome. As she passed them, they each held their treasures forward, so that the blessed mercy of God would surround her and keep her safe. Margaret clutched her reins and strained to feel the holiness affect her. What was it supposed to feel like? Tingling? Uplifting? Shouldn't she feel full of the holy spirit? She tried to concentrate her emotion but all she was aware of was her nerves.

Inside the cathedral, the familiar scent of incense and the damp stone gloom enveloped her. She had been here so many times before, or places just like it, houses of God with their particular mood. Here were all the familiar ingredients: the tiled floor, the columned aisle, the vaulted ceiling, the paintings and icons, the bright glass in the windows, the lines of humble, colourless men, the notes of the organ. Through the narrow dark path, in single file, up the worn steps, into the very heart of the place, where the presence of God was the strongest.

'This way, my lady.'

Margaret went forward as the priest indicated. The shrine was bright in the gloom with the glow of candles and the glint of gems. Behind the railing, it looked like a miniature church, with its three gothic windows, carved stone and ornate decoration. And here, finally, she felt the presence. It was strange, the feeling. The intensity, the peacefulness, the conviction and courage. It never tired; it never faded. Perhaps it was even stronger today because this was the start of her journey; perhaps she needed to feel God watching over her for the unknown adventure ahead. He would deliver her, no matter what the Earl of Warwick had planned.

She knelt, crossed herself, and laid her purse upon the top step.

'Protect and preserve me, blessed Saint Erkenwald. Steer me through the dangers. Keep my heart strong in courage and bless me with good health and many children.'

There was a moment of stillness. Then she rose, stepped back and stood with bowed head for a moment.

Cecily appeared at her side, leaning upon Hastings' arm, Elizabeth and Suffolk behind her. 'Well chosen words, my dear. Would you place this for me?'

Margaret took the little gold tablet from her mother's hands, and a sudden rush of regret seized her. Mother was the one person she

196

regretted leaving. And in the coming years, when she would be a wife and bear children of her own, the sea would lie between them.

But this was her destiny. She choked back the feeling of loss and, turning back to the shrine, placed the tablet beside her purse. Elizabeth crossed herself and put down a little statuette of silver.

'For your safe journey, sister, and a long happy life as a wife and mother.'

As they turned to process to the bishop's palace, Cecily dismissed Hastings and took her daughter's arm. They walked slowly down the aisle, over the ancient, polished stones. At the door, where the daylight waited to reclaim them, Margaret saw Warwick standing with the horses. At his side, was her own brother, George, who had grown tired of waiting and had broken away from the royal group. Their heads were bowed together, their faces earnest.

'Mother,' Margaret said softly, as they turned away down the path to where the bishop was waiting, 'I do not trust the Earl of Warwick.'

'None of us do, dear, dreadful man.'

'But George does. George is his friend.'

'My George?'

'Mother, you must be vigilant. Yes, your George. Please, be vigilant.'

And the bishop spread his arms in welcome.

From the light, it was difficult to tell what time of day it was. Perhaps a grey morning, the first hours after Prime, or it could be the setting-in of evening with the dinner hour approaching. It was impossible to tell since she'd stopped hearing the bells.

She opened her eyelids to let in a tiny slither of light. The room was still, quiet and dark, and the nun assigned to sit at her bedside had folded her hands in contemplation. But of course, it didn't matter. Day, night, all were one now; they were the hours for the living, to make them run about like mice, busy about their tasks. She was beyond all that now.

'Sister Eleanor? Are you awake?'

She turned her head slightly.

The nun leaned forward. It was Agatha in her brown habit; the same Agatha who had welcomed her into the convent four years ago. Sister Agatha, whose gentle kindness she had come to rely upon with the worsening of her illness. How quickly it had progressed, how unexpectedly in one so young. And the doctors couldn't help her. None of their herbs or fumigations had made any difference, and when the physician bled her, it just left her weaker.

Once or twice in her thinking, she had sinned. There had been a moment in the church when a sudden wave of pain took her and she clutched a pillar. The thoughts had come unbidden, railing in anger against the injustice of it all and the agony of what might have been. Queen of England, imagine that. That had been Easter. Then, just about a month ago, as her body had started to shut down, she could not help herself, one night, waking at midnight, and giving way to tears. Just two weeks ago she had been able to sit in the sunshine in the garden, even to read a little. But that was past now. God was calling her to his side, and soon she would ascend into the true bliss of heaven.

And he, perhaps he… No, she pushed that thought aside.

'Sister Eleanor, we will pray together.'

She felt the cool, smooth hand take hold of hers. A vague sensation about the fingers. Agatha was speaking softly, with a rise and fall, a rhythm that felt familiar. Eleanor closed her eyes and let the words carry her. She was drifting as sleep came forward to reach her, drifting away. Finally, it seemed like the last six months of pain was over. From that frosty morning when she had woken with a sore chest, to this moment: still, quiet, eternal. And the relief closed over her.

'Sister Eleanor? Eleanor?'

But the words fell upon deaf ears.

Edward stood by the fireplace as the servants cleared away the dishes. They had dined lightly in the abbey's private quarters while waiting for Margaret and her entourage to arrive. It was a quiet place, founded by the Cistercians at Bow, four miles to the east, beyond the city walls, and lying between the marsh and the Channelsea River.

Elizabeth was seated in the alcove where the window had a view across the marshland. Her eyes were drawn out beyond the abbey walls, her mood reflective. Finally, the last servants left, the doors closed and they were alone.

'You are thoughtful, my love?'

She turned, with that slow, wide smile that he loved. 'I suppose I am.'

He crossed the room to stand behind her, putting his arms about her neck. Elizabeth leaned back into his embrace.

'What is on your mind?'

The queen sighed. 'I was thinking of Margaret, starting out on a new life, in a new land.'

'Ah yes, Margaret. She is happy in this match, surely?'

'Oh yes, she will be. But I remember the newness of it all. Suddenly being part of a court, a queen, to whom everyone looks, and some resent.'

She saw Edward begin to speak and raised her hand to cut him off. 'No, I never once regretted it but it was not easy. And there is Margaret, starting anew in a different country, with all its funny ways and a language she doesn't understand.'

'Margaret will face it as a challenge.'

'Of course she will. She will do extraordinarily well. It's just, well, the enormity of it, I suppose. Her bravery.'

'She is a York. If she was a man, she would be out on the battlefield.'

'But instead, as a woman, she is sent into battle in the marital bed.'

He laughed and bent to kiss her neck. 'Is that how you see it, a battle?'

She turned her head away, teasingly. 'A battle, with a conqueror.'

'But the losing side is the one to receive,' he said, his blood racing, moving his hands across her bodice.

Leaning forward, he began to plant kisses on her cheek. She began to turn, her mouth opening in anticipation of his, warmth seeking warmth.

Then a knocking came, brisk and loud, upon the door.

Edward stood up to his full height. 'Damn it, I shall send them away.'

'No, it will be Margaret. Come, this is her last goodbye.'

He drew in his breath. 'Indeed it is; our appetites can be served later.'

The knocking came again.

'Confound it! Someone is in earnest. Come,' he called, 'come.'

Hastings was at the door, fresh from his horse, his breath still short from haste. 'My lord, the princess's party approaches. I rode ahead to prepare you. They come upon us by and by.'

Edward and Elizabeth exchanged glances.

'Come then, to the courtyard,' the king confirmed. 'Make haste; we shall take our leave of our sister there.'

As Edward strode down the corridor towards the open doors, the sound of horses' hooves on stone reached them.

'They have made good speed,' admitted Hastings at his side. 'Even your mother is in her litter!'

The abbot appeared before them, bowing, with clasped hands. 'Ah my lord, I was about to come to you.'

'No matter,' the king replied. 'I am here. Will you join us?'

The courtyard was filling with riders on horseback, dismounting and ordering their clothes. Margaret and Cecily were being tended by the monks and Richard was not too far off, having his man servant remove his cloak. He had grown since Edward saw him last, even in a matter of weeks. He was taller but not broader yet, in the early stages of youth, his limbs like those of a young colt. And yet, there was always something unusual about the way he held himself, never quite erect, as if he was perpetually being called back, just at the moment he was turning away. It was his shoulder, of course. The physicians had their poultices and dietary recommendations but the boy never managed to stand straight. Perhaps when he resumed his training.

Edward's attention was drawn by the approach of Cecily, slow and stately in a long gown of emerald green.

'Mother.' He went towards her, kissed her soft cheek. 'How was the journey?'

'Hell all the way from St Paul's,' she replied quickly. 'I was jolted and shaken about like a sapling in a storm. But still,' she conceded, 'if it is God's will, it is God's will.'

Edward smiled. 'My apologies, Mother. Next time we shall line the roads with silk for your comfort.'

'Humph!' she snorted. 'Saucy boy.'

As the years had passed, Cecily had become more forthright, more outspoken. Perhaps it was age, or her status, or her dislike of Edward's marriage that made her feel entitled to express every discomfort. He knew that she was in pain, that her bones caused her sleepless nights and that she still deeply grieved for their father. Without his love and wise influence, she was a little adrift. Her faith and her children had been the anchors keeping her steady.

'And where is George? Where is my George?' she asked, scanning the courtyard.

'He will be on his way, no doubt,' Edward reassured her. 'Now come, and my sisters, Margaret and Elizabeth, you must be tired from your journey. Come and take some refreshment.'

There was hippocras, with its warming spices, wafers baked thin with cinnamon and tarts with a deep custard filling. Edward saw Cecily settled in a chair by the fireside in the abbot's luxurious parlour, Margaret and Elizabeth facing her. The queen took a cushioned seat beside them. The inner chamber had been reserved for the royal family alone: the king, his wife, his mother, his sisters and brothers while the lords and guard were resting in the hall. Richard stood at the hearth but their brother, George, had noticeably not joined them. Edward assumed him to be still with Warwick.

'You do not intend to travel all the way down to the coast, Mother, I hope?'

'Indeed I do; why should I not? Your father would expect no less.'

'Father would wish for your comfort and good health. Margaret is in good hands. She has Hastings, Warwick and Lord Wenlock, and George and Richard.'

'None of whom feel a mother's love. I am resolute. Do not attempt to deter me.'

'Very well.' Edward knew when he was beaten. 'But you should stay in Canterbury a while, to rest, before you make your return. Archbishop Bourchier is of the party, I believe. He will accompany you.'

She seemed to accede to this, unfurling her fingers towards the fire, slowly and painfully.

'It is many months since I saw the palace. I should like to see Becket's shrine again too, while I am there.'

'And you, Elizabeth?' Cecily turned to the Duchess of Suffolk. Will you ride down to the coast with us?'

'We will say our goodbyes here,' she replied, with a look to her husband, who stood by the king. 'We are departing into Suffolk. There is some trouble there among the landowners; a feud is threatening to spiral out of control. It affects Norfolk too.'

'Serious?' asked Edward.

'Ours is not so bad as that between the Duke of Norfolk and the Paston family, but it could become so unless we intervene. The usual dispute over property.'

'I will give it my attention upon my return,' promised Edward.

'My lord?'

The king turned to see the abbot waiting at the door a little uncertainly.

'Yes, what is it?'

'It is the Duke of Norfolk, my lord.'

'Norfolk? Well, show him in.'

Norfolk had clearly been riding hard although he had not been among Margaret's original party. His heavy face was flushed as he bowed low.

'We were just speaking of you. You have sped from somewhere, good friend?'

'I have come from the Tower. I followed your route and am glad to have caught you before you went further.'

Edward was at once concerned. 'Pray, continue.'

'I have, until late, had the charge of a prisoner who was committed to the Tower for certain slanders and treasons. He is of no consequence, a fool of a pastry cook with no wit, well, none until Oxford and I made him speak.'

'What did he say?'

'My lord, forgive me. I hesitate to speak such godless slanders before the ladies.'

'Speak up, boy,' insisted Cecily. 'We would all hear you.'

Edward nodded. 'Go ahead. I suspect it is something touching one of them.'

'Indeed it is, my lord. It was the same scurrilous slanders concerning the Lady Margaret.'

Cecily let out a grunt of annoyance. 'Not the bastard child story again? Have they such little wit that they cannot think of anything new?'

'It was the same, my lady, forgive me. But this is not the reason why I have ridden here so fast today. There is more. Our pastry cook was paid to speak thus, to spread these slanders abroad by one who lacked the bravery to do the deed himself.'

'And did he name him?' asked Edward.

'He could not give me a name. The man who paid him was a servant but although he wore a cloak to cover his livery, our cook saw the badge when it fell open.'

They all looked up, expectantly.

'Warwick?' asked Cecily, making the word sound like a crack.

'No, my lady, I'm sorry to say. It was…'

He faltered.

Edward frowned. 'It was what? We must know our enemy.'

'Forgive me, my lord. It was York.'

The name dropped like a stone amid them. Glances were exchanged, of doubt, disbelief, confirmation. Margaret was the first to break the silence.

'York? My own family. My own brother! I have seen how close he is with Warwick, and where is he now when he should be with us? Plotting with Warwick.'

'Not George, surely?' asked Richard, his young face heavy with turmoil. 'Why would he? He is one of us.'

Edward struggled to master his emotion. 'He is also ambitious and secretive, and I fear, disloyal. He has been asking me, of late, for a marriage to match your own, Margaret, which could have been his right, but I refused him. Something gave me warning, cause to hesitate.'

'Why so, Brother?'

'He is still my heir until the queen and I are blessed with a son.' He looked briefly at Elizabeth. 'And this will come in time. But I cannot marry him out of the kingdom, nor equip him with foreign wealth and allegiances outside our family. He must wait his turn but he took it peevishly, like a child, and the resentment has hung heavy on him.'

'You married when you wished,' said Cecily, softly, but all heard her.

'I am the king,' Edward retorted. 'George is not. He must be ruled by the king.'

'And is this quite proven?' she continued, in defence of her son. 'That the blame lies with George?'

Edward turned away, annoyed. 'Who would you suggest instead, Mother? Myself? My wife? Richard? Or did you do it yourself?'

Cecily half rose in her seat. 'Utter nonsense!'

But Edward's face was set, his eyes cold and hard. 'The plot is closer than we think. I will accompany Margaret all the way to her ship. I will go and rouse the men; we will resume our journey in a moment.'

'But,' cried Margaret, rising, 'will you speak to George?'

The king paused at the door. He took a deep sigh and looked back. 'I will not. If he is the author of these slanders, I will give him the chance to amend his behaviour and return to the fold. Come now, busy yourselves about our departure.'

On the rise at Margate, they watched the fleet of ships leave the bay and head out towards the North Sea. The small boats had already fallen away and the wind caught the great white sails of the carracks, swelling them full and round like billowing clouds skimming the waves.

'There,' said Queen Elizabeth from her golden litter. 'She is truly on her way now. Godspeed, Margaret, and preserve you queen as of Burgundy.'

Edward turned at the sound of her voice. He had headed to the promontory with Hastings and Norfolk while the rest of the party waited on the road. They had delivered Margaret to the harbour, through the town, then ridden to high ground to wave her off. Cecily had insisted on accompanying them all the way, clasping her daughter and kissing her cheek before the princess took to the sea. Now she sat silently, even sullenly, turning the beads of her rosary between her fingers.

'Do you think she can see us anymore?' asked Richard, shielding his eyes against the light.

'I wouldn't think so,' replied Elizabeth. 'She will still be able to see the coastline, perhaps only parts of Essex, but not for much longer. It is a strong wind; it carries her quickly.'

'Ah,' spoke up Cecily, 'here is George. Now we shall have this nonsense put to bed.'

Three riders had appeared, mounting the road to the watching place. The wind whirled around them, up in that high spot with only the clouds scudding behind. Edward recognised George, Warwick and Lord Wenlock. The sight of Wenlock gave him some relief, hoping that although he was Warwick's friend, he was a solid reliable man, who would stand for no treasonous talk.

George rode up close, turning his horse around so his back was to the water. 'It's a good wind. It'll blow them straight into port.'

'You think?'

'So the forecasters say, and so say my legs, shivering in its breath.'

Edward dismissed this attempt at light-heartedness. 'Have you been with Warwick all this while? We missed you at the abbey.'

'Much of it, and Wenlock. My apologies, I was not aware we were wanted.'

'Are you accompanying us back to Canterbury?'

'I will, and then I am going north to Middleham, where Warwick is going to continue my training.'

'Oh.' Edward turned his eyes out to sea. 'Is your training better conducted there than at Westminster?'

George laughed. 'It's a change. Change and variety are good for learning. We will have Warwick's land. Does it not suit you, Brother? Do you have other plans for me?'

'Nothing at present, beyond your obedient education, your loyalty, your service to the crown.'

He looked at his brother's face sharply: the lively eyes, the wide, hungry mouth. He wasn't sure, but perhaps George flickered a little under his gaze?

'Maybe you are looking to arrange a marriage for me, Brother?'

'But you are young still, George, surely?'

'I am in my eighteenth year!'

'As I said, still young. And who would you have, George? Which princess of Europe have you cast your eye upon this time?'

'No princess. Someone far more suitable. You know that Warwick has two daughters?'

Edward tensed but tried not to show it. He cast a look back to where Warwick and Wenlock were talking to Cecily. 'Did he put this suggestion to you?'

'I can think for myself, Brother.'

'Yes, that is what concerns me. You are too young yet. Complete your training; be patient.'

George frowned. 'Does that mean I have your permission to go to Middleham?'

'For a fortnight but then I want you back in Westminster.'

'Why?'

'Where else would my brother be, but by my side?'

And he turned back to the brightness of the sea to find the ships had vanished from sight.

FOURTEEN

Treachery, July 1469

There was a depth to the darkness. An absolute stillness that seemed crushing as Edward lay there, eyes wide open. Around him, the men were sleeping. Beyond the curtain, his guards would be vigilant, watchful in all the corners and shadows lest anyone dare come that close. And in that enclosed stillness, all were breathing, breathing, but with the softness of the land.

Outside the tent, where the red and gold canvas was laced tight, the royal guards were lined up in their murrey and blue, with Edward's badge of the sunburst sewed upon their chests, and further yet, was the little sea of tents where the soldiers slept. Something had woken him, although he could remember no bad dreams, no cries of alarm. He lay still, his ears keening into the night.

Since he'd been a child, he'd had this strange sense, some presentiment of danger about to occur. He used to think he was over-cautious, seeking out threats in every shadow but, with age and experience, he had learned that it was more like an instinct, like the highly developed senses of animals, hunting at night, crouching above their prey or freezing in terror to avoid the attack. Somehow, he had not heard but sensed a sound, a change in the air caused by movement, a sort of vibration in the earth as men marched.

An owl called close by. But it was not that.

'Hastings?'

The bed on the other side of the room shifted. 'Is it morning?'

'Hush. Listen.'

They both lay still. The darkness seemed to fold in about them, closing down, smothering.

'What is it?' Hastings whispered.

'I don't know, but there is something. I woke unexpectedly. I feel uneasy.'

'I thought the rebels had been dealt with. Montagu executed the leaders.'

'Maybe.'

'You suspect him?'

'He has proven himself but he is still a Neville.'

Edward swung his legs off the truckle bed. 'I need to see that all's well.'

As he pushed open the curtain, the guards scrambled to attention. 'All is quiet here, men?'

The first one answered, a tall, broad chap with red hair. 'Save for the wind and the owls, all is well, my lord.'

Edward passed through into his main chamber. Here, the tent had been constructed about a central pole, making a circular room. Evidence of their evening's planning remained: the maps spread out on the table, the candles snuffed out almost at the wicks, the cushions and carpets to keep out the cold, the brazier full of ash. Here they had sat until late, discussing the unruly state of the north: Hastings, Suffolk, Norfolk, the Stanley brothers and Stafford. He had listened to their advice. It was safe to leave Elizabeth at Norfolk. It was safe to travel north. It was safe to take only a small retinue. The threat had been defeated. The night was dark and quiet.

'Some wine my lord?' A servant had brought a glass in anticipation.

Edward drank, refreshed, and pulled the tent flap aside. The night was fresh and clear. Stars crowded above.

'My lord?'

It was Richard Woodville, Lord Rivers, his father-in-law, warming his hands over a brazier.

'Rivers? What are you doing up?'

'It's my shift for the watch. I'm here until the first cock crows and then my Anthony and John take over. Did something wake you?'

Edward strode over to the glowing coals. 'Yes. I don't know what. I came to check all was well.'

'So far as I can see. Perhaps you're restless, with the rebellion on your mind.'

'You may be right. I understand Robin of Redesdale is still at large?'

Rivers nodded. 'It's possible. It's difficult to know for certain when these rebels use false names. If he does survive, he has gone into hiding.'

'Do we know who he may have been? Or who was behind him?'

'It may have been exactly what it seemed, part of the Neville-Percy conflict. Some have suggested Sir John Conyers.'

'Conyers? The steward at Middleham?'

'It's only a rumour.'

'Maybe. But I like it not.'

Although George had always returned from training at Middleham and gone about his duties at Westminster with a mild manner, he was always itching to return to the castle, and to Warwick's influence.

'I will send for Warwick in the morning,' he decided. 'And see what he has to say about it. And George, I will send for George too. He should be at my side at a time such as this.'

He turned to go but Rivers put a hand on his arm. 'But you are well? And Elizabeth is well?'

And in that moment, Edward felt what it was to not have a father: the pain of loss and absence, the love for flesh and blood that could not be replaced.

'We are well, I thank you.'

The morning dawned damp and hazy over the valley. The view over the Lincolnshire hills was magnificent with their green rises and purple valleys, and the sky hanging low, with clouds burning off. Clumps of trees made dark spots across the middle-distance and the spire of a church was just visible behind them. Thomas Stanley shivered in the mist as he looked towards the horizon.

'God, I love this country. Feels like coming home.'

Hastings laughed. 'Has this ever been your home? I thought your lands were further north?'

'I know what he means,' said Edward, beside them. 'This is England at its finest, this perfect view.'

They stood together for a moment in appreciation of the world unfolding before them, a world which was theirs for the taking. Edward's kingdom and dominion; Edward's realm, in green and brown and blue.

'What is the plan for today,' asked Anthony Woodville, striding across the grass from the tents. 'Do we press on to Nottingham as discussed?'

'I think it best,' said Edward. 'At least I can get news there, send out letters and get supplies. We will depart shortly.'

'Look,' added Stanley, 'we have the perfect vantage point. Look there, a rider approaches.'

They followed his gaze to the left. It was true. A lone horseman was making his way along the road that bisected two fields of sheep, driving his horse hard, in great haste.

At once, Edward felt a sense of unease in his stomach. There was something; he knew it. And this, whatever this might prove to be, was it.

'It's Worcester,' Stanley noted, as the figure came closer. He was travelling in earnest, head bent, losing not one second.

They walked down the hill towards the bottom of the camp, where the road gave out.

The great Westwick gate loomed above them, marking its welcome to the city. Elizabeth looked out of the litter at the men gathered outside the walls, waiting to welcome them to Norwich. The mayor and dignitaries in their colourful robes, guildsmen in furs and chain, and the goodwives in their finest gowns, with all their faces turned in expectation.

She nudged the two little girls on the seat facing her. They had fallen into a slumber, miles back on the road with the steady tread of the horses, and she had let them sleep, grateful for a moment of quiet. It was difficult to put the gnawing fear aside, to trust that all was well, that Edward was safe and would return, and that the rebels had been silenced. Until you knew differently, there was nothing to do but put your faith in God. She hadn't wanted to travel to Norwich. She'd begged Edward to let her stay in the peace and safety of Fotheringhay; even Cecily had written to say that she might. She would have had the place to herself, too, with the old lady down at Sandwich, reliving memories of happier times.

Little Elizabeth and Mary woke slowly, rubbing their eyes. She knew it had been an unusual choice to bring them with her. She might have easily left them in the nursery at Westminster with baby Cecily, who was now four months old, but while she was apart from Edward, she loved their company and their little ways: they distracted her from her thoughts. Even surrounded by all her household and ladies, there was still a loneliness without family.

'Come, my lovelies. Look, we are here. Sit up, smile and wave. All these people have come to meet us.'

The litter drew to a halt before the bowing mayor. Faces surged up on all sides.

'My most esteemed lady and queen, the city of Norwich welcomes you and the princesses. We hope you will have a peaceful and prosperous stay with us.'

And a hand thrust up towards the window.

The sudden movement made Elizabeth jump. She had learned to fear the assassin's dagger, the secret move, the thrust spear. But this hand contained a leather purse, round and full of coins. She took it with a gracious smile.

'I thank you, Mayor Aubrey, for your kind welcome.'

'We will now escort you through the city, my lady, where our children and guildsmen have prepared some pageants for your entertainment.'

'We are most grateful.'

The litter rumbled on, under the shadow of the gates and into a little square, where a stage had been erected, covered in red and green and decorated with angels and the royal coat of arms.

'Look, girls, look.' She pointed and the two princesses scrambled over to one side to best see the performance.

A group of children began to sing in harmony and two large figures of giants strode up onto the platform. At the side of the litter, one of her ladies brought wine and spiced cakes. Elizabeth ate and drank as her daughters giggled. She tried to forget the danger to her husband. Trust in God; faith in God.

* * *

Edward stared at the paper, incredulously. 'And these are their words? You are sure?'

Worcester nodded, panted, still out of breath. 'I came as soon as we heard. There is no mistake.'

'I can't believe it. I can't believe the betrayal. Warwick I suppose is no surprise, just bitter disappointment, but George, George, my own brother.'

'I suppose he was influenced by the earl,' offered Suffolk, trying to mitigate the blow.

'I expect he was, but a man with a sound head and loyalty would not have been so easily influenced. George is a weathervane in the wind.'

'Is it treason?' asked William Stanley, hesitantly, fully knowing the answer.

Edward could not bring himself to face that, not yet. He turned back to face the camp.

'Time and again I refused him that marriage, for good reason. I knew he was ambitious; I sensed his restlessness. I knew that giving him too much power would be dangerous; so, like a coward, he runs off to Calais and marries anyway. Do we know who conducted the ceremony?'

'The Archbishop of York, George Neville.'

'Of course. Warwick's treacherous brother. No doubt still smarting because I removed the great seal from his safe keeping! And now this! Read it again, Worcester. The bit with the names.'

Worcester took a breath and held up the sheet. 'The king our sovereign lord's true subjects of divers parts of this, his realm of England, have delivered to us certain articles remembering the deceitful, covetous rule and guiding of certain seditious persons; that is to say, the Lord Rivers; the Duchess of Bedford, his wife; William Herbert, Earl of Pembroke; Humphrey Stafford, Earl of Devonshire; Lord Scales; Sir John Woodville and his brothers, and others of their mischievous rule, opinion and assent, which have caused our sovereign lord and his realm to fall into great poverty and misery, disturbing the administration of the laws, only tending to their own promotion and enrichment.'

'God's blood!' raged Edward. 'I will give him great poverty and misery.'

For the moment, he could barely think, barely see. But the image of little George came back to him, riding in the orchard at Fotheringhay, as a sturdy boy of eight or nine, or even younger, toddling across the courtyard towards their father, upon his return, or sitting upon dear Edmund's lap, while their brother read to him. His gorge rose. And he dared not think of his mother, always grieving her losses, and young Richard, sixteen and growing with his spine curved. And he could not think of George. He could not. Instead, Edward folded himself inwards, contained and controlled himself. Physically, he became very still, conscious of every move.

'What make you of this, Hastings and Baron Stanley? Your wives are sisters of the earl.'

'We knew none of it!' Hastings protested at once. 'And my wife is not her brother's keeper.'

'Mine neither,' added Stanley, indignantly. 'Warwick is a disgrace to the family.'

Edward nodded. 'Where are they now?'

'On their way north,' replied Worcester. 'They came through Canterbury and London, gathering troops. Now they are heading this way, and the rebels are rising again.'

'But this is treason! Clear as day! Treason!' Suffolk burst out, looking to the others for confirmation.

'And what is their aim?' Edward asked, looking round at the faces of his friends. 'To what end do they pursue this course? Would they kill my friends? Depose me? Kill me?'

'They dare not be so bold,' said Rivers from behind the king. He had walked up from the camp and heard all. 'They dare not strike at you, so they hide behind the coward's mask of attacking your friends. They are jealous, ambitious, greedy. They want power to fall into their laps without true desert. Edward, you have been more than generous with them. You have ignored your doubts, promoted Warwick although he continued to work against you with the French. I have heard certain things spoken by the men here; I am convinced he is behind this latest uprising, and now he will use it to try and seize control. You cannot afford to be lenient. He is not a man to be forgiven, to give up his ambitions, to retire quietly. This is treason. He is a traitor.'

'And my brother?' Edward smarted at the harsh truths.

'He is young and foolish. His head has been turned. He has what he wanted now in this marriage, so he can learn to repent; he can have one more chance.'

Edward nodded. 'There is a threat to the lives of all those named in their letter. They are distributing this?'

'Yes,' confirmed Worcester. 'Copies of it have been found between here and Dover.'

'They are inviting attack upon those named. Rivers, we know you are a particular target of theirs. You should take your sons and retire to Grafton, as soon as possible. Go through Norwich and collect Elizabeth.'

'But, my lord, I would stay here to fight with you.'

Edward turned towards him. 'I know you would. And I love you for it. But the threat to your life is grave. I will summon Pembroke and Devon to raise their armies. We must part before the two sides meet or else you will be too easy a target for them. Listen, they will say they are opposing you, in fighting. If you are not there, who can they oppose but me, their king? That will give them pause for thought.'

'Very well, I follow your thoughts. I will take John and speed back to Grafton; I will send Anthony to Norwich again so that we are not in one group should we meet rebels on the road.'

'Godspeed you, good father. I will summon you to court in due course, once the danger has passed.'

Edward turned to face the road north. 'Give the orders to clear the camp. Send to all my loyal friends to join me at Nottingham. We will deal with this treason.'

Jacquetta saw them approach from the window and her heart leapt. Anthony first, on horseback, followed by the guards and the golden litter, drawn by horses. She hurried out of the door and down the path. Evening was starting to gather in the sky, creeping in at the corners, stealing across the lawn. The cool scents of a summer night were rising from the flowers. They had arrived just in time.

Elizabeth was dismounting. Jacquetta hurried to help with the girls, scooping up little Mary in her arms.

'I was praying for your safe arrival. You saw no trouble on the road?'

'Nothing, Mother, no.'

'You get inside,' urged Anthony. 'I'll post the guards in the outbuildings and at the gate.'

Elizabeth took her eldest daughter's hand and followed her mother. Grafton welcomed her with its familiar atmosphere and smells: flowers, bread, fire, old stone. And her sisters were waiting: Mary, Martha and Anne at first, and then the others, hanging back in the hall.

'Come in. There's food. You must be starving, then we'll put the girls to sleep in the top room.'

'Thank you,' breathed Elizabeth, unable to articulate anything else. As her mother drew her towards a chair, Elizabeth turned, caught her unexpectedly in her arms and buried her face in Jacquetta's neck.

'Oh, there.' Jacquetta put her hand on the back of her daughter's neck as the girls looked on in surprise. 'You're home now, home and safe.'

Elizabeth eased into the chair, pulling her two girls either side and urging them to sit.

Servants brought plates with pies, baked meats, nuts, fruits, curd tarts.

'Curd tarts,' smiled Jacquetta, 'with saffron, when we knew you were coming.'

Anthony strode into the room, stripping off his cloak. 'All well in here?'

'All well.' Jacquetta smiled.

He took his seat at the table and took a glass of wine. 'I must say, it's a relief to have made a quiet journey. We heard talk of skirmishes and rebel groups but we travelled by the back roads. It took a little longer, but it was safer. I suppose that is why we arrived back before father and John. I had thought they would be here already as they were heading straight here while I detoured to Norwich.'

'Richard and John?' asked Jacquetta. 'I've not heard word from them.'

'I expect they will arrive tomorrow,' said Anthony, tucking into a pie. 'Perhaps Edward had some other purpose for them.'

'Perhaps,' the older lady whispered, her hands coming to rest on the table before her.

Later, after they had tucked the girls into one bed under the eaves of the house, Elizabeth and Jacquetta sat together in the solar. It was dark and the candles had been lit on the table and mantle. It was only then that the queen gave way to tears.

Jacquetta came to her side. 'Hush now, all will be well; trust in the Lord, and in your husband.'

'I know,' Elizabeth replied. 'I know but it is so bitter. A brother's betrayal. I can't imagine it. Can you think if Anthony were to… He never would, ever, he would rather die first. The king's own brother, after all his kindness.'

'George is young. He has been led astray…'

'That is what everyone is saying! But I am not sure. I think this is the result of George's ambition. He knew full well what he was doing. And as for being young, Edward was king at the same age.'

'I was giving him the benefit of the doubt but you speak the truth.'

'And I am so far from Edward. I fear for him. What can Warwick's intentions be?'

'Edward has been too generous to him already. He must cut the ties.'

'But how? How can it end?'

Elizabeth shivered. The fear crept up over her like a fog, impossible to avoid. 'The worst thing is, I am helpless sitting here. I would be helpless at Westminster, even helpless at his side, but at least I would be at his side. I can pray, that is all. Pray and trust. Otherwise, I may as well be a piece of furniture.'

Jacquetta's face darkened. 'I understand. The helplessness is the worst thing.'

'I honestly don't know how I can bear it, how I will sleep tonight.'

'I will make you up a draught, a caudle with my special mix of herbs. I have some fresh lavender put by, honey, rosemary, cinnamon.'

'Thank you. But I just wish it were over.'

'I know. It will be soon.'

A servant girl knocked. 'Shall I stoke up the fire, my lady?'

'Yes please,' replied Jacquetta, and they watched as she raked through the coals and added a few small logs.

When she had left them, Jacquetta stared into the flames.

'There was a game we used to play when I was a girl, Well, it was not so much a game, but it made us feel better in times of trial. Would you like to play it?'

Elizabeth nodded.

Jacquetta went to a small chest and brought back a piece of paper. Before her daughter, she tore it into small strips and divided it between them.

'Upon these, we write the names of those who would wish us harm. Then we cast them into the flames and watch them burn.'

Elizabeth looked sceptical. 'Is this not witchcraft?'

'It is merely names written upon paper. It is better than sitting here helplessly. You do not have to take part. I am happy to do it myself.'

With a flourish, she took a quill and, balancing upon her knee, wrote the name of Warwick. Then she folded it small, threw it into the fire, and they watched the paper twist and burn brightly, then disappear into ash.

'You see? It is that simple.'

'You think it works?'

'I think it cannot do harm, unless to those we name, so be it.'

Elizabeth reached for the quill. Taking a paper, she wrote boldly, 'George.'

'George? There is to be no forgiveness then for the young Duke of Clarence?'

'No, he knows what he is doing. When brother turns against brother, there can be no forgiveness.' And she threw the paper into the hearth.

'And these,' said Jacquetta, holding up the final pieces, 'we use to write the names of our loved ones, and we tuck them into our bosom and sleep with them close to our heart.'

'This part I like most,' said the queen, uncurling her paper, and writing out her husband's name.

'Has the messenger from Pembroke come yet?' asked Edward, reining in his horse. He was standing at the crossroads, his retinue in the hot sun, surveying the land ahead.

'Nothing formal,' said Hastings, 'but a boy came from the scene who thought the earl had met with Warwick's army already, before he had rejoined Devon.'

'God's blood! What do I do? March north, or east? The wrong decision might cost us the battle. Where the devil are they?'

'The boy said he had come from north of Banbury,' added Stanley, 'from close by the village of Edgecote.'

'So, what is that from here, east, I think?'

'I believe so, my lord.'

'Then east we must ride. If only it brings us closer to the scene, we can get updates as we approach, or we will meet the messengers on the road.'

'East it is,' added Suffolk. 'It is the best intelligence we have at the present time.'

The king gave the signal and the procession began to move forward. The front riders pressing ahead to check the road, Edward and his close advisors at a trot, with the soldiers marching behind, perhaps four hundred, perhaps five. Soon the king broke ahead with his small band, surging along the country roads in search of confirmation.

They had been riding about an hour when the roofs of a village came into sight, and beyond them, the distinctive shapes of tent roofs in an encampment. With the soldiers a half hour behind, Edward had perhaps a dozen men with him. He called them to a halt at once.

'Wait! Look!'

They pulled up their reins and looked over the scene. Sloping fields, hedgerows, roofs. Lines of smoke spiralling up to the sky.

'Where are the outriders?' asked Stanley, who had chosen them himself from among the men.

'They should have returned,' said Edward, 'informed us of this. Whose camp is it ahead? Could this be Pembroke or Devon?'

222

Then suddenly, from the trees at the side of the road, appeared a line of men, their bows trained upon the king and his men.

Rage flooded through Edward. 'Lower your weapons at once by the command of the king. Put down your weapons! He who refuses is guilty of treason. I am your king!'

Some of the men looked hesitant while some stood firm.

'By whose command do you threaten the life of your king?'

'By my command.'

Through the trees strode the Earl of Warwick. He came to the ridge overlooking the road and surveyed the group. His face was ruddy, his hair cut short, his eyes hard.

'Lower your weapons, men. There is no challenge to the king's life by his loyal subjects.'

'Loyal subjects!' Edward retorted. 'Traitors, every one of you. And where is George?'

'George awaits you at Middleham, with his wife.'

'She is no wife of his.'

'Their marriage is as legal as yours. Maybe more so. And if the child Isabel carries proves to be a boy, he will be heir to your throne.'

So that was the plan all along. Edward could have kicked himself for not working it out sooner.

'Does your ambition know no bounds, Warwick? Will you have my life and England too?'

'Not at all. It is a happy union between the houses of York and Neville and will provide the country with a male heir, which you have so far failed to do, in what, five years of marriage?'

'You will release me and my men at once.'

'There is no need. The battle is over. Your enemies have been defeated.'

'What do you mean?'

'You have been poorly served, Edward, by your friends. Pembroke and Devon were so busy quarrelling about where to camp that they split their armies. It was so much easier to defeat them that way. Poor Pembroke was left quite without any archers at all. They are in my custody. As are Rivers and his son. As are you, my lord.'

'I am no one's prisoner. I am your king. You must release the others at once.'

'Dismiss your men. You are invited to be my guest at Middleham Castle.'

'Your guest? Invited?'

'Come,' said the earl, seeming to soften. 'Let us take this opportunity to talk.'

'Do not trust him,' urged Hastings. He has shown his true colours.'

'George is waiting for you,' reiterated Warwick. 'We can sit down together and talk about this. We never rose against you, only those who sought to influence you against us. We can find a way forward.'

Edward was thinking. The moments hung heavily upon them, with the line of archers by the trees and the encampment ahead.

'Will you agree to let those men go free?' he asked. 'Pembroke and Devon, Rivers and Woodville?'

'We can discuss their actions, certainly.'

Edward turned to his men: Hastings, Suffolk, the Stanleys, Norfolk, Worcester and the others. Their concern reflected back at him.

'My lord,' urged William Stanley, 'this would be madness. He does not dictate to the king.'

'No,' replied Edward, 'he does not, which is why I must go with him as my own choice, as his guest, not as his prisoner.'

'But why?'

'It may be the only way I can save the lives of his hostages.'

But Hastings could not accept it. 'No, you are the king. The king! He cannot rule you.'

'You are right, of course, Hastings,' replied Edward, mastering his emotions. 'No man must rule the king. The decision is mine.'

He turned to Warwick. 'For the sake of our past love, Cousin, for the sake of my brother, and the poor souls in your captivity, for their loyalty to me, and for the sake of the realm, I accept your hospitality and will accompany you to Middleham until such time as our business is complete.'

Turning back to his men, he added, 'Trust me. He is not so foolish as to make an attempt upon my life. Go spread the word and ensure I have loyal men waiting in Yorkshire for the moment I choose to leave. Then we shall see what reckoning Warwick has coming.'

'My lord.'

Edward's attention was called back to the earl, who had dropped upon bended knee on the grass verge.

'I am humbled by your graciousness, my lord and king. I offer you my true apology for any actions that had the appearance of treason and I hope, with our talks, you will find yourself able to forgive me, and allow me to demonstrate my true loyalty to you.'

His words fell upon silence.

Edward returned to his circle. 'Hold true.' He spoke softly. 'Hold true and bear witness to this. Spread the word. Go to my queen, to her family, and we shall all meet again soon in Westminster.'

'My lord?' asked Warwick, with a hint of impatience.

Edward took hold of his reins. 'To Middleham then, where my brother anxiously awaits me. I am happy to accept your generous hospitality and opportunity for you to convince me of your loyalty, and I hear the hunting in the area is always good. Hastings, I shall send you a fat stag so that you might know I am faring well. Lead on, Warwick, your king commands it.'

The pinkish stone of Kenilworth projected up from the hill. It was heavily fortified, with wide, solid walls and a huge ditch. There would be no escaping, Rivers saw, as he was led out of the main keep and into the courtyard. They brought John behind him; he could hear the boy arguing with his guards.

A makeshift block had been set up on the stones. It stood there like a tomb.

So this was it. All these years had brought him to this. Loyal service, love, friendship, fatherhood. All ended here.

His captor handled him roughly.

'Are we to have no trial?' John cried. 'No justice? You cannot kill the king's relatives and think he will spare you.'

But Montagu simply looked on as they were brought forward.

'You cannot do this!' John struggled. 'The king will have your heads for treason. The battle is over. Prisoners deserve justice.'

Rivers turned to his son, heavy with the inevitability of the day.

'John, my son, best of sons, make your peace with God. You are soon to enter the kingdom of heaven.'

John stared back at him, mouth open wide.

His captor led him forward, forcing him down upon his knees. There was no time to picture the faces of his wife, his children, his grandchildren. Earl Rivers closed his eyes. 'Into your arms, O Lord, I commend…'

Jacquetta looked up to see them coming through the meadow. They were distant at first, a male and a female figure on the path with the grasses tall on each side. Their demeanour was serious but they walked with a mixture of purpose and reluctance, Elizabeth a little way behind Anthony. She was so proud of them both; they had grown so tall, so strong. They brought the scent of summer with them.

Behind her, the girls were splashing on the bank of the river. She'd given in to their demands to paddle and led them to a shallow spot, where the reeds ran green and bright. Little Elizabeth was picking out pretty stones to show to her sister.

Jacquetta raised her hand to wave. She saw that Elizabeth wanted to respond; her daughter's hand travelled upwards, as far as her shoulder, but it did not quite resolve into an answering wave. That was when Jacquetta realised something was wrong. And as they drew closer, she saw their faces were pale and serious.

'What is it?' she mouthed, although they could not hear her. The girls laughed, splashed their feet. Sunlight slanted down and danced on the grass at her feet.

'Mother?'

It was Anthony who spoke. He had picked up his pace, crossing the last stretch between them with long strides.

Jacquetta held herself still. Fears crowded in, the natural fears of any mother and the terror of what was coming.

Anthony took her in his arms. She was pulled close against his chest and he would not let her go. It was Elizabeth's face she could see approaching, streaked with tears.

'It's father and John.'

She paused, waited, willing time to freeze there.

'Mother, the rebels took them. They're gone.'

She wondered if she had heard correctly. 'Gone?'

'They're gone, Mother. A messenger came from Kenilworth. They were executed, both of them.'

'No, no, it's a mistake. They have not.'

She tried to pull away. Elizabeth's hands rested upon her shoulders and her voice shook with emotion.

227

'There was no trial. The battle was over. It was done in cold blood.'

'No,' insisted Jacquetta, cold as the feeling drained out of her, 'there has been a mistake, you'll see. They will come riding up tomorrow, wait and see.'

Anthony tried to speak again but she cut him off.

'No, no, it is a false report put about by Warwick. They would not dare. Richard is the father of the queen.'

'Mother?'

'Elizabeth, you must take over with the girls. I need to go and make preparations for their return, make sure the beds are ready.'

'But Mother?'

Elizabeth reached out to try and stop her mother as she passed.

Jacquetta brushed past, holding up her hands. 'No!' She hurried back towards the house.

'I'll get the girls,' said Anthony. 'You go after her.'

FIFTEEN

Prisoner, August 1469

And, by God, he owned these stones, these walls. Edward strode into the hall as if he owned the very air they breathed, spine erect, head held high. He walked like his father, with command, with authority, with the blood of York in his veins, with decades, or centuries of royal blood. He occupied the centre of the space as if it was the centre of the world, tall, broad, young, strong.

Warwick stared back at him, diminished in his own home.

'Where is my brother, George?'

'He is out hunting. He will be back shortly.'

'That is what you said when I asked last time, and the time before. Can it be that my brother avoids my sight? Can George, Duke of Clarence, your king-in-waiting, actually be a coward?'

Edward turned and looked about the place. He knew it well, having been here before, always as a guest but never under such circumstances. At the grand table, he had dined with Warwick, his wife and daughter; on this very floor, he had danced to the music of the Middleham waits. The former memories seemed incongruous

229

now. He turned, heavy with the changed circumstances and looked intently at the earl.

'So, come on then, my old friend, what's the plan?'

Warwick opened his mouth to answer but Edward continued. 'Because so far as I see it, your situation is unclear. You have tied yourself into a knot and cannot now untangle the threads. Maybe you believe you have overthrown me, deposed King Edward; if we take the escape to Calais, the forbidden marriage, the treasonous manifesto for a start, that would be bad enough, but then you return, incite rebellion, raise men against me and kill my loyal servants. No, wait!'

Warwick was trying to intervene.

'No, wait, you have done all this and more. Now you have me here, for what purpose? Do you intend to kill an anointed king, Warwick? Place my brother on the throne instead, my cowardly, disloyal, vain brother, who would just as soon as stab you in the back if it served his purpose? And why? In the hope that you can control George? So your grandchild inherits the throne? Do you think my family would allow that? My allies? The kings of Burgundy and Scotland? You think your friend, Louis, would not come to terms with me if I wished it? You think the English people would accept him, accept you, with my blood on your hands?'

'Edward…'

'No!'

Warwick waited. He was being uncharacteristically quiet during this exchange, his dark head held to one side, as if he was prepared to tolerate whatever Edward said. The king took it as a sign that he was aware of his guilt, even ashamed.

'So, let us say you are not fool enough to kill me, even to make it seem an accident. What then? You think to rule in my place? With what authority, with what power? Where are your supporters? Who has come rallying to your cry, Warwick, who? Are my council rushing to follow your orders? Do you have any orders to give?'

Furious, Edward turned away towards the door. 'And if I try and leave now? Return to my family and my throne? Will you prevent me?'

As he moved closer, two of Warwick's armed guards stepped in the way.

Edward laughed, fell back. 'Of course! Treason, gentlemen, treason.'

'It's for your own safety,' Warwick insisted, refusing to rise to Edward's tone.

'Of course! My own safety. Not yours. Not to prevent me coming and going at will, as a king should do. So, what now, Warwick? You are going to rule in my place? What of the country out there? What of London? You know it needs a steady hand. Where is your seal, your council? Why would you rule when there is a perfectly good anointed king living, king by right and conquest? My father and yours would be turning in their graves, Cousin.'

The last word was delivered with a bitter sting.

'I have called a parliament to assemble at York, later in September.'

'A parliament? In whose name? On whose authority?'

'In the name of the council.'

'Has the council been consulted? Did they agree to my imprisonment here?'

'It is in the service of the king. They will see that.'

'You might let the king decide upon his own service. That is the prerogative of kings. Or do you seek to speak for me?'

Edward's blood was up. Boiling over with rage, he stepped towards the earl, who stood firm, maintaining his composure, square chin held high. His stillness served only to annoy the king further.

'You have gone too far, Warwick. And what of my friends, Devon and Pembroke? Where are they?'

'I have sought only to serve you and act in your interests, to remove those who wished you harm.'

'Utter lies. You have sought only to protect and advance yourself.'

'I hope you will come to appreciate what I have done in your interests.'

'Appreciate?' Edward could not keep the sarcasm out of his voice. 'Of course, all I needed was time. And you, you decided what was best for me? If the shoe was on the other foot, Warwick, if you were king and I had acted thus, would you hesitate to bring down the full force of the law upon me for my treason?'

Warwick took a step backwards. 'I cannot reason with you in this passion. Cool your heels in here, or in your chamber if you prefer. We will talk again at length.'

He turned and walked away.

'And if I want to walk in the grounds?' the king called after him but received no reply.

Archbishop Thomas Bourchier looked at the faces assembled around the table. The Westminster chamber, with its stained-glass windows, was full of the heat of the summer. Yet, the place looked bare; the men had dwindled. Here were his own brothers, Henry, Earl of Essex, William and John, and the Lords Worcester, Arundel, Oxford, Exeter, the Stanleys, John Stafford, a swathe of bishops and others. They were grave in expression. The absences among them were notable.

'My friends and colleagues in the chamber will be the first to acknowledge,' he stated, 'that I have, hitherto, been a supporter of the Earl of Warwick, sometimes a defender of his actions and choices, even when he favoured the French marriage and spoke against the Burgundian match. I have been his friend, a true and kind friend, willing to listen to his position, and afford him the consideration of his rank and experience.'

The room looked back at him solemnly.

'And yet,' Bourchier continued, 'I cannot countenance his recent acts. I must disassociate myself entirely from the earl and reject all he has done since his departure to Calais.'

A murmur ran around the chamber.

'Friends, word has reached us of the beheadings of the Earls of Devon and Pembroke, so recently members of this chamber, welcomed to sit among us, who gave their best and most loyal service to the crown.'

Some voices spoke up softly, in disbelief, and others exclaimed aloud in anger. A few sat in silent grief, having already heard these tidings.

'Yes,' continued the archbishop. 'William Herbert of Pembroke, and his brother, Richard, who fought so bravely at Towton, were taken captive and executed after the battle. Our good friend Humphrey Stafford, Earl of Devon, another veteran of Towton, escaped the scene but was pursued and killed by a mob in Bridgewater.'

'But this is outrageous,' said the Bishop of Rochester, rising to his feet. 'It is not long since all these men sat around this table, engaged in business for the peace of this realm. It is little more than treason for Warwick to turn upon them like this, for nothing more than obeying a summons by their king.'

'Not just them,' added Bourchier. 'Warwick has turned upon our king, whom he now keeps at his leisure in Middleham Castle.'

'Should we send a delegation north to Middleham?' asked Arundel.

'At the present, Hastings, Suffolk and Norfolk await the king's instructions at York. I do not believe another army at present to be the best option, and it is not ours to summon. If the king requests it of us, I shall send out commissions to you all, but until then, the most pressing matter is the state of the capital. Kempe, will you speak of it?'

Thomas Kempe, Bishop of London, rose to his feet. He was a lean, grey-faced man, with a slight list to the left.

'It is true. The city is in the most dire condition of disorder and lawlessness. My carriage was almost set upon as I came here today, this morning, within curfew hours, by a group of apprentices. Shops have been looted, damage done to properties, and attacks in the streets can barely be contained. We have doubled the watch. The curfew will be shortened and harsh penalties inflicted, but the lawlessness grows and threatens to spread beyond our control. The people speak of Warwick and the king, but they do not understand the situation.'

'I confess,' interjected William Stanley, 'neither do I.'

There was a murmur of agreement.

'This is true,' Kempe acknowledged. 'We cannot expect the people to understand and the chaos created by the absence of a king fills them with terror and turmoil. Those of an evil disposition see it as an opportunity.'

'London needs its king,' said Bourchier. 'We might not send an army but we might send a letter of appeal to Warwick, calling upon him to resolve the London chaos, or else to release the king so that he might do so.'

'That is an excellent idea,' agreed Oxford. 'I will put my name to it.'

'And I,' added Essex.

'And I,' came the echo from around the room.

'Then let us draft it, and not a moment too soon.'

There was a knock upon the outer chamber doors.

'Who the devil can that be?'

A clerk brought a letter. Bourchier broke the seal and read the contents. A few moments passed before he raised his eyes heavily to the room.

'This is from the keeper at Kenilworth Castle, written in haste.' He took a deep breath, his voice weak and threatening to break. 'He writes to inform us of the beheading of Richard Woodville, Earl Rivers, and his son John.'

The news was met with silence. The assembled council could scarcely believe what they had heard.

Bourchier put down the paper. 'The queen's own father. We have known of the long-standing animosity between the earl and the Woodville family; he has made no secret of his dislike of the favour shown to them as the result of the king's marriage which he opposed. But the country was at peace. Such acts belong to a state of war; it is only Warwick who has brought us to this. These men were defending our king against the threat created by Warwick; there was no justification for their deaths.'

'Was any form of trial held?' asked William Stanley, grimly.

'No, the letter confirms it. It states that they were executed without ceremony.'

'And Anthony?' his brother, Thomas, asked.

'The letter makes no reference to Anthony, so we must believe that he remains alive. It appears that the Woodvilles were not even part of the battle. They were intercepted on the road.'

'I can scarcely believe it,' stated Norfolk. 'We were with the Woodvilles when the king bid them return to Grafton, mere weeks ago.'

'Come,' said Bourchier, with a new sense of purpose. 'Let us draft this letter with a different feel. We will make our disgust at Warwick's actions clear and refuse to recognise or support any leadership or regime he offers. Above all, we will demand the immediate release of the king and the cessation of all violent acts against his subjects.'

A while later, as the light was fading, the Stanley brothers made their way through the hall and into the courtyard. Thomas, Baron Stanley was the elder by a year, slightly taller, darker and flamboyant. He was the father of five children so far by Warwick's daughter, Eleanor. At his side was William, slighter, his features wider, his manner austere. In recent years, he had taken a wife but she was ailing. Court rumours suggested that the marriage had not been a happy one; it was true that Stanley was more frequently at the king's side than hers, as one of Edward's most trusted confidants.

'To supper,' Thomas urged, wrapping his cloak about him. 'Shall we join the hall or return to the city?'

'The hour is late; it's growing cold. I don't want to be out on the streets at the moment.'

'The hall it is then. And we'll eat all the sooner for it.'

William saw her in the doorway ahead. A fair-haired woman with a child of eight or nine. She was staring at them most urgently as if she wished to speak.

As they headed towards the double doors that led back inside, she stepped forward.

'My lords?'

She had been pretty once, but now she appeared tired, her finely-shaped eyes lined at the corners. The child was a girl, a sweet thing with tangled hair.

'Should you be here?' asked Thomas, somewhat abruptly.

William saw her patched kirtle, the worn shoes. 'Go ahead. I will deal with this.'

He turned back to her as his brother strode on ahead without a word, thinking of his stomach.

'How can I help you?'

'Sir, thank you. I was asking, and they said to find Lord Hastings, but I heard he was not here. I know he has the ear of the king.'

'You can speak to me. What is your business?'

'My name is Mary, sir. Mary Denny. Until recently I lived in Yorkshire, near the king's residence of Fotheringhay.'

'You were a servant there or a member of the household?'

'I sold them produce sometimes, for the table.'

Stanley nodded. 'And why have you come to London?'

'I tried to speak to the duchess, Lady Cecily, a few years ago but she sent me away. I've come for my daughter's sake.'

Stanley looked down at the girl, who met him with wide eyes. 'What's your name?'

'Grace,' she replied boldly. 'Grace, maybe Denny, but I don't know what I should say.'

Stanley looked at the mother. 'What does she mean?'

Mary summoned her courage. 'She is the king's daughter. I have tried to sustain her myself but I cannot find work. I want her to have just a little, just the simplest of alms from her father.'

'You are sure?'

'The king will remember me. He will know.'

'He does not know already?'

'I spoke with the Lady Cecily, asked her for help. Then I waited. I thought he might come or send for her, but there was nothing. So we came to London and I have been working in a cook shop but it was destroyed by looting. We have nowhere, nothing.'

Stanley saw that the child was shivering. The woman's words rang true with him; there would be time to investigate her claim later.

'Come, come inside. The king is away at present but we will find you a space, somewhere to sleep, something to eat.' He took the girl's chin in his hand. 'Does that sound good?'

She nodded and grinned. And he saw she had the look of Edward about her mouth.

'Thank you, sir, thank you so much. God bless you.'

'Come, this way, the king would not want his own flesh and blood to go without.'

* * *

The hawk soared high above them, caught a current of air and drifted upwards. Hastings followed it with his eyes until it dropped again and swooped behind the trees. The clearing on the edge of the forest was ideal for hawking, just as the landowner had promised.

'You see her?' Suffolk was pointing into the greenery. 'Look, she's there, upon the second branch up on the left.'

Hastings and Norfolk looked in the direction he indicated.

'No.' Hastings shook his head. 'I can't find her.'

'Me neither,' confirmed Norfolk.

'Right, wait,' Suffolk held out his arm with the huge leather glove as a perch for the bird. He rang a small silver bell, making a tinkling sound in the air.

The three men stood still, turned towards the trees. She was barely perceptible at first, just a shimmer in the shadows followed by a clap of wings. Her movement was so smooth and fast, so fixed upon them, that it was only when she was very close, almost above them with a great swooping sound, that the full scale of the bird impressed itself upon them. And then she closed inwards, folded her wings to her body, and settled upon Suffolk's arm.

'Good girl.' He rewarded her with a small treat.

Hastings looked around. 'Excellent, so far so good.'

'You think we should try and push a little further now?' asked Norfolk, following his gaze.

Beyond where they stood, the forest petered out to fields and the road through the valley.

'There's been no movement this morning, no one in or out from this direction,' said Hastings. 'I think it safe to move closer, at least so the castle is in sight. If Edward can see us from a window, he can get a message to us.'

Suffolk handed his hawk to the care of his squire. He nodded directly east. 'Let's walk across this way, pretend to be seeking out a better distance to fly the bird. I think we can safely come nearer.'

They walked a way further, through swathes of green land lined with trees, and fields full of sheep. Presently, a square of grey walls appeared, with the keep and chapel and towers protruding within. Ravens topped the walls and spirals of smoke stretched up to the sky. The outer court was crowded with low roofs. There was something foreboding and ominous about the look of the place, made even more so by their knowledge that the king was held captive within.

'Middleham Castle,' said Hastings, 'what are your secrets?'

Suffolk was surveying the area. 'We will let her fly here; the distance to the rise is more than sufficient. And we will be able to face the castle to watch discreetly. If I place myself at the far end, I can send her down towards you. Norfolk, your young eyes are probably the sharpest. You go to the far end, where you are best able to see the place.'

'Right.' Norfolk was already off, striding down the field towards the point where it dipped. The squire hurried after and helped him to attach the glove. The view of the valley stretched out before him, clearer here, perhaps the distance of three tiltyards, maybe four. The windows of the castle were visible now as dull dark spots against the stone. It was sufficient, for now. Any messenger from the king would not have to travel far.

Norfolk turned to see Suffolk and Hastings up on the rise. He lifted his arm to indicate that he was ready for the hawk and braced himself to take her weight.

The bird was a distant speck at first, a long line of stretched wings gliding effortlessly through the air. She lifted in the air, then fell low, and suddenly loomed large above him. He stood strong against her, unflinching, and felt her drop onto his hand, her talons wrapped about his fist. It was something of a personal triumph. He had never been a natural hawker. As a boy, he'd avoided the sport, preferring to ride or shoot arrows at the butts: now he could hit a target from further off than most men. He'd never taken to birds. He'd appreciated their beauty but disliked their unpredictability, and only in recent months had he worked more closely with them, honing his skills. Now he looked at the sheen of red and brown on the feathers of the magnificent creature on his arm.

He turned, pretending to survey the scene, considering her next flight. But his eye caught movement. A rider had been dispatched from the castle and was heading towards them. Looking up the rise, he saw that the others had spotted it too.

It was best to continue as if they had not noticed. He gave the signal and saw Suffolk raise his arm. With a powerful forward stroke, Norfolk sent the bird back into the air and watched it descend upon the duke. They repeated this twice more, disturbing the air with the creature's strong wing-beat, before the rider drew up on the road beside him.

Norfolk was relieved to see it was a mere youth although he was dressed in Warwick's livery. He did not recognise him and he hoped the servant wouldn't know them either.

'Gentlemen, what is your business here?'

'Nothing but a bit of sport,' Norfolk explained, 'for me and my fellows. We are the guests of Sir John Lloyd, whose estate lies to the west.'

'All this land belongs to the Earl of Warwick.'

'Oh, does it,' replied Norfolk, feigning innocence. 'Please accept our sincere apologies. We must have strayed further than we thought. We were seeking a suitable stretch to fly our bird and the three of us are strangers to these parts.'

The youth gave a curt nod.

'Does the earl mind if we hawk here? We mean no harm and this is the best spot. We will be gone soon, back to our supper at the hall.'

'You should move back to the lands of your host. The earl has important guests and their safety is paramount.'

'Important guests? Is it anyone we might have heard speak of?'

'You should move back to your host's lands.'

'Right away?'

The youth stared back at him, fixed and sullen.

'Very well, we shall retire. We meant no harm.'

'What are your names?'

'Never mind that, we are moving at once.' Norfolk gestured to Hastings and Suffolk, and began to walk away across the field. The pair, holding the bird between them, met him halfway. The liveried youth was still at the roadside, high on his horse, watching them retreat.

'We are trespassing on the earl's lands and have been asked to leave. He even asked our names but at that point I conceded and walked away.'

'He's still watching,' observed Hastings, looking back over his shoulder. 'He's going to watch all the way until we're completely out of sight.'

'Very interesting,' added Suffolk. 'They're clearly watching from the castle. We dare not get so close again; we should wait in York until Edward can send to us.'

'It's so frustrating,' railed Norfolk, 'to think the king might be at one of those windows.'

'We'll write to the council and inform them of what happened today. They may have instructions for us.'

'Such a state of affairs.' Hastings shook his head. 'I would gladly wring Warwick's neck with my bare hands if the opportunity arose.'

'You and half of England,' agreed Suffolk.

* * *

Edward watched the figures retreat into the green middle-distance. From the hall window they were nothing but tiny specks and their bird was invisible to the eye.

'Hawkers who strayed too far,' said Warwick, at his side. 'They've got the message. They won't come back. Probably local men, forgetting their place.'

His rider was already turning back on the road. The winding length of it stretched beneath them.

'You don't want to eat?' Warwick returned to the table where bread, meat and cheese was set out on gold plate, and flagons had been filled with wine.

'I've no appetite. And how do I know you do not intend to secrete some poison into my food and give out word that I have died of an illness?'

'You think your council would stand for that?'

'No, most likely not, but it would be too late for me.'

'I would not poison my old friend.'

'But you would rise against him and keep him captive? Wait, is that George? Or is it my assassin?'

A figure had appeared in the doorway, half in, half out of the shadow.

Warwick beckoned him forward. 'Clarence!'

George came reluctantly. The meeting had been inevitable but he had delayed it as long as possible. He was looking tired, unsettled, his dark hair cut short, his eyes shifty, conscious of the knowledge of having done wrong but bold enough to brazen it out. Something had changed in him lately. He had lost that old childish innocence, and the sweet, playful boy who loved to hunt and ride, whose eyes had been dazzled by feasts and dancing, had vanished. He was harder on the outside, darker on the inside.

'Welcome, Brother.'

'Really, George? This is my warm welcome? Being disobeyed, deceived and betrayed by my own brother, then brought here as a captive, and you offer me welcome?'

George shrugged. He strolled over to the table and began picking at a piece of meat. Warwick continued with his meal.

Edward watched them both steadily. 'I had not realised, until now, Brother, that you have no shame, no honour. Woe betide this family for it. Think how you break your mother's heart, setting brother against brother, and think, George, of what your father would say to you now, if he could? What counsel would he offer you?'

George slowly consumed a pie.

'George, what does your conscience say to you? How can you make your peace with God?'

'I have done everything for the best,' he replied, between mouthfuls, 'haven't I, Warwick?'

'For the best?' railed Edward. 'How can it possibly be for the best?'

'For my best,' said George, shamelessly. 'And for the good of the realm. Warwick understands.'

'It has been regrettable,' the earl added, 'that a stance had to be taken against your favourites, and that you had to be taken into our care. Temporarily, while the situation resolves. Regrettable but necessary. George has played his part in that.'

'No. It was not necessary. It was entirely avoidable. You have both acted with treasonable intent.'

'It was not treason to execute traitors,' George flared up. 'The Woodvilles have been influencing you against me and Warwick for years. You have favoured those upstarts over us to the detriment of the realm.'

Edward saw Warwick rise with a gesture of warning, but it was too late. He felt cold suddenly, despite the fire.

'What have you done? Warwick! What have you done? Tell me my wife is safe.'

'She is safe. I have not moved against the queen.'

'Who then?'

Warwick snapped at George. 'You see what your indiscretion has done?'

'How could I know you had not told him?' the duke retaliated. 'You don't keep me informed.'

'Prisoner I may be,' thundered Edward, 'but do not test my patience further.'

Warwick rose to his feet, leaving his meal. 'Earl Rivers and his son, John, were taken after the battle at Edgecote.'

'They were not at the battle. I sent them home to safety.'

'They were taken on the road and executed as traitors at Kenilworth.'

'Executed?'

'They were traitors.'

'Executed? My father-in-law and brother-in-law, the flesh and blood of the queen. How dare you?'

Edward felt the anger mounting inside him, boiling almost to the point of explosion. He bit the rage back, for the moment, but his hands were shaking. He thought of that moment when he had bid Rivers and John farewell: the good advice and warm wishes from the older man.

'A time will come,' he said through gritted teeth, 'when I am not contained within these walls, when I will have my strength back, and I can act. And then, when that time comes, I promise you, I will act.'

George looked back at him nervously. 'We acted for the best. It was done to remove your evil counsellors, just as our father did in the past.'

'It is not the same. There is no comparison. Father always worked for the family interest.'

'As we have.'

'Earl Rivers was my family. And John, my brother. God rest their souls. Your own greed and vanity drove you to ally with this traitor, and it has cost the lives of innocent men. Good men. This is on your conscience, George.'

'I am married,' George blurted out. 'My wife is to have a child. If it is a boy, he will be the heir to the kingdom.'

'This kingdom already has a king! And God will bless me with a son in time.'

Warwick and George exchanged looks.

'And Mother, George?' Edward continued. 'You would break her heart?'

'If she has any left,' added Warwick, sharply. 'She has been no friend of the Woodvilles.'

'You will not speak of my mother again,' Edward said coolly. 'I will be going hunting tomorrow. Prepare my horse. No one will stop me.'

And as he strode out of the hall, the guards stood aside to allow him up to his chamber.

It was summer. The height of the summer. The air was warm and the grass long and lush with that vividness of green after it has just been awakened and grown.

They were walking in the forest, hand in hand. She couldn't see his face but she knew it. She felt it there as she felt his presence beside her. There were birds flying overhead and flowers spread around their feet. Close by, a stream was babbling with water and children were laughing.

He was saying her name, over and over, softly, as he did when he looked into her eyes. And she stopped, turned to look up at him, to respond to his kiss.

But he was gone. Suddenly, nowhere to be seen. And the sky

darkened and rain poured down upon her, and all the birds began to screech like owls.

'Elizabeth, wake up.'

She opened her eyes with a start. Jacquetta's face was before her, her greying hair loose, her nightgown dishevelled.

'You were dreaming. It's alright. You're safe.'

They were sharing the big bed in the top room at Grafton. Elizabeth's daughters and sisters slept on the truckle beds spread around the floor.

'I was dreaming?'

'Yes.'

'Then he is not here. We are still in the nightmare.'

At this realisation, her eyes began to well up with tears. Her mother took her in her arms.

'What did you dream?'

'That he vanished. He was there beside me and then, suddenly, he was gone. God keep him safe.'

'There. No news is good news. We must trust that he is safe unless we hear otherwise. With every day that passes, it is more likely that he will return.'

Elizabeth thought of her father and brothers, of the silence that preceded their deaths, but she said nothing.

'You must rest, to be strong for his return. The council want us to go to Westminster for our safety. It will be the easiest place for him to find you. He is bound to go straight there.'

'Maybe,' Elizabeth replied. 'If you think it safe. We'll discuss it in the morning.'

'Very well. Let us try and get back to sleep.'

'You don't think, do you,' she asked, her mind troubled by midnight fears, 'that somehow we cursed them? With our little game of the names cast into the fire? You don't think that we invoked some sort of evil magic and brought this upon us?'

'No, not at all,' replied Jacquetta. 'It was a game, nothing more. You must not think it. There is no such thing as magic. There is only the good and evil that is in men. Now go to sleep.'

But as she rolled onto her side, preparing to sleep, her face was wet with tears.

'It is hers,' the man stammered, holding out the strange mannequin in his hands.

Richard, Earl of Warwick, looked down at it, with its misshapen limbs and long, unwieldy head. It appeared to be fashioned from some crude metal, perhaps lead. How the man had found it or brought it to his castle remained a mystery.

'What is your name?'

For a moment, the face looked blank. The eyes boggled and the mouth flapped open.

'Good God, man, it is a simple question. What is your name?'

They were standing in the great hall with a fire roaring behind them in the grate. There was work to be done that day and the precious hours of daylight were ticking past.

'My name? My name?' It was his struggle to remember that first made Warwick suspicious.

'My name is Thomas Wake.'

'And who is Thomas Wake? Do I know you?'

'I live beyond the village, at the crossroads, with my mother. She keeps geese.'

'And you, Thomas Wake, what do you do?'

'I'm a labourer. I do any jobs that come my way.'

'And what is this strange thing you have brought before me?'

He peered down into the man's hands again. Wide, crude, dirty hands, streaked with soil, the nails black and chipped.

'This figure was brought to me. It was found by Harry in his house.'

'Harry?' Warwick looked around, beginning to lose patience.'

'Harry Kyngeston of Stoke Bruerne, he found it in his house after the soldiers left. And he's an honest man, Harry, ask anyone hereabouts.'

'Which soldiers?'

'The ones who were once with Earl Rivers.'

'Oh?' The earl was interested again. 'Let me see it.'

He took the strange man-form into his hand. It had the appearance of a crude soldier or a man-at-arms, with what might be a sword in its hand.

'But it is hers, you see,' urged Wake, becoming excited. 'She made it, Lady Rivers, as an effigy of you, my lord earl. So that she might harm you. You see how it is broken in the middle? She has used it to try and inflict harm upon yourself.'

Warwick's first rational response was to laugh. The local people had such strange ideas about the forces of the world and in hidden dark acts, that every rain fall, or every sick calf was attributable to acts of foul play. Then a second light began to dawn in his mind.

'How do I know this, Wake? How do I know you have not picked up some child's toy and brought it here out of a sense of grudge against Rivers and his wife?'

He stared into the man's pale eyes, wondering how easily he could be bought.

'I would swear my life upon it, my lord.'

'Might you? Then I have a use for a man like you. Truthful, loyal, dedicated. You want to help me, Thomas?'

'I do, my lord.'

Warwick nodded and wrapped the mannequin in towards his body.

'I will need to keep this safe. You must tell your story to my clerk, who will write it down, for I need to take it to London.'

For a king, his heart was beating too fast. It shouldn't be, he should have command of the situation, but he was also a man with the mortality and frailties of a man. A swift knife could dispatch him from this world. He was not immune to that just because he wore a crown. And yet, he was the Edward who had led his men at Mortimer's Cross, when the three suns had risen in the sky; he was the Edward who had fought through the snow at Towton; the same Edward who had defied Warwick and married where he chose. He was the king. This land was his for the ruling, this castle, these men, all given at his pleasure. He was free to come and go as he pleased. And go he would.

He had little more than he stood up in. His cloak, boots, the clothes he wore when he had been taken on the road. The route was clear. He left his chamber and walked along the corridor to the staircase. Servants stood aside to let him pass. The stairs took him down to the hall. Warwick and George, seated at the table, did not rise as he entered, and he passed through. Without a word, he headed for the double doors where the guards had recently barred his way. His heart beat faster as he approached. If he was allowed through the door, he would make it outside. If they blocked him here, the situation would take a far more serious turn. He did not want to have to fight his way out, but if it came to it, there was little choice.

No guards appeared.

'Enjoy your hunting,' called George.

Edward did not turn, did not reply. He kept on walking out into the courtyard and towards the stables. A boy brought his horse, ready saddled.

Without speaking it, they had admitted defeat. Warwick was no fool. He knew they had reached an impasse, and it was better to let

Edward walk out than to keep him prisoner indefinitely. He would ride to York where his friends awaited him and, from there, back to London. With a churning bitterness in his belly, the king mounted his horse and threw one look back at the castle. Those inside could no longer be trusted or counted upon as kin. These bloody days had changed everything.

SIXTEEN

Slanders, October 1469

The city of London lay waiting on a cool October morning. The rhythms of life, of voices and lutes, of cartwheels and animals, rolled out through the streets. Feet trod the pathways, stepping over mud and dung, avoiding puddles, seeking out the dry, flat spaces. Rats darted out of their way; birds clamoured for scraps. Under their feet, water pulsed through hidden channels, surging to meet the Thames.

Along Cheapside, the market stalls were set out in two aisles. Riders had to force their horses through the middle, driving the shoppers aside. Powerful and tall, the beasts' haunches moved slowly alongside the colourful awnings, the men astride them level with the upper storeys. Across the tables were spread leather goods and tools, old clothes, crates of apples, bowls of herbs and vegetables with the earth still clinging to their roots. Children sat around the cross, kicking their heels and throwing acorns. It was gold in the sunlight, having been newly gilded and mended early in Edward's reign. A little boy looked down into the stone trough of water where the horses drank and saw the clouds reflected above.

In the yard outside St Paul's Cathedral, a preacher stood upon the stone steps, calling out the word of God. A group had assembled around him, listening as he declaimed the works of the devil and his evil influence upon those who had chosen a life of sin and luxury. He had been on pilgrimage to Rome, to Santiago and to Jerusalem: he almost drowned in a storm crossing back to England, but God had saved him for this purpose. His indulgences were for sale, with the seal of the Pope, a good price to guarantee the path to heaven. Above him, the city bells began to ring, travelling out all across the city, along the streets, in through open doors and windows, waking the sleepers, summoning the faithful.

On the river, a hundred little wooden vessels bobbed on the water, carrying people and goods out of the city. Some stayed in the deeper pool of London, docking by Billingsgate, where the big ships came from the east to unload their spices and strange fruits. Others braved the rapids of the bridge, where the water ran white under the archways, and boats had been smashed against the stone, and lives lost in the swell. Some swam smoothly over the water on the other side, where the waters ran past the backs of courtiers' homes, Blackfriars and the Savoy Palace, and round the bend towards Westminster and beyond. They all heard the boom of the cannon emanating from the Tower to announce the return of the king.

As soon as he'd left Middleham, Edward had summoned his friends to his side. Hastings, Suffolk and Norfolk had been waiting for him at York; Essex, Arundel and Richard, Duke of Gloucester, who had just turned seventeen, had ridden up to join them so that they might all accompany him as he went south. They'd progressed slowly through towns and villages, giving Edward a chance to display himself as a returning king with his loyal council. Crowds turned out, through loyalty and curiosity. Men proclaimed him along the road and some even joined his journey. And now, the huddle of London was almost upon them: the vastness of that capital, throbbing with life and intrigue. Where plans were made, wars wagered, and hearts won and lost. He remembered the moment, as a boy, when he had ridden in ahead of Edmund to join their father at court. They'd come from the quiet greenness and flowing rivers of Ludlow to the corridors of Westminster. And for a moment, he caught their faces, their voices. He recalled Edmund's attempts at composure when he turned briefly at the gates and caught his brother unawares. He'd been nervous, Edward could see, but he had done his best to hide it. That time felt like a different age now.

The bells were calling. They came down the other side of the hill, along the road that led through fields and orchards, towards the city walls. Edward could have taken the road to the west, and circumvented the city entirely, but he wanted to show his face through the streets, riding high, so the people knew he had returned. At the Charterhouse, the mayor and aldermen were waiting, lined up in their red and purple gowns, and what must have been a hundred guildsmen in their blue robes. The mayor came forward to greet him, and the city waits sounded their trumpets of welcome. Then John Rotherham, Bishop of London, stern of manner. Together they processed slowly down the hill, where people had come out to line the street, but their faces were solemn. Before they reached the descent, Edward paused and looked over the city ahead.

'Is London quiet today?'

'Today, yes, my lord.'

'But not yesterday?'

The mayor and bishop exchanged glances before Rotherham spoke. 'We have been troubled in your absence, my lord, by lawlessness and rioting. The people are restless.'

Edward nodded. He had known the consequences of his imprisonment would be far-reaching. Justice and peace must be restored and he knew he could do it, only the stain of Warwick's betrayal hung heavy upon him.

'I will speak with the watch, accompany the nightly patrols. There will be harsh penalties for those who break the law. We will ensure that peace returns.'

'Thank you, my lord.'

'And my council?'

'They await you at Westminster, ready for your command.'

'Gather the men close. We'll ride in a tight band, three abreast, and give a show of strength. Send the trumpeters ahead to announce our arrival.'

A dozen men in livery began the march forward, each carrying a dull bronze-coloured bugle. The king watched as they passed through the gate ahead and heard the blast of the instruments in unison. The mayor sent forward his guards, marching in format. Edward then spurred his horse into action and beckoned to the others to follow at a steady trot, in order to see and be seen. He rode tall, head held high, but eyes attuned to every movement. Through the gates they rode, where the houses were banked up against the walls, and people had gathered at the sound. Some of the faces were blank, uncertain, as people were interrupted, half-hurrying about their daily business, but others waved, and a few voices cheered, and then the cheering spread and began to multiply.

'The king, the king!'

As they rode further in, more faces appeared, coming out of houses and shops. A marketplace paused; a church emptied. Sellers halted calling out their wares; a preacher was silenced; children stopped playing.

'Long live the king!'

Edward waved graciously, a feeling of relief spreading through him as they passed down to the junction with Cheapside and turned westward in the direction of St Paul's. The city looked unkempt, there was no denying it. The streets were unclean in places, and one or two shop fronts on Goldsmith's Row bore damage. But the welcome was warm. The cathedral bells pulled them closer.

'My lord, my lord!'

A figure darted before the king, causing his horse to rear up. Edward clasped the reins and braced himself against the movement, pulling the beast back in line. At his side, Hastings had automatically reached for his sword.

A man cowered before them, old and broken-looking, hands held up in defeat. Edward saw at once that he posed no threat.

'Please, my lord, my shop was looted and I have no livelihood. I'm fifty this winter, with a family and no means of supporting them. I can't build it up from scratch again.'

'And I!' called another voice from the other side, a woman with her head wrapped in a scarf. 'I'm a widow. My tavern was attacked. I can't afford the repairs.'

Edward held up a hand for silence.

'I hear your grievances. In my absence, many wrongs have been committed. Bring your complaints to Westminster tomorrow morning and I will hear you all. Those who have lost their livings shall be recompensed.'

The old man dropped to his knees. 'God bless you, my lord, bless and keep you safe.'

And the king rode on to the clamour of support.

From her private chapel at Westminster, Cecily could hear the bells. The noise poured in through the window, with its brightly coloured glass saints, even into that quiet place of sanctuary. She was on her knees before the altar, where she had set up her gold tablet set with jewels and the painting of the Virgin Mary. But even the velvet cushion she knelt upon could not prevent her from feeling the hard stone floor below. After an hour of prayer, the muscles in her legs were trembling and her feet were numb. She turned to her daughter, Elizabeth, Duchess of Suffolk, who was standing patiently behind her with bowed head.

'Help me up.'

Elizabeth placed her arm about her mother's shoulders and helped her rise. Cecily could have gladly sought a chair, her bones aching with fatigue, but proud and regal as ever, she remained standing, the better to meet the occasion.

'Go slow, go slow, let these old feet wake from their sleep.'

They stood together in a pool of sunlight as the tingling life crept back into the old woman's toes.

'Your husband is returning.'

'I believe so,' Elizabeth added, 'and Edward.'

'Yes,' said Cecily, grim with anticipation but full of relief. 'So he is.'

'You are not pleased?'

'Of course, I am pleased that he is safe.'

'But?'

'But how should any mother choose between her sons?'

'I did not think,' said Elizabeth, offering her mother her arm, 'that either of them had asked you to.'

They left the quiet confines of the chapel and headed down a brightly lit corridor, hung with tapestries, that took them through the royal apartments. Guards stood aside at the furthest door to allow them to pass into the public areas of the palace, the rooms where the courtiers were gathering in anticipation of the king's arrival. Cecily nodded towards the White Hall, her breathing coming short and rasping. Any exertion cost her dearly these days.

'We will wait in there, away from the rabble.'

The White Hall was dignified, formal, but smaller than the great hall, where the king would initially be received. It was the place where the king's closer circle could enjoy a degree of privacy. Cecily headed towards the fireplace, where chairs had been placed, but she was not the first to have had that idea.

Hearing them approach, Queen Elizabeth, Jacquetta, Duchess Rivers, and Anthony Woodville, rose from their seats. Cecily halted in her tracks.

Elizabeth, Duchess of Suffolk, took the lead by bowing low before the queen, forcing her mother to remember protocol and bow her head as low as she might without pain. The atmosphere between them was very different to their last meeting.

'Rise,' commanded the queen, 'and be seated.'

Anthony stepped aside so that Cecily might take his chair. They all watched in silence as she eased herself into it, no longer able to make the choice of standing equally before them.

'We had not heard of your arrival,' Elizabeth of Suffolk offered.

The queen and Jacquetta seemed loath to answer. It was Anthony, again, who stepped into the void. 'It was late last night, after we heard Edward was on his way.'

'You had a safe journey?'

'Safe enough, thank you.'

And with that, a brutal silence fell between them, each side seething with unspoken words. The spectres of Earl Rivers and John Woodville loomed large between them.

It was Elizabeth of Suffolk again who acted as mediator. 'Please do believe, we were truly sorry and distressed to hear of your losses.'

Cecily tensed at the words, wishing her daughter hadn't uttered them.

The queen inclined her head with grace, indicating goodwill towards her namesake. But Jacquetta could hardly bite back her anger and shook her head with bitterness.

'And where is George now? Where is the darling Clarence? Is he forgiven? Or is he already planning his next move against my family? Who would he take next? My babies? Our queen?'

'Mother!' Elizabeth Woodville placed her hand softly on Jacquetta's arm. 'It was not done by these women.'

'It was done by the son she raised.' Jacquetta turned back to Cecily, who was sitting dignified and composed, trying to rise above it all. 'A son with such arrogance and ambition, and such little family love and loyalty that he would rise against his own brother.'

'You are wrong, madam,' said Cecily, evenly. 'The only ones he rose against were those who were threatening to influence the king for evil. It was the ultimate act of loyalty to protect the king.'

'To influence the king for evil?' Jacquetta cried. 'Did my husband and son influence him that way? The grandfather and uncle of the princesses? You can dress this up in any way you wish. I understand why you must. It must be an unbearable grief, as a mother, to see one son turned against the other, to realise that you inspired so little love and family loyalty that it would come to this. We may have lost our two dear loves but they were prized above all riches, and they knew it. Our family love transcends the grave, Cecily. What of yours?'

Cecily's face was very white. 'Do not speak this way to the mother of the king.'

'You want to talk about protocol? About rank? Because the father and brother of the Queen of England have been murdered. You think the king will be pleased about it?'

'Those who were a threat to the king have been removed.'

'No, they haven't,' whipped back Jacquetta. 'The threats to the

258

king reside at Middleham Castle. Will you be removing your errant traitor son?'

'Be cautious when you throw around the accusation of traitor…'

'Was George? Was Warwick? They named me as a traitor too, and Anthony. What would you do now, order our arrests?'

Cecily began to rise slowly to her feet but the queen raised her hand.

'No,' said Elizabeth. 'We are leaving. We are going to meet my husband first as befits my rank. You will wait for him to come to you here.'

Cecily froze in her chair as the three of them walked out in front of her. 'Upstarts,' she muttered under her breath. 'Upstarts and impertinents. There is witchcraft in their success, mark my words. Witchcraft!'

Elizabeth saw him before he saw her. She knew him anywhere: the particular shape of his shoulders, the way he moved, the way he held his head. He was at the far end of the hall, having dismounted and entered through the main gates, surrounded by members of his council. And she knew it was incumbent upon her to remain upon the dais, poised, dignified, regal, overseeing the hall until he was ready to come to her. She should wait, like a queen, like a queen in control. But suddenly, she felt the urge of overwhelming love. It washed through her like a tide, pulling her towards him. And she could not control her feet, queen or no queen. She had to hurry down the length of the hall, as courtiers and councillors stepped aside, towards the place where he stood.

'Edward?'

He turned. He saw her. Their eyes met and locked, and he was compelled to hurry towards her. A few paces more and they met, with arms wrapped tight about each other, clasped in relief. She shyly raised her head to meet his kiss, conscious of the crowd.

'My love,' he whispered. 'Thank God.'

Cardinal Bourchier stood at the head of the table and surveyed the assembled council. They were greater in number since their last meeting, with the addition of Hastings, Suffolk and Norfolk, and now, the king and young Richard, Duke of Gloucester. Edward had resumed his usual chair, an ornate piece carved with the arms of the house of York, which had stood empty since July.

'My lords, I am certain that you share the gratitude I feel in being able to welcome back our king, Edward, the fourth of that name, and wish to join me in giving thanks for his delivery from harm and his restoration to his rightful place among us.'

The chamber sent up a roar of agreement. Edward rose to his feet.

'I thank you for your welcome. Those of you who have remained in London during my absence, during difficult times, I thank you for your efforts. I was met in the city today with good will, and I was able to see for myself some of the damage and the concern of my subjects. When you leave here, spread the word that I shall be hearing petitioners in the great hall tomorrow. We will restore our city to its greatness.'

'It will be proclaimed at St Paul's and at the great conduit, and all the crosses,' promised Bishop Rotherham.

'We must speak of the events of the last months,' continued Edward, his face turning grave. 'It cannot be avoided. The way the situation unfolded took me by surprise. I will be the first to admit that I did not act as soon as I might have.'

'But you didn't…' began Hastings. Edward silenced him with a look.

'I must consider my part in this before I can judge that played by others.' He looked up across the chamber. 'Yes, my lords, dissention was growing in my own house and I did not act to quell it. I was too slow to accept the evidence of my own eyes, and too unwilling to believe that such a threat might come from so close to home. Thus, I must take my part in the responsibility for the upheaval and the deaths that have resulted from it. I was not the perpetrator but I did not act soon enough to prevent it. I was too trusting. I believed in family and loyalty.'

'As you should!' added Bourchier.

'We must look to remembrances of our dead. Memorials and services will be held for our dear and loyal friends and servants, William Herbert, Earl of Pembroke, and Humphrey Stafford, Earl of Devon. Their families will be provided for, as will those of the soldiers who died so bravely in the field at Edgecote. There will also be memorials to those close to me, whose lives were taken so injudiciously, without justice. I speak of my own father-in-law, Earl Rivers, and my brother, his son, John Woodville. Their names will never be forgotten.'

'Amen to that,' pronounced one of the bishops, and the word was echoed on the lips of the assembled group.

'But, my lords,' said the king, drawing himself up to his full height. 'There cannot be talk of reprisals. There will be no penalties imposed as these will prevent us from moving forward in amity. I have considered this question at length and I require your forbearance. I have written to the Earl of Warwick and my brother, George of Clarence, insisting that they submit a full and binding apology for their roles in this situation, and if I receive it, I have assured them that they will be forgiven.'

The chamber murmured.

'My lord,' asked Bourchier, 'may I speak?'

Edward indicated that he might with a wave of his hand.

'Thank you. My lord, you began your speech with the recognition that you had been too forgiving, too trusting already. Surely this must be a moment for action? A time to send a clear message. Treason was committed. If you ignore it, you will appear weak in their eyes and lay yourself open to further attacks?'

Edward nodded. 'This is a position I have considered, and I have prayed and deliberated long over my course. I do believe the main force behind the uprising to have been the Earl of Warwick, and it was he who deprived me of my liberty at his castle. I believe, therefore, that if he gives me his apology, it is then the task of the earl to prove his loyalty to me. I intend to send him to the northern border, where we have heard reports that the standard of the late Lancastrian Henry VI has been raised by his kin. He can display his regret by suppressing their campaign.'

'And the Duke of Clarence?'

'I believe my brother to have acted rashly, foolishly, but not maliciously. He was led astray, but his intentions were never to depose me.'

'Can we be certain of this?' asked Bourchier. 'Now that Clarence is married to Warwick's own daughter, he surely has divided loyalties?'

'I will bring my brother to court and keep him close.'

The archbishop nodded. 'Very well, very well. Might we ask your brother what he makes of this; I mean your other brother, Richard of Gloucester? As he is the other son of York and must have an opinion on this?'

All eyes turned unexpectedly to Richard, who had been sitting quietly listening at the side. The youngest member of the council, he was accustomed to following and absorbing the information of his elders. But seventeen was almost a man, even if he was as small and slight as one of his sisters, pale from lack of sleep, brought on by the pain in his back.

'Richard?' asked the king. 'You heard Bourchier. Are you happy to speak your mind on this?'

The lords turned, some amused, some interested, to hear the first pronouncements of a youth they recalled clinging to his mother's skirts. Richard gazed back at them all with dark, limpid eyes. They might underestimate him if they chose but here, at last, was his voice.

He climbed slowly to his feet. He was learning to master his balance so that his list to the side was countered and the pain concealed. His face was a mask that showed no sign of his struggles.

'My lord, I would speak if you permit it.'

'Speak away, Brother.'

'It grieves me to admit that our brother, George, Duke of Clarence, is an ambitious and scheming traitor. He has conspired against you and caused the deaths of your loyal friends and relatives, and he will not repent in his heart. His apologies ring hollow because he will always aspire to more. You can't afford to show him leniency or charity because he shares our blood. If you do not deal with him harshly, he will rise against you again, and next time, he may defeat you.'

The council chamber sat in stunned silence.

Eventually, Bourchier turned to the king. 'The young duke speaks the truth.'

Edward's mouth was set firm. 'Charity and forgiveness are the teachings of God. What kind of king would not practice mercy? George will see the error of his ways and repent. We are the York family. It is what father would have wanted.'

'But, my lord,' began the archbishop.

'No!' Edward snapped. 'I will not take counsel on this. I extend my brother my charity. It is for no man here to meddle with my conscience or my soul.'

There was a moment of silence.

Then Bishop Rotherham rose slowly to his feet. 'Before we conclude our business, there is one final matter that must be brought to the king's attention.'

Edward's head snapped up. 'Something more?'

Rotherham looked uneasily round the room. 'We have received an approach by a Leicestershire man by the name of Thomas Wake. He has an accusation to put to your lord.'

'An accusation, against me?'

'No, my lord, against the queen's mother?'

'Against Jacquetta? For shame, what can this be?'

'Forgive me, my lords, I only bear his message and am filled with as much disgust towards it as your good selves will be when you hear of it.'

He drew out an object wrapped in cloth, about the length of a man's forearm and slowly unwound the material. A strangely shaped metal figure was inside, with long thin limbs, broken in the centre. Rotherham held it up for the chamber to see.

'This item has been sent to us by Wake after it was discovered in a house in Leicester where soldiers in the service of Earl Rivers had been billeted.'

'What is it?' asked Edward.

'Wake claims it is the effigy of the Earl of Warwick, created for the purpose of witchcraft with the intent to do the earl harm.'

'What utter nonsense. Why bother us with this?'

'Only, my lord, because Wake makes the ridiculous claim that it was the creation of the queen's mother.'

A gasp was heard in the chamber. The words were repeated in varying combinations of doubt and anger.

Edward's face was set like stone. 'The queen's mother? Countess Rivers? On what foundation does he base this allegation?'

'This is indeed a terrible slander,' agreed Bourchier.

'And one intended to harm her, just as much as the axe that took her husband. Come, Rotherham, what is the basis of this?'

'I fear it is the work of Warwick. Wake is known in the area of Warwick Castle, and likely to be one of his tenants, or at least, his man.'

Edward rose to his feet. 'Good God, if Warwick is behind this, I will have his blood!'

'Be cautious,' urged Bourchier. 'This could inflame the situation again. That is precisely what Warwick hopes for, if indeed he is behind this.'

'He's right,' added Hastings. 'Whoever did this is seeking to test you. They want a reaction. Do not give it to them. We will simply cast this child's doll into the fire and speak no more of it.'

'And Jacquetta will not know.'

'She will not.'

'But there is nothing, no actual certainty that this plan was devised by Warwick?'

Rotherham looked uncertain. 'The locality certainly suggests it. Wake states he took it to Warwick Castle but he will speak no more on it.'

'Perhaps, my lord,' spoke up the Duke of Norfolk, 'you might permit Oxford and I to loosen his tongue a little?'

Edward nodded. 'You are all wise in your counsel. Our rejection of this trifle will test the earl. If he does intend to hurt me, he will strike again in some other way. There will be other occasions when I can press his loyalty.'

'No doubt there will be soon,' Bourchier agreed. 'The earl is not well known for his patience.'

'My lord?' Hastings had been waiting for the king in the garden doorway.

'William? What is it?'

'I would speak with you on a matter of some delicacy.' He gently stroked his sandy beard with its flecks of grey.

Edward looked down the corridor. Elizabeth was waiting for him; they were to dine together in their private chambers. 'Be swift then.'

'I will. But it is a private matter. May we step outside?'

The autumn afternoon was fading and the light in the garden dimming. The leaves on trees and bushes were already turning, despite the sunshine of the last few days. Yellow, orange and brown were as common hues as green, and the paths were lined with the mulch caused by night-time rains. At the far end, a man and woman were watching a girl who was playing amid the remaining flowers. Edward frowned at them vaguely, recognising William Stanley but not the others.

'It is a personal matter, my lord, of yours, of which I speak.'

'Of mine? Be brief, man.'

'During your absence, a young woman came to court with a child. A girl of almost nine years. She claimed it was your child.'

Edward shook his head as if he could not absorb this.

'A woman, and a child which she says is mine? I know of no such thing.'

'She gave her name as Mary Denny, my lord. She says she visited you once at Fotheringhay Castle.'

And there it was again, fresh in his memory: the soft evening light, the golden-haired girl with the cat-like eyes and pert mouth. He recalled her shape as they danced together and the softness of her skin, yielding in the darkness of the woods.

'I do recall her.'

'She seeks provision for the child, nothing more. She awaits your pleasure, my lord.' Hastings nodded across the grass to where Stanley stood beside a fair-haired woman and a girl, bending to inhale the scent of a herb bush.

Edward turned and looked with fresh eyes. The girl could be his; the age fitted, so far as he recalled and, even from that distance, she had the look of him. It was a strange sensation, a new knowledge that transformed her from hundreds of other children of her age into one who bore his blood in her veins. Royal blood.

'What is her name?'

'Grace, my lord.'

Edward walked forward. The woman spotted him and turned, dropping her knee at once and bending her head. As soon as he was close to her, he spoke softly.

'Please, rise.'

She looked up at him, her eyes both hopeful yet questioning and fearful. She was still beautiful about the eyes, and the wide, generous mouth had not changed although her face was worn with time.

'You are well, Mary?'

'Very well, my lord. Thank you for seeing us.'

'The child is mine? There is no question?'

'None at all. She is your daughter.'

He nodded. 'I will ensure you are both provided for.'

For a moment he watched her, playing unconsciously among the blooms. Then when she paused and looked up, he called her by name. She came at once, with a quickness of manner and bright, enquiring eyes. Lord Stanley came too, nodding his greeting.

Edward looked down at the girl. 'Good day to you, Grace.'

'Good day, my lord.' She dropped something like an awkward low curtsey, which he imagined her mother had taught her.

'How do you like court?'

She gave a shrug. 'It's big.'

'I suppose it is,' he replied, 'if you aren't used to it. You have been amusing Lord Stanley?'

'A most quick wit and pretty manners,' Stanley confirmed. 'But she has quite worn me out already. She needs some employment for her hands and her mind!'

'How would you like to stay here, Grace? You could be helpful and busy, and there are lots of entertainments here and interesting people. I can find a place for you in the household of my sister.'

'Mother too?'

'Yes, your mother too.' He looked back to Mary. 'If that is what you wish?'

The slanting eyes were already swimming with tears.

'Then it is settled. You will have board and lodgings here at the court and you may exercise in this garden and have other privileges relating to the royal blood. She will have the best of everything, and in return, she will be known as Grace Plantagenet.'

'Thank you, my lord,' Mary enthused, 'thank you so much. I had feared you would prove of the same mind as your mother.'

'As my mother?' The king stopped dead. 'You had already spoken to her? Mother already knew about her?'

'Um, I…' Mary faltered, looking between Edward and Stanley as if she had done wrong.

'Come, you have nothing to fear. You had formerly spoken with her?'

'Yes, I was desperate. A few years ago, I went to the castle at Fotheringhay. I'd hoped to find you. I did speak to your lady mother but she sent me away. I fear she did not believe me. Did I do wrong?'

'Not at all. It was not you who did wrong.' Edward looked back at the child, with her wide smile. 'I wish you had come sooner.'

The fire was kindling nicely in the grate. Cecily judged it the right time to drop the scented pastille onto the flames. It dropped through the twigs and settled on the log where it would soon begin to glow,

268

releasing its spicy scent. Behind her, at the table laid out with sweet-meats in her private room, George was pouring a glass of spiced wine. His wife, Isabel, Warwick's daughter, sat in the corner, sewing in her lap. She was a slight, dark-haired girl of nineteen, whose face had once been pretty but now wore the heaviness of disappointment. She was stitching a garment for the child she was expecting in the spring.

'Duchess Rivers is here,' Cecily explained, without taking her eyes off the flames. 'And the older son, Anthony. You would be wise to stay out of their way for a while.'

'I am more than equal to anything the upstarts have to say or do.'

'And you have proved it, but do you want to be forgiven?'

George drank noisily. 'Only to make your life easier, Mother.'

'You think it makes no difference to yourself? You would happily live an outcast from court for the rest of your life? And your wife and child? If it is a boy she's carrying, it might one day be king.'

Isabel resumed her sewing without a word.

'Yes, yes,' George conceded. 'I will play the game for your sake, Mother. But don't expect me to enjoy it.'

'Does Warwick dare show his face?'

'He is going north. He has accepted Edward's challenge to put down the Lancastrian murmuring on the border. That should win him some time, and some favour.'

'And then what?' The old woman turned. 'Then what? Another plot? Another ridiculous waste, setting yourself against your brother? You are lucky he has his father's soft heart. If he had mine, he might have already put you to death.'

As she spoke, the door flew open without warning. George drew his sword and Cecily recoiled into her chair. Only Isabel seemed unmoved.

Edward strode into the chamber, expecting to find his mother alone. Instead, he faced his brother's drawn sword. Shamefacedly,

George immediately slid it into its sheath, while Isabel carefully slipped onto bended knee.

Composing himself, Edward merely stood and waited. Realising what was required of him, and with a look to his mother, George bowed low.

Edward did not give him permission to rise. 'It would appear you are back at court, without having come to ask my leave to be here, or my forgiveness.'

'We just arrived,' George replied. 'I was making sure my wife was comfortable after the journey, for she is with child, and then I would have sought you out at once.'

Edward looked to Isabel, still kneeling. 'You may rise.' And then he glanced at his mother in her fireside chair. 'And you? You knew he was planning to return?'

Cecily threw up her hands. 'He just walked in. Should I have called the guards?'

Her tone set Edward on edge.

'Mother, did a woman come to you at Fotheringhay, a few years back, with a child? Asking for my help?'

'Child, what child?'

'My child. A girl. She would have been four or five then. She spoke with you but you sent her away.'

Cecily pursed her lips. 'I don't recall. It was probably a beggar.'

'No,' replied Edward, 'it was your grandchild.'

He looked at the pair of them, from his mother to George, and from him back to Cecily again, and sensed defiance in their eyes.

'You will both stay here this afternoon, confined to your chamber. Cool your heels until dinner. Then you will come and pay respects to my wife and her family.'

'Edward!'

George stepped forward angrily. 'You don't mean it! Come on!'

But the king had left, closing the door behind him. George tried to follow but found his way barred by two guards.

'Edward!' he shouted after his brother's receding back. 'Edward!'

SEVENTEEN

The Rebels Defeated, March 1470

'For you, my lady.'

Elizabeth, Queen of England, looked up from her sunny spot in the alcove. She had chosen it because of the unseasonable warmth of the day, with its sheltered, south-facing aspect overlooking the Thames. The warm light played upon her shapely face, fair hair twisted up behind it.

The servant girl was holding out a letter.

Her sewing fell idly in her lap as she reached to take it.

'Thank you.'

'There is also this, my lady.' The girl placed a largeish parcel on the table, bulky and wrapped in black cloth and twine.

'Thank you, you may leave us.'

Elizabeth waited until they were alone.

Her sister, Anne, now wife to William Bourchier, brother of the archbishop, sat beside her, her long hair braided about her ears in the new style. Jacquetta had been keeping them company, reading out sections of the Arthurian legends, but now she placed her book down on the table. 'Who is it from?'

Elizabeth turned the parchment over. The seal was stamped in red wax, showing a young woman in a flowing dress, riding side saddle, with a bird of prey perched on her hand. Elizabeth recognised it in a moment.

'Oh, it's from Margaret in Burgundy.'

'I wonder why she writes. Perhaps she is expecting too.'

That summer, it would be two years since Margaret's marriage but, as yet, no child had been conceived. Elizabeth though, had the rounded belly of early pregnancy and was expecting her fourth child by Edward in the early autumn. Her sixth in total. Her older sons, Thomas and Richard, now fifteen and thirteen, were studying the Latin Bible with their tutor.

A swift crack broke the seal. The letter was folded several times and gradually revealed its lines of close, neat hand. Elizabeth scanned it quickly.

'She seems happy. She writes about their horses, saying Charles loves to ride, and the beauty of the Burgundian countryside. And Mary, Charles' daughter, is thirteen and growing very pretty but even more clever.'

She continued to read. 'She asks after us all. She is thinking of building a new chapel. Sends us her blessings. No, there's no mention of a child.'

'Sometimes these things take time,' said Jacquetta. 'I will dry some special herbs for her. You can send them in your reply.'

'And she sends us some yards of Burgundian cloth,' added Elizabeth, brightening as she reached the end. 'Go on, Anne, do the honours.'

Anne did not need to be asked twice. She was already at the table, unwrapping the coarse cloth on the outside and drawing out a length of something silver and shimmering. Holding it up to the light, she let the fabric hang loose so the sparkles were highlighted, before draping it about her body.

'Stunning,' admitted the queen. 'Radiant, Anne!'

There came a rap of knuckles upon the door.

'Come,' called the queen.

Edward, her husband, strode into the chamber in his riding habit of brown velvet and gold tissue. His brows were knit, his manner purposeful.

'Ah, Edward, we have just had a letter from your sister in Burgundy.'

'Margaret? She is well?'

'Yes, yes, she seems so, although no child yet. See what she sends us!'

Edward gave a brief nod of approval to Anne's display. 'God be praised for her good health; a child will surely follow.' But his brow was still set firm.

'What is it? You seem troubled.'

'I too have had a letter. You recall my Master of the Horse, Thomas Burgh of Gainsborough?'

'Burgh, why yes.' The name brought to mind a shortish man with receding hair.

'He writes to tell me that a local dispute has got out of hand. Gainsborough Hall has been attacked by another local man, Sir Robert Welles, son of Baron Welles, and Burgh finds himself cast out. It has provoked a divide in the area that threatens to widen, drawing in old disputes. I must ride north and put an end to it.'

'Must it be you? Is Warwick not close to hand? He could use it as another opportunity to prove his loyalty.'

'Burgh appeals to me direct. I think it cannot harm to show my face in the area. I will be gone a week or two, nothing more.'

Elizabeth rose slowly to her feet, one hand in the crook of her hip. Edward came forward to meet her and put his arms about her, pulling her to his chest.

274

'You must take good men with you,' she spoke into his warmth. 'Keep them about you at all times and stay vigilant.'

'Of course. I shall return safely to you soon.'

He kissed the top of her head.

'And you too, Jacquetta, stay safe. I know you will watch over her for me.'

'You are certain of this?' The older woman asked, cautiously, her senses having become more attuned to danger since the death of her husband and son. 'There is no hint of danger to your person?'

'Burgh is a good man, a trustworthy man. He has given me loyal service and deserves to be restored to his estates.'

'And the other? This Robert Welles?'

'A local landowner who needs reminding of my laws.'

'Where is Warwick?' asked Jacquetta.

'At Middleham with George and his wife. Her child must be due any day. I will send for them to join me.'

'Very well,' replied Elizabeth. 'You are the king. You must choose your course but be wary of your enemies and warier still of some of your friends.'

'I will take the counsel of good men like Hastings, Suffolk, Norfolk and others. I will keep you informed of my progress. God bless you, my love. I will see you dressed in that Burgundian tinsel upon my return.'

He leaned down and placed a kiss full upon her lips.

Warwick glowered at the paper. Black ink upon white, criss-crossing horizontal and vertical, swimming before his eyes. Then he looked across to George, who was pulling arrows out of the straw butts by the trees. They had been shooting that morning, feeling the pull of their muscle as they drew the long bow, then the release as they loosened their grip and saw it fly. The Yorkshire sky loomed bright and wide above them.

George had shot better, without question, hitting the mark almost every time. Warwick had squinted, faltered, blamed the sun, and privately admitted that his eyesight was not as sharp as it had been when he was a younger man.

George strode back towards him across the lawn with half a dozen arrows tucked under his arm. He had the air of a caged beast, barely entertained, verging on rebellion. He nodded at the paper.

'What's that then?'

'Your brother summons us. He wants our help.'

'Does he indeed?'

George picked up the bow and began to line up a new shot. The distant butts were painted in concentric circles: blue, red, black. He narrowed his eyes and drew back.

'For Edward!'

The arrow shot home. They could see, even from that distance, that it was almost dead centre.

'An excellent shot, but was it the right mark?' Warwick observed, wryly.

'Mark enough for now. What does he say?'

'He writes from Waltham Abbey but he is coming north. The dispute between Burgh and Welles has got out of hand.'

'Robert Welles?' asked George, thinking. 'He has no love for the king.'

'Indeed, he has not. I have heard that he speaks for the old regime when he thinks he is in safe company.'

'For the Lancastrians?'

'For the old Henry VI, still in the Tower. He will be most angered to hear the king is riding against him to protect the interests of his Master of the Horse.'

'But is Edward really riding against him? I thought...'

'Aye, but that is what Welles must hear. I will write to him at once.

276

And then I shall write to the king, promising that we will meet him at Fotheringhay.'

'*Shall* we meet him at Fotheringhay?' George echoed.

'At the head of Welles' rebel army, we shall.'

'Then make it a little further north; leave my old home alone.'

'Sentiment is no strength, George, remember. Keep practising. I go to write.'

Warwick's eyes adjusted slowly to the darkness inside the castle. He knew his way instinctively, through the hall, up the staircase to the solar, where he knew his wife kept paper and ink.

'Richard? Is that you?'

The Countess of Warwick came to greet him at the door, her finger pressed to her lips. She wore her hair dressed high in the fashionable style, but it was streaked with grey.

'Hush, Isabel is sleeping at last. The child is so heavy and large, she can scarce get any rest.'

'Very well, I only came for necessaries to write a letter. I will not intrude upon her.'

'I will send Anne for them, bring them down to the hall for you. What are you planning?'

'I am replying to the king's summons.'

His wife knew his tone. 'Oh? I sense trouble.'

'Not at all. I am fulfilling the role of the loyal servant, for now.'

'And later?'

'Later, we will see.'

She took him by the wrist, unexpectedly. Her face was sharper than usual. 'Isabel is close to her time. I give it three weeks, maybe four, but the condition in her hips is severe, causing her discomfort; do not do anything that will risk her health.'

Warwick looked down at the hand, plaintive upon his sleeve. 'Remove your hand, madam. I shall do what requires to be done.'

She recoiled. It was a gesture that spoke of past conflict. 'Remember how it was with me, Richard, when my time came. Remember the children that were lost.'

'I do,' he said briefly. 'I think of the sons God never granted you.'

'Me?'

'Send Anne down to the hall with the paper.'

Even the hang of the branches here was familiar. Edward passed from the sunshine into the shade where they overstretched the road. Just beyond this was the turn, the little rise, and then the green bowl of land in which his home sat. It never aged; it never changed. This old road from the south was like an old friend, where he had ridden with father and Edmund, countless times, in anticipation of a welcome. The chimneys would be pumping out smoke, the orchard full of apples, Mother presiding over the dinner and little George and Richard, plump with childhood, tumbling on the grass. It was a memory he cherished, like a pearl in his mind, but it also brought with it a sting of pain. Such jewels were lost before their value truly realised.

He mounted the rise and there she lay. Fotheringhay Castle, solid and grey in the sunshine. Hastings reined in his horse alongside.

'It appears peaceful.'

'It does indeed. We shall spend the night here. George might already have arrived and then we can press forward.'

Hastings said nothing, but followed the king as he urged his horse forward. Down the sloping road, over the moat and in through the castle walls, one after another. Serving men came out into the court-yard to take the horses, and the old woman at the door welcomed them warmly, but it was not Cecily, nor her kin, only the old cook from the village. Inside, the house felt cold and smelt slightly of damp. The grates had been old for weeks, maybe months. There was no trace of family; it seemed an age since any of the Yorks had resided there.

'Light up the fires and prepare the rooms,' Edward commanded. 'Bring wine and bread. Send word to the kitchens. We dine as soon as possible.'

Hastings strode into the centre of the hall where the Duke of York used to play with his dogs and call to his wife to dance. Now, as he looked around, it was quiet.

'George is not here.'

'No,' replied Edward, with pursed lips. 'He is not.'

And the silence of Clarence's absence echoed through the castle.

'My lord?'

They turned to see Suffolk in the doorway with a man dressed in Warwick's distinctive livery. Edward started at once at the sight of him, thinking it signalled that the earl and George had arrived.

Suffolk shook his head. 'You will want to hear what this man has to say.'

He was an oldish man, with hair greying at the temples and thin on top, perhaps forty or fifty in years. His eyes were clear and honest and a long scar graced his right cheek.

'King Edward,' he began, 'you will not remember me but I fought with your father at St Albans and with you at Towton, where I received this wound. I have, these past nine years served the Earl of Warwick at Warwick Castle, and sometimes at Middleham, where I have been in service this last month.'

'What is your name?'

'I am John Stevens, my lord.'

'You are welcome, John Stevens. Has the earl sent you? Is he on his way?'

Stevens looked nervously at Suffolk.

'Go on,' Suffolk urged. 'Tell him what you just told me.'

'The earl has not sent me,' the man continued. 'He does not know I am here. I have left his service to bring you this message. The earl is not you friend, nor is your brother, the Duke of Clarence. They conspire against you, to bring you harm. They have gone to Leicester to join with Welles who is raising an army against you. They have spread the word that you have come to punish the men of last year's uprising and will make examples of them in the streets.'

Edward hung his head, deep in thought as he absorbed this information.

'And you are sure of this,' Suffolk asked.

'As sure as anything. I have heard them discuss it many times and I saw a letter written by Welles which they left behind.'

The sting of betrayal was so great, delivered in his family home, that Edward could barely lift his head.

'You are certain that my brother, George, Clarence, was part of this too?'

'I am sorry to report it, my lord.'

'How many men do they have?'

'I heard almost a hundred thousand, but many joined them in the mistaken belief that you plan to punish last year's rebels. They would not rise otherwise.'

'Thank you, Stevens. You have served me well and you will be rewarded for it. You can remain here, take a position in this house if you wish, or go south to Westminster with my recommendation.'

'Thank you, your lordship is very kind but I have family in York and I will return there. I bid you good day and God preserve you.'

As the man left, Suffolk drew closer to speak, as did Hastings, who had heard all from the doorway.

'He has done it again. Despite all your kindness.'

'Their treason goes beyond belief.'

Edward held up a hand to stay their words. 'Now is the time for action. All talk, all forgiveness, all charity is passed. The harshest penalties must be enacted against the traitors. While Welles awaits us at Leicester, we will pay a visit to his family home and take his father, Sir Richard, hostage for his good behaviour. That may cool his ardour for a fight. They will see a new king who does not forgive a betrayal.'

He strode to the door, calling to the men. 'Bring back the horses; we must depart immediately!'

Looking at Suffolk, he added, 'Brother, I have a task for you of the utmost importance. Ride north to Stamford. It is some ten miles. There, seek out John Lyons at the sign of the sheaf, close by the church. Tell him the king commands that he bring out all my cannons, all of them, which have been in his safekeeping. He must raise men in Stamford in my name. We will meet you on the road south of the city.'

'Very well, my lord, God be with you.'

'What would you have me do?' asked Hastings.

'You will ride with me to bring in the traitor's father. Let Welles see his head upon the cross at Stamford.'

'And Warwick? And George?'

'Who will they hide behind when Welles surrenders? I will bring the traitors out into the daylight. Come, haste, we must use our advantage.'

Welles looked up and down the line of men. He was a red-faced man in his late twenties, with a shock of fair hair and a prominent mouth. The son of a local landowner, loyal to the Lancastrians, he had been raised to know his rights, his place in the world, and to fight for it.

Welles squinted. A faint drizzle was driving from the north like a mist in their faces. He had come too far to back down now no matter what the king did or said. It was a matter of honour, of family; his dispute with Burgh had to be resolved. And of course, like Warwick said, the king would side with his Master of the Horse. Unfairly. It wouldn't have happened under the old regime; Welles had been favoured then, advanced even.

Welles shaded his eyes with his hand. On the line of the distant hills, roughly on the line of the Great North Road, he could see that men were moving and the standard of the king was being raised. The colours, fluttering on the breeze, would be visible to the volunteers massing behind him. That distinctive murrey and blue, and the gold sunburst, would creep into their hearts. It was inevitable with Englishmen.

The royal standard was a blow, unquestionably, but it need not be decisive. If he could gather them together, explain that they were fighting for their liberty, their lives, against an unjust punishment, he could keep them focused. But they were already starting to whisper among themselves and point over towards the king's camp. It must be done soon.

The Earl of Warwick was riding towards him up from the hollow. The sight of the earl, and the men massed behind him in livery, gave Welles a boost in confidence. And then there was the king's own brother, the Duke of Clarence, overseeing his army to the right. Welles told himself he had the best military campaigner, the larger numbers and royal blood on his side. He could do this.

'Warwick! The king has raised his standard. We must address the men, build their morale.'

But the earl looked sombre in spite of their advantages.

'Welles, stop. Listen. I bring bad tidings.'

'What more can there be?'

'The king has taken your father and holds him hostage at Stamford.'

The news hit him like a storm but Welles stood his ground.

'He does? To what purpose?'

'To persuade you to leave the field.'

'But how? My father? How?'

'I don't know how. Our messenger says Edward threatens his life if you do not withdraw.'

'But my father is innocent in this. Is there any word from him?'

'I don't think so.'

Welles turned away, looked at the sky. The grey clouds were parting.

'Do you think this is a bluff?'

Warwick considered. 'It is unlike Edward, certainly. It is not his usual style but I do not think he would make a threat like this unless he intended to act upon it.'

'What can I do? The men are already taking heed of the royal colours, look!' He pointed across the divide to where the colours blazed.

Warwick nodded grimly and beckoned to a servant. 'Clarence and I will raise our standards. That will give them a distraction. George!'

Clarence came riding up with the look of a man who was ready for action. His face was set firm against his brother, against family, against the house of York, whoever served him least well, but there were glimmers of doubt about the corners of his mouth. Doubt at the great wave that was carrying him forward. Doubt at these new allies.

But then, just at the moment that the flags were being raised, the sky was rocked by a deep booming sound, like thunder.

The men instinctively ducked.

'What in the name of our Lord was that?' Welles exclaimed.

'Cannons,' confirmed Warwick, drawing back up to his full height and looking around. 'Wait for it; the ball will strike. Wait, wait. There!'

A short distance away, there was the sound of a dull explosion as the earth flew up close to the front line of men. The air was filled with cries and shouting. Men began to scatter but they were uncertain which way to run, and the roar of a second and third blast filled them with panic.

'Stand! Stand your ground!'

Warwick gripped his reins as his horse reared up in fear, almost throwing him to the ground.

'God's blood, this will do for them.'

The second shot fell short but showered them with a spray of earth, making the remaining men cower and run for cover. The third hit the battalion in the middle, propelling bodies into the air. George urged his horse back towards the camp, out of the line of fire.

'Should we attempt to fight?' asked a desperate Welles. 'If we get the men to run towards the guns, there will be losses, but we might make ground, take some victories?'

Warwick looked around. The front line was littered with bodies. Groaning and dying men lay twisted and bloodied. Limping and wounded soldiers were calling for help while others headed for the camp or made for the bushes. The sharp smell of blood and smoke reached them.

Welles felt his gorge rise and choked himself back, to hide his response.

'These men are not going to fight anyone,' the earl admitted. 'There is nothing to do but concede defeat and flee.'

'What are they doing?' Welles' sharp eyes had spotted Clarence's band over to the east who were struggling with their clothing. As they watched, each one threw their livery to the ground and made their escape in their jerkins.

Warwick gave a wry laugh. 'Of course. They don't want to be taken as traitors. Worse still, failed traitors, bearing arms for Clarence.'

'Look!' A man was pointing across the field. This time they saw the bright stars of gunpowder and a fourth and fifth boom followed, sending the remaining men into chaos. 'The king's men are advancing!'

It was true. There was motion on the distant hill. A long rippling motion as the line began to move forward with the advance of thousands of feet. A long blue wave descending.

'We must flee,' Warwick urged. 'Welles, leave this place at once; go into hiding. We are undone. Clarence and I must head for the coast and make Calais our refuge once again.'

The cannon balls fell either side of them, shaking the ground beneath their feet and showering them with earth.

'Make haste!' cried the earl, wiping the dirt and sweat from his face. 'Make haste!'

The Countess of Warwick had seen them approach and hurried down to the hall. Middleham had been still, quiet, nestled in a bowl of spring light, waiting for news. She left Isabel and Anne in the solar, with the maid playing the lute, and the hours ticking away. Isabel was so heavy, so full with child, that her time must come very soon. She had experienced twinges in her back but her waters had not yet broken.

The solar had been furnished in advance with necessary items: a wide mattress, cushions, firewood and supplies of spices and wine. There were embroidered panels ready to hang over the windows, and carpets for the floor. It was important that no draughts could reach her while she laboured. The midwife in the village was waiting to be summoned with her potions, poultices and herbs.

The countess heard her husband shouting as she descended the staircase to the hall.

'At once! Move! All of it!'

'Richard?'

He turned at the sound of her voice. She could see the focus and the rage in his eyes. Clarence was sulking beside him.

'Pack up a few chests. Whatever is light and ready to go. We must leave at once.'

'Leave? We cannot leave.'

'We can and we will. Today, within the hour. Or else you will find yourself not only attainted as a traitor but imprisoned and possibly executed.'

'But Isabel is about to enter her confinement. You go, I will stay with her and join you once it is safe.'

He strode up to her and seized her by the shoulders. 'You do not understand. It will never be safe. Isabel is the wife and daughter of traitors. This time the king will show us no mercy.'

'What?' she quavered. 'What has happened?'

'Edward will be here within the hour, at the head of his victorious army, and he will not spare us. Pack yourselves up. We leave at once.'

'Leave? For where? Where can we go?'

'First, to Calais.'

'And then?'

'Then I hope to prove that my enemy's enemy can become my friend.'

EIGHTEEN

My Enemy's Enemy, July 1470

She couldn't quite define these feelings, this wave of mixed emotions that rushed over her, taking her by surprise. Nine years since she had sat on the dais at Westminster. Nine years since the English people had knelt before her, hailed her as their queen. Six years since she had set foot in the land she was meant to rule. Six years since Beaufort had fought to reclaim the throne for her and lost. She ran her finger through the dust of the windowsill. It had grown thick. How those years had dragged, each day an eternity. Her husband a prisoner in the Tower, the Yorkist usurper on the throne, her son being raised in France, his rightful claim in tatters.

Margaret of Anjou had turned forty this year. When she had arrived here, fleeing after Hexham, she was still young. Almost. She had swept home with a chest full of dresses, her heart bitter but still able to entertain hope, her back still straight, her limbs lean. And yet, what six years could do to a woman! Now she ached when she rose in the morning. And she could not bear another child, even if she had wanted to. Yet, despite it all, she was still the anointed Queen of England. In this grey stone turret room, overlooking the Loire at Amboise, her coronation at Westminster Abbey felt like it had been a dream.

There was a knock upon the door, the knock she had been expecting, scarcely believing in its truth, since early that afternoon.

'Come!'

She stood proud, steeling herself. The emotions coursed through her. Curiosity, anger, pride, fear? No, not fear. She did not fear this treacherous little man; it was more the anticipation of making him kneel at her feet, the thrill of a chance that this change brought her. It may be the day that her luck finally turned.

The short, wide form of Louis XI appeared in the open doorway, draped in his velvet and ermine robes. Margaret bowed at once as he entered, grateful that he had offered her the hospitality of his castle. The French king had once been an ally of England, coming to terms with the Yorkists soon after Towton, but the friendship had always been with the Earl of Warwick, and France now served to bring Edward's enemies together.

Louis stepped into the room, surveying her with his heavy, squat features.

'He is here.'

Margaret took a deep breath.

'And what does he want?'

'To make all his insincere apologies and promises, to flatter you with false words and praise your dynasty to the heavens after he helped cast it from the throne.'

Margaret could not help the smile from playing on her lips. Louis was known for being direct.

'But,' the king added, 'he is also your best chance of returning to England and toppling York.'

She nodded. 'I loathe this man. I loathe him from the depths of my soul and I can never forget the part he played in my downfall. But if I can use him, I will. If he can bring me back to England, whatever his motives might be, if he can restore my husband to the throne and make my son accepted as his rightful heir, then I am prepared to hear him.'

Louis nodded. 'I think that is wise. Many of your old friends are no longer with us or have settled for Yorkist lies, or lands, in a sort of bought loyalty.'

'They may abandon Edward when they hear of my return.'

'They may. There are Lancastrians in England who will flock to your side and fight in your name. But this may be the last chance.'

She nodded grimly. 'I like it not, but I like where it might take me.'

Louis headed for the door. 'I shall have him brought up to you.'

Those moments felt like an eternity. She knew all the stones around the door, in their various colours and shapes, and the way they fitted together, like the back of her hand. She knew the play of light upon the floor, the angle by which it fell at this time of day. She knew all the noises of the castle, and of those outside.

Finally, the footsteps came. Slowly climbing the staircase. She sensed a reluctance in them. A heavy tone of defeat.

He was smaller than she remembered. His dark hair was flecked with grey and his face more worn than she remembered. He looked somehow diminished. She was glad she had worn the silver dress and rubies.

'My lady.'

He came a little way into the room, which was barely ten paces across, and dropped to his knees, bowing his head. And she saw at once that this figure of terror, this military leader, this giant of the

York circle, a man she had feared and loathed, was actually only a man, a mere man with a lined neck and narrow shoulders, his hair thinning on the top.

She did not ask him to rise. Instead, she waited many minutes before speaking to him directly.

'Well, well, the Earl of Warwick. I wonder what ill-wind blows you to my feet.'

He waited patiently. She paced the room before him, enjoying his complete capitulation.

'So, you have fallen out with Edward. England has rejected you. And you dare to think you might find a welcome here?'

He began to lift his head.

'Oh no, you do not speak yet.'

She poured herself a glass of wine from the jug on the table.

'What do you want of me, Richard, Earl of Warwick, that you have sought me out and disturbed the peace of my exile? You, who have placed me here, who have caused my own people to rise against me, who have toppled me from my rightful throne, imprisoned my husband, your lawful king, and cast his true heir out into the wilderness. What can you possibly want from me that you think I might be disposed to grant you? Tell me.'

She waited as he began to summon his response. But when he drew breath, she interrupted him.

'No, wait. Let me think fully of all the wrongs you have done to myself and my kin. All the wrongs you have done to England for the sake of your own ambition and a dynasty of usurpers. There are so many instances of your duplicity, your malice, that I need run through them all, lest any be forgotten in the passage of the years. For they go back so very far, back to the cruel slaughter of my dear friend, our loyal servant, the Duke of Somerset, and more recently, the death of his son and heir, Henry Beaufort. Did you make it your mission to seek out all my friends and slay them?'

The dark head hung low again. She sensed there was little fight left in him, little strength, but she did not ask him to rise.

'My lady, I offer my humble, deepest apologies. I cast myself upon your mercy. Circumstances in the past placed us on opposing sides and I served what I believed to be the true king, of God's intent, to the best of my abilities. I regret that I was wrong and that I was the cause of your suffering and loss.'

'We have always been on opposing sides. I have heard nothing yet to the contrary. Nor have you told me why you have sought me out here to disturb my peace.'

'I humble myself before you. I believe we can work towards a common aim.'

'How do I know that I might trust you? You who have always been set against my cause and might be still now, for all I know, bent upon my destruction. This might be a plot, to rid your king of my claim forever.'

'My lady, I am a wanted man in England. I have been attainted as a traitor, all my lands and titles forfeit. I was forced to flee with my wife and family; my elder daughter Isabel lost her child during the turbulent sea crossing. I have nothing left, nothing. I am here to cast myself upon your mercy.'

She listened in silence to this tale of woe, still sceptical but softening at the mention of the women's suffering.

'But I believe I can restore my fortunes if they are allied to yours. I can draw on support in England, and part of the York base will remain loyal to Clarence. Together we can defeat Edward and restore your husband and the Lancastrian regime.'

'On the condition that you are forgiven and rewarded, I suppose?'

'To live out my days in peace under a Lancastrian king would be more than all the riches I can imagine compared with the dangers I face from Edward.'

'So, you are driven here by necessity, not by choice. I am your last chance. What's to say you might not find another necessity, should your luck change again?'

'Madam, forgive me, what better offer have you received? Whatever ill-wind might blow upon us now, we will never receive a Yorkist welcome, so what better strength might we find than to combine our forces and stand together? I pledge myself to fight in our joined cause although it might cost me my life. I can offer no greater reassurance than that.'

She thought for a moment, turning away. Eventually, she said softly, 'You may rise.'

Warwick got slowly, stiffly to his feet. 'Thank you, my lady. Does this mean we might begin negotiations?'

She poured some wine from the table into two goblets and handed him one.

'I believe we might.'

The boy was seventeen but he was still very much a boy. He was a little taller than his mother as he stood beside her at the table, with her dark hair and eyes, but the strange, shapeless face of his father, Henry VI. He had an ungainly, forward lean to his demeanour and long arms that hung at his side which spoke of a readiness for action, perhaps an over-readiness. A restless energy emanated from him as he shifted from one foot to the other, a relentless desire for movement and action. His eyes were dark, roving the hall, responsive to movement.

Warwick stood flanked by his countess and two daughters. George stood, glowering sullenly, a little way off.

'Come forward, Anne Neville,' the Lancastrian queen demanded.

Anne was a slight girl, fourteen or fifteen, with her father's dark eyes. She had stronger features than her elder sister and a fresher look, although Isabel's recent trials would have worn any face into lines of care.

Anne dropped a curtsey, then looked up at Margaret of Anjou and at the tall boy at her side. He met her with a steady gaze and an unfathomable expression.

'You understand,' asked the queen, 'the nature of the discussions that have taken place between myself and your father?'

'I do, my lady.'

Her voice was soft, faint, as if it had been under-used.

'Speak up, girl.'

'Yes, I do, my lady.'

'And you give your consent to be betrothed here today to my son, Edward of Westminster, Prince of Wales.'

Her eyes flickered over to those of her mother but the countess quickly turned hers away.

'I do, my lady.'

King Louis made a gesture to the bishop, waiting in the shadows, who had come from Tours.

'The bishop brings a fragment of the true cross upon which you will place your hands and speak your vows. After that, you will be bound together in the eyes of God, as closely as if you were man and wife, until the day the final ceremony is completed.'

The man in purple shuffled forward and held out, in his upturned palms, a thin slice of dark wood.

Anne sighed at the sight of it. This was part of her father's plan, a stage in his return, one part of a process that would bring them home. She had just this small role to play and he would do the rest, setting sail across the sea, fighting battles, bringing the country in line. And she would be Princess of Wales and, one day, queen. All she need do was to smile, to agree, to speak a few small words. It should not be difficult. She would remain here in this beautiful chateau with her mother for a while, until it was safe to return. There was no difficulty in that. No difficulty.

And yet, her gorge rose at the sight of the wood. A long splinter, sitting on the bishop's fat palms. She had seen Isabel in the belly of the boat, doubled in pain as she bled, white-faced and animal-like. She had prayed with her in the genuine belief that their end was approaching, while the waves tossed them like feathers. Together, they had wrapped the dead child in linen before Isabel turned aside and vomited, purging away the pain and grief. And now it was her turn.

This boy, this stranger, had been chosen for her because of his royal blood. She had always known it would be this way, it was her lot as an earl's daughter to be wed to a husband chosen by her parents, but she had not imagined that so much could ride upon it.

'Place your hands upon the fragment,' the bishop urged in a crackly voice.

She could not. Her hand froze. The boy did as he was told, putting a long brown paw clumsily on that of the bishop. All eyes were upon her and there was not one other single place she might go, nor friend in this foreign country from whom she could ask assistance.

'Place your hand upon the fragment,' the bishop insisted. They were all looking at her.

'Anne!' her father urged.

Reluctantly, she lifted her arm and put her hand gingerly above that of the boy. Not touching, but above, so she could feel his heat but not his skin.

The bishop placed his hand over hers. 'Will you promise, Edward Plantagenet, Prince of Wales, to take this woman, Anne Neville, as your wife, to contract full and lawful marriage with her in the future and, until then, to not forsake her, and to live clean and godly to the glory of our Lord?'

He was close. She could smell the perfume of his leather jerkin and the sweat of his skin beneath it.

'I promise.'

'Anne,' asked the bishop, 'do you promise to be wed to Edward, Prince of Wales, at some future time and keep yourself always to the service of your Lord.'

She heard herself speak. Somehow she had answered. Her lips had framed the words and she had consented. The boy was looking at her.

'Now you are betrothed to be man and wife. I look forward to joining you together for the final stage of holy matrimony in the weeks to come.'

'Thank you, bishop,' replied Louis, who turned his fleshy features towards Warwick and the queen.

'You are content, my lady, my lord?'

Margaret inclined her head. 'I am. It was well done.'

Warwick nodded. 'Now we are one in this purpose that will see your son and my daughter upon the throne of England.'

'Come,' said Louis, 'let us repair to the hall and seal this moment with a feast.'

And she felt her feet moving, her mother at her side, her hands carefully feeling in front of her. They moved together, in procession, down the corridor and into the hall, and no one spoke. There was a table laid out, with wine and dishes, and a huge centrepiece of carved marzipan and pastry, set with fruits. But it was as if she was still on board ship and everything was swimming.

She was placed next to the boy, who spread himself across the seat as if he owned it, and began to eat at once. They were upon a little raised dais, with his mother on his right, and Louis beyond her, just the four of them. Elevated. The others were seated according to their degrees and served by men in the French king's livery. Members of the French court, ladies in elegant gowns and gentlemen in furs and jewels filled the remainder of the trestles, eyeing the young couple at the top table with curiosity.

He leaned across her to reach a plate. Her father was eating, talking loudly, drinking. And then there were the smells: heavy, rich meats, in sauces she did not recognise; piquant green and sharp vinegar; garlic and cloves. The combination of them together made her stomach clench.

'Don't you eat?' asked the boy, his mouth full of meat.

She did not look up.

He laughed. 'Doesn't eat and doesn't speak.'

She picked up a piece of bread and pretended to chew the crust.

It was not long before Warwick rose to his feet, making some preliminary ramble about good food and his gratitude for French hospitality.

'And I can avow that this is the best outcome that I might have dared to imagine,' he added, 'thanks to the kindness and charity of our good queen, Margaret, whose kindness has given me cause for hope, and will set England back upon its path to the restoration of the Lancastrian dynasty.'

There was a murmur of applause among the French courtiers.

'With perfect charity,' he continued, 'our charming queen has overlooked my past mistakes and is prepared to trust me with this great mission. The Duke of Clarence and I will be returning to England at once, where I hear there is much support for us in the south-west. Those who have lived quietly under the Yorkist, lamenting the loss of the true king and waiting for his restoration, are coming forward. I have received a communication from Jasper Tudor, half-brother of the old king, who will raise troops in Wales. Together we will gather an army and rid England of the usurper before he has stirred from his idle bed!'

There was much cheering at this last remark.

'And be in no doubt that we have all we require to succeed. By Christmas, the good old King Henry and his gentle queen will be seated again upon England's throne and their loyal servants will be rewarded.'

'A toast! cried Clarence, holding up his wine glass. 'A toast to…'

'Yes,' interrupted Warwick, cutting him off. 'Let us drink a toast and make an oath of allegiance. To Lancaster and England.'

Warwick raised his glass and the company on the trestles lifted theirs in response, their faces turned towards the queen, her son, and his newly betrothed.

'To Lancaster and England! Amen!'

'To Lancaster,' she heard them say, 'to Lancaster, to England.'

And her lips began to shape their response. 'To England,' Anne said softly, thinking of the green fields around Middleham Castle and her chamber, where her unfinished sewing had been left on the bed as they departed in haste. 'To Lancaster, to England.'

The boy looked down at her and his brown eyes were warmer. 'That's right. To Lancaster and England. Our England!'

He didn't think of Elizabeth. She was his wife and queen, the mother of his children. She would be waiting for him at Westminster with her beautiful smile and her kind arms, as was her place. It was simply the way of things. It did not mean he could not appreciate the way this woman moved, with her dark hair streaming down her back and the curve of her back in the shift, and her hungry, eager mouth. He put down his goblet as she turned back round to him. Her lips were pert and full. That old feeling overcame him again, that dizzying, animal drive he'd kept at bay for so long.

She'd been Hastings' find, this woman. Once the uprising had proven to be a few discontented landowners, they'd decided to tarry in York, take up the hospitality of the city before returning south. The wind was cold in this part of the world and they'd taken rest and shelter, feasted and drunk well, until Hastings had struck a deal with a tavern owner near Coppergate. They'd been there two weeks, Richard and Anthony too, although they had been more engaged in riding and studying than in the delights Hastings had introduced to their rooms. Briefly, it felt as if they were young again, as if the battles and betrayals of the past years might just melt away, when the wine kept coming.

She turned to him, eyes enticing. Her body moved towards his, barely concealed, ripe and full. It would be easy to pull that shift aside and grip her flesh.

He leaned forward in his chair and met her kiss. There was no harm in it, after all. It was as simple and necessary a pleasure as eating or sleeping.

She leaned closer and wrapped her arms about his shoulders, then slid them down his back.

He stretched up to her hungrily, taking handfuls of the loose material about her hips. His tongue sought hers.

But someone knocked at the door and then knocked again, insistently.

'My lord? Edward? May I?'

He recognised the voice of Anthony, Earl Rivers, and indicated the woman to wait, frowning in displeasure. She sank sulkily into a chair.

It was hard to keep the impatience out of his voice. 'What is it?'

The door opened enough to let in the light. 'My lord, I would speak with you on a matter of some urgency.'

'What is it, Anthony?'

'My lord, with the greatest respect, it is time to return to Westminster. The city was unruly during your last absence and…'

'Go away!'

'My lord, I must urge you…'

'You wish to urge me? What is the rush? What does it matter if we tarry a few days more? You are welcome to go south if you please. Why do you counsel me thus?'

Half visible through the door, Rivers looked uncomfortable. 'My lord, I do believe the capital will become unruly again without your presence. I have also heard worrying reports about the Earl of Warwick.'

'Warwick? There are always worrying reports about Warwick but I have driven him out. He is an attainted traitor, and if he dares set foot in my country again, he will pay the full price.'

'Even if he lands with an army?'

'What army? Of Frenchmen? We are more than a match for any army Louis might lend the earl.'

'There are stirrings in the West Country too and in Wales, among the old Lancastrian supporters.'

'Then let it be put out that I expect the full loyalty of all my subjects and those who fail me will be made an example of.'

Still Anthony did not leave.

'Good God, what is it, man?'

'I believe the time for action has come, my lord. I urge you to go south, as soon as we can. Today. We have tarried here too long.'

'Nonsense. I will not be ruled by your anxieties. Leave me be. We will discuss our departure in the morning.'

'By then, my lord, it may be too late…'

'Leave me be!'

The door closed.

The rooms had been prepared exactly to her specifications. Elizabeth surveyed the bedchamber, cradling her large belly. The child would come any day now as he was kicking so strongly and had already turned. She was certain he was a boy as he sat lower and felt more strenuous than her girls. The Tower had not been her first choice as the best place to deliver him, but it was warm and protected and she would be safe until Edward's return. If he travelled swiftly, he might be back before she went into labour to give her his blessing.

She ran her hand over the bed curtains. Red and blue velvet, embroidered with the York arms, and cushions made from cloth of gold and silver. The walls were hung with tapestries, depicting women in a garden who were surrounded by flowers and minstrels playing. These were fine rooms. They had previously belonged to the old king, Henry VI, who was now confined in more austere surroundings in one of the other towers, not too far away. This wide bed would welcome her child. This hearth, built up into a blaze against the autumn storm, would warm his limbs, while her ladies helped her recovery. With each child she bore, and this was her sixth, she learned a little more, but that did not mean it got easier. The hours of pain that lay ahead were still to be dreaded.

'Is there more linen?' asked Jacquetta, coming in from the next room. 'I thought you had ordered more but I can only find a dozen sheets.'

'I think they are in here,' Elizabeth replied, pointing to the chest under the window.

Her mother lifted the lid, releasing the smell of lavender and rose petals.

'Ah,' she moved her hand through the contents. 'Here we have sheets, linen, cloths, everything you need. But I have ordered more firewood to be stored up as the season looks set to be chilly. The kitchens are well stocked and they expect a new arrival of spices tomorrow when the ship comes in.'

Elizabeth nodded, feeling the child move strongly in her belly.

'Mother, come feel.' She took Jacquetta's hand and placed it on the spot. 'This one is such a kicker.'

'Yes, yes! I feel him.'

'You said 'him' too. I heard you. You think it is a boy?'

'I suppose I do. You think so too?'

Elizabeth nodded, feeling another kick and a turn. 'He wants to come out soon.'

'He will. Nothing will stop him when he decides the time is right. Are you in any pain yet?'

'Just my back, nothing else.'

'I will make up a poultice. Anne has the ingredients.'

'Maybe I will try and sleep for a while, build my strength.'

'A wise idea.' Jacquetta stroked her daughter's arm. 'Do you want to eat first?'

'No, I will send for something when I wake.'

Jacquetta turned back the covers to reveal the clean white sheets underneath. Elizabeth slipped off her soft leather shoes and left them on the floor as she buried down into the bed. Her mother leaned forward and kissed her forehead.

'It will be over soon enough and then he will be with us. Have you thought what you wish to call him?'

'Why, Edward, of course.' The queen smiled and closed her eyes.

'Of course,' replied her mother indulgently and crept from the room.

'But how?' raged Edward, incredulous. 'What of my fleet in the Channel? What of all those ships that cost so much from our coffers?'

Norfolk knelt before him. The king had forgotten to ask him to rise. 'How Norfolk, how?'

'Your fleet was scattered by strong winds, my lord. There was nothing that could have been done. It is the season for storms.'

'Then do not wise sailors seek a port?'

'These were unexpected, a change of wind. Might I rise, my lord?'

'Yes. Of course. Rise.'

They occupied the dining room of the York tavern, a dark-panelled space with painted friezes of hunting scenes. An unfinished meal was spread out on the table with plates of meat, rapidly cooling where they had been abandoned. Wine glasses stood half full. Norfolk's news had interrupted their midday routine.

Young Richard was standing at the door, awaiting Hastings and Rivers who had gone to secure fresh horses.

'So where is he?' persisted Edward in anger and dismay. 'Where is Warwick? And George?'

'We heard they landed in Devon and are marching across country. Jasper Tudor has joined their cause, raising forces in Wales, but it is not yet known if they have come together. It is rumoured that they have tens of thousands of men.'

'Tens of thousands of my subjects? Supporting Warwick?'

Norfolk looked uneasy. 'They are raising men under the Lancastrian banner. Warwick has betrothed his daughter to the former king's son.'

'He has another daughter? Pray to God he has no more.'

'They denounce you as a usurper and plan to restore Henry VI to the throne. The last report we received had them approaching Chertsey.'

Edward fell silent. The weight of his recent inaction hung heavily upon him.

'I fear you cannot fight them, my lord. You have only us here, and their numbers grow.'

'What will you do?' asked Richard from the door.

'I need to think. If we cannot return to London, our only chance might be to flee north, or even to take ship.'

'Here they are!' Richard spotted Hastings and Rivers approaching.

'We have horses, enough for us all, at the sign of the Cross,' explained Hastings. Rivers hung back, looking sullen.

'My lord,' added Norfolk, 'I am afraid I bring more bad news.'

'What is it? What can be worse?'

Norfolk looked anxious. 'I have heard, and it may be mere rumour, I cannot say, and I hope it proves to be untrue…'

'Heard what?'

'I fear that Oxford may have gone to join Warwick.'

'Oxford? Who I thought was my friend?'

'He is related to Warwick by marriage, as is Stanley.'

'Stanley too.'

There was a stunned silence.

Edward's breath was laboured. 'Stanley has betrayed me?'

'Thomas Stanley, the report suggests. The whereabouts of William is unknown.'

Two men from his intimate circle, with whom he had fought, ridden, feasted.

'Did I not do enough for them?' he asked. 'Did I somehow fail them? All these years at my side were they secretly waiting, hoping for a Lancastrian return?'

'I think,' suggested Hastings, 'it was more like opportunism.'

'They must see Warwick as being the greater chance, Henry as the better king. My God!'

He sat down, heavy with the news.

'If my friends do not believe in me, if they join enemies bent upon my destruction, my claim is not worth fighting. And my wife and children, what of them?'

The others looked to each other with anxious eyes.

Anthony stepped forward. 'This is not the time, Edward, to lament these losses. We must leave now, ensure your safety, plan our next move.'

'He is right,' added Richard. 'Warwick is not popular; the old king is mad. Even if they succeed briefly, their power cannot last. Not against yours when you are back to your strength again.'

Edward heard their words and took heart from them.

'If they have a French army, we will bring them a Burgundian one in response. We must sail to the coast. Norfolk, you must stay. You must take this news to London, spread the word among my loyal friends and ensure my family is safe. Warwick has no quarrel with you. Play his game; bide your time. Write to us in exile. We will return.'

'I loathe the very thought of it,' Norfolk grimaced, 'but I will ensure that your loved ones are unharmed.'

'Come,' cried the king, 'take me to the horses. We leave at once.'

It was dark. Someone was calling her. Her own name came drifting through the strange landscape into her conscious brain.

'Elizabeth?'

304

She remembered her child before she made the decision to move. It was instinctive, the desire to relocate her limbs slowly and gently, and to keep her belly supported.

'Elizabeth, you must wake.'

It was her mother's voice.

The queen opened her eyes a little and blinked. It was dark but candles were still lit, or had been lit again, since she slept.

Jacquetta was leaning over her bed, hair dishevelled with a gown thrown over her shift. Behind her, the servants had gathered, and her sisters, ranging in size.

'What?' she asked, suddenly afraid, her hands going to her stomach. 'What is it?'

'We must leave here, tonight.' Jacquetta was solemn, serious. 'Warwick has landed and is marching to London.'

'Warwick? He is in France.'

'No, he has landed in the west, taken us by surprise.'

'Can the guard not arrest him?'

'He has raised an army with help from the French.'

'Where is Edward?'

'We received a note from Norfolk, who has just reached London. Edward and Anthony have fled to Burgundy.'

'To Burgundy?'

It did not seem real. She wanted to close her eyes again, go back to sleep, realise that it was all just a dream.

'You must get up, get dressed,' urged her mother. 'Girls, make yourselves ready. Take what you can carry. There is a barge awaiting us to take us to Westminster.'

The nightmare was not fading. 'Why Westminster? But mother, I cannot possibly travel. Not in my condition.'

'The alternative is to wait for the Earl of Warwick to arrive. The man who caused the deaths of your father and brother, who branded me a traitor. Goodness knows what his plans are for us now. The Abbot of Westminster offers us sanctuary in his house. Come, we must go at once. Warwick rides ever closer. He will be here before morning.'

Elizabeth swung her heavy legs out of bed, reached out for the arms that offered to help her stand. Slowly, she rose to the vertical. The baby seemed to be still, resting, thankfully. She cast her feet about for her slippers.

'No, you will need something stouter than that. We must take the river, even at this hour. You know how cold it gets. You must dress as if it is the depths of winter.'

She nodded, letting her women begin the process of changing her clothes. They brought hose and boots, kirtle, jacket and cloak, cap, hood and gloves lined with fur. The queen stood passively, almost still dream-like, and let them dress her. The material was stiff, unyielding. She caught her fingernail on a thread. Jacquetta hurried about the place, gathering essential items and directing proceedings.

'My child will not be born here after all.' Elizabeth spoke wistfully. 'Poor little one. A child of the sanctuary.'

'We cannot know it,' replied her mother. 'We must trust in the Lord. We may be back here safely soon enough if it is his will.'

'No, the child will come soon. I feel it, perhaps even tonight.'

Jacquetta came to face her, held both her arms in her hands. 'You cannot deliver him yet. You must hold on until we are safe. You must not push.'

Elizabeth nodded. 'We must go then, and make good pace, because I fear he will not listen to me.'

Jacquetta helped her to her feet, and threw a last look around as the women made their final touches. Laces, ties, gloves.

'You are ready?'

Elizabeth nodded. 'Ready.'

'Out we go,' sighed her mother. 'Fugitives into the night. Who would have thought that fortune would have cast us so low again?'

She blew out the candle.

NINETEEN

Lancaster Returns, October 1470

But London was still there. As they left the Tower and headed east, Henry could scarcely believe what he saw. That huge, hot mass of bricks and bodies, of flame and smoke, life and death, where the streets were arenas for betrayal and violence, love and triumph. Somehow, like a miracle, its walls were standing in spite of everything, when all he had seen were the inside of cold walls, the burning altar, his chaste bed. The markets were busy, the houses had expanded, children had been born and grown. Trees and plants had doubled, trebled in size; animals foraged along the waste and bells rang in church towers. And the colour, the noise. Towering above him, crowding in on all sides. Oh, good God, the noise! The shattering of voices, the clatter of hands. It was too bright, far too bright.

Henry stopped and shielded his eyes with his hand.

The crowded streets, the buildings, the people, all came rushing up, assailing him, as if they would batter him down, press him into the earth. God in heaven, what strange new chapter was this?

And there was shouting. Wasn't there shouting? Strange, disjointed syllables that seemed somehow familiar. Wasn't that once his name, over and over, coming from the crowds? Henry, Henry, they called, as if that was his name still, after all this time. But were they accusing him, or cheering? Was he being led to his death, with all these strangers, with their distorted faces baying for his blood? They were too loud, too bright. They were walking too fast. He cringed and cowered, flinching and ducking behind his hands for protection.

'The king is not well,' George observed. 'See how he reacts. He shirks away as if in response to unseen enemies.'

He was walking with Warwick, immediately behind the tall figure in the stained blue gown.

But the earl's face was set firm as he waved to the London crowds. 'He will adjust. It's his surprise at his release, the contrast with his cell.'

'I fear it is more. He has lost his senses entirely. Mark him!'

'Keep it together until Westminster. It is essential that the people see him.'

'But they also see that he is not fit to rule them.'

'I do not intend that he will rule them. He is only our excuse.'

'But this will serve to spread fear. Look, see how he bolts.'

Henry had been surprised by a dog jumping up in the crowd and flinched away to the extent that he almost broke out of the line of procession.

'God's blood!' muttered Warwick. 'He is little more than a child, but he is the legitimacy we need.'

He stepped forward and took the king by the hand. Henry looked round in surprise, his grey eyes wondering at the gesture.

'All is well,' the earl reassured him. 'Just walk straight and true at my side.'

'To where?' stammered Henry.

309

'Back to Westminster. You remember Westminster? Your palace. You will soon be there again.'

'Westminster? Does it still stand?'

'It is standing waiting for the king.'

'For the king?'

Warwick felt the hand in his tremble.

'For you, my lord. But never fear, I shall guide you in all things.'

And they walked on, under the watch of the citizens and the peal of bells. House by house, street by street, the word spread. Whispered over walls, carried along on the backs of carts, spreading out beyond the gates into the suburbs, ridden north, south, east and west, to the very limits of the country. The Lancastrian king is back.

Henry cast his eyes ahead. The road lay straight and true before them. Clouds moved quickly overhead, parting to let the light stream down.

Somehow, he knew not why, he had been cast out of his quiet, dark cell, the womb-like home that he had known for five years, with its routine of meals, prayer and sleep. He had believed himself to have committed the remainder of his life to God, almost felt relief in the prospect of living out his years in silent contemplation, of achieving a state of grace beyond his deserving, of coming closer to the Lord before He finally called him to his side.

However, it seemed that there was to be this final act. God's plan for him lay down a different path. Perhaps it was his fault for having turned his back upon his kingship: after all, he had been chosen, crowned, anointed by God for his special purpose, and here was the Lord reminding him of his obligations, through the instrument of the Earl of Warwick.

He looked up to see birds flying overhead. So long, so many years since he had seen the expanse of the sky, seen birds like this, free on wing.

Warwick still had a firm grip upon his hand. He must go wherever this man led him. This final chapter must be lived. They turned the corner into the Strand where an even larger crowd had assembled. The guiding hand drew him to a halt.

Warwick turned to address the people.

'Behold! Here is your true king. The Lancastrian Henry VI.'

There was cheering and some clapping while others looked on in confusion.

'I have released your king from his cruel imprisonment in the Tower, where he was locked up after the usurper replaced him. Now he can rule over you again. Behold your most merciful Christian King Henry VI.'

'Where is King Edward?' called out a voice from the back.

Warwick spun round. 'The usurper, Edward, former Earl of March, has fled the country in terror with his tail between his legs. Your true king is restored to the throne. Long live King Henry VI!'

The crowd tried to echo his cry but its chorus was patchy and broken. The words seemed to fall in two halves, 'long live' and 'King Henry,' but the name came out more as a question hanging in the air. Others merely looked on.

'To Westminster!' cried Warwick, desperate to move on. 'Your king will soon be back at Westminster, and the queen and Prince of Wales will join him. Pray for them.'

Stirred by these words, Henry lifted a feeble, shaking hand to wave his blessing over the heads of the people. The hand flopped left and right like a dying bird. Warwick snatched him away.

He had been grateful to spot land. The crossing had been violent, with the ship tossed so high upon the waves, he expected every minute to be swept overboard and drowned. The wind and rain had been filled with so many curses and prayers, and Edward had even given the captain the cloak off his back to steer them safely to shore.

After hours in the blackness of the night, drifting wildly across the North Sea, with all its shades of cruelty, they had spotted land. A flat, wide, pale sort of land he knew to be the Netherlands, and Edward had dropped to his knees upon deck and thanked the Lord. And the rage in his heart and the fire in his blood came rushing back at once, with all the force of a flood. Had Warwick been before him at that moment, he would have strangled him with his bare hands, foul traitor and false friend he had proven to be. But the time would come for that, he told himself, as he watched the little vessels setting out from shore to help steer them in. There would be time for Warwick to experience his reckoning. First, Edward must grow his own strength, return to being a full, true king, active for his people, for his country, for his destiny. He must remind himself that he was a son of York.

A wooden craft with cream sails was bobbing alongside. A Burgundian, in velvet with a clipped beard, stood up from among the rowers.

'English ship?' he asked in a heavy accent. 'You have a cargo to land?'

'I am Edward, King of England, brother-in-law to Charles of Burgundy. Conduct me at once to your governor, Louis de Gruthuyse in Bruges.'

The man in the boat looked stunned. 'At once, Your Grace, at once. I will send out a fleet to collect you and arrange for horses to transport you. You are most welcome to the Low Countries, Your Grace, most humbly welcome.'

Gruthuyse's house stood in the centre of Bruges, in a pale pink-yellow L-shaped building on the corner of a cobbled market square. The guard brought Edward and his party right up to the door, where the governor stood waiting, dressed in his long furred gown. He had a distinctive pinched face, a long nose, barely any discernible jaw, and the whole effect was of a sandy colour: skin, hair, beard and eyes. He had previously been to England on diplomatic missions and Edward recognised him at once.

'My lords,' he spoke, stepping out from the ornate carved entrance, 'you are most welcome as guests in my home for as long as you need.'

Edward dismounted, his limbs suddenly stiff and tired with the ordeal.

'I thank you for your kindness in our hour of need. We will never forget it.' He turned to indicate the others in turn. 'These men have shared my journey and must share my exile: my brother, Richard of Gloucester, my brother-in-law, Anthony, Lord Rivers, and William Hastings. I am sure you remember them.'

'Indeed, I do. You are all most welcome, friends,' he insisted. 'And you must be tired and hungry. Come inside.'

Inside, a long hall hung with exquisite Flemish tapestries; a round table was set before a blazing fire. The men came in thankfully, heavy with their journey and the uncertainty of their flight. The last two days had been particularly hard on young Richard, just eighteen, who had suffered terribly during the crossing, but now he looked around in wonder at his surroundings. With kind hands and words, Gruthuyse guided them to seats piled with cushions. The warmth of the grate began slowly to revive them.

With tired smiles of gratitude, they drank the deep Burgundian wine, with its woody tones, and ate the spiced meats, rich slabs of pate, curd cheeses and pastries glazed with syrup and fruits. For a while, none could speak as they enjoyed the simple comforts of warmth and food.

Their host watched them, keeping them company with a glass of wine and spiced cake, judging the right time to speak.

'I have dispatched a messenger to Duke Charles and to your sister, the Duchess Margaret,' Gruthuyse explained eventually. 'They are currently in Mechelen, so he should arrive before morning. Do you think it is Warwick's intention to set himself up as king, with the Lancastrian as the front?'

Edward nodded. 'I do not doubt he will seek to rule through Henry's authority. He tried before and failed when he imprisoned me last year, but if he has Henry as a puppet, he can give a semblance of legitimacy, or so he must believe. He has denounced me as a traitor and an enemy of the people, a usurper of the very Lancastrian regime he fought so hard to defeat. while he makes himself a friend to our bitterest enemies.'

Gruthuyse looked puzzled. 'I do not understand how he managed to achieve this, with so much support so quickly that it took you by surprise.'

Edward looked at his friends with shame in his eyes before resting them upon Anthony. 'I was remiss; I confess it. I thought I had defeated him and I grew complacent when I should have acted. My good friend and brother, Earl Rivers, counselled me to act, and I am ashamed to say I did not take his advice. That's how the earl gained ground and time. But the seed for this, the ambition and treason has long been growing, and the old Lancastrian heartlands in the north and west never really forgot their allegiances.'

'And he has support from France?'

'He was always a lover of the French,' replied Richard.

'Yes,' Edward added, 'he has never forgiven me for not accepting the match he proposed with Bona of Savoy, and he resisted my sister's match even though he received honours for his service. When this is over, my policy against Louis of France will be most warlike.'

'And Burgundy will support you, with a full heart,' Gruthuyse nodded.

'What I need is money, men and ships. Sufficient to return to

314

England and land in some place sympathetic to my cause, from where I might send out summons to arms. I shall be eternally grateful to the duke for his assistance. This time I will rid England of the Earl of Warwick, once and for all.'

'And Clarence?' asked Hastings.

'George is a fool and a coward. He will crumple upon my return and come to my side. I do not doubt it, but if he is truly so false as to stand against me in battle, he will suffer the same penalties as his elective friends.'

'It must be so,' added Rivers, speaking for the first time. 'This must be ended or your throne and that of your children will never be secure.'

Edward nodded. 'And my wife is left alone in London with our daughters, due to deliver our next child. For all I know, she might have borne it already, or suffered and been called to God, and I am not there to see the child or offer her comfort. I do not even know if they are safe.'

'Mother is with her,' Anthony offered. 'She will ensure they come to no harm.'

'And word will come soon from England,' Gruthuyse said. 'You will hear from them, I am certain.'

But Edward had become very still, very composed. When he finally spoke, it was through teeth tense with energy and hatred. 'If anything happens to them, I shall tear Warwick limb from limb with my own bare hands.'

'Then let us begin,' said Hastings. 'Let us begin at once. As soon as we are rested from our journey, we will send out more letters requesting support from our English and Burgundian allies and begin to plan our return. You will be back on the throne of England before the spring.'

'Never doubt it,' Edward replied. 'For a while I had forgotten that I was my father's son. No one will stop me from retaking what is rightfully mine.'

Henry had new robes. Borrowed robes. They hung down in wide folds from his shoulders, almost like curtains engulfing his frail body. The material felt heavy and luxurious, with the purple velvet spaced with panels of cloth of gold. He was unused to the weight of it and the strange way it moved about his legs. There was so much material behind him, brushing against his calves, that it felt as if someone was there, continually touching him. Continually seeking to caress his legs. He moved again, kicked out, shook it off.

'Sit still.'

Warwick was seated to his right while the king was at the head of the table. George was placed on the other side. The white chamber had been prepared for a special dinner, being smaller and more intimate than Westminster's great hall, more conducive to conversation, less likely to overwhelm the king. Henry looked at the tapestries with their scenes of hunting, the cupboard bearing gold and silver plate, the branches of wax attached to the walls that made the place burn bright.

'All you need do is smile and nod, be gracious,' Warwick instructed. 'Your loyal friends wish to come and give you their welcome and celebrate your return.'

'How many?' asked the king.

'On this occasion, a mere handful: your brother, Jasper Tudor; my Lord Stanley, I mean Baron Thomas Stanley; the Earl of Oxford; Henry Stafford with his wife, Margaret, daughter of John Beaufort; and her son, Henry, a boy of twelve or thirteen. A small party, nothing more.'

'Forget the people. Try and enjoy the food and wine,' added George, out of his depth in the strange corridors of Henry's mind.

Warwick shot him a withering look. 'Right, if we are ready?'

He gave the signal to the guards who admitted the guests. Oxford came first followed by Thomas Stanley, both eager to see the state of the king's health and accrue the benefits of their new-found loyalty. Each paused and bowed low before being shown to their seats. Next came Tudor, striding tall and broad with royal blood, who insisted on walking right up to Henry and embracing him.

'Brother, such a sight you are to behold, restored to us by the grace of God. Praise be, praise be.'

Henry stiffened at the contact.

'The king will need time to adjust,' explained Warwick.

'No doubt,' agreed Tudor, 'and I will be here to assist with that. And my young nephew, Henry, your namesake. Have you met him yet?'

At the sound of his name, the boy appeared in the doorway led by his mother. Margaret Beaufort had been widowed early, with the death of Edmund Tudor from plague, and had remarried the quiet, solid Henry Stafford. She appeared demure, pious in her bearing, with her plain gown and headdress. She had the appearance of an older woman, with her drawn, lined face, but she must only have been in her mid-twenties. The boy was slender, dark-haired, with a slight cast in one eye.

The trio came forward when summoned and bowed low in a carefully rehearsed move.

'My nephew,' spoke the king, surprising everyone. 'I have a nephew.' He turned to Warwick. 'Can he sit by me?'

'He will sit with his mother, but it is close enough,' said Warwick, surprised. They were shown to their seats.

'I have a nephew!'

'You have a son too,' added Warwick, frowning. 'A son in France who will inherit your throne.'

The king was silent.

'We speak of your son, Edward,' said George, concerned by the set of Henry's face.

317

'Edward? Hasn't he fled?'

'Not Edward of York who usurped your throne. Your son Edward, Prince of Wales, who is in France with his mother, your wife and queen. They will be returning to England soon to join you.'

'My wife.'

'Yes, Queen Margaret.'

The servants brought in the first round of dishes, placing them gently on the table before the king. They then laid them before the guests. Hands reached out, breaking bread, lifting up portions of meat.

Henry stared, bewildered at the spread. His hands fell like weights into his lap.

'Might I pass you something, my lord?' asked Warwick, putting down his portion of meat. 'There is roast pork, baked chicken, venison pie. Or something lighter? A pottage or cheese tart?'

'I can't eat all of this.'

'No one expects you to. But you may have a little of whatever you like. Here.' Warwick spooned some meat onto the king's plate. 'The king must eat. Your people expect it.'

'It's too rich.'

The earl placed a bowl of pottage at the king's side and put a spoon in it. 'There. That will do then. But you must have a little to give you strength to rule.'

'Is it true,' asked Jasper Tudor from his place next to George, 'that the usurper is being sheltered in Burgundy?'

'That is what we have heard,' Warwick replied. 'No doubt he will seek assistance from his friends but we have France on our side. The former Earl of March will be intercepted the moment he sets foot on English soil again if he is brave enough to do so.'

'Oh, he will try,' said Oxford quietly. 'He certainly will.'

No one heeded his comment and Warwick continued. 'As soon as the tides are favourable, Queen Margaret will sail with Prince Edward and Princess Anne. Yes,' he explained, seeing their surprise, 'I have married my younger daughter to the prince as part of our alliance. The sooner she bears an heir, the better.'

He did not see George's face blanche at this comment, nor the memory cross his face of the child he had lost on the sea crossing, the child that was supposed to be the Yorkist heir once Edward had been removed.

'But until then,' the earl went on, 'we are among friends. Let us eat and drink and rejoice that the rightful king of England is back in Westminster again.'

'A toast,' replied William Stafford, rising to his feet and raising his glass, 'to King Henry and the Lancastrian line.'

'To King Henry,' they echoed with force, drinking glasses full of wine, with hearts full of hope. 'To King Henry and the Lancastrian line.'

'Did you hear the cheering?' asked Jacquetta. The light was fading outside the window, with its thickly paned glass.

Elizabeth was lying on the edge of the bed. A wooden cradle was pulled up alongside it, which she rocked gently with one hand. The room was dark, framed by the ecclesiastical arches that defined its shape, and lit by flickering candles. On the far side, the younger girls sat sewing.

'I did. I thought it might wake him, it was so loud.'

'It must have been Warwick returning with the old king. They passed right by us.'

'You do not think Warwick will try and force us out.'

'Out of sanctuary? I should hope not.'

Elizabeth propped herself up on one elbow. 'But what if he does? He is unscrupulous.'

'Then we would flee to Burgundy or back to Luxembourg, where I spent my childhood. I still have family there who would help us.'

'You do not think he will harm us?'

'Two women and a bunch of children? Would he make martyrs of us?'

The baby in the cradle began to stir. Elizabeth leaned over and lifted him out, a long, warm bundle in her arms.

'He is hungry, see his mouth, how he already knows to seek the breast.'

She lay back down, placed the infant beside her and loosened her gown. It only took a little guidance before he began to suckle.

'It is a good thing he has taken to it so well,' remarked Jacquetta. 'At least one of us will not go hungry.'

'The abbot will not let us starve.'

'He will not; he is a good man. And there have been tradesmen of London, a butcher and a baker who brought supplies to the steps outside for the love of our family. We are not forgotten. All we must do is remain calm, pass the days here until Edward returns. It might be any day.'

Elizabeth was quiet, watching the pull of the child.

'He will return; you know it.'

She nodded, but her eyes filled with tears. 'I know he wants to. But there are so many dangers between him and us, not least the sea, even before he has to face Warwick.'

'You cannot think that way. You will only torture yourself. There is nothing we can do from here except to pray and keep in good spirits. Trust in God. He will not fail us.'

Elizabeth closed her eyes.

Jacquetta turned back to the window. It had fallen quiet again outside. 'I expect they are feasting,' she guessed, 'to celebrate his return. But Henry was not fit to rule before Edward. He can hardly be a better king now, after the long years of his incarceration. I wonder how long Warwick can keep up this pretence.'

It was the largest library he had ever seen. The walls were lined with shelves, upon which lay heavy leather-bound volumes, some as books, others as collections of manuscripts, some rolls and some images. The air was a mixture of dust and paper, with a dryness and particular tang of paint and ink. Edward and Louis were perusing the shelves, which ran from floor to ceiling. The ambassador, Oliver de la Marche, was seated by the hearth.

'It is a remarkable collection,' Edward was saying. 'We have some similar books in our university libraries, at Oxford and Cambridge, and in our monasteries, but I have never seen such a wide selection of different manuscripts, and the illumination is exceptional.'

'We have very fine artists here in Burgundy,' remarked de la Marche. 'Many of them study in Florentine and Milanese studios, and bring their skills back to adorn our court.'

'I would very much like to see them,' said Edward. 'I hope Charles will invite me to be his guest soon, for the weeks pass.'

Marche shifted uncomfortably and looked at Gruthuyse. Edward caught the expression.

'What is the matter? What am I missing?'

'I believe,' said Gruthuyse uncomfortably, 'that the duke does not wish to compromise his good relationship with England. He wishes to help you but he feels that he might invite hostilities if he received you at his court.'

'Invite hostilities!' Edward was incensed. 'Yes, I wish to invite hostilities against the traitor who has displaced me from my throne and my kingdom. Duke Charles' good relationship was not with England, it was with me! Does he seek now to make peace, to make friends with my oppressor?'

Gruthuyse spread his hands in apology. 'The duke is happy for you to remain as my guest and will provide you with financial assistance but he cannot be seen to be entertaining you.'

'In case he gives offence to Warwick?'

'It is simply diplomatic relations.'

'It is a gross betrayal of friendship. And what does my sister, his wife, have to say?'

'I believe she is writing to you, my lord, to express her support. They will fund your ships.'

Edward pursed his lips. 'And if I were to ride to his court, where is he now? Would he turn me away? Would my sister turn me away?'

'The duke and duchess wish to see you restored to your throne as soon as possible.'

'Then they must help me! I have received a handful of replies to the letters I have sent out; many friends are willing to help with money and supplies, but it is not enough. With the duke's assistance, I would be gone far sooner and an awkward diplomatic situation would be avoided.'

Gruthuyse nodded in acknowledgement of this. 'I will write to the duke again.'

'As will I,' said de la Marche. 'We will see what can be done.'

Edward turned away and pondered the fire.

'I understand the nature of politics. I understand the delicate international balance all too well. But a time must come when a ruler commits their colours. And that time is in the defence of family. Blood must come first and I gave the duke my own dear sister as his wife. When I am restored to my throne, not if, when, I shall not forget those who stood with me. Nor those who stood against me. I make this my solemn promise.'

Gruthuyse looked solemn. 'Your words strike me at the heart. I will compose a letter this very evening and dispatch it in the morning.

Burgundy will always be a friend to England and England is in need of a friend today.'

Edward clapped him on the arm. 'Thank you. That was spoken like a true brother.'

TWENTY

The Final Stand, March 1471

For a long time, there was nothing but whiteness. Absolute stillness and silence.

He stood close to the bow, holding fast to the wooden foremast as the ship rose and fell. The grey waves broke against the side and the fine sea spray wetted his face. There had been nothing to see for hours, save this thick, close white veil, allowing no light to penetrate. Still, the ship inched forward, trusting, hoping, ever closer. They had been at sea for almost an entire night and day.

'Still no sign?' asked Hastings, coming up behind him.

'Not yet, but our course is set fair, so we must be on the right path. It's this poor wind dropping and lifting that slows us.'

'Better a poor wind that lets us creep into shore than a fierce one that would smash us to pieces.'

'You speak the truth. How fares Richard?'

The young Duke of Gloucester had suffered terribly from seasickness upon the return voyage, on account of not being able to see his surroundings through the mist.

'Rivers is with him at the bow. Our landing cannot come soon enough for him.'

'Nor for me. There is so much work to be done.'

Hastings nodded, conscious of the enormity of the task that lay ahead. 'You have a plan?'

Edward nodded. 'I will put out that I do not return as king, but only to claim my lands in York, inherited from my father. That way Warwick cannot justify an attack upon me. Then we will march south, gathering troops as we go. By the time we reach London, we will have the numbers to meet them.'

'I have my men in the Midlands who will readily join us.'

'And Rivers has contacts in East Anglia and Lincolnshire. I am hoping that the Duke of Norfolk will come to join us and raise his forces.'

'He will. Norfolk is a true and loyal friend.'

'And William Stanley too, unlike his treacherous brother. He will come out of hiding when he hears of our return. Bourchier too, who as archbishop, has had to play Warwick's game, but he will drop him as soon as he can. They will come to us.'

Hastings nodded. 'And this time?'

'This time there will be no mercy.'

A sound from above drew their attention, a strange, high crying. Hastings shielded his eyes to look.

'What was that?'

They heard the noise again together, saw the blur through the clouds overhead. Edward realised what it was.

'Seagulls. We must be nearing land.'

Then, through the mist, the king saw it. The distant tip of greenness, undulating, as it called to him. A long line, flanked with white, where it ran down to the water. England.

'There, look, you see!'

'Yes! We have arrived!'

The captain appeared on deck behind them. He was a grey, grizzled man, with skin tanned and salted from years on the waves. 'You've seen it then? Lad in the crow's nest called down. It's Ravenspurn in Yorkshire.'

'See,' said Edward, turning to Hastings, 'see how God favours us, bringing me home to my own county? Call the others; the end is in sight.'

Warwick stood at the head of the table in the council chamber. George sat on his left and Henry VI, in ermine robes, to the right. Further down the table, the places were half filled, and the men occupying those seats looked at each other with unease. Here was Archbishop Bourchier and his brothers; the Duke of Oxford; Thomas Stanley; Henry Stafford; Warwick's own brothers, Montagu and John Neville, Archbishop of York; and Henry Holland, Duke of Exeter, once married to Edward's own sister, Anne of York. Among them were others formerly loyal to York, swept along in fear and change, and those like Norfolk and William Stanley, who still honoured Edward in their hearts and were seeking opportunities to act in his name.

'This bill will punish those who speak against the king,' the earl was urging darkly, eyes flashing as he waved a sheet of parchment before them, 'and those who provide shelter or support to the usurper Edward of York. We have, at great cost, restored the rightful line of Lancaster, and must be seen to quell any efforts to restore the traitor. Even idle words of praise for the old regime must be suppressed.'

'Do we take you to mean,' asked Archbishop Bourchier, slowly, appealing to the other councillors, 'that any conversation overhead, say in a tavern, or between man and wife, or by the maids washing linen, any conversation considered critical of the new regime, or supportive of Edward, is to merit the severest of punishments?'

'I do mean that,' replied Warwick. 'We cannot have treasonous talk spreading through the realm, causing discontent, leading to rebellion. It is too dangerous.'

'So a man might, in his cups, make a joke, or repeat a story he has heard among friends, and suffer death for it?'

'Is it acceptable to speak treason so long as it is among friends then? Or with wine as an excuse, Archbishop? Would you have the whole country wagging its tongues against its leader?'

'Might you be so fearful of this treasonous talk, Warwick,' asked Bourchier, 'because you have, yourself, recently seen how effective it can be? I refer to your own campaign of sowing discontent against the Yorkist regime?' He stopped just short of calling them lies and slanders.

Warwick turned to the archbishop with the full fury of rage in his eyes. 'Everything that has been done, has been done with the purpose of restoring the true line of England and bringing King Henry back to the throne. Would you suggest that it was wrong to have done so? Because that would be treasonous talk, of exactly the kind I intend to punish by the most strident means.'

Bourchier held up his hands. 'That is not the purpose of my speech as you are aware. I fear such harsh penalties being used against idle and drunken tongues, which will punish the weak rather than your real enemies.'

'That is likely because your master was in possession of an idle and drunken tongue, my lord.'

The slur against Edward created a ripple around the room.

'That was not the master I knew and served,' replied Bourchier, softly but firmly, before resuming his seat.

It looked as if Warwick might respond but Norfolk rose quickly from his seat. 'Might I ask, my lord, for some charity and clemency to be shown towards Queen Elizabeth and her children, who are, at this time, sheltering in sanctuary here…'

'Elizabeth, wife of the former Earl of March, you mean. Our queen is Margaret.'

'I mean Elizabeth, who has been our queen these past six years. She has recently borne a child in sanctuary and is in great need of charity for her sustenance and that of her family.'

At this, King Henry lifted up his head and spoke clearly. 'The women and children must be provided for, mustn't they? The innocents must be fed, as God told us. The little ones must not suffer. Ensure it.'

Warwick looked at him amazed; it was the first time he had spoken since they entered the chamber and now he issued a command.

'My lord,' continued Norfolk, addressing himself directly to Henry, 'they are living in poor conditions, cold and afraid, without the support and protection of their men. They need not only regular supplies but the promise that no harm will be done to them on account of their family name. The earl has previously taken action against the queen's father and brother and attempted to slur the name of her mother, an elderly lady of noble blood, formerly the wife of your own uncle, John of Bedford.'

'Is this true? We cannot have them in need or fear. I give my promise here today that no harm will come to them or their kin, and we will arrange provisions to be sent from the kitchens here. The earl will support me in this.'

Henry looked to Warwick but the earl was staring at him with a fixity that contained surprise and rage.

'Thank you, my lord,' replied Norfolk, ignoring Warwick. 'I knew that your kindness and faith would not permit you to let their suffering continue.'

'It is probably better, my lord,' Warwick added, trying to regain control of the chamber, 'if you leave such trivial matters to me.'

'On the things I do not understand, yes,' said Henry, 'but not when it comes to the little children.'

'He is regaining himself,' muttered George, so that only Warwick might hear. 'He is finding his voice again.'

But Warwick brushed him off with an angry gesture.

'Let us return to the matter of law and order in the city,' pronounced the earl, looking out at the council. 'Now that the king is back in Westminster, the treason and slander laws must be put in place to protect his reputation. In recent years, governance here has grown slack, with rioting and lawlessness taking hold.'

'With respect, my lord,' spoke Bourchier bravely, 'as you have been absent from the capital for so long, you may be unaware that the former lawlessness erupted only as a consequence of the period King Edward was your captive at Middleham Castle. Upon his return to the city, he took measures to contain and repair the city, which were proving a success.'

For a moment Warwick was speechless. Norfolk jumped into the void.

'There is no doubt, as we have seen in recent years, that the city benefits from the presence of a strong and capable king.'

'A king who is respected and loved by his people,' added William Stanley from the back of the chamber, 'who has earned their trust by proving himself to be present when required. Any recent disturbances were the result of circumstances beyond the king's control, as any hypothetical king would discover.'

'And our dealings with the mayor and aldermen have always been the most cordial and productive,' added Bourchier, 'and were of the utmost importance in the speedy resolution of conflict. Yet I see the mayor is not represented in council today; was an invitation issued?'

Warwick appeared close to the point of explosion.

Sitting back, George watched as the earl balled his fists under the table. And he saw at once that Warwick, for all his audacious schemes and martial ability, lacked the easy charm of Edward, and the ability to appease. People would never like him the way they did the son of York, and they would not willingly serve him, and so because of it, he realised with a sinking stomach, this regime was already doomed.

A clerk hurried in, down the side of the chamber, carrying a note. The movement broke the awkwardness just at the point where tempers were reaching the boil.

Warwick read the note with concentration, then handed it to George. He was still reading when the earl addressed the room.

'Edward, former Earl of March, has landed on the coast of Yorkshire.'

At once the chamber began to stir. Men half rose in their seats as if to leave at once and desert the present company.

Norfolk's eyes met William Stanley's and then Bourchier's.

'Stay where you are!'

Warwick's command halted them all.

'The former Earl of March is a usurper, an oppressor and destroyer of your sovereign Lord, Henry VI and of the noble blood of this realm. A great reformation of his abuses has taken place, for the common weal of all the people and to amend all the great, mischievous and inordinate breaches of the law. Anyone departing from this point with the intention of aiding, abetting, or joining forces with the invader will suffer the full penalties of the law. You are tasked, at once, to raise your troops and meet with me in opposition to the traitor, fulfilling your duty to king and country, to the glory and safe delivery of your families. Failure to do so will result in death.'

The chamber was as silent as the grave. No man moved as these words penetrated the crowd. But then, as if by deliberate choice, they began to collect themselves, made their apologies and hurried away, in groups of two and three, or singly, until there was only Warwick, Henry and George remaining.

'They are hurrying to obey your command,' smiled the king. 'They will return soon with their armies. I will pray for their souls.'

'And I must do my part,' added George, rising to his feet. 'I will summon my men and send you word.'

Warwick barely heard him. He gave a dismissive nod, white-faced with the consciousness of a man on the verge of drowning. Nor did he notice when George slipped from the room, nor the party of Norfolk, Bourchier and Stanley awaiting him in the cloister outside.

Margaret stood on the cliff path, her face set against the wind. For three weeks the northern French coast had been battered by wind and rain. As soon as the storm paused for breath, its direction changed, leaving them sitting on the shore in despair. The ships were ready and loaded with cargo, bobbing in the bay.

Ahead, on the path, walked her son and the Lady Anne. They had been married last December in a ceremony at Angers Cathedral, but they were still young. Especially the girl, who seemed even smaller and slighter than before. She was the same age that Margaret herself had been when she had come to England to be married, but Margaret had already been so well-grown and tall, her body that of a woman, with the monthly flowers. She had seen no signs of consummation, even though the pair occasionally shared a bed and the chamber maids assured her that the girl had her courses regularly. What they most needed was an heir, a boy, to keep the line going. Her son, Edward, would fight in England. She knew he would; this was what all his training had led him to, but he was only one. And one was not enough.

She turned to the sea captain. 'There is no change?'

'No change, my lady, the wind still bears down from the north.'

It was true. She felt it harsh and brackish upon her face.

'So we must wait another day or two?'

'It is in God's hands.'

She nodded. Everything was in God's hands. There was no point getting frustrated. She would go to the little chapel again, get out of this rain, take the girl with her, and pray as hard as she might.

'How the people cheered!' exclaimed Richard, as they rode through the gates of Coventry.

'It was truly heartening,' Edward agreed, riding at his side. 'And there were many offers of support and men joining us. It fills me with hope.'

The thick, pale walls of the castle in the centre of the city loomed ahead. Somehow, word had spread. Again, in the streets, people came out to wave and cheer, shouting for Edward and for York, even though the skies threatened rain. The men following them dispersed, some into the castle keep, some finding billets in the inns and hospital that lined the way, and others seeking the marketplace.

'We are but few at the moment,' admitted the king, 'perhaps two hundred, a little more, but once we reach my heartlands, we will be in the thousands.'

Once they were safely inside the walls, the drawbridge was brought up behind them and guards placed at all vantage points.

'I feel we are safe here,' said Edward, dismounting. 'There are pockets of Lancastrian support in the area, but the old Beaufort line is almost gone save for a few youths.'

'No doubt they will lend their colours to Warwick,' said Rivers. 'The scouts say he is marching north and hopes to engage you here.'

'Here? I am not ready to fight yet and he knows it, which is why he seeks the advantage. If we can reach London, the mayor will welcome us and the city will loan us funds. And there is Bourchier too. And if we have London, we have won the battle, like in sixty-one.'

Braziers were burning outside the hall, lining the way inside. The constable was waiting upon the steps to bid them welcome.

'You honour us with your presence, my lord. The castle is at your disposal. All is secure.'

'Thank you. We will dine at once.'

'There are gentlemen waiting to see you, my lord. I currently have them in my parlour, but will send them through to you, upon your request.'

'Very well. Let them come to the hall and present themselves as we eat but accompanied by a guard.'

'Right away, my lord.'

The hall was square and panelled with dark wood. Fires had been kindled in the grates and rich tapestries dug out and hung in honour of the king. A makeshift canopy of cloth of gold was draped above the place where Edward sat. Plate glinted on the shelves and a gallery of minstrels and tumblers awaited instruction.

They had barely taken their places at the table when the far doors opened.

Edward recognised his visitors at once and rose to his feet.

'Norfolk! Stanley!'

They fell upon bowed knees before their king. The emotion rose up in Edward's throat at the sight of his friends, and he gestured them towards him, clapping them upon the shoulder and taking them by the hand.

'You are most heartily welcome, my friends.'

'We came as soon as we heard,' explained Norfolk. 'We walked out of a council meeting when the news was brought.'

'A meeting held by Warwick?'

'With his puppet king at his side. We were half a day ahead of him on the road.'

'Tell me,' Edward urged. 'What news of my family?'

'Your wife and children are doing well, including your son.'

The words brought him to life. 'My son? I have a son?'

'A fine boy, my lord, a strong boy. Your wife has named him Edward. We have ensured they were well treated. They are safe in sanctuary at Westminster. No man dared touch them.'

'Your mother has removed to Berkhamsted, seeking a life of retirement,' added Stanley, 'and Grace and her mother have been housed safely at Eltham.'

'God be praised,' cried Edward, his heart soaring. 'A son, a son at last. An heir. Edward. That's a blow for Warwick and George and their schemes. We will show the people of London my boy when I am master in Westminster again.'

'How is George?' asked Richard, tentatively.

'He chafes, as always,' replied Norfolk. 'Warwick has quite forgotten him amid his new French alliance. He has a more powerful son-in-law now, in the Prince of Wales.'

'Poor George,' said Richard sadly. 'He always chased after the shiniest baubles, but he was never one of them. And Mother?'

'Your mother is in good health.'

'But Warwick's power is fading,' added Stanley, 'and he knows it. Bourchier was strident in his opposition and Henry's presence did him no favours. He races north now in a show of desperation.'

'And George with him?'

'Aye, George at his side.'

'Come and sit,' urged the king. 'I thank you for all the pains you have taken on our behalf; they will never be forgotten. Eat with us and tell us how things fare in London, and what Warwick plans. It is only a matter of days before we come face to face again.'

Night was falling outside. The wax brackets burned brightly in the hall; the minstrels were playing and the spiced wine was being passed along the table. Edward was recounting the story of their flight to Burgundy when the constable approached in haste.

'My lord, forgive me, it is your brother.'

'George? What has he done now?'

'He is here, at the gates, asking to be admitted. Quite alone, save for his squire.'

At once, Edward was beset by conflicting emotions. All the anger, frustration and sense of betrayal he had locked away in his heart rose to the surface. 'George is here? Has he stated his purpose? Is he armed?'

'He does not appear so beyond his sword. He wishes for an audience with you.'

'I'll bet he does!' burst out Rivers. 'Now that he knows he is on the losing side.'

'Does he deserve an audience with you?' asked Hastings. 'Do you feel disposed to grant it?'

'He would be well served if you turned him away alive,' added Norfolk.

Edward looked at Richard, knowing that he would see the same struggle reflected in the young man's face. Richard's dark eyes, so like their father's, spoke volumes of his suffering.

'Richard?'

The duke sighed. 'Hear what he has to say.'

'And then? If he throws himself upon our mercy?'

'I cannot answer. Once I thought he deserved the worst of punishments or else he would act again, just as he has. Now, I find I cannot say.'

'Nothing is guaranteed,' replied Edward, before turning to the constable. 'We will hear him. He has one chance. Remove his sword and bring him in.'

The jovial atmosphere in the hall turned to ice. The musicians halted their instruments and crept away; servants carried plates back down to the kitchens and did not return. The men gathered themselves together in a group on the dais and waited: Edward, Richard, Hastings, Rivers, Norfolk and Stanley, formidable in their allegiance and conviction.

'I hope you do not regret this,' murmured Rivers, as the far door opened.

George appeared very small in comparison. Small and humbled, his body folded inwards somehow, his head hung low, all the fight drained out of him.

The constable indicated that he might go forward. He took a few steps into the centre of the room, then fell upon his knees and prostrated himself, flat upon the floor, face to the rushes.

It was an unexpected move. The men on the dais waited, expecting him to rise but he did not.

Eventually, Edward called out from the other end. 'Get up!'

George stood waiting, thinking there might be another instruction, but none came. He looked at the panel of men ahead, as if they were a frieze carved in stone, holding his destiny in their hands. Six pairs of eyes stared back at him.

Eventually, he took a step forward, then another. He walked slowly, each step painful. Before the table, he came to a teetering halt.

'Brother…'

No one answered.

'Brother,' he began again. 'I have come to beg your forgiveness

336

and throw myself upon your mercy.' He knelt for a second time. 'My treachery has been unforgiveable. I do not deserve an audience with you, let alone your kindness. I can only beg, for the sake of our family name, for the memory of our father, the love of our mother, and hope that the charity you always hold within your heart will spare me. I will retreat, live in exile, should you desire it. I will enter a monastery, live out my years wherever you wish, spend my days in making amends for my crimes. I forgot myself. I was led by the earl. I let my selfish greed and ambition overcome my nobler virtues. I have betrayed you, a better man than myself, and my true king. Humbly, I appeal for your mercy.'

'He makes a good speech,' whispered Norfolk.

'Aye, he has never failed at that,' replied Hastings. 'Hot air is his skill.'

Edward was torn. The others could see his conflict, barely sensing the depths of it, but they held back. It was the king's decision to make, as a monarch, as a man, as a brother.

'How can I possibly trust you again?'

'I give you my word. I will swear an oath. You can take my life now, or at any point when I might show disloyalty again.'

'I have no wish to take your life.'

'Then allow me to dedicate myself to your service. You will never have cause to doubt me again.'

'You have already given me cause enough. This is not the first time.' The anger began to rise in Edward, surpassing the initial surprise at George's arrival. He took to his feet. 'I was forced to flee my country, amid storms that might have drowned me. I was alone, save for the loyalty of these good men, and my true brother; in fact, all these men seated here with me are more my brothers than you. And my wife and children, fled into sanctuary at night, in fear, while my wife laboured with child. All for your stupid vanity. There is no good reason why I should forgive you. The sight of you fills me with loathing. If it were not for our blood ties, I would act at once.'

George hung his head low. 'I deserve all that and more, much more. Let me be of use to you. I know Warwick's intentions.'

'Then do not tarry, tell us!'

'He has married his daughter, Anne, to Edward, son of Henry VI. They are waiting with Margaret of Anjou for a favourable wind to bring them to the West Country. He has Tudor, Exeter, Oxford and the young Beaufort men, the brothers of Henry, who was Duke of Somerset, and plans to draw you down there to engage where he has the most support. Perhaps close to the cities of Exeter or Gloucester, wherever he can lure you.'

Edward turned to his friends, spoke softly. 'This suits my plans well. While Warwick engages in the west, we shall march directly south and enter London. If he wishes to fight me, he can come and find me.'

'What of this knave?' asked Rivers.

Edward turned back to his brother. 'You can earn your forgiveness. We might have some use for you, although your treachery will never be forgotten. The constable will conduct you to the castle cells where you will pass the night. Tomorrow you ride south with us. You will not ask what we do, or where, or when; you will not speak unless spoken to, nor will you approach any of my men. You will hold yourself fast to my cause and be obedient in all things, and grateful for the chance to redress your wrongs. Constable!'

The king turned away so that he did not have to see his brother being escorted from the room.

'Open these gates! Take me to them at once!'

The mayor's hands shook with speed. London had opened its gates and cheered home its Yorkist king as he knew it would. Now

338

the aldermen were emptying the arsenal of its hoard, and men were gathering in the streets, calling his name. But Edward's first impulse was to ride to Westminster.

The keys jangled and rattled. The outer gates finally yielded and swung back on their ornate hinges. On the inside of the precincts, the abbot was waiting.

'My lord! It is you, at last! Come this way.'

He conducted the king through the shadows around the abbey, down dark passageways without light, into the inner sanctum.

'I can report that they are all well. Oh, what joy that God has brought you back to us.'

'I have heard of your infinite kindness to my family. It will never be forgotten.'

The final door stood between them with its rusty oak lock. Edward hurried past the abbot, banging upon the wood with his fist.

'It is me! Edward! Unlock the door.'

There was movement inside. Whispered voices.

'I swear, it is me here, with the abbot. I am returned!'

And then he heard her voice. 'Edward? Is it truly you?'

'My love, I have returned. Open the door.'

The long bolt made a screeching sound as it was drawn. He pushed against the strong wood impatiently but it did not budge. Then there was a second dragging of metal, and a third.

'See how secure they have been here,' nodded the abbot.

Finally, the door yielded. At first, the darkness within blinded him, but he did not require the use of his eyes, as the arms of his wife wrapped about him, pulling him to her. He breathed in her scent again, his lips upon her hair and cheek.

'I can't believe it's you,' she said. 'We have waited so long, but we never gave up hope.'

'No,' said Jacquetta from the shadows behind. 'We never gave up hope.'

'Daddy!' The little princesses came forward, Elizabeth at five, and the smaller ones, taking hold of him about the waist and legs.

'Come inside, come in,' urged the queen, meeting his eyes at last. Hers were brimming with promise. 'There is someone else you must meet.'

Elizabeth led him to the cradle. The boy was sturdy, solid, over six months now. She scooped him up in his blankets and held him forward for the king to take.

'A son! We have a son! His name is Edward!'

He took the boy with both hands and held him up level with his face. The child struggled and mewed a little. Edward brought him close and kissed him upon the forehead.

'Welcome, Prince Edward, future King of England. Welcome to the world, my boy. As soon as I have rid it of our enemies, I will return to you and our lives together can begin.'

Behind the hedge, the mist pooled deep and white. The time was drawing near, the hour coming closer. He felt it in his chest where his heart pounded in anticipation. In partial battle armour, his visor up, Edward drew his commanders in close as the day was already beginning to fade. Around them, the field was patchy with the mass of men waiting quietly, and the dark waving shapes of trees.

'The scouts have returned with information. There will be no fighting tonight. We must wait until first light. There's no point trying to meet them like this. They lie on the other side of the north road and we will move in as soon as the mist fades. They've overshot us with their cannons and believe us to be much further away. At least we'll have the element of surprise.'

'They are lined up, facing this way?' asked Richard, slightly stiff in his armour, facing his first battle. His back still pained him, but all the training he had undertaken and the doctors' ointments applied to his spine had made it bearable.

'They are facing all ways at the moment, and I am only guessing at their position from the direction of their guns.'

'Damn this mist,' said Hastings, looking around. 'It will be the undoing of us.'

'No,' said Edward, 'it will be the undoing of Warwick. We will make it our cover and our friend. We will use it to steal close and give us the advantage. Do not fear it. Embrace it as a cloak and hold our ground.'

'What will the formation be?' asked Richard.

'You will take the right flank, if you are happy to do so. You will have Norfolk and Suffolk with you. Hastings, you will take the left flank, and George will be beside me in the centre.'

George, Duke of Clarence, subdued, lifted his head. 'I will fight beside you even though Warwick himself stands before me.'

'As he may well do,' said Edward.

'Who does he have with him?' asked Rivers.

'Montagu, Exeter, Baron Stanley, Tudor and Oxford. Their numbers are greater than ours, but that has never stopped us before. The morning cock is about to crow, and when it does, we shall ready the men to move forward on foot.'

'What do you mean to do with Warwick?' asked Hastings. 'Do we try and take him alive? And his brothers, and Exeter, and Oxford? Do we bring them captive to you if the chance presents itself?'

Edward took a deep breath. 'This is the last stand between myself and Warwick. One of us will not survive this battle. There will be no prisoners.'

Warwick stood behind the line of cannons, peering out across the white scrubland.

'Do we keep firing?' asked Oxford, appearing out of the mist. 'Do we have any indication that we are hitting our marks?'

'Keep up the fire. We must weaken them as much as possible before the morning. They were last sighted approaching on the south road, so we must be hitting some part of their forces.'

'If you are sure.'

'It's all we have at the moment.'

'Very well, I will give the order to continue. We have ammunition sufficient for another three hours.'

'Thank you. Have you seen Exeter?'

'Not this past hour. He went to rally his men over to the west.'

'His men are troubled?'

'Not so much troubled, I believe, but uncertain in the mist. They came for a fight but sitting around in uncertainty is unsettling some of them. Exeter will put them straight.'

'And George? Has George returned?'

Oxford tried to keep his voice light, untainted by the rumours that were flying around camp. 'Not yet, my lord.'

'I have heard what the men are saying. His banner was sighted among Edward's men.'

'I cannot know, my lord. It may be a ruse to affect our morale.'

Warwick nodded. 'Send me word the moment he returns.'

The sky was beginning to glow with the pinkness of dawn.

'Now!' cried Edward, lifting his sword high above his shoulder. 'Now is the time to advance. Come men, I have been driven from my kingdom by this friend turned traitor, who would bring about the destruction of this realm for the sake of his own ambition. For England, for the York kings, and for my son, Prince Edward, heir to this land, to ensure his peaceful rule.'

'For Prince Edward,' echoed George at his side and Richard from beyond, 'for his peaceful rule.' The body of men behind them cheered and repeated their words. Edward turned to face them.

'My followers, friends, men, today we give our all. Your king, your country and your God might ask of you the ultimate sacrifice here upon this misty field. If we should win, we win peace and good health for all, and if we lose, we ascend to the right hand of the Lord, to bask in his eternal glory, with the eternal gratitude of the house of York. Everything is at stake. We fight today for our liberty and our lives. To preserve the rights granted to my father. To preserve the peaceful rule of the family of York. We take no prisoners and we fight on until the end. God bless you men; he will guide your hands and keep you safe. Onwards, with your king, onwards to the fight!'

'Onwards to the fight!' And the company erupted in a motion of limbs.

The terrain was uneven, sparsely covered with grass, dotted with bushes and trees. The spaces between were still thick with mist, which not even the fingers of first light could disperse. It was impossible to see the distant forest, but they knew it was there, and almost at arm's reach beyond it, the armies of the Earl of Warwick.

The enemy came out of the whiteness in groups: two, three, four, stumbling and dazed, into the furious onslaught of sword and pike. Voices roared up through the mist as they recognised that this was the place and this the moment, and called for assistance. Edward's men moved swiftly and decisively, cutting down their foes the moment they became visible. Men, born from the mist, only to fall back, bleeding, into its pockets. The roar of the cannons had ceased. There was only the striking metal of conflict and the groans of the wounded.

He came with sword swirling. Some anonymous minion of the earl, bent upon destruction, cutting a swathe through the Yorkist men. He was taller, broader than the others, almost as tall as the king.

Edward did not see him at first. He was engaged with the centre, parrying the men who urged towards him, catching their blows, hurling them aside. The giant came from the left, hurtling down the line, breaking men as he raced through them. Edward fought on unawares, but the giant saw the king and flew over with his sword raised to the place where the king stood. He was bent on death, bent on murder and destruction, bent upon doing his master's will. He was the instrument, bringing death to the field. And, believing himself to be the danger, this made him blind to other dangers.

Already, George was behind him with his weapon raised. Before the giant came within reach of the king, inching forward to claim his life, he felt a sudden strike. The thrust of long, cold steel pushing through his guts. And he knew it was over before it had begun. He fell to his knees, mouth frothing with blood, just as Edward turned to witness his death. As the giant crumpled, he revealed George, standing in his shadow, sword drenched to the hilt.

Gasping at the narrowness of his escape, Edward strode to meet his brother, clasping him about the shoulders.

'You saved my life. That is more than amends. Now fight beside me and together we will win this day.'

Suffolk came rushing up out of the mist. 'I come from Richard. The right flank has prevailed and Warwick's army has crumpled, but I have heard that Hastings' left side are scattered.'

'Bring them back,' cried the king. 'I will ride to Hastings myself and round up the men; they must return so we can press our advantage on the right.'

'I will go,' said George. 'You are needed here. I will serve you with my life. I give you my word.'

Edward thought for a moment. 'Go, with my blessing. And God be with you, Brother.'

George receded into the mist. The men continued to appear and Edward pushed forward at them, cutting down his opponents and gaining ground.

'My lord, my lord!'

It was Rivers, slightly blooded about the face.

'Anthony, you are injured?'

'A mere scratch. But the mist has proven our friend. Oxford has fought through Hastings' side, but then his men doubled back and encountered Montagu. Such were the conditions that they took each other for the enemy and are cutting down their own allies!'

'A blessing indeed that they do our work,' agreed Edward. 'And what of Warwick? Has he been sighted?'

'Last seen heading out to support the right flank.'

'Then I will seek him out. We are pushing through easily here. If I can take Warwick, we have won the day.'

'I will take your place here,' said Rivers, raising his sword.

'Good man.' The king clapped him upon the shoulder and sped away.

'Richard? Richard?'

Gloucester heard the voice cutting through the white wall before him. At once he recognised the man who had trained him in swordsmanship, the cousin who had fought with their father, who dined at their table, whose visits to Fotheringhay he remembered as a little boy.

True enough, the mist parted to reveal Warwick, bleeding from the shoulder, staggering across the little hillock that separated the two sides.

'Richard? My boy, is it you?'

Richard clasped his sword in both hands. On all sides, his men were engaging, breaking through the ranks, making the grass run red with blood.

'Richard? Do not fear me. I want to talk. Where is George?'

He called back across the divide. 'The Duke of Clarence fights nobly with his family.'

Warwick nodded, staggering to a halt. 'He has turned traitor to us both. How can you trust him?'

'He is my brother. I know who I might trust.'

The mist swirled between them. Warwick attempted to move closer but Richard held up his sword.

'Do not come a step closer or I shall not hesitate to kill you.'

'You? Kill me? A boy like you, kill the man who has taught you so much?'

The boy brandished his sword higher. 'Yes, I give you my word that I will.'

'Where are your brothers now?'

'Do not come closer.'

Warwick swayed. Blood ran from the wound on his shoulder. 'You can't win, Richard. Don't you see? You can't win now. Henry is restored to the throne and his heir, Prince Edward, remember the Prince of Wales, has set sail for England to land any hour. He is a man now, and married, and he's coming to fight for his country. You must face the truth. I have the superior numbers today and your dynasty will be defeated. There is still time to save yourself. Flee. Flee this place and live, or else join with me.'

346

There were times in his life when Richard had experienced pain. Pain as he grew, pain in his shoulder and back, pain when the doctors tried to treat him. Pain upon the loss of his father and brother Edmund. Each time, he had taken that agony, squashed it tight and buried it deep, deep within some well in the bottom of his belly. And perhaps it had all been for this. All that suffering, and all the strength, had been in preparation for today.

Now, with the mist surrounding him and his sword held high, he stood taller than he had ever been.

'I would rather die than join you.'

'Well, that may happen,' Warwick sneered. 'I am surprised you have not already been cut down, a slow, twisted-spined creature like yourself.'

And all the strength and all the power surged through Richard's slender frame. He was conscious of every movement but it was as if something outside himself carried him forward. He strode across the divide, swinging the weight of his sword about him, building momentum until he had it drawn back and ready to release. It happened so quickly, so unexpectedly, that Warwick could do little but look on in surprise as the distance between them closed.

He delivered the blow at waist-height. By some chance, the sword sliced through metal, through leather and through flesh with ease. It passed through half of Warwick's middle, before getting stuck, lodged in bone and flesh, drenched in blood, before Richard drew it out. The effort made a terrible sucking sound, and a crunching, as Warwick stood, sliced and broken, his mouth open, slowly filling with blood. His eyes glazed over. He fell upon his knees.

Richard stepped back, balancing his weight against the sword. The blood ran down the shaft and over the handle onto his hands.

The lifeless form of Warwick crumpled forward, face-first into the dirt.

'Richard?'

Edward and Hastings came out of the mist, the king's sword held forward, its blade clean and gleaming bright.

Slowly, the duke turned to them, full of the enormity of what he had done.

Edward looked from him to the body on the ground. 'You found him? You found Warwick.'

Richard realised his hands were shaking. 'It was him or me.'

Hastings went to the body and pushed it over with his foot. Warwick rolled back to reveal the slice through his midriff, gaping open and still wet and red. 'He is dead. There is no question about that.'

Edward turned to his brother. 'You've done it. By God, Richard, you have done it! The battle is won.' He shouted at the top of his voice, 'The day is ours.'

Around them the mist moved and the men circled as the word spread.

Richard nodded. 'The day is ours.'

Margaret knelt upon the stone floor and closed her eyes. The scent of incense hung heavy in the air, but all the nuns had been ushered out to give her peace. She was aware of Anne, kneeling beside her, hands clasped in prayer, but she paid the girl no attention.

The crossing had been rough. The little fleet had almost been beaten back several times, but their sails caught a new wind and carried them forward to the coast at Weymouth. And that was where Jasper Tudor had been waiting to break the news. They had taken to their horses almost at once, riding through the Severn valley without a chance to catch their breath. The green forests and white gushing rivers marked their route out with a sort of unexpected beauty, a kind of permanence in spite of everything. Margaret had urged her horse forward with new purpose, or a new desperation, knowing that Warwick would not be joining them. His corpse lay bleeding in a field at Barnet. They would have to win this battle themselves.

Her forces had been refused entry to the city of Gloucester. Gloucester, upon which she had pinned her hopes. Behind the city teemed the River Severn and the safety of the Welsh hills, where Tudor's men waited to join them. But the gates were already closed when they approached, and the walls defended. There had been no choice but to press on, exhausted and thirsty, to find the next bridge, leaving some of their artillery behind. And then, there was Cerne Abbey, offering to shelter them; this tiny place with its pitiful little sanctuary was everything she had now.

'Oh, do stop your snivelling. God wants your prayers not your tears.'

Anne sniffed and held in her grief.

Margaret clasped her hands tighter and stared at the candle flames flickering on the altar. Their brightness was hypnotic.

They were all boys. Just boys. Her son, Edward, was only seventeen years, and of the young Beaufort men who had ridden to meet them at Bath, only Edmund and John were of any real age, yet still inexperienced in battle. At least they had Tudor and Lord Wenlock, veterans of the field. There were others, too, who had come out of hiding as Lancastrian supporters, recalling their grievances and making their promises, pulling out old livery coats and sharpening blades.

'Mother?'

It was her son, Edward, standing in the doorway. She felt a pang of emotion at the sight of him.

'We must move on. The Yorkists are closing upon us. We must leave now and aim for Tewkesbury.'

'Tewkesbury?'

'They march apace, Mother. We must be able to choose our ground, not be caught by surprise and have to fight as we stand.'

'Of course, of course. Make our horses ready.' She tugged at Anne's sleeve. 'Come girl, up you get. It is time to go.'

Across the field, Tewkesbury Abbey was pale in the sunlight. The meadow stretched down from its end walls, broken by the stream, where cows had been grazing up until the moment the armies had arrived. Crows nesting in the tall trees overlooked the large formation of men in their murrey and blue livery, gathering in three parts. They saw the banners unfurled in the wind, flapping with their sunburst design, and the glint of sunshine upon the silver cross raised by the archbishop. Then, with the blasts of trumpets, the crows scattered and flew south along the length of the field, over the forest clumps and hedges to where the second army lay, with the banners of Lancaster's red rose and the three feathers of the Prince of Wales.

As the sun steadily climbed, they were ranged in the same format as Barnet. Richard, then Edward and George, then Hastings, ready for action. The king stared out across the field.

'They're grouping,' said Edward. 'I expect Wenlock will lead one portion, and Beaufort's brother, maybe also the prince, if he is ready for it.'

'The terrain is poorer for them,' observed Hastings. 'They will be marching against the incline, through the stream.'

'If I was commanding from that position,' Edward observed, 'I would branch off to the side and pass through the woods there, which is why I have stationed two hundred archers among the trees, to head them off.'

'That will drive them back into the centre,' added George, 'if they are not shot down first.'

'And we'll keep the side lines tight,' Richard confirmed, 'so there is nowhere else that they might run.'

'There, look!' Edward pointed. 'The banner of the Prince of Wales as he styles himself. There is only one Prince of Wales, and he is in his cradle at Westminster. And there is only one King of England. The old Lancastrian is returned to his cell in the Tower. Today, we fight to reclaim our right. Three of us together again, the sons of York.'

He signalled for the trumpets to sound. Their blasts rang out across the field, making the crows rise, and the figures of their distant enemies twitched in response.

Edward lifted his sword. 'I commit my cause and quarrel to Almighty God, to our most blessed lady, his mother, Virgin Mary, the glorious St George and all the saints. Advance!'

The lines came forward, man after man, equipped with whatever weapons they had been able to lay their hands upon. Through the tall grass they trod, over the stones, across the deep ruts. And here and there, the stream had made the ground boggy and the going was tough. Across the divide, some with shouts and cheers, some with cries, some with prayers on their lips, and others silent as the grave, they came. And in those moments, as the two sides were ever closer and closer, each man carried in his heart the awareness of death and the imminent contact with other men, bent upon their destruction, driven by the need to survive. There were already voices and cries of pain and death before the weapons clashed. The Yorkist archers had unleashed their arrows, making a chorus of whistling in the air, followed by the terrible thud of metal and wood sinking into flesh.

Suddenly, the space between them narrowed. They could see the faces and the eyes of the men opposite. The first blows fell, steel upon steel, or upon wood, or wood on flesh. The first men on the front line began to fall.

'Onwards!' cried Edward, wielding his sword towards a block of three men. 'Put down your weapons, traitors, or die a traitors' death.'

He brought the blade home against one man's skull and turned and struck another through the chest, before the third turned and ran in terror.

'I am King of England!' he cried. 'Who among you dares to face me?'

'They break!' shouted a soldier. 'Beaufort's flank has broken; they head down the lanes.'

'Pursue them!' the king replied. 'Cut them down.'

A body of men ran to the left where the Lancastrians had weakened, but the king stayed and fought on. Still they kept coming, more and more men, to meet their deaths upon his sword. As the sun rose higher, as he began to tire, the armies on both sides began to thin away. The fighting moved up closer to the abbey behind, where some Lancastrians were attempting to seek shelter.

'Edward!'

He parried a blow and turned to follow the voice. It was George. His heart filled with relief at the sight of his brother still standing, unhurt.

'Edward, the so-called Prince of Wales, has been taken. Wenlock is dead. The Beauforts are dead.'

At the sound of this news, the men fighting around them began to scatter in the direction of the river.

'Edward is taken?'

'Yes. And begs for mercy like a child. I have dispatched William Stanley to take the French queen, who shelters nearby.'

'Take me to him. There will be no mercy today. Men! The day is ours!'

It was that particular greenness of England in May. That season when the world sprang back to life after lying dormant through the long months of waiting. The trees spread their canopies overhead, full of birdsong, and branches grew their arms out across the paths, heavy with life and flowers. Roads began to sprout grass and the air was sweet again. In her chamber at Berkhamsted, Cecily, Duchess of York, was drawn to look up from her devotional book at the sheer beauty of the scene outside her window. Emerging from a London chapel, Archbishop Bourchier gazed out at the sky, which was the most unusual shade of blue, and at the line of birds singing on the roof leads. Butterflies looped and swam over the meadow at Grafton Manor.

In the Westminster garden, outside the council chamber, Elizabeth walked with her child in her arms. The boy was almost eight months now, strong and happy. He was putting on weight well, pulling himself up and would be walking soon. Her elder daughter, Princess Elizabeth, was at her side, picking at buds with her little fingertips, fascinated by the blooms. The moss paths were flanked with flowers, early daisies and blue-faced stars, and the orchards beyond were a sea of pink froth. Jacquetta sat on the bench, stretching out her limbs in the sunshine. The other girls sat at her feet, plaiting grass and making flower chains.

Elizabeth felt the sun upon her face. It was done. The messenger had been and gone and their prayers of thanks had been offered up to God. The Lancastrian force was defeated, their enemies killed or captured, and the name of her father and brother avenged. George had proved his loyalty and now, surely, the coming years would unfold like this beautiful spring, in glory and peace? She kissed the top of her child's soft head, breathed in his baby smell.

In the Tower, in his monk-like cell, the old Lancastrian king prayed upon his knees, mumbling the words that had become as familiar to him as breathing. It was safer here, away from those crowds, the heavy robes and the expectation. He was old. He felt it in his bones, and all he wanted now was to live in quiet contemplation. Through the grille in the door, his gaolers watched, wondering when the order would come.

On the road north, a small band of riders were making as fast a pace as their horses allowed. Some were wounded, others sullen, some desperate. At their head was the Earl of Oxford, lashing the reins, not daring to turn and look back. He had backed the wrong side, supported the wrong king, turned his back upon England. Now, on this lonely northern road, he put his hopes in Scotland. To the west, along a road that cut through green fields, rode Thomas Stanley, rehearsing his speech of forgiveness. He had broken from the losing side at the last moment and headed fast to Westminster to throw himself upon the king's mercy. It was his last hope if he was to avoid a traitor's death. It was only a question of luck as to whether Edward would admit him and give him a chance to speak. He would go first to his brother, to William, and ask him to intercede on his behalf. Brother would not deny brother.

In the darkened room, Margaret Beaufort rolled up her sleeves. On the bed before her lay her husband, Henry Stafford, his bare limbs drenched in sweat and crusted with blood. The stench of suffering rose from him. Gently, she dipped her fingers into the pot of ointment and drew out the thick, grey unguent.

'This will sting,' she whispered, 'but it will help. Try to lie still.'

But as she daubed his wounds, all she could think of was her son and Jasper Tudor, in flight from the battlefield. France would shield them for now, after this York king had snatched back his throne, but only God knew when she would see her boy again.

From the west, the party was marching in cavalcade. The deep rutted country roads resounded with their feet. The loyal friends, tired but triumphant after their bravery: William Hastings, closest friend to the king, trustworthy to the end, with his laughing eyes; William Stanley, steadfast and stoic; the amenable Duke of Suffolk, brother-in-law to the king; the Duke of Norfolk, grown into a man since that snowy night Edward had appeared at his home; and Anthony Woodville, Earl Rivers, brother of the queen, full of the wisdom of learning and of life.

Behind them rode the French queen, her hands tied, humbled and defeated, too broken from the loss of her son to even allow tears to relieve her dark eyes. For Edward, her Edward, Prince of Wales, was dead, cut down by his namesake after the battle, his body lying in Tewkesbury Abbey awaiting burial. George, Duke of Clarence, was finally forgiven and returned to his family, riding beside her, charged to keep her safe.

Next in line, riding on a palfrey, came Anne Neville, the young widow, entrusted to the care of Richard, Duke of Gloucester. He was beside her now as they passed through the burgeoning countryside, transformed into a man, a knight, a victor, by the last few weeks. They rode in companionable silence, their horses level in common purpose, neither willing to break away.

And then, sitting high in saddle despite the hours of fighting, Edward, King of England, tall, noble, his hazel eyes bright with success. A man in his prime, returning to claim his throne. The past years had brought him to a point of maturity. He was no longer the enthusiastic youth who shone bright and carried all in his wake. He had suffered, been betrayed, and emerged as a wiser man, refining that caution that had always been his sixth sense. Now he knew to trust his instincts, not to override them with charity, and to act with speed and decision. It had taken much out of him, these trials, but he had fought back and reclaimed his throne. He had another chance, and he was not the man to waste it.

The people saw them coming. They came out of their homes to wave and cheer. Bells in the steeples of every village began to ring. Children held up bunches of flowers. Women passed wine, bread, cheese to the hungry travellers. Vicars waved censers.

'A victory,' they cried, 'the king has won a great victory.'

'Lancaster is dead. Long live York!'

'God save King Edward! God save the king!'

And he rode home to London with their blessings ringing in his ears.

CPSIA information can be obtained
at www.ICGtesting.com
Printed in the USA
LVHW011226140222
710786LV00001B/2